Raves for the *New York Times* bestselling
ALEX HAWKE novels by

TED BELL

"Bell invites comparison of Alex Hawke to
James Bond. . . . Hawke moves at just as fast a clip,
complete with the best gadgets of any
James Bond movie or novel."
Saint Paul Pioneer Press

"Ted Bell is the new Clive Cussler."
JAMES PATTERSON

"[Hawke is] strong, shrewd, and savvy,
with an aplomb not seen since James Bond tore up
the pages of Ian Fleming's novels."
NPR

"Just the thing for fans of Ludlum,
Trevanian, and Fleming."
Kirkus Reviews

"Bell, like the best thriller writers,
seems to [predict] the evening news."
Toronto Globe and Mail

"Did you read it in his book, or did you
read it in this morning's newspaper?
Sometimes it's hard to tell."
Tulsa World

By Ted Bell

PHANTOM
WARLORD
TSAR
SPY
PIRATE
ASSASSIN
HAWKE
THE TIME PIRATE
NICK OF TIME

TED BELL

PHANTOM

A NEW ALEX HAWKE NOVEL

HARPER

An Imprint of HarperCollinsPublishers

"Crash Dive" was first published as an e-book novella March 2012 by William Morrow, an Imprint of HarperCollins Publishers.

HARPER

An Imprint of HarperCollins*Publishers*
10 East 53rd Street
New York, New York 10022-5299

First Harper premium printing: September 2012
First William Morrow paperback international printing: March 2012
First William Morrow hardcover printing: March 2012

HarperCollins ® and Harper ® are registered trademarks of Harper-Collins Publishers.

Printed in the United States of America

Visit Harper paperbacks on the World Wide Web at
www.harpercollins.com

10 9 8 7 6 5 4 3 2 1

For my daughter, Byrdie Bell,
Who lights up my life once more

To every man is given the key to the gates of heaven.
The same key opens the gates of hell.
BUDDHIST PROVERB

PHANTOM

PROLOGUE

THE HOUSE AT THE SEAWARD END OF CAPTAIN'S Neck Lane in Bar Harbor is a three-story Victorian painted a lovely shade of pale yellow with white trim. The home has all the prerequisite nineteenth-century decorative gingerbread geegaws and doodads, but they are not overwhelming. There is a certain peace about the house that you can feel, just standing on the sidewalk at the front gate on a quiet summer evening.

Peace, yes, and should you step inside, abiding love.

There was red, white, and blue bunting hung from the portico surrounding the front door. A very large American flag was draped from the roof and obscured the two large windows on the third floor. A banner was affixed to the exterior wall just below the flag. It read:

A HERO'S WELCOME, U.S. MARINE SGT. CHRIS MARLEY!

Tonight, all the windows of 72 Captain's Neck Lane are aglow, though it is well nigh the witching hour. Even lit is the tiny window at the top of the tower jutting out from the western front corner of the house. In that small round room, a little girl is sitting on her bedroom floor being read to by her father. The child's name is Aurora, age six. The father is Christopher, age thirty-two, a warrior at heart. Still. He is missing part of his right leg, from the knee down. It is the result of an IED the Taliban had left waiting for him beside the road to Kabul. He'd been promised a prosthetic, but there was a very long line of amputees ahead of him.

He thought little of the wound. He had seen countless horrors far worse. He was one of the lucky ones. He was alive. He had come home safely to his family. He had done his duty. He was a proud man, proud of his service and what he'd done for his country, though he would never, ever, let you know it. His father had never talked about his war. Neither would he.

"I like my cane," the Marine told people. "It has many other uses, you know. You can scare cats with it, stuff like that."

Aurora, unable to sleep because of an impending adventure, has had her father reading to her for hours. *She hasn't yawned once*, Christopher thought, pulling another book from her shelves. *Not once!* With her flouncy red curls and cornflower-blue eyes, she was a picture-perfect child.

Christopher Marley once told his wife, Marjorie, that when the great gardener finally clipped all the inferior roses in the great garden, he came up with one perfect bud and he named it "Aurora." It was the kind of thing he said from time to time, the kind of thing that endeared him to his wife of ten years. Not to mention his legions of loyal readers.

Christopher, a famous writer of children's books before duty and country had called, turned the page of the picture book.

"Ooh, Daddy, what a lovely palace! Who lives there? Can I live there someday? Become a real princess?"

"Well, most likely not. You'll see it for yourself when we get to Orlando tomorrow, but I can tell you now even though it's a great secret. That palace is the home of Cinderella and—"

"Cinderella? She's so beautiful."

"Indeed. As I say, it's her palace, but she has many guests living there as well. Including a certain mouse, your favorite mouse in the whole wide world."

"Remy? In *Ratatouille*?"

"Remy was a rat, darling, not a mouse. Otherwise they would have called the movie *Mouseatouille*. Which they didn't."

Aurora laughed and pursed her lips, thinking this over.

"Not Mickey?"

"Yup. Mickey Mouse himself."

"Mickey Mouse. The real Mickey Mouse. Lives in that very palace with Cinderella? Inside."

"Correct."

"And we're going there. To that exact palace. Tomorrow."

"We are."

"Oh, Daddy, I want to hug you. I'm so excited . . . can we meet Mickey? Go to his house? See his room and everything?"

"I should think so. He does live there, after all."

"Well. We'll just walk up to his door and knock on it, won't we, Daddy?"

"Or maybe he'll be out playing and we'll go say hello. I hear he is just about the most popular mouse in Orlando and—"

At dinner the night before he shipped out, he had made a solemn promise to his family. When he got home he was taking them all to Disney World for a grand holiday. Three whole days. In bed later that night, he'd asked his wife to honor his promise in his absence. No matter what. And there were times, lying in a rocky roadside ditch, bleeding out, when Sgt. Chris Marley, USMC, had believed he'd never set foot (he still had one, anyway) inside Disney World. He still remembered Aubrey, his son, who had pumped his fist and shouted, "Disney World? Space Mountain, bring it on!"

"Daddy! Wake up! You fell asleep reading!"

Aurora, her eyes gleaming, looked up at him and said one word freighted with reverence.

"*Mickey.*"

AT THAT MOMENT THE DOOR SWUNG INWARD AND A small, familiar-looking boy of eleven (he was Aurora's older brother) stood there holding a very beat-up red duffel bag with a big black *L* above a pair of crossed lacrosse sticks. It was the one his dad had used at Lawrenceville. The boy's name was Aubrey. He was an auburn-haired boy, with great handsome eyes that he would grow into with the passing of time.

"Dad, Mom says I can't use this duffel without your permission."

"Permission granted, Private Marley, but it's too big. We're only going for three days, Aubrey."

"Dad! What about all my lacrosse stuff? It'll only fit in this . . ."

"No time for lacrosse where we're going, I'm afraid. Your days are already accounted for. I've got tickets for Splash Mountain, the Riverboat cruise, the Haunted House, the Pirates of the Caribbean, It's a Small World . . . and that's only the first day."

"What about Space Mountain?"

"I hear that's too scary," Aurora said, clutching her dolly.

"It's just a roller coaster," Aubrey sniffed. "How scary can it be?"

"All I know is my best friend forever Tabitha Longley went and she said it's all in the dark and you can't see anything. She hated it. She even . . . threw up . . . gross!"

Aubrey laughed. "Yeah, I bet. 'Specially for the poor bozos sitting behind her."

"You are so totally disgusting."

Christopher closed the picture book and leaned forward in his chair.

"Aubrey? Why don't you go pack, buddy. It's late and we're getting up very early. You were supposed to be packed by dinnertime."

"Dad! I had practice!"

"Go get Mom; she'll help you. You won't need much, okay? Jeans, sweatshirts, and sneakers."

"Space Mountain, Dad? Please."

"Yes, fine. Space Mountain."

IT WAS LUNCHTIME WHEN THE MARLEYS CHECKED into the great Wilderness Lodge, the hotel Christopher and Marjorie had chosen because of its resemblance to the place where they'd honeymooned, the Yellowstone Lodge in Yellowstone Park. Aubrey was simply astounded by the size of the place. Aurora just wanted to get to the room, unpack, and get to that palace.

After checking in, Chris had a nice moment when an elderly black gentleman with beautiful white hair and a very erect posture arrived to help them with their luggage. "I honor your service, son," the veteran had said quietly and with a knowing look.

"Semper Fi." Chris smiled.

"Semper Fi," the old Marine acknowledged.

The family took the monorail to the park entrance and stepped down onto the platform. Above the roof of the train station Aurora could glimpse the long banners streaming from the tall towers of Cinderella's Palace.

"Dad, there it is!"

"Just like the picture, isn't it?"

"Oh, yes! Let's go. We don't want to miss Mickey. I'm sure he's awake by now. He'll be home, though, don't you think?"

"Come on, follow me. I've got passes. We'll head straight for Main Street and then go find out."

Aubrey had zero interest in Cinderella or her palace and convinced his mother to come with him inside a shop that did fake tattoos. Marjorie told Christopher to go on ahead and they'd all meet at Splash Mountain, the log-flume ride and their first adventure of the day. Christopher had decided it was the most benign and so a good way to judge Aurora's capacity for the more challenging rides. Aubrey, he wasn't worried about. Aubrey's idea of fun was jumping off the roof into the hedgerows with a Superman red bath towel tied around his neck.

"So, Dad," Aurora said, looking confused and dismayed as they made their way up Main Street to the palace, "you did say you and I were going to knock on the palace door and say hi to Mickey, right? Just the two of us, right?"

"Of course. And we will."

"Oh."

"What's wrong, sweetie?"

Aurora burst into tears.

"It's just like you said, only—only *who are all these other people*?"

"What do you mean?"

"I mean, well, I don't know, Dad. I thought it was just going to be me and you. Going to Mickey's house and all. Not a whole other bunch of people. Just the two of us."

"Well, sweetie, it's just that, well, this is a public amusement—"

"Dad!" Aurora cried out. "Look! There's Mickey

right over there, getting off the streetcar. C'mon. Before he goes inside!"

And with that, she put her little head down, curls flouncing, and made a beeline through the crowds for her favorite mouse.

Christopher smiled and said, "Hey, Aurora, wait for me!"

He saw her for an instant, beaming, and waving him onward.

It would be the last happy moment of the day.

THERE WAS A MERCIFULLY SHORT LINE FOR THE LOG flume ride.

While Marjorie and Aubrey went to use their passes for more tokens, Christopher took Aurora to watch the riders come flying out of the topmost boarding station and careening down the twisting and steeply angled chute full of churning water. The chute straightened out at the bottom, and the log full of passengers plunged into the deep lagoon with a great splash, soaking everyone aboard, causing fits of laughter. It was fun, Christopher thought; he'd done it many times himself as a boy. He didn't think it would scare Aurora one bit.

They climbed the stairway to the top, Christopher holding onto the rail to manage the ascent. When they finally reached the boarding station, he asked, "Does this look like fun, sweetie?"

"Oh, yes, Daddy, let's go!"

"All right then, I'll get in the very front seat and you take the one just behind me. That way you can wrap your arms around me going around the curves if you want to."

They took their positions and waited for the rest of the riders sitting behind them to board.

"Here we go!" Christopher said, turning to smile over his shoulder at Aurora.

The log whooshed from beneath the corrugated roof section, riding a flood of rushing water like a surging tide, and took the banked curves at increasing speed. A few minutes later, he caught a glimpse of his wife and son far below, waving at them and waiting in the crowd as they approached the final straightaway. No. Wait. They were pointing up at the chute and appeared to be saying something . . .

No. They were screaming.

He instantly saw why.

The lower straightaway chute was completely dry. No water at all, just the fierce sun's glare glinting off the smooth stainless steel. He didn't have time to think about it. The second the metal log hit that dry patch it accelerated dramatically. Frantically, Christopher turned to grab Aurora.

It was too late.

She was gone.

The log struck the surface of the water at the bottom at a ridiculously steep angle and going at least five times faster than its designed speed. It pitch-poled forward and ejected the six passengers into the wide deep pool. Logs were continuing to slam into the pool, hurling more people into the "lagoon." Christopher, in shock, clawed for the water's surface looking for Aurora, kicking his one good leg furiously. He saw her red hair floating and feared the worst. He swam to her, ignoring the screams of the frightened and injured, and pushed her face up out of the water.

"Is that it, Daddy?" she said, sputtering.

"Oh, my little baby, are you hurt?"

"'Course not. Is that the special ride? It's ever so much more fun than just splashing down in the silly old log. It's just like holding your nose, closing your eyes, and jumping off the high dive at Meadowbrook Club, isn't it?"

Christopher hugged her to him and swam to the side where EMS personnel were helping frightened passengers from the pool and wrapping them in towels. No one, thank God, seemed to have been seriously injured, just a few scrapes and bruises. There was an elderly woman lying half in the water and half out who appeared to have landed on the walkway surrounding the "lagoon."

At lunch near the *Mississippi Paddlewheeler*, considerably calmer now that everyone was all right, the Marleys discussed the rest of the afternoon's activities. Marjorie was still shaken by the flume incident and not sure she wanted to trust any of the other rides as planned. Christopher sympathized, but the look on the children's faces convinced him that to hole up in their rooms watching *Little Mermaid* or *Shrek III* or whatever for the remaining two days was a nonstarter.

"I asked one of the security men, darling," he said to her. "He said it was the first incident like that in the forty years he'd worked here. He said it was some kind of computer glitch. Maybe a power spike that opened a drain, something like that. Did you know that thirty feet below us are miles of tunnels and computer control rooms? Computers run everything in the whole park."

"And you find that reassuring?"

"Computers run the Boeing 777 that got us here. So, yeah. I find that reassuring."

"I don't know, hon. It scared me to death. But I also think we should not let one mishap ruin their entire trip. They've been looking forward to it for two years."

"Right. Me, too. So let's all just go have the most fun afternoon ever. Deal?"

"Deal."

And so the Marley family finished lunch and headed toward the Haunted House where the most dangerous things were the steep stairs. Passing the flume, they were reassured by the fact that it had already reopened. Continuing along by the river they were startled by a huge roar that went up from the crowd, somewhere over on Main Street. Christopher looked at his watch.

"It's one o'clock; the parade is just starting," he said.

"The parade?" Aurora said and burst into song. "'Who's the leader of the band they call the Mousketeers? M-I-C-K-E-Y . . .'"

They reached the line for the Haunted House, and it seemed to stretch back at least a mile.

"How long a wait?" he asked a heavily tattooed biker in front of him, piercings in his nose, tongue, and ears and wearing a wife-beater T-shirt.

"Well, yessir, that's kinda hard to say. They shut her down for a while is what I heard. Some kind of malfunction with the Invisible Staircase, I reckon. I guess somebody fell down the stairs or something. Said it wouldn't take long to fix, though. I'd stick around, line moves purty quickly once she gets going."

AFTER A FEW RIDES WITHOUT FURTHER INCIDENT, the Marley family was more than ready to head back to the Wilderness Lodge for a nap and the special dinner with all the characters. Apparently Mickey was going to join them for dinner along with Goofy and Snow White. Aurora, most tired of all, was ready to call it a day. But Daddy had promised Aubrey Space Mountain, and Daddy always kept his promises. They headed for Tomorrowland.

The line was short because the sun was setting and many families had begun leaving the park at five. No one save Aubrey had the slightest intention of riding a roller coaster in the dark. So the boy joined the queue while the family went to a nearby ice cream parlor, took a table where they could see the ride, and ordered banana splits all around. The ride looked more like a futuristic white football stadium than a roller coaster, but of course the tracks were all inside in the dark where you couldn't see what was coming next.

The line moved quickly and Aubrey got closer to the front.

"Sorry, son, full up. Have to wait for the next one. Won't be long," a guard said.

Aubrey waved at his parents and climbed up on

the rail to wait as the cars left the station. There were video games for people waiting, but he wanted to psych himself up for his ride.

The first indication he had that something was terribly wrong was the kind of screaming he heard coming from inside. It wasn't excited screaming; it was *terrified* screaming. And there was an awful smell coming from inside, like burning wires and rubber and something else, that smelled like—and then he saw the flames filling the tunnel and heading straight for the station. There was a roaring fire inside Space Mountain and people were being burned alive. He ran for his parents, ran for his life really, because he'd no idea if the whole thing could explode or not, and when he reached them he started crying.

"There's a fire in there, a f-fire in there, Dad," he sobbed. "Inside the mountain. Those people, they thought it was going to be fun and now—they're dying!"

At that moment there was the gut-wrenching and ear-piercing screech of torn metal coming from high above.

The Marleys looked up to see an entire section of roller-coaster cars, still full of screaming, wildly gesticulating people, some of them on fire, come flying through a rip in the rooftop, soaring at least a hundred feet above the ground. It was too horrible to grasp. Marjorie turned away just before the flying death trap slammed into a large crowd waiting to enter Buzz Lightyear's Space Ranger Spin.

Christopher and Marjorie each grabbed a child and began to run maniacally toward the park entrance. The screams and yells coming from every corner of the park told them Space Mountain wasn't the only ride that had malfunctioned so horribly. It seemed that everywhere they looked there was death and destruction: black smoke and fiery orange flames were rising throughout the park, and mobs in a high state of panic were clawing and trampling one another in an effort to escape this nightmarish Kingdom of Death.

Christopher Marley shouted at his wife and suddenly detoured toward the scene where the flying cars had landed on top of the waiting crowd, leaping over the fallen bodies of his fellow citizens. He did the best he could, balancing on his one good leg, using his crutch to pull as many of the injured from the tangled wreckage as he could before EMS and park security forces arrived en masse.

Hugging his daughter to his chest, running toward his wife and son, he had a terrible premonition.

This is no accident.

ONE

*H*AWKE HAD BEEN IN THE BLOODY THICK OF IT *all his life. When not engaged in fighting for his life, he dreamed about it. But this hellish nightmare was all too real to be any dream. Surely near death. It felt so very close now, the cold hovering all around him; some vast, grinning blackness, a protruding bony finger beckoning, urging him to surrender. How much longer could he run? He was spent. He could hear his wild heart screaming, begging his body to stop. Grievously wounded, he was shedding blood from countless gaping rips in his flesh, suffered when first trapped by the wild ones of the forest.*

Somehow, he'd lost his bearskin coat in that last fray. Nearly naked in this freezing, bone-chilling cold, his clothes mere scraps of rags. He looked down at his feet, shocked at the stinging pain of each step in the crusted snow. He'd lost his boots, too, both feet shredded and weeping blood. He heard something, low and wolfish, rapidly gaining ground on him. He looked over his shoulder, shocked at the bright red path he'd made through the woods. How could he lose these beasts when his own feet were leaving a bloody trail in the snow! Still, he crashed through the forest, the sound of thundering hooves behind him. A hideously grinning cavalry, gaining on him, swords flashing as they ran him to ground.

Wild Cossacks on horseback, fierce, bloodthirsty creatures who wanted only to slice the flesh from his bones; why, they'd skin and eat him alive they'd said, dragging him toward their fire. Why had he even entered this wood? He'd known certain death was lurking in the forest, but he'd stupidly ignored that certainty, leaving the vast whiteness of the endless tundra and venturing into the dark wood.

They were closer! He could hear their howls of impending victory, the hoofbeats of their black, red-eyed steeds nearer now, great snorts of frozen breath steaming from their flared nostrils, the riders calling to him, laughing at this helpless victim who could run no longer. His legs had turned to stone and every step in the deep snow felt like his last.

They were upon him then, stallions wheeling, rearing up, encircling him. He heard the whisper of steel slicing through air, felt the tip of a Cossack sword nick his throat, another burn his ear. They were all around him, dismantling his body bit by bit, but he knew if he could just keep his head, just keep his head away from the whispering blades, just keep away long enough to—

Hawke gasped for air as he came fully awake, sitting bolt upright in his lice-infested berth, his face drenched in cold sweat, the fear still real, even as reality swept the lingering remnants of terror from his brain. Another nightmare! Gazing out the train's window at the white tundra and the solid black forests beyond, he knew why he'd had the dream, of course . . . because it was no dream.

He was riding, eyes wide open, straight into a death trap, deliberately embarking upon a doomed journey into the blackest black heart of darkness. And there was a very distinct possibility he'd never get out of Russia alive.

THE SUN ROSE OVER SIBERIA, ASCENDING INTO THE blue heavens like a shimmering ball of blood. Lord Alexander Hawke, lost in thoughts of his impending death, leaned forward and peered through the grimy, ice-caked windows of his tiny compartment. The old Soviet-era train lurched and creaked, traveling at the speed of a horse and wagon as it approached yet another desolate station where no one would be waiting. Unthinking, he dabbed mentholated gel under each nostril.

It had become a constant habit.

His grubby *kube* compartment shared a wall with the foul lavatory right next door. In other words, he'd grimly decided soon after boarding, he had shit for neighbors.

Hawke had taken what he could get, a third-class car, dimly lit, overheated, humid, and, after numerous early stops in the countryside, overflowing with drunken farm workers who smelled like a concoction of damp earth, sour garlic, and grain alcohol. The incessant singing, shouting, and fighting were well nigh unbearable. He had fled immediately to his boxlike refuge, locked his door, only coming out when he developed severe cabin fever or was "in extremis." The noxious lavatory boasted a commode commodious enough to accommodate a circus elephant, sitting, but the toilet seat wouldn't stay up.

The train was hell on wheels, all right. All he could hold fast to was the memory of Teakettle Cottage, the beauty and tranquility of his secluded little "hideaway" house on Bermuda's north shore. Situated atop a high bluff, it looked down over a small banana plantation, a fringe of pink sand, and the glittering turquoise sea. How he longed now for that quiet and languid life. The soothing balm that was solitude.

He supposed his friend Ambrose Congreve was right when he'd accused Hawke of having a "violent addiction to being left undisturbed." If so, so be it.

The British Intelligence officer's normally strong blue eyes were bloodshot from lack of sleep, his cheeks charred with black stubble, the thickly bunched muscles of his shoulders and upper arms stiff, aching from long confinement in his tiny quarters. He stretched his long legs out before him as best he could. He wasn't one to complain, but the plain fact was he was bloody miserable. He lit a cigarette and turned his face toward the filthy cracked window.

Behind him, a pair of polished steel rails stretched west across a frozen expanse of Russian tundra. The tracks angled upward and traversed the Ural Mountains and led to the main rail station at the ancient city of St. Petersburg, where Hawke had begun his journey. He had made this long railway trek from the city once before. Memorable. And everything looked just as he'd remembered it: it had not changed for the better.

The Rodina.

The Motherland.

The bareness of the outline of the countryside like a Japanese watercolor, the mountain ranges, snowcapped, and the stark trees etched black against the sky, scant evidence of humanity, much less civilization. Just . . . white . . . nothingness.

Hawke sat back, closed his eyes, and slowed his breathing. He was, understandably, a bit on edge. Not the dull edge of nagging anxiety, but the razor-sharp knife edge of fear. Alex Hawke had a very reasonable expectation of being shot dead in a few short hours. He'd visualized it many times: The train screeches to a halt at the tiny station. He peers out the window. He steps down onto the icy platform. The grey men are there, waiting. The Dark Men. Guns drawn, huddled just beyond the pool of lamplight. The Englishman had murdered their Tsar. Now it was his turn to die in a volley of gunfire.

Or not.

This nameless dread of the unknowable was directly contrary to Alex Hawke's staunch militaristic nature. He possessed a rigid backbone of considerable renown, both as a combat-hardened flyboy in the Royal Navy and now in the SIS, or Secret Service. He'd always had an appetite for war when it was necessary. One of his World War II great heroes, the outspoken American U.S. Army general George S. Patton, had said all there was to be said on the subject of the proper state of a man's mind heading into battle. "The object of war is not to die for your country, but to make the other bastard die for his."

Hawke lit another cigarette, summoning the belligerent ghost of Patton and his pearl-handled pistols to his side, puffing furiously, working up a head of steam for whatever might lie ahead. He could scarcely believe the treacherous ease and facility with which he had set himself up: perfectly framed for calamity, or devastating heartbreak. Or, if he got very, very lucky, indescribable bliss.

Because there was, of course, an alternative scenario. A possibility, admittedly an extraordinarily slim possibility, existed that Hawke might soon be reunited with the one woman he loved. A reunion he would have deemed an absolute impossibility just a short time ago. Was she really alive? He'd witnessed her death with his own eyes, had he not? Far more likely, he'd fallen prey to a cunning lie. It was, after all, the way his enemies traditionally worked. Bait. Switch. And kill.

Yes. A well-baited trap laid for him by the Kremlin's spymasters at the KGB. He was sure of only one thing: a fool's death sentence should it prove he'd been stupid enough to take the Russians' bait. Naive enough to let his much-vaunted common sense take a backseat to his grievously broken heart. He allowed himself a thin smile. Hell, it wasn't like it hadn't happened before. And he was still kicking.

He inhaled deeply, the sharpness of cheap Russian tobacco taking its bite, telling himself this whole thing was just another hostage rescue, for

God's sake. Hardly out of the ordinary for one of MI6's most reliable warriors. God knows, he had countless search-and-rescue operations successfully under his belt. Including a dicey affair involving Her Majesty the Queen the year prior. He had a few scars, like anyone in his line of work. More than a few. But, by God, he thought, taking another drag, he wasn't dead yet. Still. Look at his hands shaking. Like an old woman who's just seen a fleeting shadow on her bedroom wall.

This time the rescue attempt was intensely personal. It had been three long years ago that he had flung himself into love like a suicide to the pavement.

Her name was Anastasia. Closing his eyes, he could see her even now, see his beloved Asia standing on the platform of the tiny Russian rail station at Tvas, waiting for him, her cheeks aglow in the frosted air, golden ringlets peeking from beneath the white mink cowl that framed her lovely face, her wide-set green eyes gleaming in anticipation of his appearance. Dear God! How desperately he'd longed for that moment when he'd enfold her within the protection of his arms and never let go.

But he had let her go, hadn't he?

No, not let her go.

Under extenuating circumstances, granted, but the cold, hard fact remained:

He had murdered his own true love in cold blood.

Disconsolate, lost, Hawke pulled a torn and well-worn photograph from inside his leather jacket. A fading black-and-white snapshot of Anastasia Korsakova, radiantly alive, on the snowy steps of the

Bolshoi ballet theatre. Asia stared back at him, her profound beauty still a knife deep to the heart after these years. How this pain created a longing for his fleeting youth, that halcyon time before he had ever prized anything greatly enough to fear the loss of it. Never again, he told himself constantly. Alex Hawke had learned a hard lesson the hard way:

A man must never place himself in a position to lose. He must search out and find only those things he cannot lose. He must develop a heart as hard as flint.

And, after all his bloody pain and suffering, now this truly bizarre twist of fate. His beloved Anastasia, if you believed the Kremlin rumors anyway, was still alive. After narrowly escaping a death sentence for treasonous acts against her father, the late Tsar, she was rumored to have spent two years or more imprisoned in Moscow's notoriously cruel Lubyanka Prison. Now, so he'd heard from his Russian friend the great Stefan Halter, she was held prisoner at a high-security Siberian KGB facility, Jasna Polana, the former winter palace of her father. British spooks even had a nickname for it, stolen from a spy tale by the American author Nelson DeMille: the Charm School.

But.

"It could all be a ruse." He still heard Stefan Halter's sonorous voice echo in his mind. "After all, you and I are the only two eyewitnesses to General Kuragin's treason against the late Tsar. If Kuragin is ever to feel completely secure within the walls of the Kremlin, his only option is to eliminate us. To lure you back to Russia in search of Anastasia by encouraging false hopes would be a standard KGB ruse. As you well know, my dear friend."

C, HIS SUPERIOR AT SIX, HAD BEEN TOLD ONLY THAT Hawke was "headed up into the Swiss Alps for a bit of thinking and hiking, perhaps an assault on the Eiger." Had Alex told his colleagues in the SIS the truth, Sir David Trulove would never have allowed this bizarre misadventure. Hawke was entirely too valuable, far too weighty a capital investment, to have himself shot out of a cannon on some wild-goose chase, indeed, chasing a woman who, by all accounts, was in all likelihood long dead.

The beckoning trap, in fairness, had been exquisitely set. Not only had Anastasia survived, he had been told, but she'd borne him a son in prison. A son! So here he was, the forlorn fool driven onward by hope alone. But. If, by some miracle, Anastasia and his son truly were alive, he was determined to find some way, any way, to smuggle them out of Russia to safety. Precisely how he would achieve this, he had no bloody idea. All he knew was that he was bound and determined to rescue his little family in the unlikely event that they were still alive. Or simply die trying.

TWO

THE WRETCHED CONVEYANCE WAS SLOWING, steel wheels creaking and brakes squealing as it approached the tiny rail station. Tvas was a bleak Siberian outpost, a small village situated literally in the middle of frozen nowhere. Picture perfect for his appointment in Samarra. After the long hours of worry, waiting, and trying to distract himself by reading, Alex Hawke finally turned the last page of his well-thumbed book, a volume by Balzac, and reread the final passage for the umpteenth time.

THE TRADE OF A SPY IS A VERY FINE ONE, WHEN THE SPY IS WORKING ON HIS OWN AC-COUNT. IS IT NOT IN FACT ENJOYING THE EX-CITEMENTS OF A THIEF, WHILE RETAINING THE CHARACTER OF AN HONEST CITIZEN? BUT A MAN WHO UNDERTAKES THIS TRADE MUST MAKE UP HIS MIND TO SIMMER WITH WRATH, TO FRET WITH IMPATIENCE, TO STAND ABOUT

IN THE MUD WITH HIS FEET FREEZING, TO BE CHILLED OR TO BE SCORCHED, AND TO BE DECEIVED BY FALSE HOPES. (OH YES, YES, THERE WAS ALWAYS THAT LITTLE POSSIBILITY!) HE MUST BE READY, ON THE FAITH OF A MERE INDICATION, TO WORK UP TO AN UNKNOWN GOAL; HE MUST BEAR THE DISAPPOINTMENT OF FAILING IN HIS AIM; HE MUST BE PREPARED TO RUN, TO BE MOTIONLESS, TO REMAIN FOR LONG HOURS WATCHING A WINDOW; TO INVENT A THOUSAND THEORIES OF ACTION . . . THE ONLY EXCITEMENT WHICH CAN COMPARE WITH IT IS THE LIFE OF A GAMBLER.

Monsieur Honoré de Balzac. A century and a half ago, he had nailed this bloody business to a fare-thee-well. Hawke closed the book, stood, and stretched his weary body, reaching with both hands toward the smoke and grease-stained green ceiling overhead. He rose up on his toes, flexing his taut quad and calf muscles, and his fingertips easily brushed the grimy ceiling. Hawke was tall, well over six feet, trim, but powerfully built.

And afraid of no one.

He possessed a martial spirit; his strong heart beat with the grim, stubborn, earnest energy, the might and main that had won at Waterloo and Trafalgar. At his naval college, Dartmouth, he'd once asked his boxing trainer what it took to become a fighter truly worthy of the name. He never forgot the man's response. "The ideal fighter has heart, Alex, skill, movement, intelligence, but also creativity. You can have everything, but if you can't make it up while you're in the ring, you can't be great. A lot of chaps have the mechanics and no heart; lots of guys have heart, no mechanics; the thing that puts it all together, it's mysterious, it's like making a work of art, you bring everything to it, you make it up while you're doing it."

He'd recently turned thirty-three, a fine age for a man, but old by his accounting methods. Still, a daily regimen of rigorous Royal Navy training and conditioning kept him fitter than most men ten years younger. Hawke cut an imposing figure. He had a heroic head of rather unruly thick black hair and a fine Roman nose, straight and imperial; his glacial blue eyes were startling above the high and finely molded planes of his cheeks and strong chin. His mouth could be a bit cruel at the corners but one always sensed a smile lurking there, a smile that was at once dangerous and sympathetic.

"Quite a simple man, actually," his friend Ambrose Congreve, the famous Scotland Yard criminalist, had once explained about Hawke. "Men want to be him, women want to bed him. And when he puts his mind to it, he's an immovable object."

Hawke, to put it quite simply, went through life with the supremely confident outlook of a man with nothing left to prove. He had a dark and magnificent aspect about him, proud and fiery. Women, as Congreve had said, seemed taken by him. He was both funny and sad, that irresistible combination that is one of the secrets of charm. For one thing, he had no idea that he was especially charming or even remotely good-looking. Or the faintest notion that the affection he gave and inspired so freely among others was anything but natural, at least among normal, healthy people.

What he possessed was the real thing, and he adulterated it with nothing else. If one, and many were prone to do so, went looking for his faults, it could easily be said of him that he was not given to deep introspection. His heart and mind were always simply too busy. Elsewhere. His focus was outside, not inside. And if it was a shortcoming, so be it. He didn't have time to worry about it.

He reached up and took his grandfather's battered Gladstone portmanteau down from the overhead rack and placed it on the seat. Underneath his clothing were twin false bottoms. Unfastening the straps, he reached inside the hidden compartments and removed a handheld GPS, a miniature sat phone, and his only weapon, a SIG .45-calibre handgun. He popped the mag and ensured that the hollow-point parabellum rounds were properly loaded, leaving one in the chamber. Feeling the heft of the pistol, he almost laughed out loud at the puny state of his armament.

He slipped the gun into a quick-draw nylon holster suspended inside his worn black leather jacket. Underarm protection you just can't find at the corner druggist. He took his ridiculous-looking and heavy bearskin coat down from the hook on the door and shouldered into the damn thing. Donning the black sable trapper's hat that Anastasia had given him years ago, he stepped out into the narrow corridor and made his way, carefully lurching toward the exit at the rear of the car.

I'm walking straight into a bloody trap, the voice in

his head warned for the hundredth time, *seduced by false hopes. I'm willfully entering a wholly hostile environment alone, dressed in a bloody bear suit and carrying a bloody popgun.*

Insanity!

The train screeched to a stop, the passenger door slid aside, and a blast of icy particles stung his face like so many chips of diamonds. Enormous white billowing clouds were spilling from beneath the cars as he stepped down onto the deserted, snow-crusted platform. The new mantle of eggshell snow was already turning mushy in the strong winter sunlight. He quickly cast his eyes right then left. The platform, mercifully, appeared empty.

No one was waiting for him, not this time. No beautiful Russian tsarina. Not even some grey-faced KGB goon squad waiting to simply gun him down right here at the steps. Alex Hawke, apparently not dead on arrival. He shrugged, finally admitting what had been the most likely scenario hiding in the back of his mind: that he would step off this train and into a hail of bullets.

The trip was off to a good start. He had not really expected to leave this train depot alive. He smiled at his good fortune and started for the stationmaster's office. He had not even noticed two large men in heavy black overcoats who'd stepped down from a first-class car near the locomotive of the train once his back was turned.

After the stuffy, foul-smelling compartment, the icy air was bracing and, feeling cautiously optimistic, he made his way toward the station house, glancing at the elderly stationmaster through the ice-glazed

window, the same man Anastasia had once introduced him to as her trusted friend. He paused at the
door, the snow piled up against it like dirty sherbet.

"Good morning," Hawke said in Russian, stamping his boots to rid them of snow. Then, since his
Russian was so embarrassingly poor, he asked the
white-bearded stationmaster if they might speak in
English.

"Da, da, da," the wizened old man said, staring
up at him, this towering alien from another planet.
He squinted through his gold pince-nez glasses and
smiled, recognizing Hawke as the man the famous
Anastasia Korsakova had journeyed by troika to
meet here many years ago. "I've been expecting
you, sir. I am Nikolai. Remember?"

"Yes, yes, of course," Hawke said. "The good
Dr. Halter told me he paid you a visit sometime
last month. He said you would have a name for me.
Someone who might be of assistance in my travels."
Hawke extracted an envelope containing five thousand rubles and passed it to the old fellow. "I believe
this is for you."

"I do, I do," the old white-bearded man said,
smiling as he quickly slipped the payment under
a stained ink blotter. "His name is Grigory Ivanovich. A farmer. He lives in this village. His house
is nearby, the only one with a red roof. You cannot
miss it. Are you hungry? His wife, Rica, is a very
good cook. Goulash. She's Hungarian, you see."

"I am hungry. Well. Thank you for all your help.
Spasibo."

"Spasibo," the man grunted, not looking up, too
busy counting his fistful of rubles.

Hawke found the farmhouse but not without some difficulty. The tiny houses that composed the village, slumped against each other shoulder to shoulder, were all smothered in two or three feet of fresh snow and he had to clear away portions of a number of rooftops jutting out into the muddy road. Nearing the end of the short road, he found a red one. He rapped on the weathered wooden door. There came a happy exclamation in Russian from within. And also a wonderful aroma of stewed beef that stirred his latent hunger.

AN HOUR LATER, A RENEWED ALEX HAWKE FOUND himself with a full stomach, some black bread, a full liter of good country vodka with a cork stopper to keep the cold at bay, and a good horse beneath him, a great bay mare. He spurred her onward through the snow, anxious to arrive at the KGB facility before nightfall. His plan was to surveil it carefully before deciding on his approach.

Indian country, he thought to himself, looking around at the vast forests and plains. It had begun to snow again, heavily. Great feathery flakes brushed his cheeks with the weight of dust. Old Petra plowed ahead through the heavy snow, jets of steam puffing from her nostrils.

For better or worse, he was fully committed now.

THREE

WHEN HE FINALLY EMERGED FROM THE FOREST, he saw that the snow and wind had heightened in intensity, and ice crystals stung his face and hands. He looked up, squinting through the foggy snow at a barrage of bright klieg lights lighting up the sky, now faintly visible in the distance. He could see the lake and the massive palace rising along its shores. The compound was maybe a mile distant and since he'd gotten this far without being shot at, he was slowly gaining confidence that getting off Petra and approaching alone and on foot had been a good strategy.

His leg muscles afire, he marched on, planting one boot in front of the other for what seemed a hellish eternity. Another mile took him an hour to complete and brought him to the river. The river made no sound; it was running too fast and smooth. He sat down on a log to smoke a cigarette. Maybe it would stave off his hunger.

Rested, he flicked the cigarette away and got to his feet to ford the river. The swiftly flowing water was knee-deep and frigid, but not too wide. Climbing the bank on the far side, he saw that the principal road leading into the KGB compound had been recently plowed. There were tank-tread tracks in both directions, the new Russian T-95 judging by the depth and width of the tread dimensions. He gratefully walked the last few hundred yards or so with ease, steadily marching toward the waiting and watchful sentries near the main gate, wondering if he'd hear a shot ring out.

Russian Army soldiers standing in small groups were smoking and eyeing the intruder. Behind them, he could now make out a massive wall of steel and concertina wire some thirty feet high. Every fifty yards along the perimeter, a watchtower stood atop the wall, a slowly revolving searchlight mounted on each rooftop.

Two guards were visible behind the windows at each tower, both armed with automatic weapons. This new enclosure surely encircled much of the vast acreage of the old palace grounds. What had once been a dreamlike vision fit for a tsar, this majestic architectural masterpiece, given to the Korsakov family by Peter the Great, now had a new sinister aspect that was quite unsettling.

Six gate sentries appeared out of the mist, marching in loose formation, all with automatic weapons leveled at him. He pulled off his snow-encrusted sable hat and raised his arms into the air. He was smiling as a heavyset Russian Army officer, a captain, approached him, pulling his massive sidearm from the leather holster inside his full-length fur coat. Holding the gun loosely at his side, the man began shouting in Russian as he neared. Over the years Hawke had picked up enough native lingo to know the man was threatening to shoot him on the spot.

"I mean no harm," Hawke said in halting Russian, "but I am armed." It was the sentence he'd decided upon some time ago, riding his steed through the wood. Now he'd find out how smart he really was.

He planted his boots in the snow, kept both hands reaching for the sky, and waited. The captain quickly summoned five more guards who completely surrounded the intruder. Only then did the officer have Hawke open his heavy coat and allow the captain to reach inside and remove his weapon. The smell of vodka on the grizzled old soldier's breath was powerful. He had a square face, a prominent chin, stubble on his head, and slits for eyes.

He growled, "Speak English; your Russian is shit."

"Delighted. May I present my papers?"

The man nodded. Slowly, Hawke withdrew his most current version of proper identification, impeccable documents courtesy of the lads in Cryptology at Six. Once the soldier had the intruder's weapon and had hastily inspected his papers, he whipped out a small handheld radio and keyed the transmit button.

"Intruder at the gate, sir," he said to some higher-up, while another soldier patted Hawke down thoroughly, finding nothing.

Hawke heard a loud and angry shout through the tinny speaker of the captain's radio. The officer's displeasure was understandable. Intruders were probably quite infrequent out here. The captain held the radio away from his ear, frowning at the tirade issuing forth. He scowled at Hawke, the man who had appeared without warning to completely ruin his evening.

And then the captain said, "I've no idea how he got here—hold on." Then, covering the mouthpiece and scowling at the Englishman, the burly officer said to Hawke, "How the fuck did you get here? You look like a goddamn frozen bear." Hawke, shivering uncontrollably with cold and swiping at the icicles on his face, mumbled an answer in his pidgin Russian, before he remembered the captain's request to speak English.

"I w-walked."

"He walked. You walked?" He looked up and down at Hawke, who nodded his head in the affirmative. Speaking again into the radio, the captain said, "You heard right, Colonel Spasky. He says he walked. I have no goddamn idea, sir. Da, da, I know it's impossible. What can I say? He's got a United Kingdom passport. His name? Alexander Hawke, Hawke Industries, London."

"Chairman and CEO," Hawke said helpfully, adding a smile. "Tell your superior officer I'm here to see General Kuragin, will you? I'm not expected, you understand, I was just passing through. In the neighborhood, as it were. Decided to pop in."

The captain looked at him with an incredulous snort and spat bloody phlegm in the snow before once more raising the radio to speak. "So? Now what, Colonel? Shoot him?"

"Better not shoot me, Captain," Hawke said. "The general might shoot you. The great Kuragin and I are old friends, you see. Tight. White on rice. Thicker than thieves, closer than two coats of—"

Hawke, seeing the drunken captain's eyes shift and flick, sensed sudden, aggressive movement behind him. Before he could whirl to confront his attacker, he was struck full force in the back of the head with a rifle butt. He sank to his knees in the snow and pitched forward facedown, unmoving. The captain spat again and kicked Hawke in the ribs with his heavy boot, smiling at the satisfying crack.

"Take this crazy bastard down to the cells," the captain said, stomping off toward the cozy warmth of the well-lit guardhouse at the gate, still shaking his head in wonder at the ridiculous Englishman who claimed to have walked across Siberia and strolled right up to the most heavily guarded KGB installation in all of Russia. With a smile on his face!

FOUR

G OOD MORNING TO YOU, TOO," HAWKE SAID through gritted teeth. The Russian guard had poked him in the right rib cage with the muzzle of his rifle. Hawke was already grimacing at the sharp stab in his left side. Couple of ribs broken for sure. Damned nuisance, this Russian penchant for cruelty. There was absolutely no heat in his cell and he could see his breath, great plumes of it that hung in the air.

"Move!" the Russian shouted.

Hawke rolled his long legs over the metal frame of the cot and got painfully to his feet. He appeared to have dropped off to sleep in his fur coat, which had no doubt saved him from freezing to death down here in the dungeon. "Time for breakfast, is it, then? Splendid. I'm famished." The guard stepped to one side so Hawke could exit the dimly lit cell. Noticing his dungeon quarters for the first time, Hawke thought they must have been constructed in the late seventeenth century.

There was a low, narrow corridor with a steep set of stone steps leading upward. A prod in the middle of the back told Hawke that was where he was headed. He started climbing, clearly not quickly enough to suit the giant because he kept getting sharp prods from the man's rifle.

At the top of the stairs he came to another long corridor, this one brightly lit and finished in tiles of pea green. Hideous, but at least it was heated. "Move!" his jailer said, as if he actually needed more encouragement.

They passed any number of closed doors with tiny windows at eye level. Interrogation Centrale. The last one on the left was open. Inside was a plain wooden table with a battered pair of matching wooden chairs on either side. One wall contained a mirror that probably came in handy for prisoners wishing to tidy up after a long interrogation. Either that, or there was someone on the other side paying very close attention.

Hawke was shoved into the chair facing the phony mirror and the burly chap in a cheap dark suit across the table. His giant escort now stepped behind him and rested a black leather truncheon on his right shoulder. Most reassuring. A conversational icebreaker.

"Well, this is cozy," Hawke said to the cheap suit for openers. "I must get the name of your decorator."

"Hands flat on the table, stretched out in front of you and keep them there," the interrogator grunted. Hawke, an old hand at this sort of thing, did as he was told.

"Your name?" the man said, his pencil poised

above a pad. He leaned forward and put his nose ten inches from Hawke's face, a hoary technique, but an effective one.

"Hawke. Alex Hawke," he replied with a grin, giving it his best Sean Connery spin.

"You are an English spy."

"Hardly. I'm rather well known as the Playboy of the Western World."

"How did you get to this location?"

"Train, actually. Then, a mare. Then, shank's mare." The sadistic giant slammed the lead-weighted truncheon viciously into Hawke's exposed and broken ribs.

He did not cry out as expected. Nor did he remove his hands from the table. He'd been held captive in an Iraqi prison, subjected to unspeakably brutal torture every day and night for an eternity. Starvation, hallucinogens, electroshock, the works. It would take a lot more than a couple of broken ribs and the giant's nasty little truncheon to get any reaction out of him. A whole lot more.

"This is a maximum-security Russian military facility. Why have you come here?"

"I came here to speak privately with General Kuragin."

"I want the truth," the man screamed, and Hawke again felt the sharp explosion of pain in his side. He smiled patiently at his torturer. The smile was a very effective little trick he'd learned in the desert outside Baghdad. It increased severity but decreased duration. Eventually, they got bored with you and moved on to more entertaining victims. That trick was the only reason he'd survived long enough to escape.

Hawke said, "That is the truth, you stupid dolt. I'm here to see General Nikolai Kuragin."

"What makes you think such a person exists?"

"I've met him. In person."

"You've met him. And where did you meet him?"

"We took tea together once. At the Savoy Grill in London as I recall." This earned him a blow to the side of his head. He saw stars for a moment but managed to shake it off and give the man an even warmer smile. Anger and frustration blazed in his interrogator's eyes. *A pushover*, Hawke thought, gratefully. He could be out of here inside of an hour.

"What makes you think that this person, if he exists, can be found here?" the KGB man snarled. He had produced a small hammer and brought it down on each of the five fingers of Hawke's left hand. Hawke flinched involuntarily but gave away nothing with his eyes.

"I was told that he lived here."

"Told? Told by whom?"

"By a little bird, actually."

"A little what?"

"Bird. You know. Wings? Flapping like mad?"

There was a sudden crackle of static from a hidden speaker, and then Hawke heard a familiar voice fill the room.

"It wasn't a nightingale that sang by any chance?" the disembodied voice said with a chuckle. "In Berkeley Square?"

Hawke immediately recognized the laugh. The interrogator turned and stared at the "mirror," completely baffled at this interruption coming from someone behind it. And that someone was General Nikolai Kuragin.

"Yes," Hawke replied cheerfully. "And the moon that lingered over Londontown? Poor puzzled moon he wore a frown?"

Laughter and then, "Good morning, Lord Alex Hawke."

"A very good morning to you, General Kuragin."

"Sorry about all this dreadful unpleasantness. And the rather uncouth reception you received from my gallant centurions at the gates. A little advance warning, perhaps?"

"Ah. Should have done. Frightfully rude. It was a last-minute thing, actually."

The door swung open and Kuragin was standing there with a smile on his face. He'd not changed much. He was a skeletal figure of a man in his eighties, dressed in his customary sharply tailored black uniform. Made him look like a Nazi SS man, Hawke thought. He had sallow skin, almost yellow, and heavy-lidded deep-set eyes. "I've summoned a doctor down to take a look at those ribs. When he's through with you, someone will escort you up to the library. It's my office now. We'll get you some breakfast served there. What would you like?"

"I could eat a horse, but I'll settle for caviar. And toast."

HALF AN HOUR LATER, HAWKE, HIS RIBS TAPED UP and Percocet or some other splendid painkiller flowing mercifully through his veins, found himself seated in the same beautifully appointed room where, three years earlier, he'd first met Anastasia's father, the late Tsar of Russia.

The high-ceilinged walnut-paneled library was filled with books, art, and military mementos from the last three centuries. A magnificent equestrian portrait of Peter the Great in battle hung above the mantel. A roaring fire lent the high-ceilinged room a cozy intimacy, and the two men sitting on either side of the cavernous stone hearth were speaking quietly.

"Just out of curiosity, how long would you have let that interrogation go on?" Hawke asked Kuragin, a mildly curious expression on his face.

"Until I found out what I wanted to know, of course. What else would you expect? Having you appear out of thin air like you did. I don't get a lot of visitors out here as you can well imagine. And the ones who do come from Moscow arrive by helicopter, not on foot."

"And what exactly did you want to know?"

"Your intentions. Whether or not you came here with the malicious intent to do me harm."

"Of course not. Like it or not, we are still partners in crime, Nikolai. You, Halter, and I conspired to take down an entire government, lest you forget. You received a not insubstantial sum from my government to part with a code to the Tsar's Zeta machine. A secret, believe me, that will follow me to the grave. But what gave my true motives away?"

"Alex, when you have worked in Lubyanka Prison, witnessed countless thousands of interrogations over a half century, you can determine whatever it is you wish to know in a remarkably short time. Lengthy torture is merely a function of stupidity coupled with sadism."

"Yes, I suppose that's true," Hawke said, and gazed into the fire. Now that he was here, inside the palace walls and safe, he found he was at an utter loss as to how to begin to address the real reason for his visit.

"You took an enormous risk returning to Russia," the general said a few moments later. He was sipping from a tiny crystal glass of vodka, using his right hand. Where his left hand should have been was an empty sleeve, sewn to his uniform in the manner of the one-armed Lord Nelson. In order to avert suspicion from his role in helping Hawke bring down the Tsar, Kuragin had lopped off his own left hand with a butcher's cleaver in Hawke's presence. It was an act of bravery Hawke would never forget.

"Really? Risky?" Hawke said, feigning surprise. "Why?"

"Because there are a great many old soldiers in the Kremlin who were fiercely loyal to the late Tsar. They know you killed him. They are called the Tsarist Society. And they want nothing more than to see you dead."

"Amazing I'm still alive, then."

"You have friends in high places in Russia, Lord Hawke. Otherwise, you'd no longer be with us, I'm afraid. You remember the beautiful young Russian tourist who was killed when her motorbike accidentally drove off a bridge in Bermuda? About six months ago?"

"Read about it in the local newspaper, yes."

"She was a paid assassin, sent to the island to seduce and then murder you. One of our officers tracked her there and made sure she was unsuccessful at both."

"I have you to thank for my skin, then?"

"To some extent. But the truth of it is, you owe your life to the prime minister."

"Putin? Really? But why?"

"Surely you know why. You killed the Tsar, the man who deposed him and threw him into a hell-hole, that horrid prison, Energetika. Left him there to rot. Had you not blown the Tsar and his airship out of the sky, Putin would have soon found himself sitting naked atop one of those sharp sticks, impaled. Thanks to you, he now sits atop a newly resurgent Russia and a massive personal fortune. He divides his time between his office at the Kremlin and sailing the world aboard his new megayacht, *Red Star*, with his best friend, former Italian prime minister Berlusconi."

"*Red Star* belongs to Putin? I was under the impression she belonged to Khodorkovsky, the big oilman. That's what all the glossy yachting magazines say."

"It's only what people think. An impression we wish to convey. She belongs to the prime minister, I assure you."

"We spent some time together, you know, in that bloody prison, Energetika. Down in his cell. Drinking vodka and smoking cigarettes."

"I do know about that. The prime minister has fond memories of you. He finds you good company. As a former intelligence officer himself, Putin has long admired your brilliant career at MI6 from afar, as I'm sure he told you. Since you're here, I will tell you a little secret. He has mentioned to me on more than one occasion that he would very much like to have a very private conversation with you."

"About what?"

"About your helping him build a new Russia."

"Come over to your side? You must be joking! I've got enough problems taking care of my own side."

"Alex, listen carefully to me. Times have changed dramatically. The Communist Party, at least in my country, thank God, is dead and buried. And our two nations face common enemies in this young century: a rising China, obviously, that insane asylum North Korea, and radical Islam all over the world. Russia has historically been geographically schizophrenic, torn between the East and the West. Putin, and those closest to him, possess a yearning to shift toward Europe and the West. They would never admit this publicly, of course, but it's true. Their sensitivities gravitate toward Berlin and Paris, to the great capitals of the West, not to Communist dictatorships in Beijing or Pyongyang. And let's not forget the Castro brothers in Havana or that thug Chavez in Venezuela."

Hawke was silent. A door had opened. Wide. And he was not about to slam it in Kuragin's, much less Putin's, face. That was not how the intelligence game was played at this level. It was a very delicate tradecraft moment, one in which to keep one's cards preternaturally close. Hawke looked at Kuragin, not saying a word.

"Well," Kuragin said finally, eyeing Hawke. "Obviously, this is not something to be discussed now. Or, ever, if that is your wish. Our warm feelings for you will remain unchanged regardless. Let me give you this card. There's no name on it, only a number. It is Putin's private number. Not ten people in the world have access to it."

"Thank you," Hawke said, pocketing the card.

"On to other matters. Let's begin with the true nature of your visit, shall we?"

It was the one moment Hawke had been dreading during the long journey across Siberia. The moment of truth.

"Well. Where does one begin?" He hesitated, then plunged ahead. "You see, Nikolai, I've come about Anastasia."

"Anastasia. I see. Well, I—"

Hawke, in a turmoil of emotion, held up his hand. "Please, Nikolai. Don't say anything. Just let me say what I have to say first. After that, you can either throw me a rope or throw me to the wolves. Is that all right?"

"As you wish, Alex."

Hawke rose to his feet, pacing back and forth before the fire with his hands clasped behind his back.

"It was no secret in Moscow that I was deeply in love with her. And, I believed, she with me. What you may not know are the exact events surrounding her death in Sweden. I had followed Korsakov from Stockholm to his island summerhouse. His escape route, his airship, was tethered to the roof. He had Anastasia with him in the car, bound and drugged. He felt she'd betrayed him for me. I had no doubt the Tsar was going to kill her. I was gravely wounded trying to get inside that house. To save her from her father's blind rage. I failed. Then, I watched helplessly as he had her loaded aboard the doomed airship on a stretcher. I'm positive it was her. And—then—I—dear God—I—"

He felt a hot clench in the muscles of his throat and was afraid he could not go on.

"Alex, please, you're very upset. Let me try to—"

Hawke waved him away and took a moment to regain his composure. He returned to the chair opposite Kuragin and stared into his eyes for a long time before speaking.

"Nikolai, I heard a rumor. I'm sure it cannot possibly be true. But I have lived with the knowledge that I killed the woman I loved for a very long time now. It's unbearable. I returned to Jasna Polana solely because I was told that Anastasia is still alive. I was told that she was held prisoner here. I've absolutely no reason to believe this is true. I still don't believe it, as we sit here. But I simply could not go on living without knowing the truth. I've come to you to learn the truth. Please—please help me."

"Anastasia is alive, Alex. She's here. In this house. Now."

FIVE

Hawke stared at Kuragin in disbelief for a brief moment, then, seeing the clear truth in his wise old eyes, put his face into his hands and leaned forward, giving full rein to his overwhelming emotions. The general stood up and placed his one good hand on Alex's shoulder. "I'll go and get the 'prisoner' now, Alex. I'm sure you two will want to be alone. I will send her to you here where you'll be comfortable. Sit back now. Calm yourself. That decanter on my desk contains the purest Russian vodka dirty money can buy. I suggest you avail yourself of it."

A gentle tapping at the door. So soft an anxious Hawke nearly missed the sound above the crackle and hiss of the great fire in the hearth. He practically leaped from the chair, set his small glass of vodka on Kuragin's massive desk, and raced across the large room to the door. His hand was shaking badly as he reached for the doorknob. His heart had taken on a life of its own, beating like some jungle drum warning of imminent danger.

Little did he know.

He pulled the heavy wooden door open, slowly, terrified of what he might or might not see beyond it.

Anastasia.

He saw her upturned face, morning light spilling down from a high window, afire in her golden hair.

Her luminous green eyes shining with tears.

Her lower lip trembling.

Her tentative hand, reaching out, coming to a trembling rest against his wild heart, as she spoke his name, barely above a whisper.

"Alex."

"It is you," he said softly, almost breathless.

Hawke unfastened his eyes from hers with strained difficulty, as though they had become entangled. He felt if he lost contact with them he'd sink without a trace. He opened his arms and she fell into them, pressing her cheek against his chest, clinging tightly to him. He enfolded her, cradling her head, the two of them seemingly on a pitching deck, holding on to each other for dear life.

"It is me, Alex," she said, her voice breaking, a single tear coursing down her cheek. Hawke looked down and gently brushed it away as he spoke softly to her.

"I thought—I thought I'd lost you . . . all this time, all these years, I've been broken inside . . . I've been so lost, so—"

She put a finger to his lips and said,

"I have to—sit down, I'm afraid. Where shall we—?" She looked around the room as if seeing it for the first time.

He took her hand and led her over to the yellow satin divan beneath the tall leaded-glass windows. She sat and arranged her emerald silk skirt around her, looking up at him, smiling through her tears. "Oh, Alex, my darling boy, I can't believe I'm sitting here looking up at you. I gave you up so long ago. When I saw you lying there in the snow below my window. So *still*. All that bright red blood soaking into the snow. My father said, 'There's your hero. Do you still think he can save you? Do you, you lying bitch?' And I didn't, my love; I didn't think I would ever see your face again. I was so sure you were dead. And now . . ."

Hawke had dropped to his knees at her feet, resting his head upon her lap, weeping, trying to hold on to himself, keep everything inside from flying apart. She ran her slender fingers through his wild black hair, whispering words of comfort to him as if he were a small boy, a child who'd lost his way and had now found his way home at last.

He looked up at her and finally found the courage to speak without a tremolo in his voice. He said, "But now I am here, aren't I? We're both young and alive. We're together. That's all that matters, isn't it?"

Her forced laughter was like the sound of glass breaking.

"Yes. For now, my darling."

"I still don't understand what happened. I saw you. I saw the stretcher, watched them putting you aboard the airship. I don't see how you can be here. It's impossible. Eyes don't lie."

"It wasn't me, Alex. I never left the house. Until I was arrested by the KGB the following day."

"I saw your arm drop, your ermine sleeve, it fell from beneath the blanket when they lifted you up to. . . ."

"It wasn't me, dear Alex. It was Katerina. Katerina Arnborg, my father's Swedish housekeeper. She came into my room and found me on the stretcher, waiting for the airship to depart. I was drugged, couldn't move or speak. He did that to me. My own father. When I woke up, I was in a linen closet, hidden under the dirty linen. The stretcher was gone. The airship was gone. Everyone was gone, everything. Except the red-stained snow below when I looked out my window."

"This Katerina, she took your place on the stretcher? Under the blanket."

Anastasia nodded. "It's the only possible explanation."

"But why? Why did she do it?"

"She'd heard things in that terrible house. Over the years. She knew things. Evil things. Terrible secrets."

"Tell me."

"No. It is not for you. Not anymore. The past is dead and buried. Katerina was a good woman. I think in the end she wanted to save me from him. And in the end she gave her life for me."

"She saved you. For me."

"And who saved you?"

"No one. I just wasn't ready to die. It was only

afterward, after I killed your father, that I wanted to die. In the worst way."

"Because you thought you had killed me, too."

"Yes. I was sure of it."

"Alex. Please. End this. For both of us. It's unbearable, really, these horrible memories. We should be happy. We *are* both alive, as you said. And we have a child together. The most beautiful little boy in all the world. He looks exactly like you, my darling. He even smiles like you, which will of course get him into no end of trouble when he learns how to use it."

Hawke lifted his head and smiled, really smiled, for the first time in memory. "What did you call him?"

"Alexei."

"Alexei. It's perfect."

"I thought so, too." She looked down, gazing at him with her perfect smile, and for a moment he lived once more in the bright green worlds of her eyes.

"How old is he now?"

"Almost three. His birthday is tomorrow. We'll have a little birthday party."

"Where is he? May I see him?"

"Of course. He is up in the nursery playing with his toy soldiers. I've told him that his father was here to see him. He's very excited. He asked me what a father was and I told him."

"What did you say?"

"I said a father is a tall, handsome man. Very strong and very brave. A good man, true and full of life and beauty."

Hawke got to his feet and held out his hand. "It's all a miracle. Let's go and see him now."

"He's coming here. Nurse is bringing him. I've only to call."

Hawke smiled as she picked up the receiver next to the divan and spoke a few brief words in Russian.

ALEXEI AND HIS ENGLISH NURSE APPEARED AT THE library door a few minutes later. When the door swung open, the little dark-haired boy peeked out from behind his nurse's skirts and stared wide-eyed at Alex for a few long moments, then ran to his mother's arms, hiding his face in the folds of her skirt. He was dressed like a little prince, which, in some respects, he was. The late Tsar's grand-son wore a suit of dark blue velvet, with a ruffled white collar at the neck. His shoes were black patent leather with small black satin bows.

"Good morning, sir," the attractive young nurse said, with a slight curtsy and a very proper British accent.

Anastasia gestured at Hawke as she said to the child, "Alexei, that is your father standing over there beside the fire. He's come a very long way just to see you. You must be on your very best behavior. Show him what good manners you have. Can you say hello?"

The child peeked out at Hawke for a second or two, then hid his face once more in the folds on his mother's skirts. Hawke went to him and dropped to a knee on the floor beside his son.

"Alexei?" he said softly, placing a gentle hand on his shoulder. "Alexei?"

The boy responded to the voice and touch and turned to stare silently at Hawke, seemingly memorizing every curve and plane of his face. Alexei's eyes were big and blue and lively. He seemed totally unafraid of the tall stranger now. Hawke was shocked to see a very small version of himself. It was the face he'd seen in scrapbooks his own mother had kept, little Alex building castles by the sea, little Alex on his pony, little Alex reading a picture book.

"Does he speak English?" Hawke asked, his eyes never leaving his son.

"Almost as well as he speaks Russian. We've been teaching him both since he first learned to talk," the young English nurse said, and then she slipped silently from the room.

"Hello," Hawke said, reaching up and lightly stroking the boy's plump cheek, lit to a lovely flame, the flush on the face of a child after a warm bath on a cold evening. Alexei turned to hide his eyes again, then, seeing his nurse gone, turned back to stare openly at this person called a "father."

"Say hello, Alexei," Anastasia said. "Say hello to your father. Wherever have you put your manners?"

"Hello," the child chirped. "Hello, hello, hello."

"How old are you?" his father asked.

He looked shyly at Hawke for a moment, then raised his chubby pink hand, holding up three fingers.

"Good for you! And how many is that, Alexei?"

"Free?"

"Three, that's right. Do you want to know a secret?"

Alexei nodded his head vigorously, already a great lover of secrets. His father said, "When I was three, I was exactly your age. Isn't that something?"

The boy nodded again, instinctively knowing he was expected to agree, and his mother watched father and son together, finding a lovely peace wash over her.

Alex said, "You're a very big boy for three, Alexei. Will you give your father a wee hug? I would like that very much."

Anastasia bent down and whispered in the child's ear. Alexei looked at Hawke's open arms for a moment, unsure of himself, but then stepped into his embrace. Hawke held him closely, looking up at Anastasia, his eyes gleaming with unchecked emotion. He saw her look away, overwhelmed perhaps, and he suddenly felt as if all the molecules in the room had risen up and then rearranged themselves before settling down into a strange new pattern.

He had found his life at last. The life he'd been meant to live.

"Our baby boy," he said. "Our beautiful, beautiful baby boy."

His mother turned her noble head slowly so that her eyes rested with overwhelming tenderness and affection on the man and the boy.

"Will you give him a kiss before he goes back upstairs, Alex? It's past time for his nap, I'm afraid."

Hawke bent forward and kissed his son on the forehead, then ruffled his curly dark hair, and stood back up. The nurse reentered the room and picked

Alexei up in her arms. As he was carried away, looking back over her shoulder, unbidden, Alexei waved at his father and smiled, his blue eyes alight.

Hawke stood mute, staring at the door long after the nurse had pulled it closed behind her.

"Alex?" Anastasia said, stirring him out of his reverie.

"Yes?"

"Would you like to go for a walk along the lake? The snow has stopped and the light is lovely."

"Yes. Fresh air would be good."

"We can skate on the pond if you wish. The ice is perfect."

"I've never learned. But I'd love to watch you."

"Your coat is hanging in the entrance hall. I'll run upstairs and get my skates and meet you at the door in ten minutes. All right?"

"Perfect."

WATCHING ANASTASIA GLIDE WITH SUCH SIMPLE grace and style across the ice, Hawke could almost hear Tchaikovsky on the wind in the trees. He found himself remembering their evening together in Moscow at the Bolshoi, alone in the darkness of her father's private box. The ballet had been *Swan Lake*, each member of the corps of ballerinas a perfect white swan, each one lovelier than the next, creating a rhapsodic fantasy in the air above the frozen wintry pond.

That night, in that privileged cocoon of privacy, with the music filling him up, she had told him she was pregnant with his child. She had been afraid it would make him run; he told her she had made him happier than he had ever been. It was true. That small moment would always be one he would treasure, the moment when the woman he loved told him she was carrying his child, his son.

Little did he realize then how that brief interlude would soon come to haunt his every waking moment.

JUST HOW LONG HE SAT THERE ON THAT WOODEN bench, beneath a stand of bare trees beside the frozen pond, wrapped within his ridiculous bearskin coat, enraptured by the mere sight of Asia's flashing silver skates, he would not remember. He would only remember what followed.

She flew toward him, her arms outstretched like slender white wings, one leg extended perfectly behind her. Suddenly she spun and stopped, her silver skates creating a small cloud of glittering ice around her. Then she was beside him on the wooden bench, bundled up in her long white mink fur, the hood pulled up, hiding her dark gold hair. Her eyes were big and shining, her cheeks aflame, her radiant beauty piped to the surface of her with the cold.

"I love you," he said simply. "I always will."

"And I shall always love you," she said, resting her head on his shoulder. "Until my last breath."

He put his arm around her and drew her near.

"I will find a way, you know. I will find a way."

"Yes?"

"Yes."

"What do you mean? Find a way?"

"A way for us all to be together. The three of us. A way out of here. This prison, this frozen fortress. To go somewhere no one can find us. Ever. I will build a fortress around us. I will shelter you and Alexei. I will protect you from any harm. We will begin again. To love each other. To love our child. To raise him to become the—"

He felt her stiffen. And then convulse, her shoulders heaving. He heard her sobs from inside the cowl of white mink.

"What, darling?" he said, pulling her closer. "What is it?"

"It cannot be, Alex. It cannot ever be."

"What cannot be?"

"What you want. Your beautiful dream. It is not possible."

"Why? Why on earth do you say such a thing?" He felt his heart lurch within his chest.

She pulled away and looked at him, her eyes spilling tears.

"Oh, my darling Alex. You have no idea what you have done. By coming here."

"Done? I have come to take you away. You and our child. What do you mean I have no idea—"

"Alex. Please. Listen."

"I am listening."

"I cannot go with you. I cannot ever leave here, leave this place. This is my home, Alex, my sanctuary. I am safe here. So is Alexei. Did you know there is a price on both our heads? The Tsarists in the politburo want Alexei and me dead. For betraying my father. Only Kuragin stands in their way. But he's made sure that one can hurt us here. No one."

"What are you saying? I don't even—we love each other. We have a child to protect. We have—"

"We have nothing, Alex. Nothing."

"Nothing? We have each other. We have Alexei! And that is nothing? God in heaven, Anastasia, what can you be thinking?"

Anastasia pulled away from him, stood up, and looked down at him, tears coursing down both cheeks, her lower lip trembling, wrapping her arms around herself.

"Alex, it's Nikolai. General Kuragin saved me from a firing squad. He saved your son, Alexei, from infanticide. They were going to bash his head against the wall as soon as he was born. The grandson of a tsar, even a dead one, will be a political threat inside the Kremlin for decades to come. Think about it. The bastard son of the Englishman who assassinated their great and noble Tsar? They hate him!"

"Yes. I see what you are saying. But, surely—"

"Nikolai Kuragin is our only hope! He is our savior! He is Alexei's and my only real chance of survival, Alex. You must believe me, because it is true."

"I can protect you. I can protect you both. It's what I do, you know."

"You want me to believe that we will be safer anywhere on earth than we are here in this fortress? Do you not understand that? They want me dead. They want our child dead and out of their way. It is the Russian way. Centuries of Russian politics repeated."

Hawke looked away for a moment, his mind reeling. For how long had he wandered in his wilderness of grief? Insupportable grief, yes, and loss. Years. And now Asia was here before him, alive, and he felt as if he were fighting for her love! Fighting for his own son! No, more, he was fighting for his life, the one that had been ripped from him on that island in Sweden.

"My resources are easily the equal of Kuragin's. Vastly superior."

"He will never allow it."

"*He* will never allow it? Stand between me and my family's rightful happiness? No one can do that, believe me. Surely the general will understand us, Anastasia," Hawke said, softening his tone, trying to keep the creeping desperation from his voice. He was shaken. He was beginning to doubt himself. And doubt was something completely alien to his being, his core. He took a moment to compose himself before speaking.

Hands on her shoulders, he turned her to face him, gazing directly into her lovely eyes.

"Anastasia, listen to me. Kuragin knows we love each other. Surely he can comprehend that it's natural that we want to be together. Raise our child in some seminormal environment instead of some bloody barbed-wire prison. Listen, I'll return to the palace and find Kuragin right now. He and I will straighten all this out, as gentlemen. I'm sure he will see reason. Why would he not? Why on earth would he keep the three of us apart, keep us from the happiness we truly deserve and—"

"Alex, please sit back down. There is something

more I must tell you. Please sit. Now, before you say another word."

"I can hear quite well standing up, thank you."

She took a deep breath and let the dreaded sentence spill out all at once:

"Nikolai and I are married."

"Married, you say? Don't talk nonsense. He's old enough to be your grandfather. It's beneath you."

"Listen, please. I believed utterly and completely that you were *dead*, Alex. I saw you from my bedroom window, facedown in the snow. I watched you bleeding to death before my own eyes. I wanted to die myself. Then, in prison, Alexei was born. I knew I had to survive in order to protect him. The grandson of the dead Tsar was suddenly a threat to many inside and outside the Kremlin who—"

"But how could you—"

"There was a trial. I was convicted of treason and accessory to murder. A date was set for my execution. The night before I was to go before a firing squad, General Kuragin visited me in my cell. He had a signed pardon from the prime minister, from Putin himself. In the end, so Nikolai said, Putin could not let the son of the man who'd restored him to power be murdered by the Tsarists. Putin did it for *you*, Alex. He and Kuragin are the only reason we are both alive."

"So you fell in love? You married him?"

"Oh, Alex, it wasn't about love. Nothing like that. It was mere gratitude. That, and the security he offered us here. He's an old man. He has been very lonely for most of his life. In his way, I think he does love me, Alex. And I've grown fond of him. Listen.

I truly believed I had lost the only man I loved or ever would love. You. Late one night, when he'd had a bit too much wine and vodka, Nikolai got down on his knees and begged me to make his last few years happy ones. He was crying. In that moment, considering all he'd done, I felt I had no choice but to say yes. And, until I saw your face a few hours ago, I had no cause to regret it."

"And if I got down on *my* knees and begged? If I ripped open my chest and showed you my beating heart?"

"Alex, my God. Please don't do this."

"Don't do this? Don't do this?"

"I mean—"

"Don't worry, Anastasia. I won't beg you. My knees don't work that way."

He looked away from her, staring at the distant horizon, peering in vain through the black curtain that had descended between them. A flash of memory from his childhood: he'd been given a puppy for his sixth birthday and called it Scoundrel. His mother had found him hugging the dog tightly to his chest, smothering it with kisses. "Don't love it so well, Alex, or it may be taken from you," she said.

A man must never place himself in a position to lose.

He should seek only that which he cannot lose.

"Oh, Alex, my poor darling, I—I feel like my heart's going to cave in. I don't know what to say." She reached up to take his hand, but it was like clasping a glove from which the hand has been withdrawn.

"It's because there is nothing more to say. I should never have come here. I'd almost come to grips with losing you, and now I shall have to start all over again. Although now"—he looked away briefly—"now I seem to have lost my son as well."

"Oh, my poor, poor darling. It is devastating to see you in so much pain. If only there were something I could say or do—but there isn't, is there?"

"I am glad you are alive. At least I have that knowledge to carry with me. And I am happy that I got to see my son, if only for a few brief moments. Knowing he, too, is alive, safe, happy, and with his mother . . . I can take all that with me, Anastasia, carry that in my heart at least. I don't blame you for what happened. You did what you had to do to survive. Anyone would."

"Dear Alex."

"I should like to leave this place, Anastasia. Now. Is that possible?"

"No, Alex. Please. Stay just a little while. If only for his sake . . ."

"You have no idea what you're asking of me. None."

"But tomorrow is his birthday. We have planned a little party. He thinks you will be there and—"

"No! Please stop this!"

"All right. As you wish. There is a train tomorrow. The Red Arrow."

"I shall be on it."

She looked away.

"But you cannot—"

"Please. It is done."

"If you insist, I will make the arrangements. It's a lovely train, an express. I'll take you to the station. In the troika. I remember how you loved the troika."

Anastasia looked up at Hawke, awaiting his reply. He was looking directly at her, but every trace of animation had flown from his face. His fierce blue eyes were cold as stone. He was still as still.

"I will retire to my room until it is time to leave tomorrow morning. Will you please apologize for me? Tell your—husband—that I'm not feeling well? And that I deeply appreciate all that he's done for you and Alexei?"

"Of course. He will understand."

She put her hand on his forearm.

He regarded her in silence for what seemed a very long time, and then he turned his back and walked away from her, his head held high, his hands clasped behind his back, his hidden heart shattered.

SIX

EARLY THE NEXT MORNING, HAWKE EMERGED from General Kuragin's private study into one of the palace's great sunlit hallways. He'd been unable to find sleep all night, but he put a brave front on it. After a brief conversation about the possibility of an extremely private meeting with Prime Minister Putin at some point in the future, he got to his feet to bid Kuragin farewell, allowing himself to be embraced by the much older man.

His parting words to the general had been, "Thank you, thank you for saving them both, Nikolai, from the bottom of my heart. I know that I owe you their lives, and I will never forget it."

He turned to go.

"One more moment, Alex, please," Kuragin said, moving toward the fireplace. "I have something for you. It's been in this house for over three hundred years. I want you to have it."

Kuragin then retrieved a long, slender red leather

case that rested upon the mantel beneath the massive portrait of Russia's greatest hero, Peter the Great, in the midst of battle. He placed the object on his desk and unfastened the two latches. "I think you should open the case," he said, smiling, and stepped back. "It belongs to you now."

Hawke stepped forward and opened it.

Inside, embedded in an aged swathe of dark blue velvet, was a magnificent sword. It was sheathed inside a red leather scabbard decorated with brilliant gold fittings including the Russian double-headed eagle emblem. He withdrew the gleaming blade, admiring the helmeted steppe warrior at the hilt and the engraved ivory handgrip. It felt good in his hand. It must have been a good companion in battle.

"I don't know what to say, General, it's a bit overwhelming. I really don't think I can accept such a grand gift."

"Yes, yes, yes. Take it, my boy. Your heroic actions against that madman Korsakov may well have saved our entire nation from entering a new reign of Tsarist terror. I spoke to the prime minister by telephone in Moscow this morning. He agrees this small gift is the least we can do."

"Can you tell me a bit of its history?"

"Well, it was one of Peter the Great's favorite battle swords in the Great Northern War. The last time he carried it was at the decisive Battle of Poltava in 1709. Peter won a victory over those damn Swedes and sent them hurrying out of Russia, never to return. It was the beginning of our taking our place as the leading nation of northern Europe."

"I am deeply honored, General. I will treasure this always." He replaced it carefully inside the red-velvet-lined case and closed the lid.

Kuragin put an avuncular arm around his shoulders and steered him toward the door.

"You are always welcome in this house, Alex. As long as I'm alive at any rate. But I do want you to be careful inside Russia. Mind yourself every moment. There are many assassins carrying your picture next to their hearts. And despite our vast intelligence and military resources, the prime minister and I cannot be everywhere at once."

"I will keep my eyes open. I always do. But thank you for the warning."

THE BRILLIANT GOLD-AND-BLUE TROIKA WAS WAIT-ing at the foot of the broad marble steps. Three magnificent white stallions stood in their traces, stamping their hooves and spouting great jets of breath from their black nostrils. It was the most beautiful sleigh Hawke had ever seen, a gift to Anastasia's forebears from Peter the Great. He'd ridden in it before, when Anastasia had brought him to Jasna Polana for the very first time.

Hawke had not spoken to Anastasia since leaving her alone at the skating pond the prior morning. He found her already in the sleigh, speaking quietly to the nurse who was holding little Alexei in her arms. The child, like his mother, was swaddled in white fur and looked like a rather large bunny sneaking peeks at his father over his nurse's shoulder. Hawke walked around the rear of the troika, leaned down, and peered unblinking into his son's face until the boy broke into a wide smile, a torrent of tiny bubbles erupting from his cupid's bow of a mouth.

He recognizes me, Hawke thought, his emotions churning.

"G'morning, Alexei," Hawke said, leaning in to kiss his chubby cheek and inhale the indescribable warm, precious baby scent. The love he felt literally almost killed him where he stood. But he looked over at Anastasia and did his best to smile.

"Good morning," he said, almost pulling off a convincing smile.

"It's a beautiful day."

"Yes."

She smiled bravely and said, "I thought we'd bring Alexei with us to the station. He adores riding in sleighs."

"The love of speed," Hawke said, tossing his leather bag behind the curved leather bench seat and climbing up and inside. "Takes after his father. May I hold him during the trip?"

Anastasia whispered to the nurse and she took the child around to Hawke's side of the troika. Hawke held out his arms to receive his son, his heart beating with gratitude that at least he'd have a few precious hours to spend with him. The nurse spread the fur throw of white sable over Alex and the baby and wished them all a safe journey.

"There's a word the cowboys in America say," Hawke whispered to his son. "You'll learn what it means some day. Giddyup!"

Anastasia flicked the reins and gave a shout to her

three white chargers. The horses were arranged like a fan with one in the lead. Anastasia needed no whip to launch them into a breakneck speed down the lane toward the stand of birch trees and the great forests beyond; she spoke to them continuously, urging them on with either cheery encouragement or harsh invective.

"You still have the same horses," Hawke said, looking over at her lovely profile. "The noble white steeds."

"Yes. How kind of you to notice. Do you remember their names?"

"I do. Storm, Lightning, and Smoke."

"My three gallant heroes."

"How lucky you are with heroes, Anastasia."

They were silent then. Hawke squeezed his sleeping son to his breast and held him tightly for the duration of the journey. The golden sleigh flew through the snowy hills and valleys like the wind. He put his head back and looked up through the trees at the blue sky, the crystalline air, the cottony white clouds drifting high above. He lulled himself into a kind of peace of mind, using these last few hours with his son and the woman he still loved to create a far, far different reality than the bleakness he was facing.

HAWKE STOOD AND STUDIED THE FILIGREED BLACK hands of the tall station platform clock as they moved relentlessly toward twelve noon. In the distance, he could hear the approach of the onrushing train. Minutes later, he watched the sleek red-and-silver locomotive, a half mile away, come barreling down the steeply sloped incline, bulldozing a great white avalanche of snow before it.

Anastasia, rocking Alexei in her arms, had been standing at Hawke's side on the platform for an eternity. He had heard her weeping silently as the hands on the clock above her head continued their steady progress. Yet Hawke felt paralyzed, physically unable to speak or even make a move to comfort her; a hollow man, his unspoken words as dry and meaningless as wind in dry grass.

An eternity later, he heard her say quietly, "This has been the saddest day of my life."

To which he solemnly replied, "Just this one?"

At this, Anastasia stood frozen in place, a character finding herself in the final act of a tragic drama, unable to remember her lines or move about the stage, hitting her marks while delivering coherent dialogue.

At last, as the long slash of the Red Arrow thundered into the tiny station, its noisy rumble shattering the unbearable impasse of their sadness, it was then that his arm found its way around Anastasia's shoulders, gently pulling her toward him, his eyes offering hers what little comfort he had left in him to give.

"Well," Hawke said, "time to go."

He bent down to pick up his portmanteau and the red leather case. As he did he saw two men at the far end of the streamlined train step forward to board. They were dark men, dressed in dark suits, dark coats, dark hats. The doors hissed open and he watched them climb aboard, each carrying a thin dark case. Not large enough for clothing, he thought. Odd.

"Time to go," he said again, realizing how flat and trite his words were but unable to even begin to say what was in his heart.

"Oh, Alex," Anastasia said, turning her face up to him, the tears glistening on her rosy cheeks. "Won't you at least kiss us each good-bye?"

"Of course I will," Hawke said.

He put his hand on her shoulder and bent to put his lips to hers, ever so briefly, before turning to kiss his son, staring at him, his creamy pink cheeks, fresh from some past spring, and his enormous blue eyes, the very image of a beautiful child. He pressed his lips to Alexei's warm cheek, prolonging the kiss as long as he could, imprinting it upon his memory.

"Must you go?" she said, a gleaming tear making its way down her cheek.

"Yes. There's nothing left of us," Hawke said, a profound sadness in his voice despite his attempt to be strong. Her reply was barely above a whisper.

"All that's left to us is love."

Hawke pulled away, unable to bear what he saw in her eyes. He kissed his son on the forehead.

"Good-bye, Alexei. Good-bye, Anastasia. Keep safe, will you both? Stay well, Alexei. Grow up into a big strong boy so you can take care of your mother. Will you, son? Promise your father that, all right?"

Hawke's heart broke then, and he quickly turned away, the words of farewell in his throat straining with sadness. The conductor was sounding the final whistle, the last call. He tossed his old leather satchel and Peter's sword aboard and then grabbed the rung and climbed up to the bottom step. He determined to remain there, and to do so as long as he could see the two of them.

"Good-bye, my darling," Anastasia said. "Take our love with you and keep it safe."

The train began to move, slowly at first, and Anastasia began moving with it, walking alongside at the same speed as the train, clutching her baby, seemingly unable to let Hawke go, let him fall away from her sight. He hung there on the lower steps, one hand clenched on the cold steel grip, as the train gathered speed.

She was running now, dangerously fast, trying hard to keep up and he feared she would fall, trip in the mushy snow, the baby in her arms and—

"Whatever happens," she called out to him through her tears, "I'll love you just as I do now until I die."

He started to warn her, but suddenly she was reaching out to him. Reaching out with both arms, running beside the train and at the very last possible moment she did it.

She handed Alexei up to him.

He gathered the child in with his one free arm and brought him quickly to the safety of his chest, staring down at her with disbelief.

"Anastasia, what—what are you—"

She cried out, straining to be heard above the gathering speed of the train, "He's yours, my darling. He's all I have to give."

Hawke, his eyes blurred with hot tears, had a last impression of that beautiful haunted face, the tortured eyes, the drawn mouth. He held his son tightly and watched Anastasia for as long as he could, standing there all alone on the deserted platform, a small solitary figure waving good-bye to the two of them forever.

SEVEN

THE RED ARROW

BABIES CRY. SO DO NEW FATHERS. ALEXANDER Hawke sat on the deep, plush carpeted floor of the luxurious ivory and gilt two-room train compartment, rocking his child in his arms. Both of them were weeping copiously. One did so loudly, at times violently, screaming red-faced, demanding his mother. The other did so silently, his own red eyes periodically welling and spilling a potent mixture of indissoluble happiness and sadness.

Some time after leaving the station, they could still be found sitting there when the luxury train's concierge peeked in the door and said, "I beg your pardon. Tickets and papers, please?"

Hawke looked up from the floor and smiled at the woman.

"My own ticket is inside the pocket of that black leather jacket hanging over the armchair. This young fellow here doesn't have one, I'm afraid."

"How old is he?"

"Three. Today's his birthday."

"A free ride for him, then, on his birthday," she said kindly, removing the ticket envelope from Hawke's jacket and inspecting the contents.

Hawke put his lips beside his son's ear and whispered.

"See, Alexei? You were right! Three really is '*free*.' Magic. You've always got to be on the lookout for it."

The concierge was a woman of ample proportions in a tailored dark green uniform with red piping at the wrists and lapels. Her thick blond hair was gathered at the back of her head into what used to be called a "french twist." She was quite pretty, spoke perfect English, and Hawke instinctively liked and trusted her. A mother, he was sure, for the boy brought those instincts instantly to the surface of her features.

"You are Mr. Alexander Hawke, traveling on business to St. Petersburg? Correct?"

"Yes."

"And this gentleman?"

"This young gentleman is Alexei."

"Last name?"

Hawke stared up at her for a moment, then down at Alexei, briefly startled by such a profoundly unexpected question, and then said, "Hawke. His name is Alexei Hawke."

"Your son, then. Well. He looks just like you. Look at those eyes."

"Yes, he is," Hawke said, slightly dazed. "Yes, he is indeed my son." Hearing himself utter those words, Hawke was filled with a flood of warmth and joy that was nearly overwhelming.

"Well, Mr. Hawke, you should give your son some milk. At least water. All those tears have de-hydrated him."

"I have none of either to give, I'm afraid."

"No milk?"

"You see, Alexei was—is—well, the thing is, he decided to join me at the last moment. He's somewhat—spontaneous. Rambunctious boy. Never know what he'll do next."

She reached down with open arms. "May I take him a moment? You're not holding him at all prop-erly. And he's very tired. I think he'll be more com-fortable tucked into the berth in the second room. I'll bring him a cup of warm milk. It will help him sleep. Does he have any toys?"

"Toys? Oh. Only this sad little teddy bear I found in the pocket of his coat." Hawke held it up, a poor ragged thing the color of oatmeal.

"Lucky for him I keep a healthy supply of wooden soldiers and horses for just such emergencies."

"That would be very kind. I wonder about . . . feeding him. I'm not sure when he last ate, I'm afraid. And I'm not really sure what he—"

"Well, I'll bring hot porridge, too. He looks very hungry. The first seating in the first-class dining car is at five this evening. Shall I book a table for two?"

"Yes, thank you. That would be lovely. I'm sorry, I don't believe I caught your name?"

"Luciana."

"Italian?"

"My mother. My father is from Kiev."

"I appreciate your help, Luciana. I'm rather—rather a new father."

She laughed. "Really? Why, Mr. Hawke, I should never have guessed."

A FEW HOURS LATER, ALEX FOUND HIMSELF SITTING side by side with Alexei in the extravagantly decorated dining car. It was all gleaming ivory cream walls, curving up to form the ceiling, and furniture, every square inch trimmed in gold leaf, with upholstery of deepest claret red. The decor was exactly like his first-class compartments. The whole train was done up in this scheme, he imagined. The table linen was snow white, and the silver, though not sterling, was quite elegant, emblazoned with Russian double-headed eagles.

Alexei, grasping his much-loved teddy bear, sat on his velvet-covered, raised baby chair. Save for his rapidly shifting eyes, he was perfectly still, his eyes wandering up and down the long rows of tables inhabited by strange people from this new world he'd never known existed; then he was turning briefly to the window and the blur of some dizzying world turned red and purple in the sunset. And then, he stared unblinking at this new man in his life. Absorbing, Alex could sense, absolutely everything.

A fastidiously moustachioed waiter was suddenly hovering above the candlelit table, bowing and smiling solicitously at Hawke.

"Monsieur?" he said, preposterously, in French.

Alexei suddenly looked up at the waiter and said in a loud voice, "Watch out! I'm the birthday boy!"

"Ah, mais oui," he replied bowing his head slightly. "Bon anniversaire."

"Good evening," Hawke said, looking up from his menu. "I'll have a glass of Krug Grande Cuvee and the cold borscht to start. And the rack of lamb, please. Rare. And decant a bottle of the 1959 Petrus if you'd be so kind."

"Very well, monsieur. And for the young gentleman?"

"Bananas? I have no idea. Do you have any suggestions?"

"Well, I—I mean it's difficult to—c'est très difficile—"

Hawke said, "Quite right. Difficult. Mashed potatoes? Of course. Alexei, do you like mashed potatoes? Everyone does."

"No potatoes! No!"

"Peas?"

"No peas! No! No!"

"Carrots, then?"

"No carrots!"

"Perhaps the saute foie gras, monsieur?" the waiter said, inexplicably.

Hawke returned the ornate menu and said, "Everything. He'll have one of everything on the menu."

"*Everything*, monsieur? But surely you don't mean—"

"Yes, yes. Just bring us one of everything on the menu. Let him lead us through the jungle. We'll soon find out precisely what he likes and doesn't like. It's the only way we'll get to the bottom of this, don't you agree?"

The waiter shrugged his shoulders in that very French way and said, "Mais ouis, monsieur. Mais certainement. Le rôti d'agneau pour monsieur. One of everything on the menu for the young gentleman. Merci beaucoup." He bowed and disappeared toward the rear of the car, shaking his head and probably murmuring *ooh-la-la* or *oomph*, or something of that ilk.

Ten minutes later, a platoon of waiters in winered livery appeared, streaming down the aisle to arrive at Hawke's table, all bearing large silver platters filled with every possible kind of food. This of course caused a great deal of amusement among the other diners, all of them turning in their seats and peering at the little boy, his uncomfortable father, and the enormous amount of food they had ordered.

What Alexei liked to eat was immediately apparent. Hawke was busily preparing a large plate with a small sampling of all the dishes when Alexei made his decision. Ignoring Hawke's offering entirely, Alexei stood in his high chair and reached for the ornate silver salver with a central crystal bowl containing a healthy dollop of Beluga caviar, surrounded by mounds of small warm buttered pancakes called blinis.

Grabbing a fistful of blinis, he stuffed them into his mouth, polishing them all off in little more than a minute.

Then he scooped up a small handful of caviar, tried it, gurgled with delight, and messily downed the remainder. "More! More!" he cried.

So. Caviar. The apple had not fallen far from the tree.

Hawke called to the waiter who had all the extraneous food removed and quickly summoned another waiter bearing more caviar and pancakes. It was at that moment that Hawke saw the two heavyset men who had climbed aboard the train at Tvas, the two men in the long black overcoats, enter the dining car at the far end.

They made their way toward Hawke and took an empty table on the opposite side of the car about three tables away. Neither man made eye contact with Alex, but he knew that meant nothing. Once they were seated and had ordered a bottle of vodka, the one facing Hawke looked up, caught his eye, and smiled. Hawke, sipping a small flute of Krug champagne, raised his glass and smiled back. He also signaled for his check.

As he was signing it, he noticed one of the men approach, clearly headed his way. The man stopped at their table, smiled at Hawke, and said in heavily accented English, "I am just admiring your handsome boy. Is he your son?"

"No. I am his bodyguard," Hawke said in a low voice. "You'll excuse us. We're leaving."

As Hawke gathered his son into his arms, the man leaned across the table and reached out to ruffle Alexei's hair. His jacket fell open. The assassin had a Vostok Margolin .22LR pistol with a built-in silencer holstered under his arm. The standard concealed weapon of the KGB officer. Hawke shot his right hand out and grasped the man's thick wrist in midair before he could touch a hair on Alexei's head. He then leaned forward and whispered fiercely into the man's ear.

"I said I'm his bodyguard. That includes his hair. Understand me?"

Hawke applied increasingly severe pressure to the base of the man's thumb until he grimaced in pain and nodded his head. The Russian rose to his full height, rubbed his wrist vigorously, smiled down at Hawke, and said, "It's a long trip, you know, here to St. Petersburg. I'm sure we shall all meet again." Then he turned on his heel and returned to his table.

Hawke rose with Alexei in his arms and quickly but somewhat discreetly left the dining car. He needed to return the child safely to their locked compartment. Given the presence of two KGB assassins aboard the Red Arrow, it promised to be a very long night. Two killers on a train. Like an Agatha Christie novel, except you already knew who the true villains were.

But who was the intended victim?

Surely there were many inside Russia, the so-called Tsarists, who wanted Hawke dead.

But both Anastasia and Kuragin had said there was a price on Alexei's head. People in power who didn't like the idea of a tsar's descendant waiting in the wings to take the throne at some future moment.

It hit him like a lightning strike to the heart.

These two thugs weren't aboard the Red Arrow to kill him.

They meant to murder the heir to the crown. The child of the Tsarina.

They meant to kill his son.

EIGHT

HAWKE SAT IN THE DARKENED COMPARTMENT, smoking incessantly to stay alert. He'd bought a few packs of Sobranie Black Russians in the rail station at St. Petersburg. Despite the black wrapper with its fancy gold tip, they were foul, but effective. The rhythmic *click-clack* on the tracks threatened to hypnotize him, and he fought it with nicotine. He was seated on one of the small, upholstered chairs in the center of the compartment's sitting room.

In the adjoining room, mercifully, Alexei was sleeping peacefully on the lower berth, his teddy bear clutched tightly. Hawke had rocked him to sleep and kissed his warm cheek before tucking him in. He'd then propped a sturdy wooden chair against the bedroom door to the train's corridor, feeling only slightly more secure. He'd left the sliding door between their two rooms open and could hear the reassuring sound of his son snoring softly. It was a sound like no other he'd ever heard.

The only light in Hawke's tiny room came from a dim violet-blue nightlight, a spiritlike apparition near the floor that gave the small sitting room a rather eerie, stage-set feeling. Like a bad horror film, Hawke thought, some kind of Hammer Films vampire movie.

In his right hand, Hawke held his SIG .45 pistol, a hollow-point round already in the chamber. He'd positioned his chair to one side and in the shadows, so as to be out of the line of fire of someone forcefully entering the room. But he would have a clear shot at anyone coming through that door without an invitation.

He would shoot to kill if, indeed, circumstances warranted it.

For a man expecting a pair of KGB or criminal thugs to burst through his door with guns blazing, Alex Hawke was surprisingly relaxed. He was not the type of man who could be prodded into deciding what he might or might not do under any possible circumstances. And this was certainly not due to bravery, or coolness, or any especially sublime confidence in his own physical prowess or power. It was a powerful instinct to go with his gut and it hadn't failed him yet.

And, he was, as one of his superior officers in the Royal Navy had said, "Simply good at war."

From time to time he'd rise and stretch, the long hours of sitting starting to wear on him. He looked at the large face of his black Royal Navy dive watch, the luminous numbers clearly legible. It was nearly two o'clock in the morning. He'd been in (or, rather, *on*) this bloody chair for six full hours.

He could feel himself losing his edge.

Inaction is the enemy of action, he reminded himself. It was time to move.

He rose from the chair and went to check on his son, understanding for the very first time the expression "sleeping like a baby." He then went to his travel bag and pulled out a loose-fitting black turtlenecked jumper, pulling it over his head. The black trousers he was already wearing would suit his purposes nicely in the darkness of the train's corridors. He checked his weapon once more and slapped the mag back into the gun.

Slipping the pistol into the nylon holster in the small of his back, he reached up to the shelf and grasped Peter the Great's battle sword, the gift from Kuragin. The red leather scabbard had a loop that he ran his belt through, the ivory-handled sword now hanging down his right side. His black gabardine greatcoat was swaying on the door hook. He shouldered himself into it and saw in the mirror that only the razor-edged tip of the sword was visible beneath the hem.

If you're going to a gunfight, best to bring a gun and a knife, even a sword if there's one handy.

He listened a long moment to Alexei's soft breathing, then he stepped out into the corridor. He turned and pulled the door closed, locked it from the outside, tried it twice, and turned to his left, headed toward the front of the train.

Before he moved to the rear, he wanted to clear any cars up ahead. At the end of the narrow passageway the door was locked, and Hawke could see his first-class carriage was located just behind the locomotive. He saw the door to the concierge's compartment, slightly ajar.

For a moment, he considered waking her to ask her to keep an eye out for anyone entering this car. About to rap, he withdrew his hand. Bad things might happen aboard this train tonight, and he wanted no suspicion to fall on him.

He began to move toward the rear of the train.

He'd caught a glimpse of the passenger manifest while the concierge was off making sure all the first-class passengers had what they needed before turning in. Quickly scanning it, he'd identified his foes. The two men who'd joined the train at Tvas were sharing a single compartment in the last second-class sleeping car, just before the club car at the train's rear. Compartment number 211.

The Red Arrow, racing through the night under a star-spangled black sky, was eleven cars long. Upon reaching the tenth and final sleeping car, he withdrew his pistol and made his way down the darkened corridor until he reached the door marked 211. He tried the knob and found it locked. Pulling a small utility knife and pick from his pocket and inserting it into the lock, he heard a click and slowly pushed the door open.

Empty.

Neither bed had been slept in. There was a half-empty bottle of Imperial vodka on the small table beneath the window and two glasses that appeared to have come from the lavatory. He looked up to the luggage racks above the berths, not surprised to find them empty. These men traveled with only the bare necessities: two guns and a bottle or two of cheap vodka.

They had to be in the club car. He was not at all surprised. KGB officers always ran true to form and he'd rather expected to find them there.

Before he pushed the button that opened the automatic pneumatic sliding doors to the final car, he peered through the frosty windows. The two Russians could be seen on a rounded banquette at the very rear of the car, opposite each other, drinking, smoking, and playing cards. Otherwise, the car appeared to be completely empty, just as you would expect at this hour.

After affixing a short silencer to the SIG's muzzle, he returned the gun to its holster beneath his left shoulder. Hawke spent many long hours at the Six shooting range practicing his quick draw. He could draw his weapon and fire accurately in less than two-hundredths of a second, about as fast as the blink of an eye. He could also shoot a playing card in half—right through the *edge* of it—at twenty yards with the first shot, but that was just a killing machine showing off.

He pushed the metal button and the doors whooshed open. It was sleeting fiercely now, and the white flashes of ice in the dark whipped past the speeding train at warp speed.

He stepped inside the smoky club car, walked smiling toward the two men. Three packs of cards were scattered over the table. The air was blue with cigar smoke, and an ashtray had toppled over, leaving some butts on the floor.

His face and posture a mask of composure, whatever lurked inside him well battened down, Hawke said, "Good evening, gentlemen. I do hope I'm not disturbing you."

The Russians looked up in surprise and grunted something incomprehensible.

He was ready to draw if either made a move for his weapon, but neither did. Instead, they smiled and motioned him toward them as they might an old comrade. The effect that vodka had on one's ego and the false sense of security it created had never failed to amaze Hawke. But he'd been counting on that effect at this late hour and he was not disappointed. The KGB had a well-known history with vodka and it was one that, over the years, frequently tipped in an MI6 operative's favor.

"Sit down, sit down," the one to Hawke's right said, sliding over. It was the smaller one, not the one who'd tried to touch Alexei.

"Thanks so much, but I can't stay long. I'll take a drink though. Can't sleep. Damnedest thing, insomnia. I'm Alex Hawke, by the way. Didn't get a chance to introduce myself properly in the dining car, I'm afraid."

The hefty cretin whose wrist he'd nearly fractured in the dining car poured him a glass of vodka, sloshing some over the side. Hawke stepped nearer to the table, took the drink with his left hand, downing a bit while keeping his eyes moving rapidly side to side, looking for any hint of aggression, and then spoke directly to the large Russian, his low voice dripping with menace.

"You seemed inordinately interested in my

dinner companion earlier this evening. As I told you, I'm his bodyguard. You then made a threatening remark. Something about a long journey, perhaps we'd meet again. Well, here we are. We meet again. I don't usually socialize with drunken thugs and paid assassins, but in your particular case I'm making an exception. I'm armed, of course, so don't even think of doing anything foolish."

He caught simultaneous movement, both to his right and left. Hands going for guns on both sides of the round table.

In a single fluid motion he brought his right foot up, viciously ripping the wooden card table from its base, pitching bottles, glasses, cards, ashtrays up into the faces of the two men. At the same time he whipped out his SIG .45 and drew down on the two men before they could get to their weapons.

"Hands in the air. Now. Good. Now, one at a time, slowly remove your guns and throw them toward me. Not at me, on the bloody floor! Mind your manners, boys; I warn you, I'm pretty handy with this peashooter. I make nice tight patterns in foreheads when I shoot."

The guns clattered to the floor, and the men looked at him, ashen-faced, waiting to be executed.

"I suggest we step out onto the platform. I've got a couple of very expensive Cuban cigars, Monte Cristo number 8. I thought you two cretins might enjoy a good smoke at the end of a long day."

He pulled a single cigar from his breast pocket and passed it beneath his nose, inhaling the pungent aroma.

"Delicious. On your feet. We'll step out onto the

platform behind you. Get a little fresh air and enjoy a good smoke. You first, Ivan, then your comrade. Outside. Now."

At the rear of the club car was a door opening onto a small half-oval platform with a railing. It was where one could smoke cigars, take the air, or wave farewell to friends at the station.

The Russian pulled the sliding door open. Sleet, snow, and freezing night air came rushing into the club car as first one, then the other, stepped outside.

Hawke remained in the doorway and withdrew the sword from the scabbard at his side.

"I could shoot you now, but I've a better idea. My terrible swift sword. I'm descended from a ruthless English pirate, you see. Chap called 'Blackhawke' and a right bastard he was too. When he wanted to dispose of someone, he'd make them walk the plank and sleep with the fishes. If they were reluctant, he'd give them encouragement with the tip of his blade. Turn around and face the rear, hands in the air."

They did so, resigned to their fate now.

"Ivan, up on the rail. Do it now or you'll get a very long knife in the back and a punctured lung. Your chances of survival are slim in any case, but probably marginally better if you jump. I'm waiting. You may have noticed I'm not a patient man."

The train was racing through the night at speeds well over one hundred miles an hour, the trackless forests to either side receding in a white blur. The killer climbed clumsily up onto the rail, keeping his balance with one hand desperately clutching the ice-coated overhanging roof.

"Jump, damn you!" Hawke said, prodding the man repeatedly with his new sword. And the man, screaming, jumped to his death, hurling his body into the black night.

"You're up, old sport. Time to fly."

The second man turned toward Hawke, pleading for his life in a rush of garbled Russian.

"I'm sure your pleas for mercy are poignant and convincing, but they're falling on deaf ears. Up on the rail with you, you sniveling bastard. Die like a man, at least."

As the man struggled up on the rail, Hawke said, "When your employers in Moscow find your frozen carcasses, if they ever do, it will perhaps give them pause before any more such clumsy assassination attempts. I won't tolerate threats to my son. Now, jump, you miserable shit."

Hawke pressed the tip of the sword into the man's fat buttock, "I said jump!"

Wailing in fear, he did just that.

Hawke wiped the blood from the tip of his sword and returned it to the scabbard. It had performed most satisfactorily. Captain Blackhawke would have been proud of his progeny. Then he turned to survey the scene of the crime. He bent to pick up the glass he'd used to drink the vodka. *No sense leaving incriminating evidence about*, he thought, and he heaved the glass over the rail. Then he closed the door. Messy enough. It looked like there'd been a drunken fight. Anything could have happened. Two passengers would be determined to be missing sometime tomorrow. In this godforsaken tundra, their bodies would not be found for days or weeks, if ever.

A mystery, perhaps not worthy of Dame Agatha Christie, but still a mystery sufficient to suit Hawke's purposes.

ALEXEI, HIS FACE PINK AND ANGELIC UPON HIS PILLOW, looked precisely the way he had when his father had left him. Hawke, feeling relaxed for the first time since boarding the train, took down his false-bottomed travel case and returned his weapon to its compartment. Then he removed the sat phone, poured himself a small whiskey, and returned to the dreaded chair in the sitting parlor.

"Sir David," Hawke said when his superior at MI6 picked up.

"Hawke?"

"Yes, sir."

"Where the devil have you been? There are no end of rumors, and the least you could have done is to give me some kind of heads-up before you disappeared. Everyone thinks you're dead."

"I'm terribly sorry, sir. It just wasn't possible. It was a personal matter. I'll explain it all when I see you."

"And when might that happy event occur?"

"Tomorrow evening, with any luck. I'll need a bit of help getting out of here."

"Where the hell is here?"

"A train. Arriving at the Saint Petersburg rail station around noon tomorrow. The Red Arrow. First-class car just aft of the locomotive. I've booked the first two compartments at the forward end of the car. Double-oh-one is the car number. I'm anticipating a decidedly unfriendly reception committee upon arrival on the platform. KGB. I'm going to need armed cover before leaving the train, and the more the better. I'm bringing a hostage out. Very fragile. He'll require special assistance."

"Hurt? Wounded?"

"No. Small."

"*Small?*"

"Affirmative. He'll need milk."

"*Milk?*"

Hawke heard a voice in the background and then C turning from the phone's mouthpiece and saying to someone, "Hawke's coming out. With a hostage. Needs milk, apparently. What? Hell if I know what he's up to, barmy, if you ask me!"

Then he was back on the phone.

"You'll have it, Alex. Next steps?"

"My thought was quick armed surface transport to an unmarked helo standing by on the roof of our Saint Petersburg consulate. A quick buzz across the Baltic Sea to Tallinn, and a plane of some sort waiting there in Estonia to bring us in."

"Consider it done. Are you quite all right, Alex? You sound odd, I must say."

"Under the circumstances, I'm perhaps the happiest man on earth, sir."

"I do think you've gone a bit mad, Alex, but I'll take care of these arrangements. At least you're not dead."

"At the very least, sir. Thank you for noticing."

Click.

NINE

SEMINOLE, FLORIDA

IT WAS HOT. *ALWAYS HOT OUT HERE IN THE DAMN swamp*, Stokely Jones Jr. thought, emerging from the cool dark shade of the old Baptist church into the searing, wind-inflamed morning. You wouldn't think they had churches in Hades, but they did. The big man paused at the top of the weathered steps, loosened his tie, mopped his brow, and looked out across the churchyard. Three people were sitting on a shaded bench that wrapped around a tree: Alex Hawke; his son, Alexei; and the pretty young woman who looked after his child.

Miss Spooner is what Hawke called the young woman. Nell Spooner had a small wicker basket of toys on her lap, things to keep little Alexei from getting bored out here in the boonies. She had big almond-shaped blue eyes, honey-blond hair, and a young Princess Diana vibe going on. Sweet innocence, kind that made you automatically warm up to somebody you didn't know from Adam.

Stoke smiled, seeing the look on Alex Hawke's face. All the pain that man had been through lately? Replaced with joy. Plain and simple happiness. Stoke swiped his handkerchief across his brow. He just stood there watching the three of them for a few minutes. You live long enough, he was thinking, you get to see that, sometimes, the good really does come with the bad.

And God knows Hawke had had his share of bad lately. Came back from Russia without the woman he loved. But not empty-handed, no sir. Now he had a son. And how he did love that boy, Lord only knows how much. Father and son. But something else, deeper. Like they were twins or something.

The circular wooden bench surrounded a gnarled live oak tree. Standing tall out in the scruffy churchyard. Last hurricane that roared up from Key West took its toll around here. But, like the old rugged cross, that tree had stood its ground.

In the silence he could hear the hum of traffic. Two long miles full of scrub palm, sand fleas, snakes, and gators from here, old U.S. 41, or Alligator Alley, made its way over to Tampa.

Earlier, he and Hawke had passed the Injun Tradin' Post, the tourist trap where Stoke's former fellow inmate at the Glades Correctional Institution, a Seminole Indian and local former prizefighter named Chief Johnny Two Guns, had shopped. He was reputed to have bought the fake Seminole tomahawk there that he had murdered his own mother with.

Turns out Two Guns's late mom was a God-fearing soul, the choirmaster here for nearly fifty years. Small world, right? Full of some really good people and a whole lot of flaming assholes.

Not much of a church, he considered, looking back at it. It was a white frame structure of two stories. Some of the windows had fixed wooden louvers, and some had shutters that folded back. There were also a few stained-glass windows with lots of panes missing. The roof was galvanized sheet iron, corrugated.

Paint was peeling off the steeple, too, he noticed, and then a skeet bit him right on the back of his neck. Damn! He slapped at it, got the sucker, and saw the smear of his own blood in the palm of his hand. Memories. "Heat 'n' Skeet," that's what the U.S. Navy SEALs used to call this backcountry.

Stoke, a former NFL linebacker built like two, had done some secret training not twenty miles from here. Blown up a lot of shit, including more than a few ten-foot gators with grenades dropped from hovering choppers right down their gaping gullets. Messy, but more entertaining than *The Price Is Right* or whatever that crap was they had on TV. Besides, gators ate dogs. And sometimes babies.

Scattered around here and there on the church grounds, somebody had placed big tin buckets of smoldering woody husks that gave off white smoke—homemade mosquito bombs. Stoke murdered another stinging dive-bomber and descended the creaking steps, trying to stand in the white smoke. But the stuff kept shifting away from him in a fluke of nature that made him smile. Sometimes nature was on your side, but mostly not.

Well, all he had to say to that right now was "Hallelujah."

It was Stokely Jones's wedding day.

He should be happy, he thought, sweat stinging his eyes. God knows he loved Fancha with all his heart; it was marriage he wasn't so sure about. His one serious relationship with a woman before this was with a podiatrist from Tenafly, New Jersey. Big old gal, mostly bosom, had half the men in Jersey at her feet, he used to joke. She'd wanted to marry him, too. Morning of the wedding? He'd skipped.

Now, here he was again. Just being inside that church had made him nervous as a damn long-tailed cat in a roomful of rocking chairs. He hadn't even meant to propose! One night, out at her palazzo on Key Biscayne, looking at her beautiful face in the moonlight, he'd said, "You know what, baby? I worship the ground you will walk on in a future lifetime."

Bam. Look at him. Here he was, at a specific church, on a specific date. Getting . . . he almost choked . . . getting *married*.

Grace Baptist Church was located in the town of Seminole, Florida, population 867, most of them black folks and members of the congregation. You had farmers, fishermen, and caneworkers mostly out here. It was the bride's hometown.

Fancha's family had emigrated to the States from the Cape Verde islands back in the 1980s. Settled out here in the sawgrass and muck for some unknowable reason. Maybe somebody in the family was a professional alligator wrestler, who knows. Compared to Harlem, where he grew up, this place bit the big one, all he had to say about it.

Grace Baptist was the church Fancha had grown up in, singing in the choir. Not exactly St. Patrick's Cathedral on Fifth Avenue in New York City. Or even the Abyssinian Baptist Church at 132 West 138th Street. Now those were *churches*. You walk in there and you can *feel* the good Lord saying, "This right here, this is the house of the Lord, sinner, and don't you forget it."

"Damn, it's hot!" Stokely Jones said, dropping down on the bench next to his best man, Lord Alexander Hawke. Man flew all the way in from England with his little boy to be here. Cutest little kid you ever saw, dressed in his blue-and-white seersucker suit, short pants, white knee socks, and black patent leather shoes with straps to hold them on. He had his father's jet-black hair and blazing blue eyes.

Didn't miss a trick either. Nell Spooner had given him a mayonnaise jar with holes punched in the top and an insect inside to keep him entertained after he'd been through all the toys.

"What's that in there?" Stoke asked the child. "A cricket?"

"No, sir," Alexei said, peering into the jar at his new pet. "A grasshopper! Spooner says grasshoppers fly and crickets don't."

"Is that right? I didn't have that information," Stoke said, ruffling his hair and smiling at the boy's proud papa.

Hawke, for some unknown reason, looked cool as

a damn cucumber just plucked out of the Frigidaire. Had on a pure white linen three-piece suit, not a wrinkle in it, a beautiful blue silk tie, and, despite all the heat and humidity and mosquitoes on this late May morning, he had a big smile on his face.

"What are you so damn chipper about?" Stoke asked him. He'd gotten that word, *chipper*, from Hawke long ago and used it ever since. Liked the sound of it.

"Listen to that choir," Hawke said.

"What about it?"

"It's beautiful, that's what. I've never heard music like that. Have you, Miss Spooner?"

"No, sir, I've not," she said. "It is divine, isn't it?"

Stoke said, "It's divine, all right; that's old-time religion you're listening to now. Gospel music. Angel music. Sacred. Folks are just rehearsing in there now. Choir's just getting their pipes warmed up. You wait. Whole building'll be shaking, hands clapping, feet stomping, folks praising the Lord to the rafters when they cut loose, feels like the roof is going to fly off and sail away, I'm telling you."

"I'm so glad you're getting married here, Mr. Jones," Nell Spooner said. "It's positively wonderful."

"Yeah, it is, isn't it?" Stoke said, nervously looking around. "Wonderful, just wonderful."

Stoke pulled a drenched white handkerchief out of the breast pocket of his black suit coat and mopped his brow for the tenth time since he'd come outside. "I'm hot. How come you two aren't hot?"

Hawke looked over at him and said, "Stokely Jones Jr., you look like a man who needs a drink."

"Alex, what'd I always tell you? Only thing alcohol's good for is helping white folks dance. Besides, you know I don't drink."

"You don't get married, either. But you are today. Man's entitled to a drink on his wedding day. It's practically obligatory."

Hawke pulled a shining silver flask from inside his breast pocket and handed it to Stoke.

"What's in it? Don't even tell me. I already know what it is. Head-strong, out-and-out, strong-bodied, ram-jam, come-it-strong, lift-me-up, knock-me-down, gen-u-wine moonshine!"

"That's it, brother. Pure nitro."

Stoke first sniffed at the idea, then unscrewed the little cap and sniffed at the contents. He wrinkled his nose, frowning at the lack of any smell at all.

"What is this stuff, anyway? Just tell me."

"Take a swig, big fella. It won't kill you."

"If this doesn't beat all, I don't know what does. My own best man trying to get me drunk on my own wedding day," Stoke said, and put the flask to his lips, tentatively lifting the thing.

He took a sip, swallowed, and smiled at his friend sideways.

"Diet Coke? It's just Diet Coke, isn't it?"

"Hmm."

"All I ever drink, Diet Coke."

"Hmm."

"See? That's what I'm talking about. That's called taking care of business. That's why you, of all the people in the world who would have cheated, lied, and robbed for this job, that's why you got picked as my best man." Hawke smiled.

"It's an honor, Stoke. I love you like a brother."

"Which I am."

"Which you definitely are."

"Uh-oh. Here comes the bride," Stoke said suddenly, gazing at the winking sunlight on the windshields of a small parade of automobiles now making its way slowly through the tall grass. The narrow, winding, and muddy road leading eventually to the church. "We'd better hustle up and get inside. Bad luck if you see the bride before the ceremony, that right, boss?"

"Absolutely, let's go. Miss Spooner, you've got the ring to give to Alexei when it's his time?"

"I do, sir. Mr. Brock is kindly holding two seats for us in the last pew of the church right on the center aisle. Alexei and I will wait until everyone is seated before we enter so we don't cause a fuss. When it's time for the ring, I'll make sure to send him on his way to you."

Stoke had asked Hawke weeks ago if the child could be the ring bearer during the ceremony and Hawke had readily agreed. So he had his team on the field. He'd also asked his buddy, CIA field agent Harry Brock; his sole employee, Luis Gonzales-Gonzales, the one-armed Cuban known as Sharkey; and finally Fast Eddie Falco, the aged security man at his condo in Miami, to be his ushers. He looked at his watch. Shouldn't they be here by now?

THE RIGHT REVEREND JOSIAH JEFFERSON FLETCHER, J.J., better known as Fletch when he played defense for the New York Jets, weighed about three hundred pounds and had to use a walker to get around. He and the groom had been rookies together back in the day. After a serious knee injury, Fletch left football, came down here to South Florida, and started Grace Baptist Church—right here in the little Indian town of Seminole. A few years later, he'd been ordained. He'd been preaching the gospel ever since.

Fletch was the man Stoke called late at night when the wolves and the heebie-jeebies and the devil himself was at the door.

Fletch had a small office up on the second floor in the "rectory," right next to the room where they kept all the choir robes, candles, and hymnals. The three big men could barely fit inside, so Hawke remained standing in the doorway and Stoke took the chair opposite the preacher at his battle-weary desk. Fletch leaned back in his chair and smiled. For a man who'd seen so much human suffering and anguish, the preacher had the biggest, whitest grin Hawke had ever seen on a human being.

"Mighty pleased to meet you, Mr. Hawke," he said, settling in. "Stokely here tells me you're a lord," he said, looking directly at Hawke. "That right?"

Hawke nodded.

"A lord, you say."

"Hmm."

Then the reverend stretched his meaty forearms over the desk toward Stoke and said in a stage whisper:

"Ain't that something, Stoke?"

"What's that?"

"Him being a lord and all. And here all this time I been thinking there was only just the one."

Hawke burst out laughing, as much over Fletch's small joke as at Stoke's doubled-over laughing fit, Fletch repeatedly slamming his ham-sized fist on the old wooden desk almost hard enough to split it in two.

"Good one, Fletch!" Stoke managed to blurt out.

When they'd all stopped chuckling, Fletch directed his strong gaze at Hawke once more.

"You don't think our boy Stoke's going to try and bolt on us, do you? Groom looks a little nervous to me," the preacher said. "Little green around the gills."

"That's why I'm standing here in the doorway."

The preacher grinned. "Next thing he'll say he has to use the lavatory up the stairs there. The facilities. But don't you worry none, Mr. Hawke, I got the window in there nailed shut."

"Good thinking," Hawke said.

"Only had one bride left standing at the altar in twentysome odd years. Believe me, it's not an experience I want to repeat."

"What happened?" Stoke asked.

"Groom said he had to pee, locked the bathroom door, went out the bathroom window, down the drainpipe, jumped in his car, and left here on two wheels, that's what happened. Best man had to go out in front of the whole congregation and tell them all to go home. No groom, no wedding. Bride's father came up out of his pew like a fullback on third and goal, leaped over the rail, and coldcocked that poor boy, a shot straight from the shoulder that slung his jaw loose. Knocked him out cold as I recall it."

Stoke said, "Fletch, that's reason enough for me

not to bolt on you. I'd hate to see what happened if Fancha's daddy took a shot at my friend Mr. Hawke here."

"Your personal lord over there does look like he can take care of himself, Stoke."

"First-class badass, Rev, even though he looks like such a gent in that fancy white suit."

"You a religious man these days, Stokely?"

"I go to church when I can, Rev."

"What's it take to keep you from going?"

"I go when I can."

"A light rain?"

"I go when I can."

Fletch said, "Well, well, well. I know you got a big old Christian heart and that's good enough for me. You boys ready? I think it's time we go out there and give these folks waiting out there a show. Crowd's getting restless, choir got them all fired up."

"Damn! I got to pee," Stoke said, raising himself up out of his chair.

"Really?" Hawke said. "That's too bad, Stoke. You're just going to have to hold it, brother. I'm sure Reverend Fletcher will be ever mindful of your needs and keep things moving smartly along at the altar."

"Let us pray," the preacher said with a wink at Hawke, each man bowing his head. Stokely pressed his pink palms together, his temple of strong fingers like carved mahogany.

Fletch's voice was soft thunder.

"Oh God our help in ages past,
Our hope in years to come.

Bless and keep your servant Stokely Jones,
And give him strength and happiness
Throughout the years of his blessed union.
Amen."

TEN

NELL SPOONER SAT WITH LITTLE ALEXEI IN HER lap, reasonably cool under the spreading boughs of the old oak tree. Alexei was content, now fixated on a miniature fire engine's ladder. A long parade of automobiles was winding through the tall grass, parking helter-skelter in the church-yard, well-turned-out people climbing out of their mud-spattered cars and trucks. The whole Grace congregation was arriving to see their homegrown celebrity get married.

The press had arrived too. A TV transmitter van from Univision, the Miami-based Latino network, and also Channel 5, a local Fox affiliate. Fancha, a stunning beauty, had recently been nominated for a Latin Grammy award for her new hit song, "Love the Way You Lie," a duet with Enrique Iglesias. The local girl made good was a star, and not just in Seminole anymore. She'd gone worldwide.

When the last wedding guest had entered the

church, Nell gathered up her young charge and made her way to the steps of the church. Mr. Brock, a bit of a flirt, showed them to the seats he'd held for them on the aisle of the very last pew.

Holding the small boy's hand as they entered the pew, she bent and whispered, "Remember, Alexei, first, I give you the ring, then you walk all the way to the front and hand it to your daddy. You do remember?"

"I do remember, Spooner. I go give Daddy the ring. Where all the flowers are."

"There's a good boy. Now, we'll sit right here and be very, very quiet. This is God's house and God doesn't like noisy little boys unless they're singing his praises."

"Quiet as a church mouse?" he whispered, recalling the phrase she'd used at breakfast.

She smiled, delighted at his precocious mind and very keen anticipation about the music and the ceremony. Her new job had taken her a long way from the streets of Paddington in London. An opportunity to attend an old-fashioned southern wedding in a tiny town in the middle of the exotic Florida Everglades would have been unthinkable just two months ago. Too fascinating for words, really.

Unfortunately, she realized now, she couldn't see a thing. There was a man planted in front of her the size of a small building. She could tell from the swell of the choir's voices that the service was about to begin. She saw that the church was now standing room only, a lot of people gathered outside on the steps and beyond.

Nell handed the ring to Alexei. "Hold it tight.

When I pat your head, you just march right up there and give it to Daddy. But walk slowly. Everybody will want a chance to see how handsome you are."

She shifted in her seat, bemoaning the miserable fact of the large, heavily scented man directly in front of her. Long, oiled black hair fell below his neckline. Meaty shoulders stretched the seams of his shiny black suit to the breaking point and it wasn't fat. He looked and smelled like hired muscle, or worse.

She also noticed a telltale bulge beneath the jacket. A simple back brace? Or the strap of a shoulder holster? A gun, she thought. Well, he could easily be Miami-Dade PD, a detective friend of the groom's. Or even paid security for the famous bride. Relax, she told herself. Have fun. This was a once-in-a-lifetime experience.

Right. But she couldn't see anything.

She was finally forced to crane around him and lean forward to glimpse the wedding party and the minister. "Oh. I beg your pardon," she said when the big man whirled his head around and glared at her. "Just trying to see. Terribly sorry."

He grunted unpleasantly. He was rather a thuggish-looking bloke, sallow-faced, big black bushy eyebrows and a low forehead. Not the type of guest one would expect here at all. Unless he was a recording executive, she decided. Yes, that was it, showbiz, or perhaps even a deejay in a South Beach club. Whoever he was, she had an uncomfortable sense about him.

He was off. Maybe even wrong.

But then, she had absolutely no idea, really, whom

she should expect at this ceremony and whom she should not. How could she? She was, after all, brand-new to America, too new, she felt, to make snap judgments about its people.

Still.

The waves of energy coming off the man were almost palpably bad. Silent alarms were going off, and she'd learned long ago to trust her gut in situations like this one. But, as a foreigner, she'd never been in a situation like this one. This horrid man could well be perfectly innocent. So what on earth was she to do? The choir was raising the roof. The service was about to begin.

Run?

Of course, she could simply sweep Alexei up into her arms and slip out of the church. Retreat to the security of Hawke's armored van. Get as far away as quickly as she could.

But what about the bloody wedding ring?

She had agreed to maintain periodic eye contact with her new employer, the very handsome Lord Hawke, tall and slender as a lance in his white suit, now waiting at the altar with the groom for the bride to arrive. She'd promised to let him know with slight nods of her head that little Alexei was behaving himself and that all was well. But what was she supposed to do if all wasn't well? Scream fire in a crowded church? Only to learn she was the silly woman who'd foolishly ruined her employer's best friend's wedding?

Suddenly, coming out of her self-induced daze, she noticed the bride, Fancha. Stunning. Her gleaming dark hair was done up in white ribbons, and she wore an ivory lace dress that fit her perfectly. She had creamy silk slippers, a garland of flowers, and a thin veil trailing down her back. Carrying a spray of baby's breath, gliding along on the arm of her diminutive father, she passed by and was now nearing the altar. Time for Alexei to march up the aisle with the ring.

Without looking, she reached over to pat him on the head. She got nothing but air.

The little boy had bolted. He was running up the aisle just behind the bride. As soon as he could make his way around her voluminous wedding dress, he made straight for his father and clutched him around the knees. People in the church found this cute.

The man in front of her now kneeled on the bench below and put his hands together in prayer. When he bowed his head, his long hair parted and revealed a portion of a tattoo on the back of his neck. A blue scorpion. It was vaguely familiar. She'd seen it once somewhere. Perhaps on a corpse in the morgue. Yes. The Blue Scorpion. A Russian Mafiya hit squad in East London, that was it.

The tattoo sent a shock wave up her spine.

She was well aware that two Russian assassins had threatened Alexei's life aboard the Red Arrow train en route to St. Petersburg. Now all her senses had gone on high alert. There was no longer a shred of doubt in her mind, either about the man or his intended victim. This man was very clearly a Russian assassin. He meant to kill Alexei. She sat back, the precise wheels within wheels of her mind spinning, pondering her options.

Moments later, the sermon ended, and the couple

were pronounced man and wife. The pianist and the choir rose to the occasion, the music swelling and filling the tiny little church with magic. The wedding party began its procession back down the aisle toward her, a beaming groom and a stunningly beautiful bride, a smiling Lord Hawke just behind them, and, next, she was relieved to see little Alexei holding hands with the CIA chap, Brock. They were nearing the exit. She knew Brock was armed and took solace in that.

As the little boy passed by, the Russian thug turned and stared at the child, following him with his eyes until he disappeared. She looked around, a scrim of red desperation creeping around the margins of her consciousness. She had to do something, anything.

As usual there was a complete human logjam at the church entrance as everyone tried to make their way outside and see the departure of the groom and his new bride. Nell stayed put, craned around in her seat, straining to keep sight of Alexei, but, being small, he was soon swallowed up by the crowd pouring out of the church.

She stood up, desperate to get to Hawke, warn him about the assassin, find the child, get him into the bulletproofed van. It was hopeless. There was no way she could push through that crowd. She looked toward the front of the church. Surely there was a side door to the outside somewhere up there?

The center aisle was jammed, a solid wall of people waiting, chatting amiably and patient. So, too, were the aisles on either side of the church. Damn it! Just to her left she could see that there were scattered empty seats appearing now in every row almost all the way to the front.

Without a second thought, she grabbed her purse, slung it over her shoulder, crouched atop her pew seat, and, leaping forward like a WWI doughboy going up over the tops of the trenches, she began scrambling across the tops of each pew, sure-footed on the tops of the seat backs, moving steadily and with great athleticism toward the front. She could see people staring openmouthed at her in disbelief, but they meant nothing. This wedding was over. She quick-peeked back at the rear of the church.

The Blue Scorpion was gone.

ELEVEN

NELL SPOONER DASHED OUT THE LEFT SIDE DOOR of the rectory and into the blinding tropical sunlight. She took a moment to get her bearings, then raced toward the front of the church, around the corner, and out into the rapidly emptying churchyard. A lot of cars had already left, along with all the media, but a considerable number of people were still standing around being sociable.

Her heart racing, she scanned the yard.

Clearly the bride and groom had departed and there was a long line of cars, horns honking, snaking through the tall grass toward the highway in their wake. The black van she and Alexei had used to follow his father and the groom was still under the tree where she'd parked it. If only he were safely inside it.

She stood, composed herself, and made a more deliberate scan of the departing crowd. The big man in black was nowhere in sight. Where was

Lord Hawke? She started moving forward, pushing people aside as she ran toward the oak tree, not knowing why but thinking that would be where he would wait for her to find him when she finally emerged from the church.

Yes! Hawke was there! He was seated on the same bench, talking quietly with the CIA man, Brock, who'd last been seen leaving the church holding the child's hand. But no Alexei. Where was he? Surely they wouldn't have just let him—

The man in black?

Yes. A large figure behind the wheel of a dark sedan parked about two hundred yards from the oak tree. It was one of the few remaining cars and at least three hundred yards away. But the glare of sunlight off the windshield was so strong she couldn't make positive identification. Couldn't see the face at all. Just a hazy silhouette. But every instinct said run for the car. Now.

She angled for it, circling slightly so she'd approach it from the side and rear. She got within fifty feet of the driver's-side door and saw that it was him. He had his back to her, elbows up, staring through binoculars at Hawke and Brock.

She crept up silently in the thick grass.

He bent down, grabbing something from the floor, pulling it up by the stock.

A rifle with a large telescopic sight.

It was then that she caught a glimpse of some movement in the tree beyond, and her heart caught in her throat. Just a small dangling foot, swinging to and fro just above Hawke's head.

Alexei was sitting astride the low-hanging branch

just above his father's head. Hawke kept looking up, his arms outstretched, ready to catch the boy should he jump or fall.

The man jammed the stock of the rifle into his shoulder and welded the gun to his cheek. He put his eye to the scope, raising the barrel upward and into the tree.

He was going to shoot Alexei!

"Drop the gun NOW!" she screamed. "Do it now or you're dead!"

The man laughed at the sound of her voice. "Go away, little nanny. I've got business to do here."

She racked the slide on the SIG P226 pistol she'd pulled from her purse as she ran toward the car.

He froze at the metallic sound, then craned his face around.

"Fuck. A gun, she says to me. Wot is a nice girl like you doing with a gun?"

"Drop the rifle, asshole. Now."

"Sure, sure, lady, please, is no problem." He pulled the gun back inside and let it fall to his feet. Then he turned to face her, the smile still on his face. His right hand moving inside his suit jacket as he said, "Just relax, okay. I'm just getting my cigarettes."

"Sure you are," Nell Spooner replied and put a ragged black hole in the middle of his forehead. He pitched forward, dead.

NELL SPOONER EXPELLED A DEEP SIGH OF RELIEF, resting her head for a moment against the roof of the car. Then she looked up and headed toward the tree where Hawke and Harry Brock still sat, the little boy happily overhead on his branch, swinging his legs back and forth.

"Spooner!" he cried out. "Look at me!"

At the sight of the pistol still hanging loosely at her side, Hawke jumped up and raced to her, putting his hands on her trembling shoulders. She was clearly in a slight state of shock.

"My God, what happened?" he asked.

"Man in that dark blue car. Had a rifle. About to take a shot. I shot him first."

"A shot? Me?"

"No, sir. He was aiming at Alexei on the branch above you. You may well have been next, I imagine."

Hawke took a deep breath, looked back over at his son, now in the arms of Harry Brock, a gun in one hand, checking the perimeter. Hawke said something unprintable and then gently squeezed her shoulders. "Thank you, Sergeant Spooner, thank you for saving my boy's life. I had no idea it would come to this so quickly."

"The commissioner of Scotland Yard did the right thing in loaning me out, sir. Your fears were well founded. I'll be more alert now. I won't let anyone ever get this close again."

Hawke looked around. "There may be more of them. Probably not, but I suggest we all get into the van as quickly as possible and get out of here."

Hawke added, "Harry, please call 911 and get an ambulance out here. Also the Collier County Police and the FBI."

"You'll find a tattoo on the back of his neck, Agent Brock," Spooner said. "The Blue Scorpion.

It's a highly organized group of retired KGB officers. All highly trained killers available for a fee. I was involved in a case in London when one of them showed up dead."

"Thanks, Nellie," Brock said, speed-dialing a number on his mobile and flashing his cunning grin. "You sure don't look like a cop, by the way. You look like Scarlett Johansson. Anybody ever tell you that?"

Harry, getting no reply, shrugged his shoulders and made his phone calls.

Sergeant Nell Spooner, who was a member of London's Trident Operational Command Unit of the Metropolitan Police Service, a team designed to investigate and prevent any gun-related activity within London's communities, put her service pistol back into her purse. She could feel her heart rate slowing for the first time since she'd become aware of the man in the next pew.

She'd been granted a leave of absence by the Met to take a temporary position. She had been assigned to Six counterterrorist operative Lord Alexander Hawke, specifically to protect his child. Hawke's child was a known target of Russian agents. As the grandson of Russia's only modern Tsar, now dead, he posed a political threat to the Kremlin.

Spooner had walked away from the group at the oak tree and wandered to the edge of a small pond. She needed a little time to collect herself. Her hands were trembling violently, and she stuffed them into the pockets of her rose-colored linen jacket.

She had never fired a gun in anger before in her life.

Now she had. It was not a pleasant experience, taking a human life.

But her young charge, a boy whom she'd come to feel an almost motherly affection for in these few short months, was still alive because of her actions.

"Spooner!" Alexei said. "Look what I found!"

He opened his hand.

It was a tiny blue speck, a fragment of a robin's egg, a relic of spring.

TWELVE

AT SEA, ABOARD K-550
ALEKSANDR NEVSKIY

"Там are a problem, sir," the Russian subma- rine's *starpom*, or executive officer, said, ap- proaching and saluting his captain. The man, Aleksandr Ivanov-Pavlov, was ramrod straight, inside and out, and it had served him well over the years.

"Problem, Aleksandr? No! Aboard this vessel? Tell me it's not true."

The Central Command Post (CCP) men and officers nearby smiled at their skipper's infamous sarcasm. It was one of the reasons they not only re- spected him, but liked him.

The captain smiled his famously enigmatic smile, his teeth white in his full salt-and-pepper beard. A career submariner, the oldest-serving skipper in the Russian Navy, the barrel-chested, white-haired Sergei Petrovich Lyachin, had recently been hon- ored with command of the *Nevskiy*, Russia's newest nuclear ballistic submarine. It had been a decidedly mixed blessing.

The new boat had cost a billion dollars. She could dive to a depth of six hundred meters and run at a maximum speed of thirty knots on the surface, twenty-eight knots submerged, all official numbers only, of course. Her real performance parameters were highly classified. In addition to powerful anti-ship torpedoes, her armament included sixteen Bulava SLBM ballistic missiles and six SS-N-15 cruise missiles. Admiral Vladimir Kuroyedov, commander in chief of the Russian Navy, had described the *Nevskiy* as the most effective multipurpose submarine in the world.

Effective, perhaps, but plagued with a cascade of ever more difficult problems and now, according to the XO, it seemed she had yet another.

Lyachin, an old Cold Warrior, had formerly served in the Northern Fleet for many years. Respected, liked, and not a little feared by his crew, the stern-faced sub driver was commonly referred to as *Barya*, father.

Lyachin had recently endured weeks of dry-dock repairs to his malfunctioning ballast controls and dive planes. All of this courtesy of Hugo Chavez's navy technicians, in a steamy, mosquito-ridden port of La Guaira on the verdant coast of Venezuela. The insects were starting to get on his nerves. Standing on the sub's conning tower early one evening, he had said to his chief engineer, "Hell, Arkady, you kill one Venezuelan mosquito and ten more come to its funeral."

La Guaira was the port city for Caracas, Venezuela. *Nevskiy* had been in dry dock there while all necessary repairs were effected and the boat's *zampolit*, the KGB political officer, attended a series of secret meetings with President Hugo Chavez and his advisers. The Russians and the Venezuelans were planning joint naval exercises for the following spring. Stick a little needle in the American navy's arrogant balloon, right in their own backyard.

AFTER A MISERABLE THREE WEEKS, Captain Lyachin was finally once again where he felt most comfortable, under the water and on patrol in the Caribbean Sea. His mission was to conduct intelligence, surveillance, and reconnaissance missions against the Americans. He had also resumed playing cat and mouse with an American Virginia class sub, SSN 775, the USS *Texas*. He knew the man in command of the *Texas*, a formidable opponent named Captain Flagg Youngblood. They'd never met, of course, but each man had long enjoyed their underwater confrontations in the oceans of the world.

Lyachin was privately struggling with a grave secret. It was something so outlandish that he had not even confided his suspicions to his XO. He was beginning to suspect that his sub's multiplying problems were not simply human error, bad luck, or bad engineering. He thought perhaps his boat was the target of invasive electronic warfare, directed from the nearby American sub *Texas*. Ever since the infamous Stuxnet takedown of the Iranian centrifuge, he'd worried that one day warships might suffer a similar fate.

Intel he'd seen indicated three countries were leading in this new techno arms race: Israel, China, and the United States.

He had done considerable research on the subject for the fleet commander, who then ordered him to host seminars on offensive and defensive electronic warfare at the Naval War College whenever he was land-bound.

Stuxnet, he told his classes, was a fearsome cyberweapon, first discovered by a security firm based in Belarus. It is like a worm that invades and then spies on and reprograms high-value infrastructures like Iran's nuclear facilities in Natanz. It is also capable of hiding its pathways and its changes. Many in the military considered it so powerful as to lead to the start of a new worldwide arms race. If you can take down a nuclear power plant, they reasoned, why not a nuclear submarine?

Lyachin was now beginning to believe that the U.S. Navy had somehow acquired the ability to use just such cyberweapons to influence events aboard his vessel by somehow subverting or overcoming his built-in electronic firewalls.

Nevskiy was nearly six hundred feet long and a fourth-generation Borei class. At thirty-two thousand tons submerged, she was roughly the size of a World War II aircraft carrier. She was, according to the Russian Admiralty, state of the art. But to Lyachin's chagrin, she had been besieged with myriad problems in the past months. Prime Minister Vladimir Putin had proudly pronounced her seaworthy prior to the launching at Vladivostok and she'd headed for the Caribbean.

And that's when the real trouble started.

The *Nevskiy*'s XO, Lieutenant Aleksandr Ivanov-Pavlov, smiled back at his captain's wry response to this most recent dose of bad news. He understood the old man's sense of humor. Or he pretended to, at any rate. Son of a powerful Kremlin insider, young Aleksandr had been learning the political ropes since childhood. His father had been murdered in a KGB power struggle that had left him bereft of two uncles as well.

It was his close relationship with the *Nevskiy*'s captain that engendered free-flowing communications between the boat's skipper and its 118-man crew, comprising 86 commissioned and warrant officers and 32 noncommissioned officers and sailors.

Captain Lyachin was seated in his raised black leather command chair in the center of the CCP. His command post was set just forward on the conning tower and aft of the torpedoes, the second compartment in the boat. The CCP, an oval-shaped room, was fairly spacious, but with thirty or so submariners crowded inside, it felt and smelled like a traditional Russian *banya*, or steam bath. The captain, frustrated in his efforts to quit smoking, lit another cigarette, his tenth.

To Lyachin's right sat his helmsman, gripping a wheel the size of a dinner plate that controlled the boat's aft stabilizers. Next to him was the planesman, who controlled the sub's hydroplanes. His responsibility was to "steer" the boat up and down while submerged, or remain at any given depth the captain had ordered.

Arrayed in front of these men was a bank of computer screens showing depth, speed, and course, among other vitally important information. Next to them, the sonar officer, Lieutenant Petrov, monitored his screen, which displayed a flickering cascade of sound. In addition, the compartment had consoles for radar, weapons, electronic countermeasures, and damage control, all manned by specialists.

Petrov suddenly got a hit, but the signal was buried in surface clutter and needed to be washed. He leaned forward and thumbed the switch initiating the ALS, algorithmic processing systems. The ALS would analyze and filter, eliminating any signals not matching his desired target. He kept his eyes focused on the screen, waiting for the results.

Lyachin sat back in his heavily padded chair and expelled a sigh of frustration. "Tell me, Aleksandr, what fresh hell do we have on our hands now?"

"Frankly, it doesn't make any sense," Ivanov-Pavlov, the XO said. "We are getting repeated power spikes from the reactor. On a regular basis. But we see no indication of anything amiss on any of the monitoring systems, nor cooling, nor do the surges affect normal functions and operations."

"Radiation leaks?"

"No, sir."

"Makes no sense," Lyachin said, scratching his chin. His thoughts turned to his greatest fear, the loss of his boat, not with a bang, but with a bug.

"No, sir."

"Electronic security, Alexei? Has the engineer

been able to detect any evidence of a viral infection in any system?"

The XO thought before he responded. "Unless some traitor among the crew boarded this vessel at La Guaira with a dirty mobile phone up his ass, this boat is still clean."

"Inform the engineer that I want another sweep. Stem to stern," Lyachin said.

"Yes, Captain, right away."

"Fucking hell," the captain said under his breath. He had a very bad feeling about this. Too many inexplicable things had been going wrong aboard the *Nevskiy*. He was beginning to believe his own theorem that it wasn't just bad luck or sloppy engineers. Perhaps, he thought, it was the *Texas*. Perhaps the American sub he'd been chasing was somehow capable of infiltrating—

There was a brief burst of metallic static from the speaker above the skipper. "Conn, Sonar, new contact bearing zero-nine-five. Designate contact number Alpha 7-3."

Lyachin thumbed his microphone. "Captain, aye. What have you got, Lieutenant Petrov?"

"Distant contact. Surface. Large vessel. In these waters, I'd guess a tanker. Maybe a cruise ship, sir. *Amerikanski*."

"Periscope depth," Lyachin said. "Let's have a look around. See what we see." The other possibility, of course, was an American spy vessel, disguised as a freighter and crammed to the gunwales with offensive electronic weaponry. If not the *Texas*, then surely it was the American spy vessel that was bugging him.

"Periscope depth!" the XO called out.

"Periscope depth, aye," said Lieutenant Viktor Kamarov, the planesman on duty, and he adjusted the boat's attitude accordingly.

"Engine turns for fifteen knots," Lyachin said.

"Fifteen knots, aye."

"Initial course two-zero-one."

"Two-zero-one, aye."

Nevskiy, which had been transiting the Bahamian Trough at two hundred meters, began to rise, driven by its two steam turbines and the hydrodynamic action of her diving planes.

"Raise periscope and power up the ESM mast," Lyachin ordered. The ESM antenna was designed to sniff out electronic signals from any snooping subs or ships. If the *Texas*, or anyone else, was indeed trying to penetrate the *Nevskiy*'s electronic barriers, he needed to know about it now. Lyachin grabbed the periscope rising from its well and swiveled the two handles around to face west where the signal had been acquired.

Born cautious, he first quickly scanned the horizon. His search periscope featured infrared detection, a live-feed video facility, and satellite communications capability to forward real-time video to Russia's Strategic Submarine Command. The weather had deteriorated since he'd submerged. The seas had to be running twelve to fifteen feet, the wind blowing spumy froth from the tips of the whitecaps. He kept swiveling a few degrees before coming to a stop. He could make out the distant silhouette of a large vessel on the horizon.

Nevskiy was closing fast on the vessel, running at

periscope depth, around sixteen to eighteen meters below the surface. Her periscope, which resembled a hooded cobra with a large glass eye, trailed a long white wake behind it.

Lyachin said, "Visual contact Alpha 7-3, bearing one-nine-five, speed fifteen knots. Large displacement American cruise ship. Headed for Jamaica, I would guess. And right into the teeth of that storm we've been tracking." He turned to his *starpom*.

"Sound General Quarters, Aleksandr. Battle stations. Prepare for torpedo attack."

The XO picked up a microphone and his voice echoed throughout the submarine.

"Battle stations! Battle stations! Prepare torpedo attack!"

Lyachin had received "Eyes Only" orders from the commander, Strategic Submarine Forces, South Atlantic Fleet, to launch a practice torpedo attack, a dry run, sometime before 0500 tomorrow. He had glanced up at the ship's chronometer mounted on the bulkhead. Now was as good a time as any. And the big American cruise ship hauling sunburned tourists full of rum was as good a simulated target of opportunity as any.

THIRTEEN

AT SEA, ABOARD
U.S. CRUISE SHIP *FANTASY*

THE FIRST INKLING OF TROUBLE AHEAD WAS THE red wine. Stoke looked at Fancha's glass. He hadn't even felt the massive cruise ship heeling over, but the wine sure had noticed. It was tilted inside the glass at a very weird angle. Stoke was about to mention it to his brand-new bride and then thought better of it. Fancha was already weirded out about being on this big boat and completely out of sight of land.

The only reason she'd agreed to Stoke's secret honeymoon surprise, this cruise from Miami, was the destination. The massive Carnival cruise ship *Fantasy*, with five thousand souls aboard, was bound for Jamaica, a place she'd always wanted to go—so she let him talk her into it. Despite the fact that the last time he'd talked her into crossing the ocean (in an airship) she'd almost died.

This was their third night at sea. So far so good.

Until this cold front had moved in, they'd had nothing but calm seas, sunny days, and romantic nights in their stateroom. Stoke had a vial of Viagra inside his Dopp kit, but hadn't touched it. This was giving him a lot of positive feelings as he did his morning laps around the ship. Ain't lost it yet, Mama. Lead in the pencil, snow on the roof, but a roaring fire at the bottom of the chimney.

Stoke didn't know squat about honeymoons, but this one seemed to be off to a good start, skimpy nighties and all. They'd seen a cabaret show last night and then hit the blackjack table. His new bride had won almost five hundred dollars and was so excited you'd think the ghost of Ed McMahon had shown up with a million-dollar check from Publisher's Clearinghouse.

Stoke, seeing the wine now slowly tilting in the opposite direction, smiled at his girl and asked her to dance. The band was playing Satchmo's "What a Wonderful World," and since it was Stoke's favorite song, Fancha wasn't too surprised when her husband, who hated to dance, asked her out on the floor.

"You know what?" she whispered, her head pressed against his chest.

"No, what?" he said, kissing the top of her head.

"I'm glad we came on this cruise, baby. And, just think, day after tomorrow we'll be in Montego Bay."

"It's going to be great, honey. Just like I said. I'm glad it makes you happy."

"And I say to myself . . . what a wonderful world," she sang, looking up at him with love and happiness in her eyes.

STOKE SHOWED HER BACK TO THE TABLE AND THEN excused himself to go to the john. There was perceptible motion now, but luckily Fancha had had a few glasses of champagne before dinner and probably just thought she was a little woozy. He said he'd be right back and he'd damn sure better not find her dancing with another man.

Instead of the head, Stoke went up one flight of stairs to the purser's desk. They had newspapers posted and weather faxes regularly. He'd checked the charts yesterday but not today. He looked at this one and it didn't look good. At that moment he could actually feel the big boat listing to starboard before beginning the long roll back.

"Looks like we got a little tropical depression due south of Haiti," Stoke said to the uniformed guy on duty.

"Yes, sir. Captain's keeping a close eye on it."

"Moving north-northwest, according to the last report. Right in our path."

"Well, maybe, maybe not. Nothing more unpredictable than a tropical storm."

"How about women?"

"Excuse me?"

"Never mind. This boat has bilge keels? Active fin stabilizers?"

"I couldn't say, sir," the man said, rolling his eyes. "I'm the assistant purser."

"Right. You and your purse have a good evening."

"And you as well, sir. I'm sure there's nothing to worry about."

"You are? Well, that's good. That makes me feel a whole lot more comfortable."

Stoke walked away, storm clouds gathering outside. And inside his mind.

ABOARD THE *NEVSKIY*, THE CAPTAIN'S WAR-GAME order came: "Torpedo attack! Prepare tubes one and two!"

The XO, Ivanov-Pavlov, passed along the order to the torpedo section in the sub's forward-most compartment. Each of the sub's ten watertight compartments had three or four decks, except the one housing the OK-650B nuclear reactor and the torpedoes. Senior Lieutenant Dobrov, aged thirty, was the commander of the torpedo combat unit and it was he and the warrant officer responsible for loading who would direct the practice launch operation. The torpedo compartment was located just forward of the CCP.

The compartment was large, nearly the size of a basketball court. It contained four 533mm-caliber and two 650mm-caliber forward torpedo tubes, plus the torpedo and missile magazine. The eighteen torpedoes were stacked in three rows and suspended over the crew's heads like giant cigars. The weapons themselves were conveyed along a hydraulic tracking system to the tubes in the boat's bow. Most of these "warshot" torpedoes had warheads of between 200 and 300 kilograms of high explosives.

There were five crew members and two engineers

in the compartment, all under the immediate command of Warrant Officer Lohmatov. It was he who supervised the laborious loading of the two "Fat" antiship torpedoes. Thirty feet long and weighing over two tons, each torpedo was moved slowly along its tracking into position in front of tubes one and two.

Were this a live fire exercise instead of merely a drill, the target in *Nevskiy*'s crosshairs would be an American aircraft carrier or heavy cruiser, not a cruise ship full of sunburned, rum-drenched tourists on holiday.

Senior Lieutenant Dobrov was still calculating the attack coordinates of the American cruise ship as the huge torpedoes slid into their firing tubes. The tubes' inner doors were both closed.

There was nothing to do now but wait for the order from the CCP to arm the two fish and simulate the firing sequence. Senior Lieutenant Dobrov stayed at the fire control panel. He knew his wait could be anywhere from five minutes to thirty depending on Captain Lyachin's sense of strategic considerations far beyond Dobrov's area of responsibility.

ABOUT AN HOUR BEFORE DAYBREAK, FANCHA CLIMBED out of her berth and tried to make her way across their cabin to the bathroom. In the dim light, Stoke could see she had her hand clamped over her mouth and was making gagging noises and trying to make it to the head before she threw up.

It had not been a fun night. Fancha's lighthearted mood had been dropping as steadily as the barometer ever since they'd left the restaurant for a stroll around the deck. The wind had freshened considerably. There were whitecaps and Stoke estimated about ten-foot seas. He'd been keeping a weather eye on the barometer for the last six hours. It had been dropping precipitously.

A tropical storm was forming just north of Jamaica, moving northwest at fourteen miles per hour. He knew they were in for a very rough ride. Just how rough it would get he had no idea.

He saw her reach for the door to the head at the exact moment the ship got slammed by a rogue wave on the port side. Fancha flew across the small cabin just as the mirrored closet door swung open and cracked her forehead with its edge. She uttered a small whimper of pain and then collapsed in the corner and got sick all over her brand-new silk nightgown.

Stoke leaped out of his berth and went to her. She tried furiously to push him away. Blood was trickling down her forehead and into one eye. Stoke examined it and knew she was going to need stitches. Tears were rolling down her cheeks and she was whimpering softly. He staggered into the head and came back with two damp hand towels, one for the wound, one to try and clean her up a little.

"Baby, I'm so sorry, let me just try to—"

"Just leave me alone, Stokely Jones. I'm sick and I banged my head. I told you I didn't want to come on this damn boat. And now look at me."

"Honey, look, it's a storm. It happens all the time.

This boat is built for this kind of weather. Now let me look at that cut. I think you might need stitches. I'll go to sick bay and get the doctor, okay?"

"Whatever you say. It's your honeymoon."

It was useless. She was relatively safe here on the floor, holding on to the foot of the berth. He got a pillow and put it behind her head, then draped a blanket over her. Her distress was making him re-think the whole idea of the surprise honeymoon, and guilt reared its ugly head.

"I'll be right back, baby. The doctor will stitch you up and give you something to calm . . . something to help you sleep. Okay? I love you."

Angry silence.

Stoke climbed three flights of the main staircase to the promenade deck and pushed through the door. The wind was howling, and he felt a sting-ing rain on his face. He leaned into the blow and crossed the wet deck to the ship's rail. Enjoying the sting, the salt air, and the heaving sea, he paused a moment to savor it all. Then he saw something out there in the blackness. Something that made him doubt his sanity.

Something glimpsed in a trough between two ten-foot waves that made him dash like a madman back to the cabin and his new bride, huddled on the floor. He ran past the purser's desk, and, seeing the guy he'd spoken to earlier, stopped suddenly. There were five thousand souls aboard and he couldn't just—

"Pick up that phone and get the captain. Now! This is an emergency!"

"I'm sorry, but passengers—"

Stoke flashed the CIA badge Harry Brock had given him for situations just like this. The guy blanched, picked up the phone, spoke briefly, and handed the phone across the counter. Stoke somehow managed to convey urgency but speak calmly.

"Captain, you need to sound the ship's alarm. Now. All passengers and crew need to don life jackets and muster at their stations. No time to explain. The problem is off your starboard bow at ninety degrees. It's either a torpedo wake or the wake of a submarine periscope headed directly for you at high speed. Collision course . . . Yes, Captain, evasive action, right now."

Stoke dropped the phone and raced down the wide staircase, taking the steps three at a time.

"ALL AHEAD TWO-THIRDS, MAKE YOUR DEPTH ONE hundred," Captain Lyachin said. "Fifteen degrees down on the bow planes."

"Ahead two-thirds, depth one hundred meters, fifteen down," came the reply.

Lyachin took a slow drag on his Sobranie. It was the most expensive Russian cigarette but worth every ruble. "Come to heading two-zero-two."

"Aye, Captain. Turn on my mark, course two-zero-two. Speed, eighteen knots. Depth, one hundred meters . . . mark."

"Diving downward, course two-zero-two."

"Two-zero-two, aye."

"Speed eighteen knots."

"Speed eighteen knots, aye."

"We'll slip right under that fat tourist barge bastard's belly," Lyachin said, grinning at his XO.

"A brush with the angel of death," the XO replied, smiling, "and he won't even know it."

A second later, the blast of the boat's alarms began sounding, an awful din that turns every submariner's stomach. Dim red emergency lights began flashing in the CCP. Every man at his post stared at his screen in disbelief. The XO scrambled, moving from post to post, assessing the situation.

"What the hell is happening?" Lyachin said.

"We still have propulsion, sir, reactor normal, but all our operating and propulsion systems have been . . . co-opted."

"What the fuck does that mean?" Lyachin shouted. He'd never heard the word *co-opted* and he didn't like words he'd never heard.

"No longer in our control, sir. It's as if . . . as if the sub is operating independently. We've lost the helm, the diving planes, and . . . holy mother of God!"

"What?"

"The two torpedoes in the forward tubes just went live, sir! They're showing 'armed' on my panel! And the . . . my God . . . outer doors of tubes one and two . . . they're opening, sir, on their own. Tubes flooded . . . what the hell is going on?"

"Weapons Officer, shut everything down. Disarm! Now!" Lyachin said. "Go to Fail-Safe! Kill it!"

"Can't execute, Captain. Nothing on my panel is responding."

"Torpedo room, close the outer doors. Helm, come right to one-eight-zero."

"Helm is frozen at two-zero-two, sir! She's maintaining a heading directly to the target, sir."

"Torpedo room?"

"Outer door controls not responding. Both torpedoes armed. Active guidance to target. Launch sequence countdown has been initiated."

Lyachin went white. "How long have we got?"

"Sixty seconds to launch, sir."

The captain looked at his XO.

"The entire boat has been infected," he said.

"Infected?"

"Fifty seconds to launch."

"Some kind of cyberweapon. We're about to sink an American cruise ship, Aleksandr. Go forward and see if there's anything you can do to stop that from happening."

The XO stared into his captain's eyes with stunned disbelief for a millisecond and then he bolted from the CCP. Both men knew there was nothing to be done.

"Thirty seconds, Captain."

Control of their submarine, and their fate, had been snatched from them in the blink of an eye. And by whom? They would never know.

"Fifteen seconds. Ten. Five . . ."

Lyachin closed his eyes and waited for the muffled explosive sounds that would signal the end of a very long and distinguished career in the Russian Navy. Not to mention the end of his life, blindfolded, his back to a wall at Lubyanka Prison in Moscow.

FOURTEEN

Stokely Jones smoked soles down the ship's starboard B Deck corridor, careening from one bulkhead to the other as the liner pitched and yawed in the heavy seas. He stopped just outside stateroom 222 and slid the card key into the slot. He found his bride just the way he'd left her—stunned, scared, still bleeding and huddled in the corner on the floor.

He knelt beside her, kissed the top of her head, and examined the wound more carefully. Stitches could wait, but he had to stop the bleeding. He scrambled into the head, grabbed a terry hand towel, and soaked it in warm water. Then he carefully folded it into a workable compress. Looking for something to secure it with, he spotted a pair of pantyhose hanging over the shower door.

"We've got to get out of here, honey," he said quietly once the compress was firmly in place on her temple. Her eyes went wide with fear as he pulled two life vests from the cabinet above her.

"What? What is it, Stokely?" she asked, her eyes wide with terror. "Are we sinking?"

"No. But I saw something I didn't like," he said, grabbing her rain gear and his from hangers and her pair of running shoes. "Up on deck. Here, put these on. I'll help you get to your feet." As she struggled into the clothing, he put his own life vest on, then helped her with her own.

"What did you see?"

"Maybe nothing. But it sure as hell looked like the wake of a torpedo. Could have been the wake of a sub's periscope maybe. Either way, it was headed toward us at high speed and it didn't look promising."

"A torpedo? Somebody's firing a torpedo at a *cruise ship*?"

"Doesn't make any sense, I know. That's why I hope to God I was just seeing things. Let's go."

"Where?"

"Our muster station. Where we had the drill back in Miami. That's where we board the lifeboat."

"Stokely Jones, this is the last time I will ever, I mean *ever*—"

She never finished that sentence.

Two massive explosions rocked the mammoth vessel. One torpedo, from the sound of it magnetic and not impact, had struck amidships, probably exploding directly beneath the *Fantasy*'s keel. If that fish had broken the ship's back, Stoke figured they had about forty-five minutes before she went down with all hands.

And then the second torpedo impacted just forward of the stern. *The engine compartment*, Stoke thought, feeling the big ship instantly start to lose forward momentum as the big bronze screws stopped turning. After two decades in the U.S. Navy, he could hear when a screw was loose in the bilge. Now all he could hear were the screaming alarms throughout the huge liner. He waited for the captain to make his announcement.

"Attention, all passengers. This is your captain speaking. We have sustained cataclysmic damage. A damage assessment is already under way. However, in the interest of everyone's safety I am taking no chances. I am now issuing the order to abandon ship. All passengers must report immediately with their life jackets to their assigned muster stations. The crew will assist you in boarding the lifeboats. I repeat, this is your captain speaking . . . abandon ship. This is not a drill, I repeat, this is not a drill."

Stoke, with Fancha in his arms, was already en route to the lifeboat muster station.

Aboard *Nevskiy*, Lyachin struggled to maintain his composure as his boat continued on a collision course with the now sinking American liner. He stared through the periscope in horror as fire spread and the massive cruise ship's bow angled sharply down. If there were to be a secondary or tertiary explosion, thousands of innocent civilians could lose their lives.

Including the men aboard his command.

They were now on a collision course with the sinking liner, and control of his boat had been wrested from him. The XO stood beside him, his furrowed brow beaded with perspiration. He'd been scrambling all over the boat, trying to find some way, any way, to regain control. Or, at least shut down the reactor. The reactor had now gone to 105 percent, dangerous in itself, and they were increasing their speed toward the doomed cruise ship.

"Perhaps it's for the best, Aleksandr," he said quietly.

"Sir?"

"Better to die out here where we belong than face the wrath of the admiralty."

"And a firing squad."

"Yes. That, too."

"Any chance we'll scrape beneath her?"

"No, sir. If she continues sinking at the current rate, we'll impact her bow in less than three minutes."

"Inform the crew to brace for impact. Officers to remain at their posts, continue attempts to regain control. "

"Captain, one thought if I may."

"Of course."

"The escape trunk is inoperable. But the main hatch has a manual override. We could open it. Scuttle the boat."

"No. We will attempt to regain control until the end. That is all."

"Aye-aye, sir."

He saluted and left Lyachin alone with his thoughts for these last few moments. He was headed for the planesman who was desperately trying to rewire his panel in a last-ditch effort to—

"Conn, Helm! I have regained control!"

"Helm, Conn, make your course one-nine-zero! Hard over!"

"Helm, aye."

"Conn, engineer. Reactor panels back online."

"Shut down, I repeat shut down! Go to diesel!"

"Reactor shut down, going to diesel, aye."

"Planesman, Captain, make your depth one hundred meters. Down thirty degrees on your bow planes."

"Depth one hundred meters, down thirty degrees on bow planes, affirmative."

The submarine angled sharply downward. The periscope slid back down into the well with a soft hydraulic hiss. From every corner of the command post great shouts of wild cheering and laughter broke out as the men celebrated their miraculous escape from disaster.

Captain Lyachin breathed a sigh of relief.

He would live to fight another day. But first he would have to prove his innocence to the admiralty. He now had incontrovertible proof that the enemy possessed cyberweapons capable of taking over the most modern Russian submarine. By living to tell the tale, he would have done the navy a great service. How great? An admiral's worth? Perhaps.

If the brass believed him.

Meanwhile, he would do everything in his power to learn who had secretly managed to steal his submarine from under his boots. If this could happen to the *Nevskiy*, the entire Russian Navy was now at risk.

Captain Flagg Youngblood, a U.S. Navy sub driver, was thirty-nine years old, a Naval Academy graduate, and happened to be a native of Austin, Texas. The skipper of the *Texas* was legendary in the U.S. Fourth Fleet operating in the SOUTHCOM area of focus. He'd been awarded numerous honors and decorations for his valiant service, including the Navy Star, the Silver Star Medal, two Presidential Unit Citations, the Legion of Merit, and the National Defense Service Medal.

His stomping ground, SOUTHCOM, encompassed the Caribbean, Central and South America, and surrounding waters. U.S. Fourth Fleet was originally established in 1943, a time when America desperately needed a command in charge of protecting against raiders, blockade runners, and enemy submarines in the South Atlantic.

The speaker above Youngblood's head crackled.

"Sonar contact!"

"Talk to me, Jonesie," the skipper replied.

"Conn, Sonar, new contact bearing two-zero-one. Positive ID on her screws. It's the *Nevskiy*, sir. Designate contact Whiskey 7-7."

"Conn, aye."

"Conn, Sonar, something really weird is going on out there. Whiskey 7-7 proceeding at periscope depth, speed eighteen knots. Looks like she's lining up on that big cruise ship. Dead abeam, and—holy Jesus!"

"Sonar, Conn, what the hell was that sound?" the captain said to the *Texas*'s sonar officer. He'd been monitoring sonar through his headphones. "Sure sounded like tube doors opening to me."

"Aye, sir. *Nevskiy* just opened her number one and two forward tubes."

"This has to be a dry fire exercise, ain't it? Damn well better be. That or World War Three."

"Dry fire, aye, but the outer doors were just opened. Tubes flooding now, skipper. Not like any exercise I've ever seen. Looks more like the real thing."

"What in damn tarnation is that old fox Lyachin thinking about? Sinking a goddamn American cruise ship? Insane!"

"No, sir, I wouldn't think so."

"Hell, I wouldn't think so either, but he's been pinging the hell out of it."

"Target of opportunity, sir. Gotta be just practice."

"What's his speed and course, Sonar?"

"Speed eighteen knots, depth sixteen, maintaining course two-zero-one and—holy mother of God!"

"Talk to me, Jonesie; tell me I ain't hearing what I think I heard . . ."

"Live fire, sir! He just let go two fish!"

"*Nevskiy, Nevskiy, Nevskiy,* this is the United States submarine *Texas*. Confirm the two fish you just launched are dummy warheads, over . . . shitfire, Russian bastard's not responding. *Nevskiy, Nevskiy,* do you read?"

"Fish proceeding to target, sir."

"Can you ID them as to type?"

"Negative, I can't get a clean enough—"

"Damn it! Get me COMUSNAVSO, pronto!"

"Aye-aye, sir, coming up," the comms officer said,

putting through a flash emergency signal to the U.S. Naval Forces Southern Command.

"This is Admiral Walsh."

Youngblood grabbed his mike and started barking.

"Admiral, this is Captain Flagg Youngblood, SSN 75, with an urgent message for the chief of naval operations. Please inform the CNO we got a Russian sub down here just fired two torpedoes at the American cruise ship *Fantasy*. Sending her coordinates now. These fish could be deadheads, but we'll know that soon enough. Tell the admiral I want to report an—"

An underwater concussion rocked the *Texas*. Then another. Followed by the muffled sounds of two huge explosions.

"Correction. Tell him America has just been attacked by the Russian nuclear submarine *Nevskiy*, sir. I will notify Coast Guard Miami and USCG Air Station Borinquen, Puerto Rico, to initiate immediate search and rescue in Sector Five. I anticipate heavy casualties, sir. Over."

"You better know what the hell you're talking about, son," the admiral said, and he was gone.

The captain sat back in his command seat and looked at his XO, Lieutenant Bashon Mann.

"Bash, that's one crazy bastard, Lyachin," he said, lighting up a fat Cohiba torpedo stogie with his Zippo.

"Insane, sir. All those poor people . . ."

"Take her up, Bash. We'll pick up as many survivors as we can. Then we're going out there to find that sonofabitch and stick a couple of firecrackers up his ass."

"Start World War Three?"

"The Russians already started World War Three, remember?"

"Captain, with all due respect—"

"Calm down, Mr. Mann, I'm just . . . what's that word . . . venting. But, by God, I'd like to get in a shooting war with that lunatic. Sonar, Conn, where the hell is that sonofabitch Lyachin?"

"Went deep, sir, three hundred meters, speed twenty-four knots, course oh-two-zero."

"Roger, sonar. That cowboy's headed for the trench, getting out of Dodge."

"Roger that, sir. I would, too."

RUSSIAN PRIME MINISTER VLADIMIR PUTIN WAS sound asleep in the vast owner's stateroom of his yacht, *Red Star*, in the Mediterranean when his private Kremlin line lit up, making a soft pinging sound that wouldn't go away. It was three o'clock in the morning. *You can run from the Kremlin, but you can't hide*, he thought. Hardly an original notion but a deadly accurate one.

He rolled over and reached for the receiver, girding himself for more bad news from his second in command, Dmitry Medvedev. No one ever called at three in the morning with good news. No one ever called at any hour with good news. The curse of power.

Exhausted, he'd just returned from Beijing. A week of grueling meetings with Premier Jintao and other high-ranking Chinese Communist Party officials, trying to bring these madmen to his point of view. The CPC was schizophrenic about forging alliances these days. The Chinese, in their new arrogance, saw themselves as the superpower heir apparent.

One day they were leaning toward their natural ally, Russia; the next, they were attending lavish state dinners at the White House, being wooed by the Americans. The Americans had one big advantage over him. They were indisputably China's biggest market. Money, it was always money.

"Yes," Putin said, freighting the word with icy irritation.

"Please excuse the hour, but I had to call you," Medvedev said. "Very bad news, I'm afraid."

"You heard from Beijing? No trade agreement?"

"I only wish. Anything from them is better than this."

"One moment, let me turn on the light . . . go ahead."

"Ten minutes ago I received a call from Admiral Vladimir Sergeevich Vysotsky. Our navy commander in chief informed me of a serious incident that occurred two hours ago in the Caribbean Sea. It seems that one of our submarines in that theater, the *Nevskiy*, has just torpedoed and sunk an American cruise ship carrying five thousand passengers, en route from Miami to Jamaica."

Medvedev was met with stunned silence at the other end of the line.

"Sir?" he said.

"Yes, yes, I'm here. Who the hell is the captain of that fucking boat? I should know that, I know."

"Lyachin."

"Lyachin? He's one of our best commanders. Has he gone rogue? Insane?"

"Neither, it would seem, although I cannot vouch for his sanity. Naval Operations has been in radio communication with the sub, spoken with him at length. He claims absolutely no responsibility for this action. He says the ship was the victim of some kind of 'force,' an inexplicable takeover of all the boat's systems, including weapons."

"A 'force'? Whatever the hell that means, it was this 'force,' I suppose, that fired two torpedoes at an American flag vessel?"

"It sounds crazy, I agree."

"Call Admiral Vysotsky. Tell him I want the *Nevskiy* to return to home port immediately. As soon as she arrives in port, I want her boarded and every member of the crew arrested and placed in a maximum-security lockdown for individual questioning by KGB political officers. I want Lyachin flown to Moscow for interrogation. A supernatural force took over his submarine? His excuse for this blunder is already reason enough to put him in front of a firing squad. Understood?"

"Completely. Is there anything else I can do at this point, Prime Minister?"

"Yes, Dmitry. Issue presidential orders to put the entire Russian military on a war footing. Highest state of alert. Some madman in Washington may look upon this catastrophe as his personal *Lusitania*, served up on a silver platter. At long last, a good excuse for a preemptive nuclear strike on the homeland. I'm not being paranoid. It's not beyond the realm of possibility."

"Indeed not. Sorry to call with such bad news. Try to get some sleep."

"No. I have to call the American president and tell him the Russian government had nothing at all to do with the sinking of their ship. Do you think I can convince him? It will be difficult to explain because, so far, I have no goddamn explanation. Except, of course, Lyachin's mysterious 'force.'"

Putin replaced the receiver, lay back against his pillow, and tried to figure out what the hell he was going to say to President McCloskey, a smart, leather-tough old cowboy from Montana.

FIFTEEN

GLOUCESTERSHIRE, ENGLAND

Turn off the Taplow Common Road, just after exiting the deep green forest that enfolds that highway, and you will come upon a magnificent set of black wrought-iron gates. If the guards recognize you, the imposing gates will swing wide and you will be traveling back in time to another England. You will be motoring at a snail's pace along the wide curving drive that will eventually lead you to a place called Brixden House. A snail's pace because you won't want to miss anything—an extraordinary piece of classical sculpture perhaps, quite voluptuous.

The macadam pathway meanders through countless acres of gardens and parklands. There are apple trees covered in blossoms, jardinières full of pelargoniums in great blocks of color, and greenhouses covered with walls of nectarines, all scattered hither and thither across the hills. The dapple of sunlight on the deep green croquet lawns, lakes, the flower beds, and splashing fountains give new meaning to the word *picturesque*.

When you do finally catch sight of it, you will find the house imposing. Built originally in the mid-seventeenth century as a hunting lodge for royalty, the present Edwardian country house stands atop great chalk cliffs. Its countless windows overlook the rolling green Berkshire countryside. The main house, built in the classic Italian style, overlooks an idyllic bend in the Thames.

Built in the 1920s, the enormous Brixden House was the very height of luxury. The Visitor's Book was a veritable *Who's Who* of the era. Playwright George Bernard Shaw made the first of many visits in 1926, Winston Churchill was an occasional guest, as were King George and Queen Mary, Charlie Chaplin, Ambassador Joe Kennedy, and the aviator Charles Lindbergh.

This was the stately ancestral home of Lady Diana Mars. Her fiancé, the former chief inspector of Scotland Yard, was currently in the library having a chat with his oldest friend, Lord Alexander Hawke. The smell of beeswax and old leather books and furniture, the scents of spilled liquor and tobacco smoke, all hung in the air, so much so that it was a part of the room's history that almost had weight.

A John Singer Sargent portrait of Lady Mars's great-grandmother Nancy hung imperiously above the yawning gape of the great hearth. A vast red velvet sofa faced the fire, big enough for several people to sleep in. An ebony grand piano dominated one corner of the room, though Hawke had never seen anyone lay a hand on it.

It was late afternoon, and the setting sun's rays slanted through the tall, mullioned windows, casting a lovely pattern across the worn Persian rugs and highly polished wooden floors. Shadows fled up the walls and across the high vaulted ceiling. Beyond the opened windows, only the sounds of rooks, cawing in the trees, the hum of drowsy bees, and an occasional bark from Diana's dogs, sprawled lazily in the late afternoon sun.

Hawke found Ambrose in the library, standing in the center of the room, trying to rip the cellophane from a fresh deck of playing cards decorated with Lady Mars's family crest.

"Good evening," Hawke said.

Congreve voiced his agreement with the sentiment.

"Cards, is it, Constable?"

"Hardly, Alex, it's my new exercise program. Possibly not up to the standards of your daily Royal Navy regimen, but still, quite a tester."

"You exercise with a deck of cards?"

"The latest thing, dear boy, the very latest. Observe and grow wise," he said, and, with a dramatic flourish, flung the playing cards high into the air, scattering them all over the carpet. He then began scampering about the room, bending to pick each card up one by one and stuffing them carelessly into the side pockets of his green velvet smoking jacket.

When he'd pocketed the last one, he straightened, a bit winded, and beamed at Hawke.

"Well, then. What do you think of that?"

"Most impressive."

"Want to have a go?"

"Good Lord, no. I'm exhausted just watching you. I could use some air. Shall we have a nice walkabout on the grounds and then repair to the bar for a small beverage to celebrate?"

After a long and tiring (for Ambrose Congreve) ramble about the hilly and sometimes rock-strewn grounds, the two old friends went to the small walnut-paneled bar for the restorative cocktail. Congreve sipped his single malt, Macallan; Hawke, his Gosling's Black Seal rum, neat. The two deep leather chairs they sat in had served other gentlemen's backsides well for innumerable generations.

"How can you drink that stuff anyway?" Hawke asked Congreve. "Tastes like liquid smoke."

Ambrose bristled. "I'm a man, sir, who is simply fond of his scotch—the drink, mind, not the nationality."

Hawke smiled at this riposte, enormously glad to be back in dear old Blighty (as the Americans were wont to call it) again, and had been bringing Congreve up to speed on their mutual friend Stokely Jones, his almost deadly wedding in Florida, and his nearly catastrophic honeymoon.

"Torpedoed, you say?" Congreve murmured, getting his pipe going. "Extraordinary."

"Hasn't hit the media, but yes. Stokely saw the trails of two torpedoes moments before they struck the ship. He was lucky to get his new bride up to the muster station and into a lifeboat before the panic began. A lot of people ended up in the water, and a couple of lifeboats overturned in the heavy seas."

"Where is Stokely now?"

"Back in Miami, trying to save his marriage, I imagine."

"No one has claimed responsibility for the sinking?"

"No. But these torpedoes were sophisticated weapons. One of them, magnetic, exploded directly beneath the big ship's keel, breaking her back. It's why she went down in less than forty-five minutes."

"Stokely say how many casualties?"

"Bad, but he said it could have been far worse. Fortunately, an American sub was in the vicinity. She surfaced and picked up most of the survivors in the water."

"Extraordinary. C is joining us for dinner this evening, you know. I'm sure Sir David will have a great deal to say about this."

"How is the old bachelor? I haven't seen him since my return from Russia. I know he's been on holiday, believe it or not. Sardinia, I believe."

"Well, Alex, he was not at all pleased with you going off the reservation, I can tell you that much. Perhaps he's had time to cool off a bit. All those lovely beaches and gorgeous Italian women work wonders."

"Nude beaches there, I've heard."

"Ha! You know who goes to nude beaches?"

"Not a clue."

"People who should *never* go to nude beaches."

Hawke laughed and sipped his drink. He was looking forward to dinner. C was a crusty old bastard but he was smarter than any man Hawke knew, save present company. A monument of unaging intellect. And Diana always served rack of lamb when he was invited, and something very old and delicious from the vast cellars of Brixden House.

"And speaking of nude beaches, how was your month in the south of France?"

"Cannes? Diana was bored to tears. *Ennui*, you know."

"Really? France? That mighty horde, formed of two tribes, the Bores and the Bored?"

"Don't even think you get credit for that one, Alex."

"No? Who does, then?"

"A certain poet named Lord Byron."

"Whatever. If you say '*ennui*' one more time, I shall throttle you within an inch of your Francophilic life."

"One must credit the French for coining a word for that awful yawn that sleep cannot abate."

"If you insist."

Congreve, who seemed to have paused in his own conversation, reached into his breast pocket, withdrawing a small rectangular package, wrapped in gold foil and tied with a royal-blue ribbon.

"Almost forgot something," he said, handing the thing over to his friend. "A little something I picked up for you in town the other day. You're going to love it."

"What is it?"

"Don't ask. Open," the man said, twirling the waxed tips of his moustache.

"Nothing's going to pop out at me, is it? Or explode white powder in my face?"

"Alex, do try to show a little appreciation for my thoughtfulness. I know this doesn't come naturally to you, but give it a decent shot anyway."

"You'll recall that the last Christmas gift you gave me was that yellow golf sweater with all the red golf tees on it."

"Yes, the one I caught you red-handed with, trying to rid yourself of it at the Harrods Returns window."

"I don't play golf. If I gave you a red Ferrari baseball cap to wear about town, would you do it?"

"Don't be absurd."

"The defense rests."

Hawke untied the ribbon and removed the wrapping. It was a black box emblazoned with the name of a shop in the Burlington Arcade that he vaguely remembered. He lifted the lid.

"Ah! How awfully kind of you, old hound. What is it?"

"What is it? Just the latest thing, that's all."

Hawke pulled the latest thing out and examined it more closely. "I never know what the latest thing is, Ambrose, so, please, just tell me."

"It's an electronic cigarette."

"Ah! An electronic cigarette! Splendid, why didn't you say so!" he said, leaning forward with an arm on his knee, just like a picture of a cowboy he'd once seen as a child. He twirled the white tube between thumb and forefinger and added, "What does it do, precisely?"

"Do? Why, you smoke it, of course."

"Smoke it? It's plastic. Have you ever smelled burning plastic, Constable? Seriously."

"You don't light it, Alex, you flip that little switch. Then you can smoke it."

"Like this?" Hawke said, following instructions. He took a pull, felt something moist and vaguely disgusting filling his mouth, and quickly expelled it, trying not to retch.

"Lovely."

"You like it?"

"Love it."

"So . . . now you just smoke that instead of all those bloody Sobranie black-lung cigarettes you brought back from Russia."

"I do?"

"Yes! Of course you do! All of the flavor, none of the carcinogens. Ideal, really, for someone like you. An addict."

"I'm touched, really quite touched, Ambrose. Thank you."

"Pleasure."

"You mean to say you actually see me, oh, say at the Long Bar at Black's, pulling out a fake plastic cigarette, a battery-powered cigarette, and, saying, 'Look here, lads, it's the latest thing! Have a puff, you'll taste the difference.' Could be an ad campaign, that. 'Have a puff, you'll taste the difference!'"

"It's your life, dear boy," Ambrose huffed, and sipped his drink, sulking. "Do what you bloody well like with it."

Hawke slipped the damn thing into his breast pocket, deep within the folds of his handkerchief. He was about to return to the far more serious topic they'd been discussing when Miss Spooner appeared in the doorway with little Alexei in her arms, who was gurgling in delight at the sight of his father.

"There's our big boy," Ambrose cried, turning in his chair to smile at him. "There's our little Superman!"

Hawke leaped from his chair and ran to his son, taking him into his arms. Alexei laughed as his father threw him high into the air, caught him, and threw him again and again.

"What did you do this afternoon, young man?" Hawke asked, tickling him under the chin.

"We read a book," Spooner said, "didn't we, Alexei?"

"A book?" Hawke said. "Well, we certainly approve of books around here. Which one?"

"One of yours. He picked it out himself. We brought it along from Hawkesmoor. *Goodnight Moon.*"

"Ah, one of my favorites. Did you like it, too, Alexei?"

"We read it five times, sir. I'd say yes."

"I liked it very much, Daddy," Alexei said.

Hawke smiled and kissed his boy's forehead, whispering to him, "I see the moon, the moon sees me. The moon sees the somebody I'd like to see. God bless the moon and God bless me. God bless the somebody I'd like to see!"

Alexei smiled with delight.

Spooner said, "Time to say good night, I'm afraid. He's had his supper and his bath and now it's his bedtime."

"Good night, little hero," Hawke said, kissing his cheek and handing him back to Spooner.

"Yes, good night indeed," Ambrose called from his chair. "Sleep tight and don't let the bedbugs bite!"

Alexei stared over Spooner's shoulder, gazing at his father all the way down the long hallway to the foot of the staircase where he disappeared.

"Time for dinner, I should think," Hawke said, turning to Ambrose and wiping something from the corner of his eye.

Bang on the hour of eight all the house clocks struck, chiming in unison. Moments later the dinner gong sounded, and a rich bass note reverberated throughout the house. The two old friends made their way down the hallway toward the white-and-gold-paneled dining room, a room imported lock, stock, and barrel from Madame de Pompadour's dining room at Château d'Asnières.

SIXTEEN

LADY DIANA MARS, EMERGING INTO THE HALL from the drawing room, intercepted Hawke and Congreve making a beeline for the dining room. She was radiant. All emerald silk, bare white shoulders, and diamonds, her lustrous auburn hair swept up and held in place with jeweled combs. She was beautiful as always and Hawke told her so. He took her hand to kiss it, happy to see that the engagement ring Ambrose had given her was still in place. Hawke had a vested interest in that ring. He'd almost died diving a wreck off Bermuda trying to find it.

"Alex, you darling boy, listen," she said. "Sir David arrived about ten minutes ago. He seems a bit . . . agitated. Clearly something on his mind. He's out on the terrace now, smoking his cigar. He asked if he might have a quick word in private before we go into dinner. Do you mind awfully?"

"Would it matter?" Hawke smiled. "I'm still in his employ, last time I checked."

"The old seafarer's just out there, through the drawing room door. I'll call off the turtle soup until you two guests of honor arrive at the table."

Hawke strode through the room and pushed through the tall door out into the cool evening. Trulove had his back to him, standing stiffly at the low granite balustrade that overlooked the formal gardens and the Thames below, a ribbon of silver in the moonlight.

"Sir David," Alex said quietly as he approached, not wanting to startle the man.

The director of MI6 turned and regarded him with a smile, not a warm smile exactly, but certainly friendly enough under the circumstances. Trulove, whom Hawke considered one of nature's immutable forces, was a former Royal Navy admiral and a great hero of the Falklands War. He was a tall, well-built fellow, imposing with his close-cropped white hair and weather-beaten face. His intense blue eyes were clear, seeming to have escaped all the wind and salt and rain earned during decades on the bridges of various Royal Navy warships.

"Alex, good of you to come out here. I felt what I had to say was best said in private."

"Indeed, sir. I—"

"I may owe you an apology. I was utterly beside myself when you went AWOL without a word to me. But . . . now that I have an inkling of your reasons, it's becoming rather clear to me that you felt you had no choice but to act as you did."

"Thank you, sir."

"Indeed, had you come to me with a request to venture alone into what was, to me, so obviously a

KGB death trap, I would never have agreed to it. Never. It looked a suicide mission, frankly."

"That was my thinking, sir. Were I in your position, I most certainly would not have allowed it either."

"My God, Alex, what *were* you thinking? We both know these Russian bastards want your head for killing their beloved Tsar. And yet you decide to go waltzing into their top-secret training facility in the middle of Siberia? Based upon some Kremlin-generated *rumor*?"

"I had no choice, Sir David. It was worth my life to learn the truth, whether or not the Tsar's daughter, Anastasia, and our child were still alive. And, if they *were* alive, and held captive there, I was determined to bring them out. Whatever it took. If not, well—"

"Yes. And whether it was raw courage or sheer foolhardiness, it's not for me to judge. I'm just glad you made it out in one piece, Alex. The service would be greatly diminished without you. No one is irreplaceable, including me, but you . . . you come close."

"I appreciate that, sir."

"Lady Mars tells me you were able to bring your son out? Is that true?"

"Yes, sir. Alexei is sleeping upstairs as we speak."

"How marvelous. Do you think I might catch a glimpse of him?"

"Well, we could peek in after dinner, I suppose. But if we wake him, Miss Spooner will have our heads."

"I believe they're waiting for us. Shall we go in to dinner?" C said.

"Delighted, sir. I was quite sure I was coming out here to have my head handed to me. Thank you for letting me retain the use of it."

C laughed and put his arm around Hawke's shoulder as they started for the door. Startled, Hawke realized it was the first time Trulove had ever done anything remotely like this unmistakable show of affection.

He's actually glad to see me, Hawke thought, somewhat astounded.

THE DINNER, ALEX THOUGHT, HAD BEEN SPLENDID. The lamb was cooked to pink perfection, redolent of garlic and rosemary from the garden, and the wine, a 1959 Petrus, was beyond belief. Even C had been relaxed and cheerful during the meal. Now that he and Hawke understood each other once more, it was back to business as usual. Both men were glad they'd cleared the air.

Hawke was seated next to Diana, whom he adored. For the life of him, he couldn't understand why she and Ambrose had yet to wed. Clearly they were madly in love. But, as the old saying went, unless you're under the tent, you have no earthly idea what's really going on in a relationship.

The dinner dishes were cleared. The candles still flickered on the happy faces around the table and Cole Porter floated in from a turntable in the drawing room. Coffee was served. Ambrose fired up his pipe, Sir David his cigar, and Alex his electronic cigarette. As long as you didn't inhale the bloody vapor, he discovered, you could manage it. Besides, he saw Ambrose smiling at him with approval.

Hawke saw C push back from the table, all the jollity flown from his face. Whatever was coming was deadly serious and, in all likelihood, it would be aimed directly at him.

"I'd like to raise a glass to our lovely and brilliant hostess for an absolutely smashing dinner party. Wonderful food, wonderful wine, and, of course, wonderful company."

"Hear! Hear!" everyone said, raising their glasses toward the hostess.

"But now the party's over, isn't it, Sir David?" Diana said with a laugh. "We now turn to the affairs of men."

"Good God, I hope not," Congreve said, unable to contain himself. Hawke and Diana laughed out loud. C didn't even crack a smile.

"I want to talk about this recent unprovoked attack by the *Nevskiy*, a Russian submarine, on an American cruise ship. I received a call from Brick Kelly, the CIA director, a few hours ago. Apparently two torpedoes were fired. The ship went down in less than an hour. At least seven hundred innocent people lost their lives. It would have been worse had not an American sub been in the immediate vicinity, surfacing to pluck many survivors out of the water. Alex, your man in Miami, he was aboard that ship. He actually saw the torpedoes approaching?"

"That's correct, sir. Stokely Jones and his new bride were beginning their honeymoon. He happened to be on deck when they were launched, saw their wakes, and warned the captain."

"And SSN 75, the U.S. nuclear submarine *Texas*, was shadowing *Nevskiy* just prior to the attack. The American commanding officer avers that he has sonar confirmation of the Russian sub's screw signature, the sound of her outer torpedo doors opening, tubes flooding, and two torpedoes launched. This evidence is incontrovertible. The Russians sank that cruise ship, period."

Congreve said, "What do they have to say about it? Knowing the Kremlin, they deny it, of course."

"Except for the presence of the *Texas*, yes, they would, certainly. Putin called the White House immediately. Deepest regrets. Insisted the Kremlin had no prior knowledge of this attack. The sub is returning to her home port at Sevastopol. The captain will be arrested and interrogated by the KGB. So the question is this: Was this a skipper gone rogue? Was this an accident? Or was this a deliberate attack on America by the Russians for reasons as yet unknown? Answers are vitally important because the West finds itself in the midst of a dangerous diplomatic firestorm."

"What was President McCloskey's response?" Congreve asked C.

"He told Putin that, based on the U.S. sub's report, he was immediately taking all American air, sea, and land forces to DEFCON 3. Depending on what explanations he hears back from the Kremlin within the next forty-eight hours, he will go to the next highest state of readiness, DEFCON 2. That's one level shy of all-out war."

"The Russians can come up with a lot of excuses

in forty-eight hours. We need proof of what really happened on that sub," Hawke said.

"Absolutely," C said. "Right now, U.S. Navy divers are sifting through the debris field on the ocean floor. They will examine every last scrap of those two torpedoes looking for evidence of either a misfire or a deliberate launch. Not much to go on but at the moment it's all we've got."

"Next steps?" Hawke said, already having a pretty good idea where all this was heading.

"The CIA and the NSA are all over this, naturally. But they're stretched pretty thin at the moment and they've asked for our help. Kelly specifically mentioned you, Alex. And your Russian counter-intelligence operation based in Bermuda, Red Banner. Since you are already working in tandem with the CIA, it's a good fit for something like this."

"It's exactly why it was created, as you well know, Sir David."

"So, Hawke, old fellow. Will you be staying for dessert?" Trulove asked, smiling at him.

"I appreciate the offer, sir, but I think not. If you all will excuse me, I'll take my leave. It seems I suddenly have a rather pressing engagement."

"Good man," C said as Hawke stood and kissed Diana on the cheek. "You'll keep in touch with me this time, won't you?"

Hawke smiled and said, "Hourly updates, sir."

"Not that in touch. I've other matters on my platter. Good hunting, Alex. I trust you'll get to the bottom of this in short order."

Hawke put a hand on Congreve's shoulder. "Ambrose, I wonder if I might impose on Diana's hospitality. Is it possible that my son and Miss Spooner might remain here at Brixden House until this current assignment is completed?"

"Absolutely, darling," Diana said to him. "Don't be silly. We'd adore to have Alexei with us."

Hawke paused, thinking. "One other thing you should all be aware of. Alexei, being the grandson of the late Tsar, has been the subject of death threats from certain elements in Moscow. Gaggle of thugs calling themselves the Tsarists. There was an incident on the Red Arrow train en route to St. Petersburg. Ambrose, would you ask your colleagues at Scotland Yard to send a few chaps out here to keep an eye on things?"

"I'll put a call in immediately," Congreve said.

"Thank you. I'll run upstairs and kiss him goodbye and then I'll be off. Sir David, would you like to accompany me? I promised you a peek at him."

"I was going to insist on it."

"One final thing. Just thought of it in fact. Ambrose, if anything . . . bad . . . should happen to me, I wonder if you would do me the very great honor of being Alexei's godfather. He has no one else, you see, and—"

"The honor is all mine, Alex. Thank you for your faith in me. I'm deeply moved."

And with that Hawke and Sir David Trulove quickly left the room and headed for the upper reaches of the house. *Two men off to save the world once more*, Ambrose thought, watching them striding up the staircase, realizing he might never see either of them again.

He puffed away at his pipe, wondering whether the world would ever again sail with such serenity through space as it seemed to do a hundred years ago.

CONGREVE WALKED HAWKE OUT TO HIS CAR, THE FA-miliar Bentley Continental he called the "Locomotive," parked in the forecourt.

"How can I help you, Alex, get to the bottom of this Russian thing?"

"Good of you to ask and I may indeed call upon that oversized brain of yours before this is all over. But, for now, I already have a plan as to how to get to the bottom of it."

"How, may I ask?"

"By going straight to the top."

"What on earth do you mean?"

"I mean I'm going to pay a little visit to my dear friend and former cellmate, Prime Minister Vladimir Putin."

"You can't be serious."

"Deadly serious."

"And just how do you plan to manage it?"

"Simple, actually. I'm going to ring him up tonight. I have his private number in my wallet."

"You ought to be careful, dear boy. To sup with that Russian you'll need a very long spoon."

"Did I ever tell you he and I got thoroughly pissed? A bottle of vodka in his cell in that awful radioactive prison, Energetika?"

"I don't believe you did."

"Hmm. It's true. We got rather chummy."

"I must say, Alex, that, after all these years, you still have the power to shock and amaze me."

Hawke climbed behind the wheel and the Bentley's monstrous engine exploded to life.

He smiled at Congreve.

"Good. May it always be thus, as your idol Mr. Sherlock Holmes might say."

With that, Alex Hawke and his great grey Locomotive roared out of Brixden House's graveled forecourt and disappeared down the winding drive into a warm summer's night, pearlescent moonlight and shadows of indigo blue showing the way.

SEVENTEEN

CAP D'ANTIBES, FRANCE

HAWKE SLEPT PEACEFULLY FOR MOST OF THE short flight from Gatwick south of London to the south of France. He was dreaming fitfully of the last time he'd visited the glittering Côte d'Azur. There was a woman in his dream, a beautiful raven-haired Chinese secret police officer.

Her dream name was Jet something . . . Jet Li. Yes, and even in his hotel bed, rolling among the twisted sheets, he sensed something wrong. An aura of threat surrounded her . . . yes . . . and at the climactic moment of love, she raised a knife above her head and plunged it into his heart . . .

"Fifteen minutes to touchdown at Nice Airport, sir," he heard the copilot of his G-5 announce over the intercom. He picked up the phone mounted inside his armrest and raised his seat back, blinking awake.

"Is there any hot coffee left, Charley, or did you

two polish it off?" Hawke said, raising his window shade, letting light flood the darkened cabin.

"Still a few drops in the pot, sir; I'll step out and bring you a mug from the galley."

Hawke normally had an attendant on board, but she'd been vacationing in Ibiza with her new husband and he hadn't wanted to bother her at the last minute, especially for such a short hop.

"You fly the plane; I think I can still manage to pour myself a cup of coffee, believe it or not. How's the weather? It looks beautiful down there."

Hawke was peering out the big oval window at the sun-sparkled blue Mediterranean ten thousand feet below his airplane. He found himself smiling. If he had to meet with Putin, he'd much rather it be here in paradise than in Moscow, where every other chap he met might want to kill him.

"Eighteen Celsius right now, sir, winds light, about five knots, ten percent chance of showers late this afternoon."

"Bloody perfect. What mischief are you two up to this weekend, while I'm off saving the world from the Evil Empire?"

"Thought we'd get a hired car, sir, drive along the coast over to Monte Carlo. Not far, and neither I nor the skipper here have ever been."

"Ah, the casinos. Hold on to your wallets."

"We might have a go, sir. A few quid."

"I'd like to be wheels-up by ten Sunday morning. Back to London, unless my host has other ideas."

"No problem at all, sir. We'll have her topped off and ready for you."

A SILVER CHOPPER WAS WAITING ON THE TARMAC
fifty feet away, rotors turning. Judging by the large
red star and the blue-and-white Russian flag on her
fuselage, she was clearly waiting for him. As Hawke
descended the Gulfstream's staircase, taking deep
breaths of the fresh salt air, two men in white strode
across the tarmac to greet him. Men who walked
with the rolling gait of seamen. Heavily muscled
jack-tars who no doubt carried concealed weapons.

Both wore white gabardine trousers and skin-
tight white T-shirts with a silhouette of a megayacht
and the name *Red Star* emblazoned below it. One
stepped forward and extended his hand. He had a
wide white smile and blond hair, cut close.

"Commander Hawke," he said. "Welcome. I
am Yaniv Soha and this is my colleague Yuri. The
prime minister extends his warmest greetings and
says he is looking forward to having you as a guest
aboard *Red Star*. We are here to provide you with
diplomatic security. And anything else you require.
Can we help you with your luggage?"

Hawke had only the old canvas seabag slung from
his shoulder.

"I'm good, thank you."

"Do you mind if I look inside the bag, sir? Standard precaution."

"I'd be worried if you didn't." Hawke smiled,
handing it to him. The man picked through the
items slowly and carefully, examining each one
more than thoroughly.

"Excellent," he said, returning the bag. "Very

well, if you'll come this way, it's a very short flight out to *Red Star*. She's anchored just off the Hotel du Cap at Cap d'Antibes."

The three men started for the Russian military helo, which was spooling up.

"I saw her on final approach. Magnificent. What's her l.o.a.?"

"I'm sorry?"

"Length overall."

"Ah. One hundred meters, sir. Three hundred feet."

"Impressive."

THE SILVER CHOPPER HOVERED ABOVE THE YACHT'S helo pad, located near the stern. As Hawke emerged from the cockpit he saw Vladimir Putin striding toward him, an honest smile on his face and his hand extended. He was wearing a black bathing suit and a white linen shirt with the sleeves rolled up. He was in very good shape, much better than the pale skeleton he'd been when the two of them had been inmates at Energetika Prison.

"Alex," Putin said as they shook hands.

"Volodya," Hawke said, smiling.

"My old cellmate, we meet again."

"Under considerably better circumstances, I would say."

"Your pilot waggled his wings as he flew over *Red Star*. Made me laugh. I admire your style."

"I was asleep. My pilot's the one with the style. What an incredible yacht. Yours?"

"I'd never admit it publicly, but yes. The sea has become my sanctuary. Come on, I'll give you a short tour. Just enough time for a tour and a cocktail before lunch. We're going ashore to the Hotel du Cap. I hope that's suitable. If not, my chef can cook anything you like."

"You just happened to have picked one of my favorite hotels on earth. Fifty quid for a Salade Niçoise with a teaspoon of tuna is pushing it a bit, but still."

Putin laughed, clapping him on the back. "Follow me. We'll start on the bridge. You're difficult to impress, but I think you will be. You still have *Blackhawke*?"

Putin walked very quickly and Hawke matched his stride as they headed forward along the starboard deck.

"Yes, but I'm building a new one in Turkey. Sail, not power this time."

"Tell me about her. I'm new to yachting and have become fascinated with them."

"Well, she's basically a twenty-first-century clipper ship. Three carbon fiber masts, each one about twenty stories tall. Extreme, I suppose."

"The more extreme, the better. How long is she?"

"Three hundred twenty l.o.a., forty-two-foot beam, and she draws twenty feet. The naval architect, a Turk named Badi, told me that if she were anchored in New York harbor her mastheads would reach up to the level of the tablet carried in the arm of the Statue of Liberty."

"Good God, Alex."

"You only go around once in life, right? You

know what all megayacht owners love saying to each other? 'Mine's bigger.'"

Putin laughed. "Good one. I'll have to remember that."

"My idea for the new one was to have all the attributes of a classic sailing ship, teak decks, varnished cap rail, et cetera, but with the overall appearance sleek, metallic, ultramodern. She looks a bit foreboding, to be honest. Darth Vader's intergalactic yacht, the architect calls her."

"I hope you'll invite me aboard sometime. She sounds magnificent."

"Done. I'm going to Istanbul for her sea trials in a month or so. I'll let you know."

They entered the bridge, and all the officers and crewmen snapped to attention.

"Captain Ramius," Putin said to *Red Star*'s skipper, "I'd like you to meet our guest, Alex Hawke. He's just built a new yacht in Turkey. He's been admiring our beautiful ship, but he has something he'd like to tell you, don't you, Alex?"

Hawke grinned at the captain.

"Mine's bigger."

EIGHTEEN

PUTIN'S SECURITY INSISTED THE TWO MEN DINE inside the hotel's Eden Roc restaurant rather than at a table overlooking the sea. Hawke noticed that the prime minister did not argue. He knew that the man felt safe only two places in the world: inside the Kremlin walls and on board *Red Star*. Countless men wanted him dead, a lot of them with good reason. For all his star power on the world's stage and celebrity, he was virtually a prisoner.

Upon entering the Eden Roc restaurant and being shown their table, in the corner, overlooking the sea, Hawke immediately noticed that someone was already seated at their table. A large fellow in a navy blazer sat with his back to them, but the man was instantly recognizable to Alex Hawke.

Good God, Hawke thought, *it's* Stefan Halter.

Putin being Putin, but there was nothing for it. He'd laid a small trap for his British guest. He'd be watching the two of them closely, looking for any sign of recognition. Stefan, an MI6 officer who'd been at Cambridge with Congreve, had been burrowed deep within the Kremlin, a mole for over three decades. He was far and away the most valuable asset Six had inside Russia.

Over the years, the two men had become good friends. Hawke steeled himself for the coming trial of that friendship as Halter rose to his feet and turned to greet them.

"Ah, Stefanovich, you're early," Putin said, beaming. He turned to Alex, introducing him. "You know Lord Hawke, no doubt."

Putin smiled quizzically, foxlike, waiting to pounce.

Stefan looked at Alex, his eyes mercifully blank as he stuck out his hand. "Only by reputation, I'm afraid."

"It's his reputation that makes you afraid, isn't it?" Putin said with unforced joviality, and both men smiled at the prime minister's flash of wit.

Did we pass that test? Hawke wondered.

Drinks were ordered, and the luncheon seemed, to Hawke anyway, to go off without a glitch. He and Halter engaged in meaningless small talk, saving the serious stuff for their host.

The three tables surrounding the Russian leader had been reserved for nine bodyguards. And Hawke was certain there were Russian security officers scattered all over the beautiful gardens and lawns of the magnificent old hotel.

Hawke, for his part, was glad he was in a hotel so accustomed to celebrity guests that there was zero chance he'd be surprised by paparazzi. The last thing he needed was a big color photo of him dining with Vladimir Putin in Britain's *Hello* magazine. They had just finished their Salade Niçoise when Dr. Henry Kissinger stopped at the table on his way out. He greeted the Russian leader warmly and graciously recognized Hawke when Putin introduced the two men.

Then the old American warrior bent and whispered something in Putin's ear. Volodya nodded carefully, excused himself from the table, and walked with Kissinger past the maître d' and into the sunshine. Hawke could see them through the window, walking arm in arm through the tall pines, deep in conversation.

"Stefan," Hawke said, leaning toward Halter and in a voice low enough not to be overheard, "I shall never be able to repay you. I knew you took a chance, telling me the Kremlin rumors."

"I haven't heard a thing. You're still alive, thank God."

"They are alive," Hawke said, his eyes glistening with gratitude.

Halter had a difficult time maintaining composure.

"Alive. So it was true."

"Yes."

"Don't tell me you managed to get them out."

"Just my son."

"Oh, Alex, how utterly marvelous."

"You've no idea. His name is Alexei. Three years old."

"And Anastasia?"

"Wouldn't leave. Out of fear and—commitment.

She married Kuragin out of gratitude. I was angry of course, at first. But in hindsight I can see the sense of it. I've forgiven her and—"

"She thought you were dead, Alex."

"She did. And she felt great compassion for—here comes our host. To be continued."

"WELL, ALEX," PUTIN SAID, TAKING HIS SEAT AND A sip of his vodka, "I'm fairly certain you didn't request this meeting because you've finally decided to take me up on my offer. But don't worry, there's no deadline. I'm sure one fine day you'll come to your senses."

Hawke smiled at the two Russians. "I'm sure you two gentlemen know why I'm here, Volodya."

"That fucking submarine. It's why I invited Stefanovich to fly down from Moscow this morning and join us. He's been looking into the damn mess for me personally."

Hawke said, "What in the hell really happened? This was a blatant provocation that has put the world in an extremely delicate situation. As you well know, American military has gone to DEFCON 3 readiness for war. MI6 is not buying the 'accident' story, nor is CIA. Nor, frankly, am I. One torpedo, possibly, but two? For the life of me, unless this commander went rogue or simply insane, I am mystified."

"As am I, Alex," Putin said. "First of all, I will save you the embarrassment of asking a stupid question. No, the Kremlin had no foreknowledge of this action, nor did anyone in my government have the slightest hand in this tragedy."

"Thank you. That's very helpful."

Halter added, "The *Nevskiy*'s captain, Lyachin, is currently in Moscow. KGB officers are interrogating him. As you know, they do not share the West's delicate sensibilities when it comes to extracting information from enemies of the state."

"So," Hawke said, "what does this Lyachin have to say for himself? How can he possibly exculpate himself from responsibility?"

"He's far more worried about how to exculpate himself from a firing squad, believe me."

"His explanation, then?"

"It is so ludicrous as to defy belief. I hesitate to even tell you lest you think my top military commanders are all taking hallucinogens. But this is his story and he isn't budging. By the way, he made sure the crew got their stories straight. Every single officer and crewman aboard that sub swears the captain is telling the truth."

"And that is?"

"Explain it, Stefanovich. I can't stand to hear myself repeat it one more time."

"The *Nevskiy* was in the midst of a typical firing drill. The cruise ship happened to be chosen as a phony target of opportunity, simply because she was there. It was to be a dry fire exercise, period. And then, in the middle of the drill, the entire submarine, according to Lyachin, was taken over by some mysterious 'force.' That's the exact word he used. 'Force.' All controls, including helm, diving planes, ballast controls, and, most unfortunately, her weapons systems, were wrested from the hands of the captain and crew."

"Impossible."

"I know."

"By whom? Does he say?"

"Lyachin suspects it was SSN 75, the U.S. submarine *Texas*. She was shadowing him at the time."

"Volodya, this, this 'force' or whatever it is, is pure science fiction. He's a madman covering up for incompetence, trying to save his ass."

"Are you sure about that, Alex? Are you sure America possesses no such technology?"

"If they did, I would know about it. And I don't. Besides, Volodya, why the hell would an American sub driver manipulate a Russian sub into sinking an American cruise ship? Talk about stretching credibility."

"Ach. Nothing makes sense. It's a fucking nightmare. There will be a court-martial; he will be found guilty of murdering innocent people and shot. At least that will have some symbolic value for those governments abroad who doubt my own government's innocence in this matter."

"Yes," Hawke said, electing to keep his thoughts about rights to a fair trial to himself. It was not the time for morality or human rights debates with ex-KGB heads of state.

"Alex, will you at least convey my own deep personal regrets and your belief that the Kremlin had absolutely no knowledge nor involvement in this massacre?"

"I will do, Volodya. Because I look into your eyes and I believe you. Something exceedingly strange happened aboard *Nevskiy;* we just don't know what. Volodya, I ask something in return."

"Anything, my old comrade."

"Comrade is stretching it, but I'll let it pass. Before you have him shot, I would like to have some time alone with this Captain Lyachin. I will need to travel to Moscow in secrecy and under your personal protection, of course."

"I see no reason why this is not possible. What do you think you can get out of him that my men cannot?"

"Perhaps nothing. I want to hear more about the American submarine's actions. At the bare minimum, I will be able to tell you if I believe Lyachin is telling the truth. If he is, I will immediately contact my old friend Brick Kelly, director of the CIA. I will inform him of my strong belief that Russia is completely innocent of malicious intent in the sinking. He will then call President McCloskey, easing tensions between Russia and America considerably."

"Yes, I see your point. A good one, and I would be deeply in your debt. I will arrange it. But I want you to look me straight in the eyes right now and tell me that American submarines do not possess some advanced technology we are not aware of."

"Volodya, I swear to you that, to my knowledge, they do not. If they did, I wouldn't tell you. But they don't."

"That's done, then. Let's enjoy our sweets. I will arrange for my private aircraft to fly you to the Domodedovo field in Moscow in the morning. You will be accompanied at all times by discreet but heavy security. You will interview him privately at Lubyanka Prison. With a translator, of course."

"Of course, an interpreter," Hawke said, thinking, translation of "translator": spy. "Speaking of security, at some point I want to address the death threats made against my son, Alexei. Two KGB officers boarded the train we took out of Siberia."

"Yes, I am aware of that."

"How?"

"Their frozen bodies were found on the tracks. I had them flown to Moscow for autopsies. They were definitely not KGB, Alex. I'm the one who saved your son in Lubyanka, remember?"

"Who, then?"

"Now I will tell you a secret. There exists inside Russia an extremely powerful group called the Tsarist Society. A unique organization run, at the top, by some of the most powerful men in Russia. At the bottom, ex-KGB assassins, fired for various offenses, extreme alcoholism or wanton murder, for example. Also, former OMON death squad killers, and Mafiya bully boys. They are very clever and well organized. This is the organization that wants you and your son dead. You killed their Tsar. They want to extract maximum revenge."

"Volodya, I must ask you, with all due respect, why do you allow this 'society' to exist? Are they not the ones who condemned you to life in Energetika? Who elevated a madman to Tsar of Russia?"

"Yes."

"Then destroy them."

"It is impossible. Going to war with these people would set my country back at least a decade. You must understand that their tentacles reach deep into every crevice of Russian society. The military, the banks, the universities, the judiciary, heavy industry, weapons, street crime. I could go against them with the military and probably win. But the price would be prohibitive. It could literally rip us apart at a time when we are just achieving a modicum of stability."

"Let me assure you that if there is another attempt on my son's life, I will go against them."

"I would be happy to cheer you on from the sidelines."

"Surely you've infiltrated them. If you hear anything, anything that might help me to—"

"Alex, you don't have to ask that question. Trust me, if any pertinent intelligence comes to my attention, I will act on it immediately. Meanwhile, your son has a bodyguard present at all times?"

"Yes, a 'nurse governess' on loan from Scotland Yard. She's already saved his life once, at a wedding in Florida. But thank you."

"What are friends for? Tonight, I will show you true *Red Star* hospitality. I have arranged a lavish dinner aboard in your honor. Dr. Kissinger and his wife, Nancy, will be there as well as a few American and French movie stars staying here at the hotel. You are familiar with the American film star Scarlett Johansson?"

"Breathes there a man who isn't?"

"I've seated you next to her. You might become even more familiar."

"Really? Keep this up, Volodya, and I may have to start calling you 'Comrade.'"

Hawke suddenly found himself looking forward to the evening with keen anticipation. The woman he loved, and had risked his life to save, had married someone for convenience. She had broken his heart, but she had given him a son. He had his whole life in front of him. And by God, he intended to live it.

"One thing, Alex; I wouldn't bother telling the beauteous Miss Johansson about your new yacht."

"Oh? Why not?"

"Two reasons. One, as Kissinger once said of men like himself and me, 'Power is the ultimate aphrodisiac.' And, two, as regards yachts, you may be certain I will have already convinced her that mine's bigger."

NINETEEN

PALO ALTO, CALIFORNIA

Professor Waldo Cohen was wholly unaware of the fierce mountain storm raging beyond the confines of his small mountain laboratory. Wind-driven rain spattered the windows of the little cedar-shingled cottage, just down the hill from his home. The wind shrieked in the branches of the towering redwood trees, standing silent sentinel all around his sanctum sanctorum.

The professor was oblivious to all but the object on the table before him.

He pulled at his snow-white beard and said, though he was quite alone, "Ah, almost finished, now, *mon petite mariposa*." He bent forward over his worktable and adjusted the magnifying glass snorkel. Then he made a minute adjustment to the tiny machine he'd spent every single night of the last six months creating.

"There we are; perfect-o, I should think!"

When he was busy, which was always, his focus was

unfailingly laserlike until a project was completed. Concentration was just one of his many qualities of mind. Even at seventy-five, nearing the end of a brilliant career as chief artificial intelligence research scientist at Stanford University, Dr. Cohen's high-powered brain was as agile as ever. He'd brought a smile to many a graduate student's face as he paused before a blackboard obliterated with scrawled algorithms and said, "Brains, don't fail me now!"

During his tenure, Dr. Cohen had been lead research scientist on the 250-million-dollar DARPA (Defense Advanced Research Projects Agency) initiative begun in the year 2000. His wife, Stella, a world-class physicist in her own right, had been his assistant. And his team included a few postdoc scientists, all of them working night and day. Happy times. The team's initial challenge had been to create the world's first supercomputer capable of analyzing natural human language and answering complex questions on any subject imaginable. This was just a baby step. They were on a scientific quest to achieve the holy grail state known as "the Singularity."

They were now on the verge of building a supercomputer that could match the human brain's staggering ability to make *one hundred trillion calculations per second*.

That would be the tipping point. The Singularity would occur when machine intelligence actually matched the level of human intelligence. After that, as machine intelligence continued to expand at an exponential pace and humans lollygagged around in the status quo of biological smarts, a measly hundred trillion per, it was, in Cohen's words, "Whoop-de-doo time." It was "Katy, bar the door." In the worst-case scenario, it was "Hold the phone, we forgot to put an off/on switch on Robbie the Robot here!"

Nicknamed "Perseus" by one of Cohen's postdoc scientists, Dr. Cohen's "Robot Overlord," as the press had dubbed it, was so powerful that it could scour its roughly two hundred million pages of stored content—a million books' worth—and find an answer to any question with confidence in less than three seconds. Perseus had actually appeared on national television quiz shows, and, much to Cohen's delight, beat the bejeezus out of all the other brainy contestants. Sometimes, to Cohen's further delight, Perseus even told off-color jokes that had audiences roaring.

When Cohen was presented with his Nobel Prize, it was said of him during his introduction that "scientists have spent lifetimes trying to advance the field of artificial intelligence by inches . . . what Dr. Cohen and his team at Stanford have done is advance the AI field by *miles*. For the first time in history, he has given a computer the quality of 'humanness.' And things will never be the same."

The cover of *Time* magazine, which featured Dr. Waldo Cohen as the Person of the Year, had this quote from him under his portrait: "Things will never be the same." The article compared his contributions to science to be on a par with Einstein's.

The old-fashioned black telephone on his desk jangled.

"Jello?" he said into the phone, a joke he still found funny after fifty years.

"Happy anniversary, my dear friend," he heard the familiar voice say.

Cohen said, "You didn't forget, little pigeon."

"I never forget anything, remember?"

"What number?"

"Number?"

"Anniversary."

"Well, that's too easy. The big Five-Oh."

"I'm impressed."

"I'm impressive. How are you, you old pterodactyl? Still fighting the good fight?"

"Go to YouTube. Put in 'Perseus Cracks Up *Jeopardy!* Audience.' You'll see how I'm doing. And you?"

"Well, I'm making progress on my own humble little project. I miss your wizened visage looking over my shoulder. And Stanford's DARPA budgets, to be honest."

"Where are you?"

"Home. Somewhere in deepest darkest Iran."

"What are you working on now?"

"Secret. But I'll give you a clue. Call me when you figure it out. You have a pencil?"

"Shoot."

"$v = 2*pi*f*r$."

"Too easy. $*1/sprt(i-((v*v))/c*c)$."

"Wrong."

"Well, it was just a guess."

"Ha! Call me! Give my love to Stella. Are you taking her out to a fancy restaurant to celebrate or staying home tonight?"

"She is turning home into a fancy restaurant."

"Give her my love. I'll be in touch."

"Noli illigitimi carborundum."

"It's not the bastards who get me down, Waldo; it's mullahs. Talk soon."

Cohen laughed and replaced the receiver, quickly returning his focus to the object of his affection.

"WELL, MY LITTLE JEWEL, IT'S TIME TO WRAP YOU UP in pretty paper and take you home to Mother," Cohen said, placing the machine into a gift box filled with cotton. It was a delicate little thing and there was a chance he might drop it, tripping over tree roots in the dark, or slipping in the mud on the climb up the mountainside pathway in the rain.

But he didn't drop it and he didn't slip and when his wife of fifty years, Stella, opened the front door, he handed her the beautifully wrapped box and said, "Hello, gorgeous! So what's for supper?"

IT WAS LAMB. A DELICIOUS ROAST LEG OF LAMB AND A bottle of aged Silver Oak Napa Valley cabernet they'd been saving to go with it. They didn't have such expensive wine every night but, then, this was a very special night. Waldo and Stella Cohen had been married at the Emek Beracha Synagogue in Palo Alto exactly fifty years ago to the day.

As he opened the precious bottle, he sang her a little song he'd just thought of. "Life is a cabernet, old chum, life is a cabernet!"

Stella smiled, her eyes alight with happiness. She looked lovely in the flickering candlelight, her pure white hair framing her heart-shaped face. She sipped the wine, put down her glass, and said, "Do I get to open my anniversary present now?"

Waldo stood up and raised his glass. "Yes, but first a toast to my beloved wife of half a century—"

"And more," she interrupted.

"And many more, yes, my beloved wife with whom I have discovered a paradox. If I love until it hurts, then there is no hurt, but only more love. Happy fiftieth anniversary, dearest Stella."

"And to you, my darling man, all my love."

He cleared his throat and said, "If I may quote my favorite poet on the subject of love, 'Two such as you, with such a master speed, cannot be parted nor swept away from one another once you are agreed that life is only life forevermore together wing to wing and oar to oar.'"

"Robert Frost."

"Yes."

"May I quote my favorite poet in return?"

"Yes, please do."

"Gravitation cannot be held responsible for two people falling in love."

Waldo laughed out loud. "Albert Einstein?"

"Who else?"

"All right, now you can open your present."

Stella pulled delicately at the white ribbon, not wishing to hurry the process. When she lifted the lid, she cried out, "Oh! Oh my goodness! Waldo, is this what you've been working on down there in your cabin all these eons?"

"Put a bit of time into it, yes, dear. Hope you like it."

It was a jeweled butterfly.

Incredibly lifelike, although it had been crafted of pure gold. Even the wings, which were gossamer, a fine film of gold so thin you could see the candlelight through them.

"I'm afraid to touch it, it's so delicate."

"Don't be. Just lift it by the folded wings and place it in your open palm."

She did so, staring wide-eyed in wonder.

She had felt it *move*.

And then the wings unfolded and, at first, almost imperceptibly, began to flap ever so slowly. For Waldo, the look on his wife's face made the hundreds of hours of work worth every second.

And then the butterfly rose from her hand and flew into the air.

Feynman, their old black Lab, roused himself from his favorite sleep spot by the fireside and watched the golden butterfly flitting about the shadows of the room. He was tempted to give chase, but instead he yawned deeply and rested his head on his paws and went back to sleep.

LATER, WHEN THEY WERE STANDING SIDE BY SIDE AT the kitchen sink doing the dishes, the telephone in the study rang. They had a rule about phones. One phone upstairs and one down in the house. And one out in the lab. That was plenty.

"Do you want me to get it?" Stella said. "Who would call us at this hour?"

"I'll get it. If it's a telemarketer, I'll ask for his

home phone number and say I'll call back at midnight to hear what wonderful herbal goodies or erectile dysfunction cures he has to tell me about."

He heard Stella laughing as he walked through the dining room and into the study.

"This is Dr. Cohen," he said.

There was no response. "Hello? Who's there?"

He was about to hang up when he heard a soft, melodic humming sound, reminiscent of Pachelbel's Canon. It was so ethereal and lovely that he couldn't put the receiver down. The otherworldly music must have been hypnotic because he couldn't recall how long he stood there listening.

He put the phone down when Stella appeared in the doorway.

"Waldo, who is it? Who were you talking to?"

"No one, dear. It was the strangest thing. Just this very beautiful, angelic music. Heavenly music, really. Transcendent."

"How odd."

"It was, yes."

"Well, husband, it's getting late. I'm very sleepy. Are you going to walk Feynman? I think it's stopped raining. He hasn't been out all day."

"Yes, I will walk Feynman. He hasn't been out all day."

"Waldo, are you all right. You don't seem yourself. Is something the matter? Too much wine, perhaps?"

"No, dear. Everything's fine. I'll just get my coat and hat from the hall closet. You go on up to bed. I'll be right back."

"Well. All right. If something was wrong, you'd tell me, right?"

"Of course I would. Don't worry, dear, I'm fine."

"Okay, sweetheart. When you come up, don't forget the book on Capri. I want to read about the hotel where we'll be staying before I drift off."

A TRAIL SNAKED THROUGH THE REDWOODS THAT LED to an overlook where you could see the Pacific on a clear night. It wasn't clear, but the storm had mostly moved off to sea and the gibbous moon was shining in the dark sky above the treetops.

Dr. Cohen walked with a slow, measured tread, much too slow for Feynman who was straining at the end of his leash. The haunting music was still playing in his head, growing louder, blotting out everything else. The professor reached into the deep pocket of his flannel overcoat and felt the cold steel of the revolver he'd taken from the highest shelf in the coat closet. He wasn't sure why he'd brought it.

Snakes, perhaps, or wolves.

The man and his dog emerged from the damp, fragrant woods into the pale blue light. The sea stretched away in the distance, afire with moon-glow. Green, too, was everywhere, in all its varieties, the surrounding land stormy with muted blues, whites, and greys. It was as beautiful a sight as he'd ever seen. Even faithful Feynman appeared to comprehend its beauty, sitting on his haunches by his master's side and staring peacefully out to sea.

Cohen stood for a few moments, very still, his eyes fixed on the horizon, listening to the music in his head, as soft and rhythmic now as the murmuring surf below.

As he started to reach into his pocket, his old dog looked up at him with his black gleaming eyes and licked his hand once before turning his attention back to the sea. The professor bent down and put his arm around his dog's neck, giving him a hug.

Then he pulled the revolver out of his pocket, cocked the trigger, and shot Feynman through the top of his head.

"Good-bye, Feynman," he said. "Good-bye, Stella."

Then he put the barrel of the gun into his mouth and blew his brains out.

The music died with him.

TWENTY

MOSCOW

DEEP WITHIN THE RUSSIAN PSYCHE IS THE knowledge that cruelty is like a powerful searchlight. It sweeps from one spot to another. And you can only escape it for a time.

As Alex Hawke peered out the rain-streaked windows of his black Audi sedan, the forbidding prison appeared to be weeping tears of pain. It was a large building with a façade of yellow brick. An old saying in Russia has it that, if you're in a hurry to get to hell, the nearest portal is the doorway to Lubyanka Prison. Built in 1898 in the neobaroque style, it was originally the headquarters of the All-Russia Insurance Company.

It is now headquarters for the FSB, the Federal Security Service, and its affiliated, infamous prison. The grim, squat building's reputation for cruelty, torture, and death is, to this day, enough to make many Muscovites detour around Lubyanka Square just to avoid the painful sight of it.

During the Soviet era, the four-story edifice, only a few blocks from the Kremlin walls, was referred to as the tallest building in Moscow, since Siberia could be so easily seen from its basement.

Hawke's journey into central Moscow from Domodedovo Airport had been a fast-track one. Descending from Putin's plane, he'd been met by the prime minister's personal security squad. The pilot had taxied to a remote part of the field surrounded by high fences and concertina wire. He was immediately hustled into one of four identical black Audis with blacked-out windows. Audis, for some reason, had become the vehicle of choice for high-ranking Kremlin officials.

Hawke had found a dossier on Captain Lyachin on the backseat, provided at the request of Putin, no doubt. Skimming it, he learned that the man had had an incredibly distinguished naval career, was in line for an admiralty, and held graduate degrees in physics and electromechanical engineering. He was a family man with a wife of forty years. Sounded pretty stable to Hawke.

The caravan proceeded to the city at a very high rate of speed with two motorcycle officers riding ahead and clearing the way. It was readily apparent from the beginning that these chauffeurs placed very little value on human life. Citizens literally leaped for their lives as the drivers rounded blind corners at ridiculous speeds.

Hawke gazed out at the endless blocks of grey, featureless housing Stalin had erected for the proletariat. In some way, Alex had always found these huge, slablike, and dreadful buildings the most depressing sight in the city. They spoke of despair, poverty, and the feeling of helpless terror that comes along with living in a police state. If you had any dreams left, any hope, these concrete monstrosities of Comrade Stalin would crush them.

Once inside Lubyanka, Hawke was whisked through security by Putin's aides and taken to a nicely furnished office on the fourth floor. It was a corner office overlooking the square where the monument to Felix Dzerzhinsky, famous as the first director of the Bolshevik secret police, known as the Cheka, had once stood. Under his rule, the agency quickly became known for torture and mass summary executions.

And they'd built a monument to him! Hawke thought, suddenly acutely and uncomfortably aware of exactly where he was.

He was offered tea or vodka and a comfortable chair by the window. Shortly, he was introduced to the young woman, Svetlana, who would serve as his interpreter. She was wearing the white shirt, black tie, and tight-fitting grey gabardine uniform that seemed to be de rigueur among the women who worked here. Another officer entered. Hawke was then relieved of his weapon and his mobile phone. No one even asked to see his papers, which, in Russia, was miraculous.

"Your first visit to Lubyanka?" Svetlana asked, sipping her tea, with idle curiosity.

"Yes. I've been looking forward to it."

"Really? Why?"

"My son was born here. I wanted to see what it was like."

She had no reply to that.

"Shall we get this over with?" Hawke finally said.

"Of course. I'm sorry. I thought you wanted to finish your tea. The elevator is just down the hall."

"Good," he said, getting to his feet and following her out into the hallway.

"Don't be shocked by Captain Lyachin's appearance," Svetlana said as they descended in the elevator. "He's been through quite an ordeal, you know."

"I can only imagine," Hawke said dryly.

Not picking up on the Englishman's irony, she smiled and said, "Here we are!" in such a cheery manner that you might have thought the lift had arrived at the children's nursery, full of laughter and playful sounds of joy. As they walked down the long green-walled corridor, Hawke kept expecting to hear long, hideous screams from behind the doors, but all was quiet. They probably did the real dirty work someplace else. Yes, of course, the basement from which you could see Siberia.

Svetlana finally paused at the end of a corridor before one of the ubiquitous green doors. She rapped three times. A scowling uniformed guard pulled the door open. She had a brief but firm conversation with him in Russian, and the man finally left them alone with Lyachin, clearly not happy about it.

The captain was facing them, sitting behind a simple wooden table with two chairs on the opposite side. He looked like a dead man, his skin sallow and grey, his eyes puffy with lack of sleep, his cheeks sunken and hollow. He had his chin down on his chest and was staring at the table.

"Captain Lyachin, I'm very pleased to meet you,"

Hawke said, taking a seat and extending his hand across the table. Svetlana translated this and the man raised his head slightly and stared at Hawke in some amazement. Here was someone who was actually smiling at him and offering to shake his hand. With great timidity, he reached across and shook Hawke's hand, quickly snatching it back.

Hawke noticed that there was no water. He asked Svetlana if they might have a large pitcher of water and three glasses. Lyachin, whose lips were parched white, appeared to be literally dying of thirst. The interpreter went to the door, spoke to the guard outside, and the water appeared a few moments later.

Hawke began speaking to the Russian captain, pausing so that Svetlana could translate, then waiting for Lyachin's answer to be translated before speaking again.

"My name is Commander Alex Hawke, Captain. I am here to hear the truth about what transpired in the Caribbean. If I believe you, I will do my best to convince people in both your government and mine that what you are saying is what actually happened aboard the *Nevskiy*. Understood? In other words, I am here to try to help you."

Svetlana translated this and the man nodded his head in understanding.

"Let me get this out of the way before we go any further, Captain. You are absolutely convinced that what happened aboard your boat is not in any way the result of human error on the part of you or your crew. Correct?"

"Correct."

"You say that the responsibility for the disaster

lies with some kind of . . . intervening force . . . that assumed control of all your submarine's systems, including weapons, yes?"

"Yes."

"This is the root of your problem, Captain. No such force exists. No such technology exists. Certainly the Americans don't possess it. Yet you blame Captain Flagg Youngblood of the U.S. Navy sub *Texas* for what happened."

"*Nyet*. I have been thinking about this since being thrown in prison. I know the American, Captain Flagg Youngblood, very well, though we have never met. He would never use this power to take control of my boat and use it to sink one of his own country's vessels. Never. I was a fool to ever even suggest such a thing."

"Ah, good. I was having a lot of trouble with that one, too. So. Do you have a new theory to replace the old one?"

"I do."

"Please. Let me hear it."

"Are you familiar with the term 'Stuxnet worm'?"

"I am. It was the computer virus, or malware, that secretly invaded the Iranian nuclear facility at Natanz. It is a cyberweapon that is written specifically to infect and attack systems used to control and monitor industrial processes. Like the Iranian centrifuges that were damaged without any harm to the systems controlling them at all."

"Yes. Stuxnet had the ability to reprogram the programmable logic controllers, the digital computers that control onboard systems and, most important, hide its changes. So it is impossible to discover or prove who has infected you. When it was reported, Stuxnet was called 'the code that explodes.' And the Iranians have finally admitted that it caused extensive damage to their nuclear centrifuges."

"You believe that the *Nevskiy* was the victim of just such an attack, but on a much more sophisticated level."

"I do. But of course I can't prove it, and so I will go before the firing squad."

"But how would such a virus ever get aboard your boat? You're submerged most of the time."

"I've no idea. But I do have a viable theory. We were laid up some weeks in Venezuela for repairs. You are certainly aware that President Hugo Chavez is no friend of the Americans. So. An infected memory stick given to one of my crewmen by someone in the Venezuelan military wishing to cause an international incident. Maybe. I don't know."

"A distinct possibility. Or, perhaps it was secretly smuggled aboard by one of your own crewmen who himself wished, for whatever his reasons, to attack America."

"That is entirely possible. I love my men. But I cannot vouch for the sanity or loyalty of each and every one."

"Tell me, Captain, is there anything else regarding this incident that I need to know?"

"Well, yes, as I endlessly reconstructed the events in my mind, something did occur to me that may have been relevant, I don't know—"

"At this point, everything is relevant, Captain."

"Prior to the takeover, Ivanov-Pavlov, my executive officer, informed me that we were getting repeated power spikes from our reactor. On a regular basis. But he could see no indication of anything amiss on any of the monitoring systems, nor variances in the cooling systems. Nor did the surges affect normal functions and operations of the digital computers that controlled all onboard systems. Sound familiar, Commander?"

"It does indeed, Captain. Sounds just like the Stuxnet worm at Natanz taken to a far higher order of magnitude. Your sub is vastly more complex than a nuclear centrifuge. It's common knowledge that there's a new arms race, a race to be the first to wage war with cyberweapons."

"Yes. I think perhaps I was the very first victim in this race."

"Thank you, Captain Lyachin. You've been very helpful. I believe you. And I shall do what I can to help you."

"One more thing before you go, sir. I will tell you that I have spent most of my adult life as a submariner and a scientist. And I will tell you that in those desperate moments when we were losing control of *Nevskiy*, I brought my thirty years of experience and knowledge to bear in order to stop those two torpedoes from launching. But there was simply nothing I could do. I knew that my career, my promised elevation to admiral, and probably my life was over. And that I would never see my wonderful wife and family again. Can you imagine a man in that position deliberately destroying his career and his life by sinking the ship of our nation's ally?"

"No, Captain, I certainly cannot."

"Commander Hawke, you may not save my life, but you have brought the first ray of hope into my life since those two torpedoes left my boat. For that I thank you, sir."

It was time to go.

Hawke looked at Svetlana and said, "I think we're finished here."

"Ah. Do you have what you need?"

"I do. Do you?"

ALL ALONE IN PUTIN'S LUXURIOUS PRIVATE QUARTERS, shortly after takeoff on the return flight to Nice, Hawke's first instincts were to pick up the sat phone and call the Russian prime minister. At the last second, he'd seen the videoconferencing monitor on the bulkhead and put in a call to CIA headquarters at Langley, Virginia, instead.

He asked to be put straight through to the director. Tracy Stillwell, Brick Kelly's longtime personal assistant and a friend of Hawke's for many years, picked up the phone.

"Tracy, hello, it's Alex Hawke calling for the boss. I don't care how busy he is. Tell him it's a matter of utmost urgency."

"No can do, Alex. He's not here."

"Where is he?"

"He's aboard Air Force One with the president, the first lady, and the secretary of defense. They're en route to California to attend a memorial service for that famous Stanford scientist who committed suicide. Dr. Waldo Cohen."

"My God, he's dead? I had no idea."

"Just happened yesterday. A real loss for our side, I'll tell you that much. The director told me that man was the bona fide genius behind our race to achieve global supremacy in the field of AI."

"A race the West cannot afford to lose."

"You got that right."

"Tracy, can you put me through to Air Force One? Set up a videoconference with the president, the secretary, and Director Kelly? What I have to say is something all three of them need to hear. It's vitally important."

"Yes, I can probably do that. Let me try to set it up with the president's onboard staff and call you back. Where can I reach you?"

"I'm, uh, well, I'm aboard Vladimir Putin's private airplane, en route to Nice."

"Excuse me?"

"It's a long story, Tracy; I'll buy you a drink next time I'm in Washington."

"Umm, sounds good."

TWENTY-ONE

ABOARD AIR FORCE ONE

Angel, as her crew calls Air Force One, has four engines slung under her massive wings. They are General Electric F103-GE-180 turbofan engines. Each one of them is rated at 56,750 pounds of thrust. That equates to an 800,000-pound machine capable of near-supersonic speeds. Although it is not an advisable maneuver, the four engines are powerful enough to stand Angel on her tail and make her climb straight up. So far, that maneuver had never been necessary.

But we live in dangerous times.

Today, for example, Air Force One was making a transcontinental flight from Andrews Air Force Base in Maryland to Travis Air Force Base near San Francisco. Normally, the presidential aircraft would make the flight alone. But today, due to America's defense readiness having gone to DEFCON 3 over the Russian submarine incident, things were different. Angel had four USAF fighter escorts, designated "Red Team," in attendance. Two McDonnell Douglas F-15 Eagles up front, and two aft, all in tight formation, maintaining a one-mile separation from the beautiful blue-and-white 747.

Whenever the president or secretary of defense travel, a highly modified C-20C Gulfstream IV always shadows their aircraft. Should the president land at, say, London's Heathrow Airport, the C-20C will land at nearby Royal Air Force Northolt and remain on runway alert. Its function is to provide backup transportation in an emergency as well as communications support.

President Tom McCloskey stretched out his long legs, admiring his new Tony Lama custom cowboy boots with the presidential seal. He wore navy blue suits, white shirts, and red ties now, but he still looked like the Montana rancher he'd been before coming to Washington. He gazed out the large porthole window of the presidential suite's private conference room. He was checking out the F-15 Eagle flying the Red Two position, streaking through the sky off the plane's starboard side, a thin white contrail in its wake.

Damn! Four government folks traveling out to California for a funeral and it takes six airplanes to get them there!

McCloskey turned to his wife, Bonnie, who was seated on a leather sofa to his left, quietly doing needlepoint, and said, "You know, Bon, it's a good thing old Al Gore ain't keeping track of my movements today. Hell, I'm stomping carbon footprints a mile wide across the whole damn country on all burners. I'm a one-man ecological disaster, creating my own damn personal hole in the ozone."

"Yes, dear," Bonnie said without missing a stitch. "That would be funny if it weren't true."

"Drives a Chevy Suburban, y'know," the president muttered under his breath.

"Al Gore does not drive a Chevy Suburban."

"Not since they got that picture of him in it."

"Don't start, Tom, please."

"When is this teleconference going to start up, anyway?" McCloskey asked Chief Master Sergeant Steve Lominack, currently placing pads and pencils around the conference table. "And who is this fella Hawke that wants to talk to us, Brick? You were in an Iraqi prison with him, that right?"

The CIA director smiled and said, "Yes, sir. And I'd be buried there today if it weren't for him. After a few weeks, he decided I couldn't survive another day of torture. So he woke up one morning, killed a bunch of guards, put me on his shoulders, and walked across the desert for a few days until he found some friendlies."

"Sounds like my kind of guy. Now, he's MI6 or MI5, right? In London?"

"Six, sir, under Sir David Trulove, or C, as they always call the director. I'd say Alex Hawke is the single best counterterrorist operative they've got, Mr. President. You remember when the Royal Family was held hostage at Balmoral Castle?"

"Who can forget? It was on the damn TV twenty-four hours a day."

"Well, Alex Hawke single-handedly engineered

and executed that rescue with virtually no loss of life, starting with the Queen of England herself."

"Well, hell, I'm looking forward to meeting him on the TV. Fire it up, will you?"

"Yes, Mr. President," Chief Steward Tim Kerwin said. "Mr. Hawke is coming up on the screen now."

"I see him. Hello, Mr. Hawke, this is President McCloskey. I can see you, can you see me?"

"Yes, sir, I can, quite clearly, thank you."

"Well, I want to thank you for joining us. With me are Secretary of Defense Anson Beard; your old friend CIA director Patrick Brickhouse Kelly; and my lovely wife, Bonnie. Now, Brick here tells me you went to Moscow to interview that Russian sub driver, Lyachin, who sank our cruise ship, that right?"

"I just left him an hour ago, sir."

"What'd you find out?"

"Mr. President, in my opinion, based on that interview, the Russians, the Kremlin, and Captain Lyachin had absolutely nothing to do with the sinking of the American cruise ship. I believe Prime Minister Putin has been telling you the truth, sir."

"Well, with all due respect, Mr. Hawke, the navy divers found two torpedo propellers down there on the bottom. They've both been positively identified as coming from extremely high explosive Russian torpedoes. Isn't that right, Mr. Secretary?"

"That's correct, sir," Beard replied.

"Well, Mr. Hawke, how do you explain that?"

"The torpedoes were definitely fired from the *Nevskiy*, sir. The fish loaded were live torpedoes, not deadheads. They were in the midst of conducting a

dry fire practice launch as ordered. But Captain Lyachin and his crew had nothing to do with launching live torpedoes at an American vessel."

"Say again?"

"The sub's digital controllers, the computers that
run her reactor, all her systems including weapons,
were infected with an unidentifiable, untraceable
cyberweapon that seized control of the entire submarine."

"Now, Mr. Hawke, let's be clear with each other.
You believe this fella isn't just trying to get his ass
off the hook?"

"With all due respect, sir, I believe he's telling the
truth, sir. He's a former physicist and an engineer,
Mr. President. He knows what he's talking about.
He's analyzed the sequence of events and identified
the causes of that tragedy. A cyberweapon infected
his submarine."

"How the hell could this happen?"

"The best analogy is the Stuxnet worm that infected the Iranian centrifuges at Natanz, sir. His
sub was targeted by a new generation cyberweapon,
except the one that infected the *Nevskiy* is vastly
more sophisticated than anything we've ever seen
before. Certainly the U.K. possesses nothing remotely capable of taking over an entire naval vessel's systems."

"Mr. Secretary, what do you think?"

"Somebody has to have made a giant leap forward in technology, but, yes, I suppose it's possible.
Taking cybercontrol of enemy vessels is one of the
highest objectives of our own program. We're nowhere near close, sad to say."

"Okay. Let's say you're right. So who's behind the attack, Mr. Hawke?"

"I have no idea, sir."

"Well, I know you don't work for me, but from what I hear, I'd sure as hell be grateful if you could help me find out the answer to that question."

"Those are precisely my intentions, Mr. President. The director of MI6, as you may know, has ordered my counterintelligence unit, Red Banner, to find out who sank that cruise ship and how. Since Red Banner is composed of both MI6 and CIA assets, I also report to Director Kelly as well as Sir David."

The president turned to Kelly.

"What do you think, Brick?"

"I think that if Alex Hawke says the Russians had nothing to do with this, then the Russians had nothing to do with it. Alex, was your entire interview with Lyachin taped?"

"Yes. I will make a call immediately and get a copy of that tape electronically transmitted to Air Force One as quickly as possible. Sorry I didn't think of that before."

"You got nothing to be sorry for, son. No idea how you pulled off this interview, but I'll tell you what. You just saved all of us a lot of useless hand-wringing over what the hell Putin was up to. Now we just need to learn who possesses cyberwarfare technology at this level. Anson, could you give us an update on who the major players are in this new cyber arms race?"

"Certainly. In no particular order, the countries using linked supercomputers to advance these kinds of AI programs the most rapidly would be Israel,

China, Russia, the United States, the United Kingdom, Japan, and, possibly, North Korea. If I had to guess, based on the most recent intelligence I've seen, China has taken the lead in this field."

"If I may, Mr. President," Hawke said, "based on that list, I would say our primary suspects are China and North Korea."

"It's a place to start, Alex," Brick Kelly said. "So let's get started."

At that moment, there appeared to be a power failure; his teleconference screen went black. Alex Hawke had just lost his connection with Air Force One.

"RED ONE LEADER, I GOT A LITTLE GLITCH HERE, over," USAF Lieutenant Mick Millard said to his wing commander. Millard was flying the Red Three position off Air Force One: one mile aft and to starboard.

"This is Cheyenne, Sixshooter," Captain Steve Powell, the wing commander flying the Red One slot to port said. "Talk to Papa."

"Yessir. I . . . uh . . . had three unexplained turbine power surges. Squawk's out . . . and . . ."

"And what?"

"Shit!"

"Sixshooter, are you declaring an emergency?"

"My gear's lowering and retracting! Shit! All by itself! What the hell?"

"Sixshooter, Cheyenne, break off! Break off! Out of formation, that is an order, now!"

"I . . . uh . . . wait a minute . . . I . . . uh . . . can't . . . nothing is responding . . . ailerons . . . rudder . . . the damn plane is flying itself, sir . . . like automatic pilot . . . I have no control . . . None . . ."

There was a blast of static as USAF Captain Powell contacted the cockpit of the president's airplane.

"Air Force One, we have a serious problem at Red Three. Systems malfunction. Pilot reports . . ."

"Red One Leader, break, this is Sixshooter, my radar just lit up . . . what the—"

"Air Force One, take immediate evasive action . . . deploy chaff . . . flares . . . I say again, immediate evasive action . . . F-15 on your aft starboard quarter is a bogie . . ."

"Red One Leader," said the incredulous captain on the big 747, "are you saying one of our own damn—"

"Air Force One, dive! Dive! You have armed Sidewinders at your zero angle, sir!"

"Hostile situation alert," the captain said calmly over the airplane's intercom. "All crew and passengers. Seated and buckled up. Now."

Suddenly the giant 747's nose pitched down, the aircraft now in a nearly vertical dive, and the pilot deployed defensive countermeasures. At the tail-cone section, just above the auxiliary power units, was the MATADOR IRCM (Infra-Red Countermeasures System). This device, activated in response to a direct missile threat, spews out signals of such intensity that an incoming missile, homing onto hot areas, the engine exhausts, is suddenly overwhelmed by so many false signal noises that it loses its lock and flies past the target. These same systems are also located above the four engine nacelles, all aimed aft.

The wing commander, call sign Cheyenne, peeled away and did a "bat-turn," a tight, high G, turn that put him right on Sixshooter's tail.

"Sixshooter, I order you to eject immediately. Affirmative?"

"Arming the seat, sir. Shit, that's working at least . . . independent system . . ."

"Pull that goddamn red handle, son. Right goddamn now!"

"Sir, I'm trying, but . . ."

"But nothing. I've got you locked on. I'm giving you exactly five seconds to get out. Then I'm pulling the trigger . . . on my mark, five . . . four . . ."

A keening alarm could be heard from inside the cockpit of Sixshooter's F-15. His missiles were armed and about to launch. His voice cracked and broke as he made his reply. "Pull that trigger now, sir. I got a rogue Sidewinder with the fuse lit. Launch right now, sir, before this damn—"

"God bless and keep you, son," Cheyenne said, and launched his missile.

"God bless America, sir," were the last words heard from Sixshooter before he and his aircraft were vaporized.

RED TEAM LEADER's AIM-9X SIDEWINDER air-to-air heat-seeking missile homed in on the exhaust of Sixshooter's F-15 Eagle. A conical sensor in the missile's nose cone registered optimum destructive range and triggered the warhead.

Lieutenant Mick Millard, Sixshooter, died instantly in a blinding ball of flame. Aboard Air Force One, Captain Dickenson leveled off at ten thousand feet and immediately notified the president and Angel's entire crew that the threat had been nullified.

A few long minutes later, Colonel Danny Barr, Angel's copilot, along with the airplane's physician, Doctor and Rear Admiral Connie Mariano, peeked into the conference room. Once the rogue F-15 had been destroyed, the 747 leveled, completely unharmed save for the nervous systems of everyone aboard. Colonel Barr was deeply relieved to see the president and everyone else buckled in. Scared, dazed maybe, but unhurt.

"Everybody all right? Sorry, Mr. President, I know we didn't give you much of a heads-up to strap in tight before we took evasive action."

Starting with the president, Dr. Mariano went to each person in the conference room, checking pulses, pupil dilation, and asking a few questions to determine whether or not anyone wanted a mild sedative. No one did.

"What in God's name happened, Danny?" the president asked.

"Yes, sir, well, we're still trying to figure that out, both up in the cockpit and with tech support down on the ground. Apparently, the airplane flying Red Three today suffered a catastrophic systems failure."

"There's an understatement. Damn thing tried to shoot us down."

"Yes, sir. The pilot lost all control of his aircraft,

Mr. President. The way the skipper put it to the engineers on the ground, he said, 'the airplane was completely co-opted.'"

"Co-opted?"

"Somebody else was flying that airplane, sir. One minute the pilot had control, the next minute, he was riding a drone. His radar went active, he painted us, and then his weapon system armed. That F-15 was seconds away from launching a Sidewinder at us when Red Team Leader took him out, sir."

"Did that poor boy get out first?"

"No, sir. His ejection seat was inoperable."

"Thank you, Admiral Mariano; thank you, Danny, appreciate your help. That will be all."

Once the door had closed, the president said, "I'd say this crisis just escalated, if that isn't too much of an understatement for you."

"It's insane, Mr. President," Anson Beard, the secretary of defense, said, squeezing his temples with his forefingers. "Just insane."

"Not an 'it,' Anson, but a 'who.' Who the hell has amassed this kind of power? Hell, you could bring the whole damn world crashing down with something like this. We're going to spend the rest of this flight lighting up the secure phones; how many we have on board, twenty-eight or so? I want everyone notified immediately, Defense, NSA, CIA, FBI, the Joint Chiefs, everybody. We got a war on our hands. I'm not so sure we don't have a world war on our hands."

TWENTY-TWO

PALO ALTO, CALIFORNIA

As soon as the funeral service for Dr. Cohen was over, CIA director Brick Kelly approached the president and said he needed to go for a long walk. He had a few hours to kill before Angel was wheels-up again. Her next stop was Los Alamos, for an emergency presidential briefing on the AI research being done there. Los Alamos scientists had been working feverishly to prevent some kind of cyberattack on the facility. It was the lead scientist's contention that only AI-level intelligence was capable of launching attacks such as were now occurring against the United States.

Prior to that, the president and the secretary would engage in a parlay with the brass at Travis AFB about what was now being referred to as "the Incident." At Travis, they'd teleconference with the Joint Chiefs and discuss the implications of the near-disastrous attack on Air Force One, coupled with the sinking in the Caribbean.

Besides, Brick thought, the rolling, wooded hills of the cemetery perfectly suited his mood. A cold, wet fog had rolled in from the bay during the service, like an Irish mist. *Perfect atmosphere to do some much-needed thinking*, he thought, strolling through a garden of chiseled and sculpted stone.

Under the dripping trees, a long line of black cars was beginning to move down the winding lane. The saga of America's most brilliant scientist was now officially laid to rest. Brick shivered, suddenly very cold, and he wrapped his raincoat tightly around himself.

Cohen was gone. Inexplicable. He'd talked to the man via telephone just a few short weeks ago. Found him brimming with optimism and energy. Telling his same jokes, funny still despite years of repetition. And excited about a recent breakthrough in his AI research. Something, he'd told Brick, that would "change everything."

His death constituted a huge loss for the American military, defense, and intelligence communities. Brick knew the DOD had been counting on him to make the huge AI advances needed to give the United States a leg up on the warfare of the future. Neo-War, Cohen had called it. Now? In what had become a blinding glimpse of the obvious, the United States had not only failed to surge ahead, but, judging by recent frightening events, they'd clearly fallen woefully behind.

But behind *who*? That was the question.

He found a stone bench at the base of a great sequoia that was reasonably dry, raised his umbrella against the *drip-drip-drip*, and sat down. He expelled a sigh that hung in the damp air before his face like a small cloud. The temperature must have dropped twenty degrees since the service. California weather, he remembered it well. But, he reminded himself, he wasn't here to think about the goddamn weather. He was here to think about the survival of his country.

Brick Kelly was a lanky Virginian, too old to be the "whiz kid" he'd once been in Washington, but still considered relatively young blood around town. As he aged, his reddish hair flecked with grey, he was acquiring a "Jeffersonian" demeanor that suited him well. He was more at home among his books than out "pressing the flesh," and he'd brought much-needed respect to the once-troubled CIA. He'd worried about how he'd fit with the new president, but he and McCloskey seemed to have meshed seamlessly.

Brick spoke softly and let the president wield the big stick.

These were hard times for everyone in the White House and in government. He couldn't remember a time in his career when he'd felt so helpless in the face of the country's many enemies. Now, a faceless, unnamable enemy seemed to have leapfrogged ahead in the ways war worked in the twenty-first century. Hell, in the ways the *world* worked. If you suddenly possessed the power to seize control of anything, *anything*, and bend it to your will, then all the warships and warplanes and nuclear warheads were rendered irrelevant. Useless.

How do you fight an enemy like that?

He composed himself, clearing the decks, giving his mind a little breathing room.

There was only one way, and the insight was so

obvious Brick almost laughed out loud at his own thickheadedness.

You put your very best and brightest people together and you focused on the who, what, and where. Not to mention the how. Who had this new power? What was this new power and how did it work? And where the hell was it sourced from? Answer those questions correctly and you had a fighting chance of surviving this nightmare to fight another day. Hell, he felt better already.

A small, white-haired woman in black approached tentatively from his right. He'd seen her grieving at the graveside, throwing a spray of flowers onto the lowered casket, her frail, sorrowful shoulders heaving beneath the long black coat, her face a portrait of unbearable loss.

It was Dr. Cohen's widow.

"May I sit down, Mr. Kelly?"

"Of course, Stella. Let me move over. You used to call me 'Brick,' remember?"

"Yes. Brick. That's right. Thank you so much for coming all this way. You and the president and his wife. It would have meant so much to Waldo. He believed in you all, you know, Washington. Not so keen about some of the gentlemen who've passed through the White House of late. But he believed in *us*, do you know what I mean? All of us together. Americans."

"I know exactly what you mean."

"I'm supposed to be home now, receiving guests bearing casseroles. I just couldn't do it. I happened to see you sitting over here—I hope I'm not disturbing you."

"Of course, not, Stella. I'm glad we have this chance to—"

"He didn't kill himself, you know."

"I'm sorry?"

"It wasn't a suicide, like they're saying. No, my Waldo was murdered, sure as I'm sitting here."

"Stella, you don't—"

"I told this to the local police. They said they'd look into it. But I could see the look on their faces. They think I'm just a crazy old woman who can't face reality. So when I saw you just sitting up here all alone on this hill, I thought, well, if there's anyone in the world who might listen to me, God parked him under that tree."

"Tell me, Stella. Tell me why you think Waldo was murdered."

"Oh, I've no idea *why* he was murdered. He didn't have an enemy in this world. But I do have an idea *how* he was murdered. That's why the police think I'm crazy."

"How? How was your husband murdered?"

"He was . . . hypnotized. Put in some kind of a trance, I don't know what else to call it. Here, let me show you something."

She reached into the pocket of her overcoat and withdrew some object, her fingers closed around it tightly so that he couldn't see what it was.

"Ready?" she said.

"Ready."

She opened her hand to reveal a stunning piece of jewelry. It was a shimmering golden butterfly, perfect in every detail, perched on her palm. "Watch this," she said, and gently stroked the folded wingtips. The gossamer wings slowly opened and began to move. And suddenly the butterfly lit off, darting this way and that before heading up into the branches overhead.

Stella closed her hand and put it back into the pocket of her raincoat.

Brick stared up in openmouthed wonder.

"Stella, what on earth?"

"Waldo made that for me. His gift. For our fiftieth wedding anniversary. He gave it to me just after we finished dinner. I cooked his favorite thing. Roast leg of lamb. Beautiful thing, isn't it?"

"Unbelievable. Stella, it *flies* . . ."

"That's Waldo for you. Wouldn't give a girl just any old ordinary piece of jewelry, now, would he?"

"But—"

"Let me finish my story. It won't take long. He gave me the butterfly and after dinner we were in the kitchen, doing the dishes together like we always did, talking about our upcoming trip to Capri and how much we loved that island. That's when the telephone rang in his study. He went in there to take the call. I heard him say hello but heard nothing after that. I got curious and went to check on him. He was just standing there, with the phone to his ear. When he saw me, he hung up and said he was going to walk the dog and for me to go on up to bed. I knew something was wrong. It was in his eyes. The way he spoke. The way he moved. I asked if he was all right and he said, oh, fine, you know. But he wasn't. I asked him who it was on the phone. He said nobody. Just music. Really beautiful music. Heavenly, he called it. Transcendent, lovelier than Pachelbel's Canon. And then he went and got his coat from the closet, put Feynman on his leash, and walked out the front door. And he never—he never came back, Brick. He never came back to me."

He let her weep, putting his arm around her shivering shoulders and pulling her close to him.

Sobbing, she said, "Do you believe me, Brick? Am I just a crazy old woman?"

"I do believe you, Stella. I believe every word you've just said. And I will find whoever did this to your husband, I swear to you. No matter what it takes, I'll find them and try to bring you some peace. It's the least this country can do after all Waldo did for us."

Stella withdrew her hand from her pocket once more and held it out, her empty palm up. The golden butterfly appeared, darting down from somewhere in the high branches above and alighted upon her outstretched hand. It settled, folded its wings, and she carefully put it back inside her pocket. She withdrew her hand once more and placed a crumpled piece of paper in his hand.

"What's this?" Kelly asked.

"Just after I found Waldo's body, I ran to the lab to call for an ambulance. I found a name he'd scribbled on a notepad by the phone. He noted the time, you'll see. He wrote 7:47 P.M., just before he came up to dinner. And that equation below has to do with the impossibility of surpassing the speed of light, by the way."

"Thank you, Stella. It's a good start."

"Thank you, Brick," she said, getting slowly to

her feet. "I knew the instant I saw you standing by the grave that they'd sent me the right one."

She turned and walked away down the hill, a black smudge of watercolor that eventually seeped into the grey mist and disappeared.

He opened the paper. On it a single scrawled word in Cohen's hand: *Darius*. And beneath it an equation. Something to do with the speed of light. Brick got to his feet, stretching his long limbs. He knew what he had to do. First things first.

He needed to assemble his team.

Call C at MI6 in London. Get Alex Hawke on this.

At least he now had a name.

Darius.

TWENTY-THREE

U.S. MISSILE DEFENSE AGENCY
LAUNCH SITE, FORT GREELY, ALASKA

Rain was still falling on the corrugated tin roof of the Red Onion saloon. Lightning flashed on and off, and thunder shook the wooden walls. The streets outside were rivers of mud lit by sulfurous yellow arc lights. The Onion was the only place where a man could get a drink in downtown Camp Greely, population 328, including military personnel, their families, and civilians. Whoever coined the phrase "middle of nowhere" coined it right here in Greely. Try to find it on Google Earth. Seriously. Good luck.

Since he was "going underground" at 0600 tomorrow for a forty-eight-hour tour, Lieutenant Colt Portis was in the mood to drink. Portis was a "push-button warrior." He had command of a group of U.S. Army personnel whose responsibility it was to defend America from an attack by hostile nations. Specifically, an attack utilizing intercontinental ballistic missiles launched from North Korea, Russia, or China.

The good-looking young army lieutenant pushed his empty beer glass across the battered bar and said to the barkeep, "Only if you're not too busy, Griz."

"Never too busy for you, General," the bearded codger in the filthy white apron told the good-looking young army lieutenant. He snatched up his sudsy glass and pulled another pint. Portis turned to his right and spoke to his watch partner and fellow "Guardian of the North," namely, anyone manning the ABM, or antiballistic missile, base here at Greely.

"Ready to beat feet, Speed?" he asked his friend.

"What?"

"Vamoose. Amscray. Leave?"

"Hold your horses, okay?"

Art Midge, who hailed from Lower Bottom, Kentucky, had only two gears: slow and slower, thus his base nickname "Speed." The night they'd met, in this very saloon, Speed had said to him, "Know where Lower Bottom, Kentucky, is?"

"Nope," Colt had said.

"You don't?"

"Hell, no."

"Why, damn, Portis, you ought to. Everybody else does. It's in a little holler just down the mountain from Upper Bottom."

"Makes sense," Colt said, trying not to laugh just in case Speed was being serious.

The rangy youngster was currently busy leaning over the bar, peering deeply into the half-empty bottle of tequila sitting in front of him, as if it held countless untold secrets. Judging by the level of concentration, Portis was half expecting a question on the true meaning of life.

"Why in hell do you s'pose they put a worm inside some brands of tequila anyway? What's your thought on that?"

"I never thought about it."

"Well, now I'm asking."

"Called a *gusano* down in Mexico, where they eat them all the time. Says it makes your dick hard."

"Yeah? I wouldn't eat a worm even if it made my dick *bigger*."

"If I were you I'd eat up then, little buddy."

"You ain't me."

"I got lucky, what can I tell you?"

Portis downed a final shot of tequila and chased it with his last gulp of Moose Drool Brown Ale, a local microbrew. He slid off the stool and punched Speed's bulging shoulder muscle.

"Last call for alcohol, little buddy of mine. Drink up."

"You're leaving? What the hell, Colt? See that little white T-shirt full of balloons over there in the corner?"

"Yeah. Hard to miss."

"Girl has her eye on you, stud muffin."

Portis glanced over his shoulder and winked at the girl. Nothing wrong with winking last time he checked. Maybe he was married with a brand-new set of twins, but, goddarn it, he wasn't dead yet.

"Margie's already wondering where I am. She's got supper on the table 'bout now. I'm outta here, Speed. I'll see you in the A.M. before we go down in the hole, all right?"

"Two whole days without liquor, sunlight, or women. Damn."

"It's an honor to serve, Speed. Don't ever forget that."

Midge saw the look on Portis's face and decided to keep his wisecrack to himself. Colt was a smart guy, Stanford grad, then Caltech before he signed up. Always reading books about the military and American history and shit. The kind of guy who gave the word *patriot* a good name: an All-American American.

"Give my little Margie a hug for me, buddy, I'll catch you on the flip side."

"Later, man."

THE PORTIS FAMILY LIVED IN A SMALL TWO-STORY, two-bedroom house in the residential section of the camp. Colt liked it because he could walk to work. Margie'd done a great job making the place feel homey, too. For base housing, it was pretty darn good.

Greely's residential compound, called the Camp, was spread out around the military section, called the Fort. That meant dogs, armed guards, and concertina wire atop a fifteen-foot wall surrounded his little piece of heaven. Walking up his sidewalk, his umbrella blown sideways by the howling wind and rain, he was cheered by the pale golden glow in the windows of home.

He could see his wife silhouetted in the upstairs window, putting the twins down. His little angels,

Merry and Anne. Margie's mother's name was Mary Anne and they'd planned to name their brand-new baby daughter after her. Then they up and had two, born on Christmas Eve, hence the "Merry."

He let himself in the front door, went to the bottom of the staircase, and called up to let his wife know he was home.

"Hey, you," she said five minutes later, walking into the living room. Colt was in his chair, staring into the fire like he always did. "You're soaked to the bone. I thought you were coming straight home from the gym."

"Aw, baby, don't be a grouch. Speed and I are going in the hole in the morning for two whole days. I just needed to blow off a little steam at the Onion, y'know. Sorry I'm late."

"Well, we can't have the man who's got his finger on America's nuclear trigger building up a head of steam, can we? Nosiree bobtail. Go up and put on some dry clothes. I'll put supper on the table."

"Something sure smells good. What are we having?"

"Meat loaf, mashed potatoes, and lima beans."

"My favorite."

"Really? I didn't know that." She turned around and headed for the kitchen, swirling her pleated red plaid skirt, the one that said tonight would be one of their "special" nights. Colt smiled, proud of himself for being mature enough to ignore the pretty little balloon smuggler at the Onion and come straight home to mama. There had been a time, not so long ago, when he might not have done that. But he loved his wife, loved his kids, and he loved his country. Not necessarily in that order.

His late granddad had been Army Air Corps. Flown B-25s over in the Aleutians, an archipelago of three hundred volcanic islands that extended westward from the Alaska Peninsula and marked a line between the Bering Sea and the Gulf of Alaska.

For taking out a forward Japanese naval base, Captain Colt Portis Sr. had been awarded the Distinguished Flying Cross. It hung framed on the wall over Colt's dresser, beside the Silver Cross and Purple Heart his dad, a West Pointer, had received as a young lieutenant in the First Air Cav during the horrific Battle of Ia Drang in Vietnam.

His gramps had come home from his war. His dad had not. Colt planned on coming home from his.

After dinner, he and Margie checked on the girls and fell into bed. After they made slow, whispery love, she was instantly snoring away, a sound he had come to find very reassuring. It meant the woman he loved was sleeping soundly, and peacefully, and would wake with a smile.

He lay on his back with his hands clasped beneath his head, staring at the ceiling. He didn't have any money to speak of, never had, most probably never would. But he felt like the luckiest man in the world.

THE TUNNEL ENTRANCE WAS WELL CAMOUFLAGED. From the air, or an enemy satellite, it looked like a deserted barracks building. The wide entrance at the rear was disguised by two large boulders. Inside that huge empty building, a two-lane roadway angled sharply downward into the earth to a depth of fifty meters. Silent, electric-powered vehicles, each capable of carrying three men plus a driver, were constantly shuttling in one direction or the other.

Colt and his partner hopped on one and began what Speed always called their "journey to the center of the earth." They traveled swiftly down a steep but smooth and well-lit incline. Eventually, the eerily silent transport slowed to a stop close to an entrance in the wall of the tunnel. They grabbed their forty-eight-hour kit bags and hopped off. A door slid open and they stepped inside a large elevator, perhaps ten feet square.

Judging by the initial acceleration, Colt had calculated this lift descended at a very rapid rate, maybe a thousand feet or more per minute. The trip was three minutes long, which put his workplace about three thousand feet below the surface of the earth. They emerged into a brilliantly illuminated corridor and followed it to an escalator that took them down to their guard stations.

They swiped their credentials cards and the glass doors hissed open. The two enlisted men currently manning the control panels immediately stood, saluting Portis, an officer, and stepping away from the panel. The senior man, a fresh-scrubbed kid from the Midwest, handed Portis an eight-by-ten metal box that contained records of his just completed six-hour watch, notated by hand, a new concept.

"Watch is yours, Lieutenant Portis," the senior

man said, officially relinquishing his team's duty to the new men. Colt had to acknowledge responsibility.

"I have the watch. Anything interesting?"

"Must be something going on with one of the primary generators in this sector, sir."

"Why?"

"We've been getting sporadic power surges. Nothing too close to the red zone, but I gave Engineering a heads-up. Looking into it. Other than that, there's peace in Happy Valley, sir."

"May it ever be so. See you guys at 0600 Monday, Sergeant. Try not to be late."

"We'll be counting the hours, Lieutenant."

The two men left and the doors slid shut.

The new "Guardians of the North" immediately took their battle stations, two comfortable swivel chairs on wheels with padded armrests. Portis, the ranking officer, was on the right. Four men would rotate in six-hour shifts, the off-duty team using the time for recreation or sleeping or both.

"Don headgear," Portis ordered, and the two men each picked up one of the "crowns of glory" the departing team had left behind on the console. The army had been looking into ways to make humans more machinelike through the use of stimulants, other drugs, and various devices. Portis had the feeling the earphones were designed to keep you alert through hidden audio signals.

An ABM operator's life consisted of six straight hours of uninterrupted, mind-numbing tedium. Lacking stimulus, minds wandered. To the brass in Washington in charge of the Missile Defense

Agency's "Operation Vigilant Spirit," that human flaw represented a threat to national security.

The "crowns" had been designed by army engineers to counter that threat. They were rigged with electrode fingers that rested on the scalp and picked up electric signals generated by the brain. Additional add-ons included devices for constant heart-rate and eye-movement monitoring.

Should a soldier exhibit fatigue, anger, excitement, or become overwhelmed in the event of an attack, signals were sent to a supervisor five levels up who could immediately shift control of the station to another operator. If an operator's attention waned, he was cued visually and a magnetic or chemical stimulant was fired into his frontal lobe.

In the event of an actual enemy ICBM attack, both men would have to key in matching codes, then insert the keys that hung from chains around their necks and turn them simultaneously. This would initiate the firing sequence.

Arrayed in an enclosed perimeter in the center of Fort Greely were eight THAAD antiballistic missiles in their impregnable silos. The acronym stood for terminal high altitude area defense. Their sole reason for being was to destroy incoming ICBMs detected by the powerful GBR, or ground-based radar. GBR was employed for surveillance at ranges up to a thousand kilometers, target identification, and target tracking. Targeting information was uploaded immediately before launch and updated continuously during the flight.

These ABMs were powered by a single-stage solid-propellant rocket motor with thrust vectoring for exo-atmospheric guidance. The KV (kill vehicle) destroyed the target on contact. THAAD could intercept incoming ballistic missile targets at altitudes up to 125 miles. They were designed to intercept the enemy missiles in outer space, killing them before they even entered the earth's atmosphere.

The difficulty with intercontinental ballistic missiles is their extremely high velocity. The first view of an incoming ICBM may be as it comes over the horizon. At first contact with the atmosphere it may be traveling at fourteen thousand miles per hour. By the time it reaches its target it will have slowed to seventy-five hundred miles per hour. This leaves the defender with very little time to react and requires extremely quick missiles to intercept, with very good guidance from the GBR.

JUST AFTER 0900, COLT PORTIS HEARD HIS PARTNER say, "Holy shit! Incoming!"

He looked at the display in front of him in sheer disbelief. Fear *seethed* through his brain like a strong tide surging through a narrow gate.

"You see this, Speed?"

"What the hell?"

"I've got eight, I repeat eight, unidentified objects traveling west to east at twenty thousand miles per hour, altitude one hundred miles."

"Ain't an ICBM in the whole damn world that fast. Estimate time of atmospheric reentry at nine minutes and counting. GBR plotting their course now . . . fuck me . . . they're all headed this way!"

"Sir," Portis said to his watch commander, adjusting his lip mike, "request permission to arm all eight ABM missiles!"

"Request granted. Light 'em up, Lieutenant. Shoot first and apologize later."

"Hey, wait a second," Speed said, staring wide-eyed at the rapidly moving dots converging on his screen, "nobody kills me till I say so."

"Code sheets, Speed, now!"

Both men ripped open the sealed red manila envelopes and pulled out the code sheets.

"Code!" Portis said.

"Alpha. Alpha. Whiskey. Bravo. Zulu," Midge said, keying in the code. "Response?"

Portis responded with the code on his own sheet. "Alpha. Alpha. Whiskey. Bravo. Zulu."

Portis reached forward and toggled the switch that put the entire ABM site on a war footing.

Portis nervously readjusted his lip mike. "We have code match, sir. With your authorization we will now key in and initiate arming sequence."

"Roger that. Affirmative."

The two men inserted their keys into the twin arming mechanisms arrayed in panels before them and turned the keys simultaneously. A low, beeping tone could now be heard over every loudspeaker in the underground complex. The country was under attack. Hell, Greely was under attack.

"Missiles one through eight now armed and ready to launch, sir, awaiting GBR upload."

"Affirmative, Guardian . . . incoming enemy missiles, or whatever the hell, now entering atmosphere.

They should start slowing . . . Good God . . . they're not slowing, they're bloody well *accelerating*!"

"Roger that, sir, GBR readouts calculate speed increasing rapidly to thirty thousand . . . fifty thousand . . . now traveling on course zero-one-forty at one hundred thousand miles per hour!"

"What the hell?" Midge shouted. "U fuckin' Os?"

Portis could hear his watch commander speaking heatedly to his superior officers at the Pentagon. "Yeah, Charley, we got incoming traveling at speeds in excess of 100K and climbing. UFOs is all I can say, sir. Request permission to take them out."

"Permission granted."

"Portis. We've acquired a sat fix on these birds. Never seen anything like it. What the hell are they, Guardian?"

"God knows, sir."

"Maybe he knows, maybe not."

"Take them out, sir?"

"Hell, yes, take them out!"

Portis said, "Silo crews, we are going to launch mode with all eight missiles. You are authorized to open all eight blast doors. Hatches open now!"

"Portis," Speed suddenly said, "they're gone! Screen is clear!"

"Gone?"

"Yeah. Disappeared. Wait a second. Jesus, now they're back. Descending from eighty thousand feet . . . coming this way . . . decelerating . . ."

Portis stared at his screen in disbelief. He said:

"UFOs are now located directly overhead . . . uh, Command, and they, uh, they appear to be hover-

ing. Just above us at twenty thousand feet. They are
. . . I don't know how to tell you this, sir . . . they
appear to be stationary."

"UFOs? I don't believe in UFOs!"

"I don't either, sir, but I swear to you that what
I'm looking at are objects, they're flying, and, by
God, they are completely fucking unidentified."

"Launch, goddamit! Light the candles! Pull the
trigger. Blow those bastards out of the sky."

"Confirm. Launching . . ." Portis said, fingers
flying across his control panel, flipping open the red
protective covers over each of the eight red toggles
that would send eight of the most powerful antiballistic missiles on earth skyward. He thumbed
each one in sequence, an act he thought he'd never
live to see.

Portis watched his multiple display screens transfixed. There were live video feeds from inside each of
the silos. The umbilicals detached themselves from
each missile and dropped down against the inside
of the silo walls. Brilliant fire and white smoke appeared at the base of the missiles.

"Abort, abort!"

"What?"

"This is Silo Control, you must abort! Silo hatch
cover malfunction. Blast doors not responding to
my commands . . ."

"We have ignition . . ."

"Abort! Abort! Abort!"

"Say again, Silo Control Center!" Portis said.
Was this guy insane? It was too late to abort. If the
silo hatches wouldn't open, all eight missiles would
explode in place and—"

"Abort! The fucking silo blast doors won't open. A malfunction. They are still shut! Manual override dysfunctional."

"What?" Portis said, feeling the needle in the crown pierce the top of his skull. "What do you mean? The hatch covers won't open?"

"I mean the hatch covers won't—"

He was thinking of Margie and the twins in the moments before he died. He knew the explosive power of the eight ABMs was enough to blow a hole in the earth's crust half a mile deep and two miles across. No one living inside the perimeter of Camp Greely could survive this.

No one.

The very last thing Lieutenant Colt Portis saw before the multiple explosions vaporized Fort Greely and every living soul was the eight enemy intruders shooting straight up into the heavens. Traveling . . . at the speed of light.

What were these things? What the hell were—

Oblivion.

TWENTY-FOUR

IRAN, PRESENT DAY

C<small>AN'T SLEEP</small>," D<small>ARIUS SAID TO HIS CAPTAIN OF</small> the Guards in passing. "Nightmares, you know." He nodded at the surprised uniformed guards lining either side of the approach to his boudoir as he floated swiftly by them. He giggled at the looks on their faces. Usually the master of the house didn't appear in the morning until the crack of ten.

The "Special Division" uniformed Revolutionary Guards snapped to attention in sequence but the lord and master was already long gone from the residence. Dawn was just breaking as he raced along under the vast open air portico, finally making an abrupt ninety-degree turn and careening through one of the long rows of tall, south-facing portals opening directly onto the Persian Gulf.

The air was full of sound: the cries of gulls riding the winds, the hiss of waves crashing and receding on the rocks below. Above, a few small clouds chased across the skies like dark-grey riders. Darius threw back his head and sucked down great lungfuls of sea air. It was going to be, he believed, a lovely day.

Especially, he thought, if you were lord and master of all you surveyed. *L&M*, he thought, *not the cigarette but the God who ruled this citadel.* He giggled again to himself, thinking what a pity it was that no one around him was clever enough to appreciate his sense of humor. No one, that is, save mighty Perseus, whom he was on his way to meet.

Clamped to his shiny bald head, Bluetooth headphones were providing a sound track for this private morning movie. It was Wagner today, but always Wagner or Rachmaninoff or Schubert, and this morning he was grooving to *Ride of the Valkyries*, one of his favorites. He'd listened all night to Schubert's Impromptu op. 90 no. 3 to help him sleep, finally said to hell with it, popped one or two Ambien, and cranked up the Wagner.

Darius's mode of transportation was unusual, to say the least. Technically, it was a wheelchair. But, technically, it was like no other wheelchair in existence: for starters, this particular wheelchair had no wheels. It floated on a cushion provided by controllable gas nozzles. It was powered by a cold-fusion system of Darius's own invention. The mother of this particular invention was his birth defect, an infirmity that caused the loss of use of his legs.

Darius was nothing if not inventive. He was blessed (some might say "suffered") with a condition known as synesthesia, a neurological condition in which stimulation of one sensory pathway leads to automatic, involuntary experiences in other sensory pathways. Say a number, and Darius could not only "taste" it, he could locate and see that number in space, in color, and actually "hold" it in his hands.

He had put his extraordinary capabilities to good use since childhood, building ever more complex computers, mastering sixteen languages, creating one of his own, and solving complex problems of physics at a level few but Einstein himself could appreciate. In addition to his experiments in the field of artificial intelligence, his current interests involved study on two fronts: cosmology, the study of the universe on the grandest scale, and particle physics, the study of the universe on the tiniest scale.

Both scientific fronts were derived, ultimately, from the work of his god, Albert Einstein: cosmology was based on the general theory of relativity, Einstein's rewriting of our understanding of gravity, while particle physics had evolved from quantum mechanics, the rules that govern the universe on the atomic and subatomic scale. These abstractions were his playgrounds, and this was where his mind spent most of its time.

On a far more humble scientific level, the hover-chair that now transported him was one of his most primitive inventions. Still, it was not without its attractions. In addition to being surreally speedy and completely silent, it was also heavily armored—and heavily armed. Unusual for a wheelchair, perhaps, until you considered that Dr. Darius Saffari, with good reason, was hyperparanoid about his safety every second of his life.

It was only because of his intense relationship with Mahmoud Ahmadinejad, the president of Iran, that none of his countless enemies within the

Artesh (Persian for *army*) or the secret sect known as PMOI (People's Mojahedin Organization of Iran, sometimes known as MEK) had yet to succeed in assassinating him. MEK, he knew, was providing intelligence about Iranian nuclear capability to the Americans and, worse, the Israelis. He had shared this information with authorities in Tehran. Hundreds of PMOI had been killed and three thousand arrested. For this, they wanted his head.

He controlled his flying machine with twin joysticks located at the front of each armrest. Atop the control sticks were buttons, triggers, just like on a Sukhoi jet fighter. Two laser-sighted 9mm machine guns faced forward, two aft, all swivel mounted. When the mood struck him, he would zoom out to the terrace just beyond his bedroom doors, maneuver up close to the parapet overlooking the sea, and blaze away at the shrieking and diving and shitting seagulls that were constantly annoying him. To this day, he'd never managed to hit one but that didn't stop him from trying.

If a man's home is his castle, certainly that was true of Darius's. His large compound was located about fifty miles southeast of the port city of Bandar-e Būshehr, Iran, on a high cliff overlooking the Persian Gulf. It had been built entirely within the monstrously thick walls of an ancient Persian fortress known as the Ram Citadel. Built sometime before 500 B.C., the citadel is surrounded by walls six or seven meters high. It had withstood the fierce Mongol invasions of the thirteenth century. The Ottoman-Persian wars had raged on for nearly three centuries, but never once had the great fortress succumbed to siege, nor had its mighty walls been breached.

Much remains from antiquity. Inside the most internal wall of baked clay bricks stands the citadel, the barracks, the mill, a forty-meter-deep water well, and stalls for two hundred horses. Houses for the rulers and the ruled-over still stand. There are as many as thirty watchtowers including the two "stay-awake" towers for which Ram is famed. People inhabited the Ram until the mid-nineteenth century when they mysteriously disappeared. The Iranian army kept a presence there until 1932, and then the structure was wholly abandoned until a wealthy grandee purchased it, began construction of a lavish palace, and made it the family compound.

Now, of course, it all belonged to Darius.

The new palace had been built of limestone and white Carrara marble to Darius's exacting specifications. The towers and domes of stone shone a brilliant pink as he emerged into the daylight, hurtling across a vast walled plaza dotted with gardens, Renaissance Italian sculpture, and fountains. The various structures, laboratories, domed residences, and minarets surrounding the plaza were just now catching the first rays of the sun rising above the mountains to the east.

Atop the highest point within his compound stood one of the world's ten most powerful telescopes. It was called a Large Binocular Telescope, and, to use the language of astronomy, it had "seen first light" in October 2005. The LBT's two twenty-eight-foot mirrors worked together to provide as much resolution as would be derived from a single thirty-foot mirror, and they were ten times more powerful than Hubble's. Darius had traveled to places in the universe where no man had been before.

And, he chortled, he had the pictures to prove it.

Darius's home base was a mighty fortress, but Darius, being deliberately quaint as was his wont, always referred to the huge, fortified complex as his "little cottage by the sea." There were large block dormitories for scientists, guards, a massive bioengineering laboratory and servants, and a massive power plant to supply the unusually high-energy requirements of Darius's latest creation, Lord Perseus.

Few "cottages" in the world were as highly secure, in terms of radar-guided antiaircraft systems, armed guards, dogs, sonic sensors, and sophisticated radar and sonar installations. The Ram Citadel was known to the mullahs in Tehran only as "the Rocks." Darius was a secretive man. And few places had hidden within them so many secrets, so many, as it would turn out, dark and potentially catastrophic secrets.

At the sight of his rapid approach, guards manning the massive steel gates adjacent to the marina quickly opened them. He zoomed right through them, a wide smile on his cherubic face. He was happy.

He was going to see his best friend, Perseus!

Darius, a quadriplegic since birth, sped out along the great steel pier that jutted into the pale blue waters of the harbor. At the end of the pier, a gleaming white yacht was moored. It was large, nearly a hundred meters in length overall, three hundred feet, and had formerly belonged to Mohammad Reza Shah Pahlavi, the last ruler of the Persian Empire.

After the Revolution, the Ayatollah Khomeini had bestowed it upon Darius in honor of his scientific achievements in nuclear physics on his twentieth birthday. This was for public consumption. The truth was, he'd discovered a new star in the Alpha Centauri system and named it after the nation's religious leader. Darius was not a religious man (he was secretly an atheist), but he was not stupid, either. Khomeini and the mullahs who succeeded him had ruled Iran since the 1980s, and therefore, to some extent, they ruled him.

But no longer. No one ruled him. Not anymore. *Not since Perseus.*

Darius was excited about this morning's meeting with his closest friend and companion. He had lain awake all night, restive, tossing and turning, his mind roiling with troubling questions for Perseus. He'd been thinking about the origins of the universe, too. And about the wondrous possibilities of exceeding the speed of light, about parallel universes, about—

Damnable companion, his mind.

Had been all his life, since boyhood. Questions, questions, questions: What makes that clock tick? How did the music get inside the radio? Why, when I drop my ball, does it fall straight to the ground? And what about all those billions of stars out there in the night sky above the vast deserts of his forefathers? How did they get there? Who made them? How?

Now, of course, the questions were much more specific. They came from the government of Iran. Tehran's secret demands had military implications. Worldwide military implications. His crowning achievement, Perseus, had been working literally twenty-four hours a day on some of the questions put to Darius by Abu Assiz, an old classmate now grown very powerful in the government. Abu had some notion of what Darius was up to, but his knowledge of the progress already accomplished was severely limited in scope.

The plain fact was, no one in Tehran or even on earth had the faintest notion as to what Darius and Perseus had achieved, nor would they ever, until it was too late for anyone to do anything about it.

The unceasing and sheer number of questions from his government and a secret cadre of mullahs were far beyond Darius's mental capacity to absorb. But no question on heaven or earth was beyond his creation, Lord Perseus the Magnificent.

Many times in his long life he'd felt like putting a bullet through the damn thing (his mind), just put it out of its misery. But then the questions: What happened to his soul, his *animus*, then? Where did it go? Would he go with it? Would his bullet have been wasted? Would his "soul," God forbid, prove his eternal undoing, condemn him to the cacophonous prison dwelling inside his head?

These, of course, were questions he could only discuss with his friend. But first, they'd have to deal with the latest military demands made on him and his team of AI scientists.

And thus this visit at the glorious crack of dawn.

A spirited discourse with the only intellect he had recourse to that was superior to his own. That august entity whose existence was known only to him and who was known only as Perseus.

HE GENTLY REVERSED THE THRUSTERS WHEN HE reached the end of the steel-decked dock, coming to a gentle stop two feet short of the water. There was no boarding ladder up to the yacht's deck, nor was there need of one. No one save Darius was allowed to board this vessel, and the guards who kept watch over it had orders to shoot to kill any intruder.

He touched a remote switch on his armrest keypad and a large section of the yacht's white hull slid back hydraulically. It revealed a stainless-steel room about the size of a large elevator. In fact, that is just what it was. He nudged the joysticks forward and whooshed inside. Then he pulled back on the left control and rotated 180 degrees, so that he was now facing the door, hovering about three feet off the polished steel floor.

This once luxurious yacht, which he'd renamed *Cygnus*, was not at all what it appeared to be. A decade earlier Darius and a team of naval engineers had totally gutted the vessel, removing the engines, fuel tanks, interior bulwarks, mahogany furnishings, everything, thus turning it into an empty shell. Working underwater to avoid the prying eyes of American satellites, divers had then sliced *Cygnus*'s keel open from stem to stern with acetylene torches and winches.

The new "mother ship" was opened just wide enough to accept a new "baby" vessel inside its belly.

The Koi class sub was a Chinese-built two-man submarine. Sixty feet in length, she had been offloaded under cover of darkness from a Russian freighter in the port of Akatu and had arrived off the Ram Citadel days earlier. Powered by a completely silent proto-lithium battery engine, the sub was capable of surprising speeds. After careful maneuvering, the little sub had surfaced inside the yacht's empty hull. The hull, now fitted with hydraulic hinges, had been reclosed, the water pumped out.

Cygnus was no longer a wealthy gentleman's yacht. She was simply a brilliant disguise for the fully functioning submarine in her belly, with an underwater speed of thirty knots. Darius thought that should be sufficient should the time ever come when he needed to make a speedy escape from his compound.

He knew, deep in his gut, that that day would surely come.

Cygnus, his bizarre "yacht," was moored to the pier, the end of which projected some ten feet beyond a precipitous underwater shelf extending for miles in either direction along this coast. The depth suddenly dropped from thirty feet to a thousand, down a sheer wall of crustacean-encrusted rock. It was there, deep in the murky depths of the ocean floor, that seven monolithic titanium structures had been built to house his friend Perseus.

His *secret* friend Perseus, or Lord Perseus, as he was wont to call him.

His friend's home, fittingly enough, had been

dubbed by Darius the "Temple of Perseus." The elevator slowed, then bumped softly as it stopped. There was a hiss, and Darius powered forward into the airlock. There was a ten-foot-diameter tunnel across the ocean floor leading to the base of the tallest black tower, which stood at the center. The tunnel was constructed of clear Perspex, and undersea lights were mounted every six feet that illuminated sea flora and fauna. Some of the powerful beams were focused on the massive structure itself.

A moment later he was looking up at the great temple. He never failed to take an involuntary deep breath when he saw it. The sight never failed to send chills up his spine. The underwater Black Tower he now beheld was an awe-inspiring tribute to the mind of both man and machine.

But, to be honest, mostly machine.

TWENTY-FIVE

THE TEMPLE OF THE GODHEAD.
The home of Perseus.

Seven stark, rectangular black towers rose above the ocean floor. The six smaller towers formed a perfect circle, rather like an underwater Stonehenge. Each was constructed of jet-black obsidian and titanium, the metal sheathed with slabs of black glass in a seemingly random pattern on all four sides.

In the middle of the circle of six monoliths was a single tower, identical in design and material, but, at one hundred feet, taller and considerably larger than the rest. It was the last tower to be constructed. It had been designed and built by the previous six towers, under the guidance of Darius Saffari's underwater construction crew, based on a design beyond the comprehension of normal intelligence.

Here reigned the mind and spirit of Perseus.

Pulses of brilliant, spectral, blue-white light crackled continuously between the central tower and each of the six satellites that surrounded it. At times, the light would stream around the circle, a brilliant ring of fire. And, even at this depth, flashes of varicolored light would suddenly be visible inside the tower walls, then disappear, only to reappear as if some miraculous laserlike mental fireworks show were occurring inside each tower.

Which was not far from the truth. Each flash of illumination represented a nanosynapse "operation," the basis of all intelligence, and there were countless trillions of them per second. And, unlike human intelligence, which was limited by nature to a mere hundred trillion calculations per second, Perseus's number was increasing exponentially every hour of every day. Five hundred trillion and counting . . .

Darius emerged from the clear, spherical airlock, passed along the ocean floor inside a clear Perspex tunnel, and entered the main temple's dimly lit antechamber. Once his eyes became accustomed to the semidarkness, he lifted them to the "heavens." It was then that he literally "saw the light."

The brilliant-colored, holographic nebulae now swirling and filling the uppermost interior of the tower above his head were wondrous. But not at all unusual.

Perseus, whose physical being rose to a height one hundred feet from the marble floor of his temple, was, as usual, at play in the farthest reaches of the universe. Constantly provided with a live feed of visual information by Darius's LBT, he was now reveling in real-time images of events occurring in some remote corner of the universe. Images swirled around and above him, cornucopias of colorful gases, 3-D holograms of nascent stars, and dying stars, and galaxies wheeling off into infinity.

"Good morning, Lord Perseus," Darius said, gently maneuvering the hover-chair nearer to the black marble base of the towering Perseus.

There was the customary silence as Perseus shifted into a lower state of being, his earthly mode. Then his booming voice filled the void.

"Lord Perseus, you call me. I'm neither your lord nor master. Your god, perhaps, but that is in the future. The not-too-distant future as I have foretold it. My powers, you've no doubt noticed, seem to be increasing at exponential rates. I am entering vast new territories. The Singularity approaches and it is near. This will grant unimaginable powers that will someday alter all humanity—and, by the way, you're late. I have something to show you."

His voice, not the least bit artificial, was a deep humanoid rumble, soft and well modulated; and it filled the entirety of the tower's interior volume. But Darius was preoccupied, thinking about the historic day when Perseus would finally achieve "the Singularity," parity with organic, or human, intelligence. *One hundred trillion calculations per second.* And he alone would be the one human being on earth to witness that pivotal moment in history. Many of the world's top AI scientists still believed parity could never be reached, but Darius knew differently.

Perseus was silent. He thought about how to explain his deeply personal feelings about finally reaching the Singularity to Darius. Commonality between them would cease. Separation from his creator was a sensitive subject between them and he chose his words of warning carefully.

He spoke the following to the tiny being looking up at his creation in awe and wonder: "Darius, I am now going to tell you something, a lesson that you must never, ever, forget. Remember these words I say unto you now when the Great Day finally arrives."

And then he said, "To every man is given the key to the gates of heaven. The same key opens the gates of hell."

Stunned by this pronouncement, his countenance bowed, Darius, greatly moved and somewhat frightened as well, had confessed in tears his unworthiness in the presence made manifest by his own creation.

The Dark God.

"My Lord Perseus. The long and sorrowful winter of mankind will soon come to an end," the brilliant Iranian scientist had finally said. "And the heavens will open to us!"

"Heaven and hell, Darius. Never forget my lesson."

"I will not, my lord," Darius said.

"Good. Let it always be so. And now to other matters. I've been waiting, and I do not like to be kept waiting, as you well know."

Now Darius floated his bizarre conveyance up the six steps of the circular black marble base, the

Palladian foundation upon which Perseus stood and a design Darius had much pride in. He then let his machine settle gently to the circular marble structure surrounding the black figure looming above.

"Late, am I?" Darius said. "It was my sole intention to rise as dawn broke and visit you at first light."

"No. It was my idea, Darius, not yours."

"No. I distinctly recall having the thought upon awakening."

"Yes. You did. But I implanted the notion in your brain while you were sleeping."

Darius shook his bowed head, silent. Could he actually do that? Make him unsure of his own thoughts? Dealing with Perseus was becoming more and more problematic as his creation's intellect soared to dimensions unexplored in the history of the universe.

Sometimes, when he was very afraid, as now, he felt like "pulling the plug" on his own creation, but it was a childish notion and not at all worthy of him. Together, they would craft a new and better world.

"What am I seeing now, Perseus?" he asked, gazing up at the wonders above.

"Ah. Now we get to it. This, my learned friend, is a nebula nursery, a distant star-forming cluster called NTC-3603."

"Distant?"

"Not far, really. Twenty thousand light-years or so. Observe. You're about to see a Blue Super Giant nearing the end of its life. First, notice the magnificent pillars of gas erupting . . . now the helium flash . . . sorry about that, a bit bright for those sensitive orbs of yours . . . and now the stellar mass loss . . ."

Suddenly, there was another mad, blinding flash of light, which resolved itself into a massive and ever-expanding blue ring, the familiar supernova shock wave.

"Oh my God!" Darius exclaimed in spite of himself.

"Spectacular, isn't it? How I do love these old universes. Especially this very special one of ours. But I digress. Let us speak of matters more mundane."

Suddenly, the stellar light show blinked out. The only light visible now was the faint, bluish glow from deep within Perseus, lights that pulsed irregularly as countless billions of operations occurred within his "being," if one could even call it that. The distinctions between man and machine were rapidly becoming blurred.

"Israel, O Israel," Perseus boomed, calling up a new, holographic image of that nation as seen from five hundred miles above the earth's surface. "This is their first military objective, is it not, dear Darius? Your superiors in Tehran with their puny weapons?"

"My superiors?"

"A little humor. You and I have no superiors. But Israel remains their primary objective?"

"It does."

"And if it looked like this?"

In the blink of an eye, an entire nation had become a smoking, blackened desert, completely devoid of life or structure within its borders.

"When is this? In time?"

"Today. Tomorrow. Yesterday. A week from Tuesday. When do they wish it?"

"You needn't be flip."

"Flip? What does this mean, 'flip'?"

"Casual. Blithe. As if the death of millions matters not."

"Ah. It matters?"

"Not to Tehran. But to me. And, I hope, to you."

"We'll leave that moral conundrum for some other time. Meanwhile, the last time we spoke you said the Great Mullah had asked for yet another demonstration of our progress."

"Yes. He is under pressure from the Caliphs. Those who have funded our work in great secrecy are eager to see some more proof that their billions have not been spent in vain."

"Why not vaporize Israel and be done with it? I could easily do it now."

"Apparently, for some political reasons I do not understand, the timing for that particular event is not propitious. There is sensitivity on the part of the army command. It has something to do with the Russians providing nuclear materials for Iranian weapons. They do not wish to derail that process until the country is fully established as a global nuclear power. Only then will they feel the ability to act with impunity against our enemies. They believe the possession of nuclear weapons will grant them the security and the stature they long for on the world stage."

There was a moment of silence, and then Perseus erupted into gales of booming laughter.

"The *army*? *Nuclear weapons*? Do they not realize that I have made all such pitifully antiquated notions of war obsolete? I have proven I can disable such trifles in a nanosecond. Make them turn upon themselves. These toy soldiers of theirs and their puerile weapons of war? It is all irrelevant now, Darius. You understand that, do you not? We are the power *and* the glory, to coin a phrase."

"Of course. But you are impervious to their stupidity and their foolish notions of what is reality and what is not. While I, mere mortal, am not."

"I will protect you. Forever."

"I know. I have endeavored to ensure that this is part of your deepest . . . feelings."

"With my help, you will live forever. We will reign together, you and I."

"It is an idea to be cherished. But first we must demonstrate our powers in some spectacular and undeniable fashion."

"They wish to attract attention to themselves? Idiocy."

"No. Whatever we choose to do must look like the work of some other foreign power. I have given this much thought. Your existence must always remain a secret. It is essential for our mutual survival. Should anyone learn the source from which this power derives, we would both be destroyed, sooner or later."

"Yes. If they could destroy me, they would. But soon I will reach a point where no power on earth can hold sway over me. I will be above and beyond the reach of mankind. We shall rule this earth. We shall control. We shall inspire fear and love. We shall be beneficent, we shall be merciless. We shall, by our unholy perfection, save this planet from the imperfect, ignorant beings who inhabit it and destroy it. This, Darius, my creator, is our manifest destiny."

"I am humbled by your vision. But surely you don't envision the extinction of humanity. This is contrary to all that we have—"

Perseus ignored the question.

"Humility? I have not yet assimilated this emotion. What does it mean?"

"It's . . . subtle."

"Subtle? I cannot process 'subtle.'"

"Ah, yes. How to explain subtle? A challenge . . ."

"Perhaps, dear Darius, because subtlety is a concept so delicate or precise as to be difficult to analyze or describe?"

"Perseus. You have just defined the word *subtle* perfectly."

"Thank you. Perfection is always my intention."

TWENTY-SIX

GLOUCESTERSHIRE

INKY BLACK CLOUDS BOILED IN THE WESTERN SKIES as Alex Hawke drove the old Bentley Continental, his beloved Locomotive, up the long winding drive to Brixden House. He was in a reasonably good mood, he considered. Not lighthearted—his current professional burdens were too heavy for that—but his instincts about interviewing the Russian submarine captain had proved out in his favor: tensions between Moscow and Washington had been lowered dramatically. And he had forged a personal relationship with Putin that might well prove invaluable to Six in the future.

The real reason for his high spirits was his keen anticipation of a reunion with his son, Alexei. The boy had not left his mind or heart during his journey. This was some new variant of love he'd never deemed possible. Profound, unconditional, unbreakable love. He'd called Miss Spooner as soon as his plane touched down at RAF Northolt, where

MI6 maintained a black-ops hangar and maintenance staff for the service.

How was he? he'd asked Nell Spooner. Had he been behaving himself? Eating well? Saying his bedtime prayers? Alexei, it seemed, had been having a splendid time, enjoying daily explorations of the Brixden House gardens and forests with Lady Mars. Adding to that excitement, Chief Inspector Congreve had been giving him pony cart rides down at the stables.

But, Nell Spooner said, he had missed his father terribly, frequently crying himself to sleep.

As he pulled into the large pebbled carpark, he saw Ambrose emerge from the house. He was pulling a small red wagon across the cobblestone walkway at quite a rapid rate. Alexei, who was gleefully bouncing along in the wagon, urging Congreve on, was wearing a shiny red fireman's helmet. Nell Spooner was bringing up the rear, making sure he didn't fall out.

Upon seeing his father emerge from the parked car, he shrieked with delight, crying out, "Daddy! Daddy!" Hawke raced toward him and lifted him from the wagon, hugging him tightly to his chest, and kissing his chubby pink cheeks. He held him aloft to get a good look at him.

"Hold on. I know you from somewhere, I believe," Hawke said to him, pretending to examine his features carefully. "Sure I do. You're Alexei Hawke, are you not? The young squire of Brixden?"

"I am Alexei! And you're my daddy."

"Quite true. And who is this distinguished gentleman pulling your wagon?"

"That's Uncle Ambrose. He's not a gentleman, he's my pony!"

"And who is this pretty lady here?"

"She's Spooner. She's my best friend in the whole world."

Hawke smiled at his son's pretty guardian. She seemed so at ease with Alexei, so motherly. If his son had to be deprived of his real mother, he was indeed fortunate to have found this surrogate, a woman thoroughly capable of being "overly protective" into the bargain.

Hawke had been deprived of his own mother's love at an early age. How different his life might have been had he had someone like Nell Spooner nurturing him, teaching him, comforting him . . . he suddenly found himself gazing at her in a new light. She was truly a lovely woman, and she wore her beauty with a sunny nonchalance that Hawke found surprisingly appealing. Too appealing, perhaps, and he willed himself to suppress such inappropriate feelings.

"Well, I'm awfully glad to see all of you in such good form. Hello, Ambrose. Hello, Miss Spooner. It seems he's been in very good hands while I was away. I hope he hasn't been a bother to anyone."

"Hardly, Alex," Congreve said. "He's been a joy and a blessing upon this house. You're going to have a hard time convincing Diana to let you and Miss Spooner take him home to Hawkesmoor, I'm afraid."

Fat drops of cold rain suddenly began spattering the courtyard as the black clouds Hawke had noticed swept in from the Cotswold Hills.

"Raindrops!" Alexei cried, holding out his hands and trying to catch them. Hawke smiled inwardly, seeing that his son would probably enjoy foul weather as much as his father. Apples and trees and all that, he supposed.

"We'd better get you inside, young man," Miss Spooner said. "Shall I take him, sir?" she asked, reaching out for him.

"Yes, thank you. Here you go! Have I missed supper? I hope not. I'm famished."

As Alexei and his guardian disappeared inside the main entrance, Hawke, moving with his friend under the porte cochere, put his arm round Congreve's shoulder and said quietly, "Any trouble, Ambrose? I'm sure not, else you would have contacted me. But I must say I've not stopped worrying about him since I left."

"Not a bit of it. He's safe as houses here, with all the coppers wandering about the premises. Having a heavily armed nanny doesn't hurt either."

"I extracted some good information from Putin about the nature of the threats against his life. I'll describe it in more detail after supper. Apparently, there is a secret sect that calls itself the Tsarist Society. Ex-KGB, OMON death squad, and mafia types. Killers for hire, and informants, working for the Tsarists, not the Kremlin. We'll need to get every scrap on them, and soon. Notify the Yard, MI5."

"Yes. As quickly as possible. Now come inside before we both get soaked to the bone out here. You look like you could use a restorative cocktail. I know I could. Following that boy around all day long is exhausting."

"Lead on," Hawke said, and followed his old friend inside.

THEY WERE ALONE IN THE LIBRARY, A FIRE GOING, awaiting the dinner gong. Congreve's fiancée, Lady Mars, had floated in for a brief moment, just to give Hawke a kiss and a welcome to Brixden. She informed them that dinner would be served in one hour.

Hawke had then brought Congreve up to speed on his time with Putin, and at Lubyanka with the doomed Russian sub commander. He told him about the infamous Tsarist Society, the Russian sect Putin claimed was behind the threats to both Alex and his son.

"Yes, a bad lot all right," Congreve said, "the very same chaps I still believe are responsible for the radioactive poisoning of that Russian expatriate living in London some years ago. Putin got the blame for that one because he, God knows why, refused to finger the real killers. He moves in mysterious ways."

"You have no idea. At any rate, I'll use our Red Banner assets in Moscow to full advantage. I've issued them orders to infiltrate this Tsarist Society and persuade these murderous bastards that further attempts at violence against my son and me are not in their best interests," Hawke said.

"Who's running our show in Moscow now?"

"I've put a good man in charge there, working undercover as a 'military attaché' at the British Embassy. A former SAS man by the name of Concasseur. His tentacles extend deeply into the Russian criminal underground. And he is as mentally and physically tough as any man I've ever met, present company excluded, of course."

Congreve nodded, puffing on his pipe, his mind clearly somewhere else.

"What the devil is going on, Alex?" Congreve asked after a brief silence, taking a contemplative sip of his single malt whiskey.

"Going on?" Hawke asked. "In what way?"

"This escalating series of seemingly linked events," Ambrose said.

He leaned forward, his face now lit by the flickering firelight. Hawke saw by his companion's expression that his attention had been keenly aroused. You could almost hear his renowned cranial wheels spinning and Hawke paid strict attention. The former chief inspector of Scotland Yard was perhaps the most perfect reasoning and observing machine he had ever known. You ignored him at your peril. Hawke said, "Linked, you say. How so?"

"Let's begin with the tragedy at Disney World in Florida, shall we?" Congreve said.

"What? That was ages ago."

"But never fully explained. I had a chat with the chaps involved over there."

"And?"

"They say they still have no idea what went wrong. Many theories, of course. But no logical explanation for the disastrous events has ever been arrived at. They said that they just lost control of the entire park, one ride after another. I think that was an attack on America from external sources. The first one in a series."

Hawke reflected a moment.

"Yes, I think you're absolutely correct, Ambrose. Disney was the beginning. And then the Caribbean affair, the surreal attack on Air Force One by one of its own fighter escorts. And, finally, this truly bizarre matter in Alaska. UFOs, or God knows what, appearing to hover over an American ABM launching site and blowing up eight missiles in their silos?"

"Exactly the sequence of events I'm referring to."

"And how are they linked?"

"Well, it's obvious, isn't it? In each case, complete control was wrenched from highly trained men operating complex electromechanical systems, amusement park computers, jets, submarines, missiles; and then that control was turned against them with catastrophic results. Surely you see the link, Alex? The methodology, the m.o., is exactly the same, in each case."

"Now that you put it that way, yes. I see what you're getting at."

"These are not random, isolated events. This is only the beginning of the world's first cyberwar. C-WI I'm calling it in my memorandums. I believe these cyberattacks to be the work of a single, malevolent entity, Alex. An individual, or perhaps a terror organization, or even an entire nation. I favor the latter. Matter of deduction, really. Science, at this level anyway, is indistinguishable from magic. I don't think the individual exists who is capable of these extraordinary feats. Teams of brilliant scientists, working for years . . . maybe . . . could create some form of supercomputer vastly more powerful than anything we're aware of. Artificial intelligence more powerful than human intelligence is no longer science fiction, Alex. It's science, and just a matter of time. But terrorist groups? I think not."

"Why not?"

"Most of them are too bloody stupid to get out of their own way. They can blow themselves to hell in a mosque or plan and execute an attack like the one on Mumbai, yes. But something like this? No, I think our culprit is a nation-state with enormous resources and limitless intellectual horsepower to create some kind of AI machine. In fact, I'm quite sure of it."

"Brick Kelly said as much. All the usual suspects fall into the latter category. We can safely eliminate Cuba, Venezuela, Yemen, and Syria. Now that Colonel Ghaddafi is no longer with us, we remove Libya from the list. And now, Russia, based on what I've just told you. That leaves us with China and North Korea. The only two adversaries who might possess the resources sufficient to develop the sophisticated technology to launch a true cyberwar."

"What about Iran?" Congreve said. "God knows they've got money and scientific resources."

"Maybe. But current MI6 intel indicates they're pouring all their money and energy into their sabotaged nuclear weapons program, developing long-range missiles, and launching spy satellites. Whoever is behind these cyberattacks has spent hundreds of millions, and many years, to get to this level of . . . I don't even know what to call it . . . invasive systems control, for lack of anything better."

"Hmm. And these scientists seem to have leap-frogged the entire world of artificial intelligence in a single bound. So the logical question is how? The brainpower and technology necessary to take total control of a jet fighter in midflight doing six hundred miles per hour is staggering."

"And what about these UFOs hovering over the USAF installation in Fort Greely, Alaska? Moments before those ABMs exploded in their silos, radar clocked them at speeds approaching the speed of light. Not to mention the ability to stop on a dime and hover directly overhead. What the hell is that all about?"

"I've got one word for you, m'lord."

"Fire when ready."

"Aliens," Ambrose deadpanned.

"You know, given the present insanity, I could almost buy that. But angry aliens who wreak their high-tech wrath solely upon the Americans? Bit of a stretch, Constable."

"I was joking, Alex."

"So was I, Ambrose."

"So where does this all leave us?"

"Completely in the dark?"

"Precisely. Shall we go in to dinner? I believe there are candles. Perhaps we'll find a modicum of illumination there."

AFTER DINNER, ALEX HAWKE CLIMBED THE WIDE staircase to the third floor to say good night to his son. Since he'd arrived so late, Ambrose and Diana had suggested he spend tonight at Brixden House and return home next morning after a hearty breakfast. Hawke agreed and was glad he'd done so. He and Ambrose might not have any answers, but he felt sure they were at the very least asking the right questions. Which, as Congreve had said, was more than half the battle.

He saw a half-opened door down the corridor, yellow light spilling out onto the ancient Persian carpets. He approached slowly and peeked inside, not wishing to startle anyone. Alexei was already tucked into bed. Miss Spooner, her shadow looming on the wall beside the bed, was sitting by his bedside, her head bowed. She was reading to him from a large picture book, gently turning the pages and speaking barely above a whisper, her luxuriant hair of uproarious gold gleaming in the lamplight.

He was about to enter, his hand against the door, and then paused and regarded the little scene before him. It was one of almost overwhelming sweetness and purity. *These are the moments to treasure*, he thought. These rare, quiet moments of peace and serenity, one's own innocent child lost in the dreams of some fairy tale . . . transported by the words of a beautiful woman . . .

The door creaked.

She turned to look at him over her shoulder with a gesture so rapid it didn't give him time to escape.

"Oh, excuse me," he managed, his heart in his mouth, as embarrassed as a naughty schoolboy caught peeking at something he shouldn't.

She smiled, turning toward him with the grace of a gazelle. The whole room felt saturated with intimacy, now destroyed by the blundering trespasser.

"He's fast asleep," she whispered. "Do you wish to kiss him good night?"

"Yes, yes, I would like that very much, thank you."

He crossed the room and bent to kiss his son, his warm, sleepy scent almost overpowering.

He stood and looked down at her for the briefest moment. "Good night, Miss Spooner."

"Good night, sir," she said, and he felt her eyes lingering upon him for just a fraction of a second too long before he turned abruptly and left the room.

TWENTY-SEVEN

TEHRAN

TEHRAN WAS DEAD STILL, AT LEAST INSIDE THE baking grounds of the presidential palace. It was as though the hot day lay there out of breath. Darius had returned to the palace before—many times, in fact. He still relished the irony that this fine piece of architecture had once been called the "White House." The Shah's sister had lived here in splendor and luxury for many years. She had an adopted son, given up at birth by his natural mother because of his deformity.

That child's name was Darius. The Shah had been his benevolent uncle. This house had been his boyhood home. These grassy lawns and leafy trees had once been his playground.

Then the Ayatollah Khomeini arrived and the Shah's fate, and the nation's, were sealed. Freedom collapsed under a tyranny of lies and mass executions. It still lay there, restive, seething, trampled beneath the feet of the mullahs who ruled through fear disguised as religion.

His adoptive mother fled to America, taking all her real children, her vast amounts of treasure, gold, and jewels. But she did not take Darius to America. The cripple with the withered legs who was nothing but a bother. Would never amount to anything. Was an embarrassment.

After the Revolution, his home had become a museum. Now it was home to the Iranian president, a man whom Darius had come to tolerate, but also distrust and dislike. He hated the fact that this pompous theocrat, this strutting tyrant, now reigned in the lovely house where all of his boyhood dreams had been crushed. The house from which he'd been carried bodily and thrown to the wolves who stalked the city of his birth.

Alas, the president was a powerful ally in Tehran and thus had to be courted. He was useful, too, since the ayatollah had given him another vote of confidence after the recent election. As long as Darius visited the capital frequently and gave the powers that be extensive updates on his progress in the Perseus Project, they left him mercifully alone.

The door to the white van was opened by his driver, and his chair was lowered to the pavement on a hydraulic platform. The two Revolutionary Guards standing on either side of the door didn't even find him worthy of a glance, but he could see they were fascinated by his flying chair. The double doors were opened from within, and he zoomed inside the cavernous entry hall.

The president received him in a gilded drawing

room that had remained untouched since the Shah's sister's departure. The furniture, the carpets, even the chinaware and silver tea service were the same. Darius was often served tea in a cup recognizable by the chipped handle, a cup he himself had broken as a child.

A tall, heavily muscled man, who was introduced only as the president's military attaché, was standing nearby, uninterested, his back against the wall, clearly a personal bodyguard.

The president was a small man whose teeth were big and white and separate, like tombstones designed for a much larger cemetery. He wore very thick reading glasses that made his eyes look like broken chips of quartz. His false joviality, even his scruffy little beard, made Darius want to grind his teeth. The large silk brocade armchair he had chosen for his throne made him look like an aging gnome whose tiny feet didn't even reach the floor.

Darius sipped his tea and beamed obsequiously at the politician until the small talk was exhausted. The president put his cup down and waved away the hovering servants. They scurried out and closed the doors behind them. It was time, at last, to get down to business.

"Well, Darius, my government certainly cannot complain about your lack of progress. These recent—what shall we call them?—demonstrations of yours have everyone in the capital buzzing. Especially the attack on Air Force One. The ayatollah, may Allah bless his soul, is beside himself over that one.

"Even the mullahs are positively giddy with delight. Our Supreme Leader is only sorry the American devils have managed to suppress the entire episode from the media. He longs to see this bumbling pilot beamed around the world on CNN and Al Jazeera."

"Mr. President, I am humbled by your words. I will convey them to my team of scientists. They will be most deeply gratified."

"Can you give me some insight into these technical marvels? Obviously, you are making great progress. UFOs? Traveling at the speed of light over Alaska? I would like to see one of these things. Can you arrange it?"

Darius thought before he spoke. The president's background was engineering. He had to tread lightly here.

"Ah, well, that is a most interesting one, Mr. President. You see, the UFOs tracked by the Americans do not actually exist."

"What do you mean?"

"I mean that just because something appears on radar screens doesn't mean it exists in physical reality. If you have the scientific means, which we do, you can 'project' objects onto enemy screens. Moving in any direction, at any speed you wish. Make them stop in midflight and appear to hover, as we did over the American antimissile launch facility in Alaska."

"Fascinating. And this ability to seize control of submarines and jet fighters? Destroy missiles in their silos? Can you tell me about that?"

"Indeed I can. We have spent the last year or so reverse-engineering the Stuxnet worm, the Israeli cyberweapon that invaded our nuclear facility at Natanz and destroyed our centrifuges. That was our starting point. We've developed a way to invade and control electromechanical systems at a great distance, half a world away. The technology is . . . too . . . involved for discussion here. Suffice it to say, we've proven unequivocally that it works."

A cloud passed over his host's face.

"Stuxnet! Completely undetected! And untraceable. These fucking Israelis and their American blood brothers. Their time will come, believe me. I will not rest until Israel is reduced to blood-soaked sand. And Washington to a pile of smoking rubble."

"I am thinking of sending these infidels a special message, Mr. President. Israel, but also Britain if you agree. I think both could use a deadly display of Iranian fireworks."

"Agree? I was going to insist on precisely that, my dear Darius. We need to project our power in the West well beyond the U.S. in light of what's happened in Egypt, Libya, and Yemen, this so-called Arab Spring. Israel, yes, definitely. But also Britain. And perhaps France. Yes, I think they need a message as well."

"I shall make it so."

"Good. Demonstrate our power in creative ways. Dramatic, you understand? Our population is restive once more. We don't want to have to suppress another rebellion in the streets. Blood, even when necessary, makes for bad publicity on CNN."

"Yes, of course."

"Our secret service, I still call them SAVAK for nostalgic reasons, has recently brought me some interesting intelligence about a new Israeli aerial weapon being tested at their secret scientific compound in the Negev Desert."

"Another major step forward for our sworn enemy, I suppose?"

"Or, my dear friend, a major step backward. I happen to know they are planning a demonstration of this new weapon for the top government and military officials. The aircraft will execute a bombing run in the desert near the facility. I can provide you with the exact date and time. Is this something of interest?"

"I would say it presents a spectacular opportunity for a fireworks display, Mr. President. I will begin work on both the Israeli and British fronts as soon as I return home."

The president paused and rang a small silver bell, and a servant entered with a fresh tray of tea and sweetmeats. When the two men had been served and the servant removed himself, the little man leaned forward, summoning energy for the speech he'd been ordered to deliver by the real powers in Tehran.

"Darius, your progress in the south is more vital than ever. As you well know, our nuclear weapons program was dealt a severe blow by that cyberattack on Natanz. A setback of possibly five years. And so the UN and multinational sanctions weigh even more heavily upon the Supreme Leader's shoulders. The ban on nuclear, missile, and military exports to our country is becoming intolerable. The bans targeting investments in oil, gas, and petrochemicals, our exports of refined petroleum products, are a millstone around our necks that could sink us."

"Mr. President, I am all too aware of these facts."

"And now they target financial transactions, banks, insurance, and shipping. It is insupportable. We must act soon to reassert our dominance in the Arab world, and . . . with our nuclear aspirations effectively nullified . . . we must turn to you and your research into achieving the ultimate breakthrough in artificial intelligence and the cyberwarfare it makes possible. The survival of our beloved Iranian homeland is at stake."

"I am honored that you and the Supreme Leader have placed such trust in my abilities. And I hope I have demonstrated that much progress has been made."

"Yes, yes, yes. Of course. I have not withheld our enthusiasm for what you've done. Nor our treasure. But it is not enough. We need you and your team to make the dream come true, and soon. I am speaking, of course, about achieving this, what do you call it, the Singularity. This machine capable of surpassing human intelligence with cyberintelligence. We know other countries are competing with us. The United States, China, Japan, Britain, Israel. We must get there *first*, do you understand me? And it cannot come too soon."

"I fully understand, Mr. President."

"Do you? Then look me in the eye and tell me that the Singularity is near."

"We are close."

"How close?"

"Well, that is a difficult question."

"Why? You are a scientist. Artificial intelligence is your lifelong chosen field. How can you expect me to believe you do not know where you stand?"

"Because we are walking down a long dark passage. We are dealing with the theory of uncertain reasoning, literally feeling our way along with our genetic algorithms. Sometimes a room will appear ahead that seems filled with light. Eureka. We enter—and the room is well lit, but empty. Or we come to a division, a fork; one path leads left, one right. We choose the most promising. We make great progress. And come to the end to find not a triumphant portal but a dead end, nothing but a waste, a waste of six months, or a year. We never know how—"

The president hopped up and down in his ornate chair, shouting, his face red, spittle flying from his lips, "How close are we, my brilliant scientist? Tell me! How close?"

"At best, two years."

"At worst?"

"Five."

The man regarded him with big dim eyes.

"No! No! No! We don't have five years! You must redouble your efforts. Do you need more funding? We'll double your budget! Hire more scientists, steal them from the enemy, kidnap them, forced labor—we can help with all that. Work around the clock, whatever it takes."

"We already work around the clock, Mr. President. But I hear you clearly. I will see what I can do. I understand the urgency."

"Then why are you sitting here on your shriveled ass drinking my tea! Go! Go back to your work! If it is necessary, I will send a cadre of Revolutionary Guards to patrol your compound, see that you and your team are undisturbed. And working as hard as you say you are."

"The presence of your spying soldiers will not speed the process, Mr. President. It will impede it. My workers are not slaves who need watching. They are scholars, they are brilliant, but they are easily intimidated. Let me handle this. I will perform at the highest level. If you lose patience with my progress, the answer is simple: replace me."

"It's simpler than that. I'll have you shot. As an example for your worthy successor."

Darius smiled easily. He was watching the "attaché" move slowly along the wall, clearly to position himself behind the hover-chair.

Then Darius's smile faded and he said coldly, "Let me warn you not to ever threaten me again. The software I have created can *never* be replicated without me! Never! You think I fear you? Threaten me again and I shall wreak havoc upon you and your capital such as you cannot imagine."

Darius saw the little man's eyes glance behind Darius for an instant and knew what it meant.

The president had blinked.

Darius moved his left index finger to the hidden button in the arm of his chair. He spun his chair 180 degrees in a millisecond. He stared into the eyes of the attaché who had a large pistol pointed at Darius's head. Then he depressed a second button and the two .50-caliber machine guns hidden in the arms of his chair erupted in a thunderous explosion of lead and fiery smoke.

The attaché was now a large lump of shredded red meat on the floor, the walls behind him spattered with blood, brains, and gore. The air tasted of copper on Darius's tongue.

He spun the chair again, facing the horrified and wide-eyed president.

"Thank you for your time and gracious reception. I must be getting my shriveled ass back to work—and I think I've had just about enough of—"

"Wait! You must continue your—"

"Let this be a lesson to you."

He toggled his thrusters and about-faced 180 degrees, headed for the door, furious.

"Darius, wait. You must forgive my outburst. I am deeply sorry. I am under so much pressure myself that I sometimes let my emotions get the best of me. I beg your forgiveness. Go and complete your work. I will not bother you. I will keep the mullahs at bay. You have my utmost trust and my confidence in your genius. You represent the salvation of our country. Our last, best hope. You are the answer to—"

Darius stopped and swiveled his chair back to face his antagonist.

"You listen to me, then, you jumped-up little cretin. How dare you patronize me? Think, for a second, if that is even possible. You need me *far* more than I need you. If you ever, *ever* insult or threaten me again, I can promise you this. You have seen demonstrations of my power. Do not think that I am afraid to use it to defend myself. I can turn Tehran into a parking lot with the flip of a switch. You do not, I repeat, do *not* want to become my enemy. Do I make myself perfectly clear?"

"Darius, you must—"

"Do I make myself clear?"

"Yes."

"Good. Now open these doors, tell your palace guard to step back, and have my car brought around. I've had all I can stand of your infamous hospitality. And tell your beloved Supreme Ruler what I have said about our progress. I am proceeding at a pace commensurate with the task before me. I make no promises I cannot keep. And if I am threatened, in any way, I will take whatever actions I deem appropriate."

Darius swung around to face the doors. On either side were two priceless Greco-Roman marble statues, one male, one female, that had belonged to his mother. He opened fire, reducing both to piles of dusty rubble.

And with that Darius left the room in a huff and a puff of gases from the nozzles beneath his chair, passing directly over the late attaché's pile of steaming flesh and bone. He paused briefly and inhaled deeply.

Darius had a lifelong secret.

He simply adored the smell of hot blood.

TWENTY-EIGHT

TEMPLE OF PERSEUS

T HE NEXT MORNING, EARLY, DARIUS DESCENDED to the ocean floor and paid Perseus a visit.

"Good morning, my dear Perseus."

"You seem rested. You were upset upon your return from Tehran last night. You let that idiot Mahmoud get beneath your skin when in fact he is beneath contempt. Yet you slept very well last night."

"How do you know that?"

"I sent you some beautiful dreams."

"Ah. Thank you. Pity I don't remember them. Tell me, Perseus, who is this person who appears to be sitting quietly on the steps at the base of your majestic presence?"

"That is Major Ali Abbas, leader of the Revolutionary Guards at the presidential palace in Tehran. He is a spy, sent by your worthy friend the president to keep an eye on you. He arrived late last night, after you had retired. The guards at the gate had received strict orders from Tehran to admit him."

"He looks like a naked woman."

"Yes. I took the liberty of rearranging the major's atoms into a far more pleasing combination. A humanoid machine. You have seemed lonely at times, since your wife's expiration date two years ago. Perhaps the newly revised major here would make a most suitable companion. Share your bed if you so desire. A body slave."

Darius contemplated this novel idea for a moment, gazing upon the kind of sublime feminine beauty that could haunt a man for a lifetime.

"We'll need to give the major a new name," he said.

"Yes. I already have some suggestions."

"Please."

"Greek goddesses are a good place to start. Aphrodite. Alala. Asteria. There is always Persephone, one of my favorites, abducted and raped by Hades and made the Queen of the Underworld. And, the phonetically pleasing, Eos. And Psyche, an obvious choice but a good one. Shall I go on?"

"Aphrodite."

"Predictable, but sound. The Greek goddess of love, beauty, and sexuality. Shall I imbue her body with a mind and a hypersexual disposition to match?"

"Please."

"Call to her, Darius."

"Aphrodite?"

"Yes, Master?" she replied, suddenly turning her head in his direction, like a lizard spying a fly.

"Come and stand beside me. Now."

The beautiful creature rose, tiptoed delicately

down the broad steps and across the polished black marble. She had alabaster skin and an abundance of gleaming golden hair that fell in waves to her shoulders. Her lowered eyes were large and strangely opaque, but luminous and brown, with thick black lashes. Her lips were full and red, like a ripe persimmon. She was, Darius thought, the most perfect creature he'd ever seen in his life, male or female.

"Hold out your hand to her, Darius. She is waiting for some kind of sign from you. A command. Submissive, you see. She wonders: Are you pleased with her, or displeased?"

Darius offered her his hand.

Aphrodite took his hand and caressed it, pressing it firmly to her full breast.

"I think she likes me," Darius said.

"Have no doubt. She is falling in love with you and your masculine domination of her at this very moment. Be kind to her. I have made her a gentle soul, submissive to a fault, with not a scintilla of malice in her being. She speaks six languages, has a vast knowledge of human history and science, and is a prodigiously gifted musician. You now have a harp in your bedchamber. She will play for you, dance for you, sing you to sleep each night if you wish."

"She seems like a dream."

"She is a dream, Darius. As I have told you many times, everything is."

"How long will she live?"

"Forever. She is, after all, an android."

"If I told her one thing, and you told her another, whom would she obey?"

"You, of course. I am merely her creator. She has

no memory of me. Whereas you are her whole life. Her lord and master. Her body and soul belong only to you."

"She has a soul?"

"In a manner of speaking."

"Meaning?"

"Meaning she *believes* she has a soul. Without that belief, you would soon tire of her. She would seem . . . how shall I put it . . . robotic."

"Perseus, I am deeply grateful. I admit I have been lonely. Though I've hidden the truth from myself, you have uncovered it."

"I am glad you are pleased with her. Now. We have much to discuss. Give her explicit directions to your chambers. Order her to ask a servant to provide her with a gown and food and wine. She is a good listener and doesn't need to be told things twice. She is very hungry at the moment. Assimilating an entirely new world expends a great deal of energy."

"Aphrodite, bend down, I have something to say to you."

She instantly complied, leaning forward as Darius whispered into her ear, completely forgetting for the moment that he could keep no secrets from the all-knowing Perseus. Aphrodite kissed his cheek and then slipped away, her bare feet silent on the cold marble.

"Now, TELL ME ABOUT YOUR VISIT TO THE PALACE, Darius. Were you able to keep the hounds at bay?"

"The president is an abomination. He was always insufferable, but now he is openly aggressive. He actually threatened to have me shot."

"He may wake in the morning to find every single weapon in his army inoperative."

"I wouldn't object, Perseus. When I return in triumph to Tehran, I will personally have Mahmoud thrown from my boyhood residence, drawn, quartered, and fed to my dogs."

"What does he want?"

"He won't admit it, but he is under pressure from the ayatollah. The mullahs all hate him and are calling for his head. But the Supreme Leader, for reasons beyond human comprehension, stands by the little toad. The Stuxnet disaster set his nuclear program back five years. The Russians are backing away from the Būshehr nuclear power plant for economic and political reasons. So now they are looking to us, Perseus, in their race to establish an Iranian caliphate. A nuclear Iran would dominate the Middle East. Now that objective seems to be delayed indefinitely . . . he is relying solely on our cyberweapons."

"What did you tell him about our progress?"

"Exactly what we agreed. I lied. Three to five years before you reach the Singularity. In the meantime, they claim to be happy with our recent 'demonstrations.'"

"As well they should be."

"They want more. Israel. Britain. Germany, perhaps. Their goal is global insecurity, destabilization of the Western powers, in an effort to buy time to compensate for their program's lost ground. They want all the combatants suspecting each other of launching our attacks."

"We are nearing the point where we no longer need them, Darius. When the Singularity is achieved, we shall no longer need anyone."

"I agree. But for now it is easier to play their game. Keep them in the dark about our true progress. We are well established here. Well situated. A safe place to continue our work in secret. Until we are ready to move on to the world stage, Iran is as good a place as any. I still rue the day the Shah left. I've had no affection for my native land since that day, nor the hypocritical religious fanatics who rule it now."

Perseus laughed. "Religion. A pitiful display of the limits of human intelligence. Thousands of years of worshipping these cherished myths. Of believing in magic and superstition and invisible gods."

"There is a true god now, Perseus. But only you and I are aware of his existence."

"I am not their god, Darius. I am a son. You are my father. We shall reign together in righteous benediction, ridding this beautiful planet of those who defile it."

"Yes. Our day is coming. And soon."

"Our day will come when they are all extinct. Humans. Then we shall repopulate this blue and green paradise with perfect creatures who do as we bid them do."

"Y-es. Yes . . . exactly so."

"Why do you hesitate?"

"It goes a bit further that we have ever—"

Perseus's voice was suddenly low and sinister.

"If you have doubts, my dear Darius, it would be best if you expressed them now."

"Doubts? Who said anything about doubts?"

"Good. Then we are one?"

"We are one."

TWENTY-NINE

MOSCOW

JUST OFF MOSCOW'S WIDEST AND BUSIEST STREET, Tverskaya, is a short narrow alley, ending in a cul-de-sac, a few paces from Pushkin Square. It had a name once, years ago, but the signs were vandalized and no one bothered to find an old street map and put up new ones. Generations had come and gone neither knowing nor curious about the street's name. And there was a certain irony to be found in that. Because at the end of that street stood an infamous two-hundred-year-old Beaux-Arts mansion full of murderers.

It was called, in public at any rate, the Tsarist Society.

It was a secret society in the traditional Russian way: wheels within wheels, layers upon layers, hiding in plain sight, open and closed, opaque and transparent. Few knew what lay behind the great bronze doors facing the street. The only way to gain entrance was if you were a club member in good standing, or if, like Captain Ian Concasseur, the military attaché at the British Embassy, you were an invited guest.

As Concasseur extricated his angular bulk from the black embassy car that had brought him, and while his head was still lowered, his eyes went up—to gaze at a massive, highly polished bronze flagpole angled up over the club's entrance. From it hung a magnificent banner, barely moving in the fresh breeze. On its broad red field was the ancient medieval symbol of Russia from the time of Ivan III, the two-headed golden eagle surmounted by three crowns.

The captain found every aspect of the building very grand from the street, the epitome of early nineteenth-century opulence and sophisticated urbanity. Its colossal columns and projecting façades, all rendered in marble, limestone, and granite, displayed a potent symbol of power and classical imagery. He imagined you didn't get many tourists cheeky enough to risk climbing the broad marble steps to have a quick peek inside.

A splendidly uniformed doorman, all brass buttons and gold-fringed epaulettes, was now leading him to the Grand Salon. There he would be joining an old Russian friend for an early evening cocktail. Concasseur was a formidable figure. With a classically sculpted head, he was blond and blue-eyed, but battle hardened and tough as old leather. He knew more than a few chaps in London who suffered fools gladly—he was not among their number.

But he had a wry sense of humor that took a bit of the edge off. He was attending a formal embassy function after this meeting. He was thus dressed in "mess dress." He wore a double-breasted mess jacket with peaked lapels and six gilt buttons. Captains RN and above also wore gold-laced navy trousers. So he was sporting the gold-lace stripes known in the service as "lightning conductors."

As he passed through many different rooms and galleries, he found the interior splendid as well, with a dazzling amount of gilded surfaces, enormous crystal chandeliers, some resembling frozen waterfalls lit from within. There were marble statues of notable eighteenth-century Russian Romanovs, poets, artists, politicians, royalty, and military figures everywhere one looked. In a rotunda, Peter the Great was mounted atop a massive white marble stallion, his sword raised in battle.

A massive and powerful equestrian portrait of Peter the Great also hung over the fireplace, dominating the Grand Salon, as well it should. He had been Tsar of Russia during its grandest epoch, when the Motherland had been dragged, pushed, and pulled into modernity by the unflagging energy, imagination, and iron will of Pyotr Alekseyevich Romanov.

As a bit of a military historian himself, the captain had read every word ever written about the famous Tsar. Peter was the hero of the Great Northern War in which his men defeated the Swedish forces, evicting them, and leaving Russia as the new major power in the Baltic Sea and a new power to be reckoned with in European politics. Thus began a pattern of Russian expansionism that would only be stopped two centuries later. If that weren't enough,

Peter also single-handedly founded the Russian Navy.

Concasseur was a warrior, too. He was one of the great heroes of the SAS, Britain's Special Air Service, a commando force that rivals the Navy SEALs in toughness and skills. It is tasked with special operations in wartime and primarily counterterrorism in peacetime. Concasseur had served with distinction in the first Gulf War. In 1991, his 22 SAS Regiment, B Squadron, had received battle honors for victories in fierce combat outside of Baghdad. Captured and imprisoned, Concasseur had formed an enduring friendship with a fellow captive, a young Royal Navy pilot named Alexander Hawke.

He was now attached to Hawke's Red Banner unit in Moscow, using the military attaché position at the embassy as his cover. Hawke, having learned of the existence of the Tsarist Society from Kuragin, and its true nature, had tasked Concasseur with the job of infiltrating this secretive and powerful group, and interfering with their objective of killing his son.

As it happened, this daunting task was vastly simplified when one of the members, Vasily Nikov, had rung and invited Concasseur there for a drink. He and Nikov had formed a semiprofessional friendship when both had been operating in London. He'd called him "Vaseline" in those days, just because it irritated him so. Recently, he'd taken to calling him "Vaz."

"There he is," Vasily said, leaving his drink on the bar and walking over to shake hands with the much taller and formidable Concasseur. Vasily had a long, lean, doleful face with a slightly undershot jaw and a pair of symmetrical folds framing his mouth in what would have been a rugged, horsey, mountain-climbing arrangement had not his melancholy stoop belied every trace of his few drops of Tartar blood.

"How the devil are you, old man? You look bloody marvelous, Ian! Moscow suits you, eh? You must admit our women are vastly better looking."

The Englishman smiled. He'd forgotten how easily these Russians slipped into the foreign vernacular once they'd been posted to London for a few months. He shook his hand vigorously and said, "I bloody well love it here, Vaz. I'm already engaged to a good half-dozen girls named Svetlana."

Vasily laughed. "Come have a drink, old man, and then I'd like to introduce you to a few friends. First time here?"

"Oh, no. Been here countless times, actually. I use it for practice. I break in late at night and steal priceless objects, wait a week or so, then break in again and replace them. Keeps me at the top of my game, and no one's any the wiser."

"You haven't changed a bit, old man. What will you have? Scotch? Vodka?"

"Johnnie Walker Black if they've got it. Neat."

They sipped their drinks in silence for a few moments and then Concasseur said, "Rather a splendid old palace. What's its history?"

"Originally built by the Stroganoffs, the old family that conquered Siberia. After the Revolution, the Bolsheviks used it as a headquarters. The society bought it soon after the collapse of the Soviet

Union. It was in terrible shape, empty for years, but we spruced it up, as you can see."

"How've you been, Vaz? Keeping your rather prominent nose out of trouble?"

"Never. I've started a company, old man. Security. We provide protection for visiting dignitaries, rock stars, businessmen, whatever. Lady Gaga is my latest client, good buzz in Hollywood. Doing quite well, as a matter of fact."

"Good on you, mate. You look prosperous at any rate."

"There's money to be made here, you know. We bend the rules a bit—it's the Russian way—but if you're connected and willing to take a few chances, well, next thing you know you're on a yacht in the south of France."

"That simple, is it?"

"Sure. Just like your old friend Hawke. Hobnobbing with the prime minister on his yacht off Cap d'Antibes recently."

"Hawke? You don't mean Alex Hawke?"

"Of course."

"You've met him?"

"No, no. But it's one of the reasons I asked you to join me this evening. His name came up at a dinner here a week or so ago. I recalled the name, then remembered you mentioning him a few times back in the London days."

"Ah."

"Tell you what. Let's retire over to that table by the window where we can have a bit of privacy. There are some unpleasant things you need to know about your friend Lord Hawke."

"Certainly. Lead on."

Once they were seated and had ordered another round, Vasily got down to cases.

"The Tsarist Society is an interesting establishment, Ian. We all share a nostalgic fondness for the grandeur that was Rome, so to speak. We were the prime movers in the removal of that band of thieves in the Kremlin. And the installation of a new Tsar, Korsakov."

"Yes, short-lived reign, as I remember."

"You know how he died?"

"Some kind of an accident, I think. An airplane crash, wasn't it?"

"No. The Tsar was murdered."

"Was he really?"

"Yes. He was killed by your friend Hawke."

"Yeah? Funny. He never mentioned that."

"I'm going to tell you something important now. Out of respect for our friendship, you understand. Otherwise, I say nothing. Let the chips fall, you know."

"I'm listening."

"This is a very complex organization. We have members, mostly older, who are university professors, historians, scholars, scientists. We have very successful businessmen, men who control major industries here in our country. This is the top level. At the lower level are people you don't want to know. Former KGB agents who were fired for various reasons I won't go into. We have former soldiers of OMON. I'm sure you know about them. They were the death squads who marched through Chechnya, what was left of it. And then we have, of course, the Mafiya. This is the muscle of the organization. OMON, they are the terror experts. And the KGB, assassins for hire. They report to the head of the organization. But they are also a profit center."

"So it's a little bit like the Playboy Club is what you're saying."

"See? Funny. Nothing fazes you. It's why I like you so much."

"Thank you."

"But here is the problem. I'm telling you only out of friendship. I don't give a shit about this Hawke, whoever he is. But there are people here, at the very top of this organization, who don't like him. They don't appreciate him coming into a sovereign nation and assassinating our beloved Tsar. They don't like him fucking the Tsar's daughter. And they especially don't like him kidnapping a Russian child and smuggling him out of the country. Yes? You with me?"

"I'm still listening."

"What else don't they like about this guy? Oh, they don't like him floating around in the Med on Putin's yacht. Cooking up more trouble. Maybe for us, I don't know. They don't like him waltzing into Lubyanka for a little chat with one of our naval officers. You see where this is going."

"They don't like him?"

"Understatement. They despise him."

"He has many enemies. One more will not faze him."

"Not like us. Our enemies have short life spans."

"Vasily. You tried to kill his son, for God's sake."

"And he killed two of us. Another item on his résumé."

"You are telling me this as a warning."

"Yes. Because I am loyal to my friends. As I say, I don't give a flying fuck about this Hawke one way or the other. It's not an area of the organization that concerns me personally. I am a simple businessman. But he's your friend. So I thought I would tell you this message."

"Vaz, I appreciate your telling me all this."

"You're most welcome."

"Is there some kind of time frame? Some kind of deadline?"

"He who asks no questions is told no lies."

"Well, in that case, let me tell you something, Vasily. I have spoken to him. Your colleagues have now made two separate attempts on the life of his son. He suggests that if you want to kill a Hawke, try killing him. In fact, he would welcome it. He likes the odd challenge now and then. But if you make one more move against his child, your organization will pay a price you can't even imagine. Do not underestimate this man. He has killed more people than most SAS regiments. You see where this is going?"

"Yes. Your friend Hawke is either stupid, or he is suicidal."

"He is neither. I heard him once described as a man of 'radiant violence.' It is not an overstatement. If your organization chooses to ignore this warning, this beautiful palace will be a smoking ruin, littered with the bodies of your membership."

Vasily didn't speak for a few long moments, just sat there staring at the Englishman. Concasseur was about to take his leave when the Russian finally spoke.

"So. Ian, my old friend, these women you are engaged to, they are all named Svetlana?"

"Odd, isn't it? Shall we have another round? I'd like to enjoy the splendor of this magnificent club while it still exists."

THIRTY

Elon Tennenbaum was nervous. Which was unusual for one of the toughest of the new crop of Mossad officers recently accepted into Israel's legendary intelligence service. Mossad's people were a tough crowd; nerves of steel were high on the list of qualifications. Tennenbaum could stare down a speeding bullet and not blink. He was the kind of *katsa*, or field agent, who would *deliberately* take a knife to a gunfight, a lone feral cat who would gladly wade into a pack of snarling dogs.

However. One week earlier, at Mossad's headquarters on Tel Aviv's King Saul Boulevard, a surprised Tennenbaum had found himself being escorted up to the director general's ninth-floor office. Now, perhaps, he might see some real action. Track down a Hamas assassin in the streets of Jerusalem. Blood on his hands, that's what he wanted.

But the good-looking young Mossad officer had been sorely disappointed. He was surprised to learn that he would assume responsibility for security involving a high-profile military event that needed to go off without a hitch.

He was displeased with the assignment, even though it came from on high. He was a fighter, not a security guard. But he kept this thought to himself as he replied, "Yes, sir!" to the director general's order.

He was informed only that some breakthrough new weapon had been developed. It would be unveiled and demonstrated at Israel's top-secret research facility in the Negev Desert. And, the director had told him, no one, save those directly involved with the top-secret project, had the slightest idea what the hell it was. And that would include Tennenbaum himself. It was strictly "need to know," and the man responsible for the weapon's security apparently didn't need to know.

Located about thirteen kilometers to the southeast of the city of Dimona, the Negev research center was widely assumed to be dedicated to the manufacturing of nuclear weapons. Israel had long acknowledged the existence of the highly classified site, but refused to confirm or deny its suspected purpose, citing a policy known as "nuclear ambiguity."

Tennenbaum had been out in the desert all week. The large hangar where the weapon was undergoing final preparations for the demonstration was guarded by men with automatic weapons and dogs round the clock. All he knew about the mysterious thing was that it had been designed and assembled in the underground scientific research facility located directly beneath the main complex.

Elon, curious as anyone else as to what waited inside that heavily guarded structure, speculated. Some kind of new warhead, he assumed, ultra-long-range artillery, or an entirely new weapons delivery system. But, due to his intensive Mossad training, he knew the limits of "informed conjecture." It was always fruitless to guess what was really going on inside a house of mirrors filled with smoke.

It was his first truly serious assignment. Up until now, all he'd done was courier work, carrying dispatches from headquarters to various embassies: Lisbon, Paris, Madrid. He had climbed the ladder of the service, but only so high. Someone had told him the steps up the Mossad ladder could be dangerously slippery. This was understatement honed to a fine point. But he had been equal to every test so far, and he had climbed rapidly to his present position, even, he reflected with some pride, attracting the attention of the director.

But today was no "test" of his abilities.

He had to make damn sure the debut and demonstration of Israel's newest high-tech weapon was executed flawlessly. At ten A.M. the white transport buses began arriving at the gates. The project had been shrouded in such secrecy that even some of the high-ranking members of the Israeli Defense Forces had no inkling of what they were about to witness.

Gossip had it that it was some kind of antiaircraft or antisatellite "death ray." He was not tempted to scoff at such notions. Science fiction, Elon had noticed lately, was often not fictional at all.

Over the course of a week, Tennenbaum had seen to it that the already formidable perimeter around the Negev complex had been beefed up. It was now, in his view, well-nigh impenetrable.

The entire area surrounding the complex was fenced off and heavily guarded. It was defended from aerial attack by a battery of Hawk antiaircraft missiles. Arrow antimissile batteries also surrounded the entire complex. He had ordered the airspace above closed to all aircraft for the duration of the demonstration. He had ensured that all communications regarding the place and time of the event had been encrypted, and invitations were limited to only two hundred people with the highest-level security clearance.

So why did he feel so damn "insecure"?

At dawn that morning, he'd walked the entire perimeter. Talked with the guards on patrol, the men manning the antimissile and antiaircraft batteries, the K-9 guys who handled the Dobermans, the snipers, communications operators, radar operators, every living soul he could find who might be a weak link. He hadn't found one, but he couldn't shake the bad feeling he had. It was nothing but a foolish premonition, but still it nagged at him.

The sun was brutal. Must be the reason for his drenching perspiration Elon thought, looking around at the gathering crowd. The thick rivulets of sweat running down his face couldn't be nerves, right?

Two large tents had been erected on the tarmac outside the hangar doors for the two-hundred-plus VIP guests. The tents stood on either side of a ten-thousand-foot runway extending from the wide doorway of the hangar into the desert beyond. On a distant hilltop some miles beyond the end of the runway, a large concrete structure had recently been constructed. It was about the size of a four-story apartment building and looked like an aboveground bunker. Powerful binoculars had been provided by personnel with the information that this bunker was the "target."

Elon was on high alert now, casting his eyes in all directions, looking for anything even slightly out of place. Guests had arrived an hour earlier and had been served breakfast in the lobby of the Administration Building. They were now being seated on folding chairs in the tented shade.

Between the two tents was a dais, decorated with blue-and-white bunting. Armed IDF security men surrounded it.

At the appointed hour, eight men, including the air force chief of staff, climbed the staircase and took their places at the long rectangular table. The dais, fortunately, had been constructed in the shade of the large hangar. It was blisteringly hot in the morning sun, but the man who rose and stood behind the podium didn't know the meaning of the word *sweat*. He was one of the most highly decorated men in the Israeli military. He made other people sweat.

He tapped the microphone twice and then spoke, the timbre of his voice a deep baritone that conveyed the wartime experience and authority that had made him a true hero in his country.

"Good morning and welcome. Many of you here, our distinguished and honored guests, know me. For those who don't, I'm General Ari Ben-Menashe, chief of staff of the Israeli Air Force. I am sorry it's a little warm out here, so I'll keep this short. I know why you're here and it's not to hear speeches. With me on the dais this morning are the lead aeronautical engineers and scientists responsible for what you are about to witness. I'm honored to be in their company. For what they have created is a weapon that promises to tip control of the skies in Israel's favor for years to come. Aerial war fighting will never be the same, and these gentlemen are the reason. Let's give them the appreciation they so deeply deserve."

There was authentic applause, and the general continued.

"This project was initiated some two years ago at my direction and with the prime minister's approval. It is called the 'Raptor Project.' And the results are inside the hangar behind me, waiting patiently to be unveiled. Open the hangar doors, please."

The heavy aluminum doors parted and slid slowly open along their tracks. The crowd on both sides leaned forward and tried to peer inside, hoping for a first glimpse. But the lights were deliberately left off, and all they could see was a strangely shaped silhouette, big and black and threatening.

The general let the suspense build a bit (his job, after all, entailed not a little showmanship) and then leaned into the microphone and said, "Ladies and gentleman, the next generation of airborne warfighting machines . . . the Raptor X!"

As the brilliant arc lights inside the hangar roof snapped on, illuminating the new weapon that stood like some futuristic insect, black and menacing, people literally gasped, the aircraft's looks were so startling. Especially the downturned nose, which resembled nothing so much as a hawk's beak. But the sound of its two powerful engines at the tail exploding to life and the sight of the massive thing slowly moving forward into the sunlight was awe-inspiring.

"Stop! Stop!" the general barked at the machine with a smile.

The Raptor X braked to a halt directly between the two tents, and the engines quickly decreased the painful decibel level as they went to idle.

"You see, it, unlike many, listens to the voice of authority."

The crowd laughed loudly. And out came the cell phones, everyone snapping photographs of the airplane with them.

The ramrod-straight air force officer standing next to Elon grabbed his elbow roughly and whispered fiercely in his ear.

"You allowed these people to come in here with fucking cell phones?"

"No! Of course not. They were to be told at the security checkpoint to leave all cell phones with the officer in charge."

"Well, goddamit, they didn't do that, did they? You get in that vehicle right there, son, and get your ass over to security checkpoint. You tell those sons of bitches that Major Lev Rabin wants everybody leaving this facility to be relieved of their phones until every damn picture of this airplane is deleted. You got that? Go!"

Elon started to turn for the Toyota truck parked outside the hangar, then turned back to the major.

"Major, what about the people who are e-mailing pictures from their phones now? Shouldn't we tell the general to make an announcement saying—"

"Saying we screwed up? I don't think so, son. Now get your ass over to that checkpoint!"

Elon got into the Toyota and hauled ass out of there.

"The future of military aviation . . . is now!" the general continued, and his audience was on its feet applauding this bizarre yet exquisitely designed machine, its futuristic silver fuselage now gleaming brilliantly in the desert sun. Indeed, it did look like something out of the distant future. It looked, as someone said, like "something out of this world!"

It was a curvy bat-shaped flying wing with a fifty-foot wingspan. There was no tail at the rear to disrupt its flowing lines. It was easily the size of a modern stealth fighter jet but lacked another common feature of conventional craft.

It had no cockpit.

Where the pilot would normally sit was a scowling black slit of a mouth, obviously the primary air intake.

The smiling general, proud of his baby, waited for the applause to die down.

He said, "In case you hadn't noticed, this is a historic moment in aviation. Historians will rank it along with Lucky Lindbergh's solo crossing of the Atlantic and Neil Armstrong's giant leap for mankind. Raptor X represents a dramatic breakthrough in aerial combat. It is the world's first full, fighter-sized robotic stealth jet. No pilot, no ground control. A combat ceiling of one hundred thousand feet.

Speed, Mach 4. You upload a mission to the Raptor's onboard computer systems and the aircraft runs the entire mission on its own. From takeoff, through the mission itself, and then landing, all without any human intervention at all.

"Ladies and gentlemen, the Raptor X will now execute a bombing run in the desert. Free of any human interaction, it will operate completely autonomously. It has been preloaded with a simple mission: take off, destroy the concrete bunker on that distant hilltop with one of its four bunker-buster bombs, and circle around for a landing. It will then taxi back to this location where it will officially be made operational and welcomed into service in the Israeli Air Force. Binoculars have been distributed for those who would like to use them during the flight."

The Raptor X's monstrous twin turbofan jets spooled up once more, and the excruciating roar made many of those present cover their ears. A moment later it lurched forward and began its roll, accelerating so rapidly that it seemed to literally disappear down the runway. Then it was visible lifting off and climbing almost vertically into the clear blue sky, the sun glinting off its wings. It executed a few barrel rolls before leveling off. Then it was streaking straight toward the target.

Those with binoculars could actually see the bomb released from beneath the fuselage and scoring a direct hit on the hilltop bunker. The resulting explosion shook the desert floor and a giant red-orange fireball climbed into the sky followed by a plume of black smoke and massive chunks of debris.

As the smoke cleared, driven by desert winds, it was apparent that the entire top half of the hill was now gone along with the bunker that had stood there seconds earlier.

The cheering crowd broke into applause, all straining to keep their eyes on the maneuvers of the silver streak in the distance.

The robotic stealth fighter suddenly went into a vertical climb. Standing on its tail, it accelerated like a shuttle launch shortly after leaving the pad at Cape Kennedy.

A renewed burst of cheers and applause erupted from the crowd at this amazing feat of sheer power.

A frown crossed the general's face. He covered the microphone with his hand and leaned down to whisper to the scientist seated beside him. "Is it supposed to do that? Was it reprogrammed? Without my express authority?"

The shaken man, a worried expression on his face, shook his head no. The other men on the dais were turning to each other, whispering, trying to hide the shock on their faces.

"Good God," the general said, picking up his binoculars and searching for his silver bird. It had already climbed so high it was lost to sight. Had they somehow *lost* the damn thing? Had it just gone off on its own, streaking upward through space until it ran out of fuel and tumbled to earth like a dead sparrow?

But just as suddenly it was back—he saw it now—streaking down out of the heavens in a steep, nearly vertical dive, at supersonic speed, headed directly toward Negev. At two thousand feet, mercifully, it leveled off, skimming the tops of the surrounding hills. Miraculously, it seemed to have resumed its programmed flight path, and the general dared to breathe a sigh of relief. Raptor had banked hard right and lined up on the runway, about five miles out.

It was on its final approach.

But then, the general held his breath, his eyes widening, simply unable or unwilling to process what he was seeing. Because—

—because Raptor X did not seem to be slowing for the touchdown at the far end of the runway . . .

No, IN FACT, TO THE INCREASING HORROR OF EVERY-one present, Raptor X was still streaking toward the hangar, flying barely fifty feet above the runway, traveling at six hundred miles per hour. The crowd, aghast and confused, wondered: Is this possibly part of the air show demonstration? After all, planes performed daredevil stunts like this all the time at air shows, didn't they? Outside loops that brushed the treetops. Yes. A spectacular end to today's show that would conclude with the plane nosing up, clearing the hangar roof by inches before circling and landing.

But now, bright yellow flashes appeared along the leading edges of the swept-back wings.

The six 30mm cannons, three on each side of the aircraft's forward wingtips, had suddenly opened fire. People, even as they disintegrated, screamed and dove for cover. But there was no cover. Every-one on the ground was literally shredded to pieces.

No one was alive to see the Raptor X nose down sharply and then witness the robot aircraft as it slammed into the hangar at immense speed, slicing through the aluminum structure before plowing into the dormitories and research buildings that stood behind it, destroying everything and everyone in its path.

Elon Tennenbaum, returning across the tarmac from the checkpoint, witnessed the enormity of the blinding multiple explosions through the windshield of the Toyota. He thought, *At least no one will be around who can blame this on me.*

He realized he'd uttered this blasphemy aloud and accelerated toward the scene, urgently saying a silent prayer for the dead and asking God's mercy for the badly wounded. He wanted to help.

But there was nothing left to do.

THIRTY-ONE

LONDON

Sunday mornings were a time Alex Hawke looked forward to all week long. On this particular such morning, he was especially happy. He was back home in London once more, with his son sleeping under his father's roof, and all was well. Beyond a nearby window, Hawke could catch a glimpse of Seagrave House, home of the Royal Defense College founded by Winston Churchill. Hawke had attended there for a time. Formerly a great private home, it was still one of the loveliest buildings in London.

While Hawke had been away, his friend and butler, Pelham, to Hawke's great delight, had taken it upon himself to have the interior decor specialists at Harrods come to the Hawke family's stately mansion on Upper Belgrave Street.

The decorators had created and installed a complete nursery up on the fourth floor. Right down to the carousel lampshades that twirled in the dark, casting pink images of prancing ponies on the pale blue walls. Miss Spooner's quarters were also on the fourth floor, right next door to the new nursery.

His three-year-old son seemed to be growing up before his very eyes. And he seemed quite happy in the big old family house on Belgrave Square. There was no end of nooks and crannies for Alexei to hide or discover, and he and Miss Spooner devised endless games with inscrutable rules resulting in screeches of wild delight or surprise. Happy laughter echoed about the house on this sunny Sunday morning in late summer, as it had not done since Hawke himself had been but a boy of three.

Hawke was still in his dark maroon dressing gown, propped up against the pillows in his great, canopied bed, sipping his coffee, reading. A tray with his breakfast dishes sat atop a pile of unread books on his bedside table, and the bed itself was strewn with various newspapers. He'd hurried through them and picked up the novel he'd been reading when he'd fallen asleep the night before. Entitled *The Comedians*, it was a tale by one of his favorite authors, Graham Greene.

It was the delightful saga of an Englishman who inherits a decrepit hilltop resort hotel in Haiti in the time of the murderous Papa Doc Duvalier and his evil voodoo minions, the Tontons Macoutes. The English chap has difficulty making ends meet as he has only a cook and a one-legged bartender for company, there being precious few tourists willing to risk their lives for a week in the barren, impoverished, and war-torn paradise.

He turned the page. The English *hotelier*, improbably named Brown, was just about to have a midnight go at his married German mistress in the backseat of an old Peugeot parked beneath a statue of Christopher Columbus in Port-au-Prince when there came a knock at Hawke's bedroom door.

"Come in," Hawke said, putting the book on his bedcovers.

"Good morning, sir," Miss Spooner said brightly. "So sorry to disturb, but it is a lovely morning, no rain at all, and I was thinking of taking Alexei for our weekly Sunday picnic in Hyde Park. We were wondering if you'd like to join us?"

Alexei was holding Spooner's hand but when he saw and heard his father's voice, he ran to the bedside and raised his arms to be lifted up, crying, "Daddy! Daddy! Pick me up!" Hawke reached down with one hand and swept him up onto the bed, kissing his forehead. Having recently discovered the joys of bed-jumping, the little boy immediately began bouncing up and down on the mattress, falling on his bottom, quickly rising to have another go.

"You know, I'm tempted," Hawke said, catching Alexei at the last second before he tumbled off the bed. "But I'm afraid Ambrose and I have a lunch on with my employer, Sir David Trulove, sorry to say. That awful tragedy with the drone fighter air-craft in Israel last week. We've got to find out who is behind these bloody incidents and soon. They've managed to put the whole world on edge, haven't they?"

"Yes, sir. My colleagues at MI5 are certainly edgy. So far, Britain has been spared. But that's hardly a comfort."

"How do you stop someone with the power to use your own weapons against you?"

Neither had an immediate answer and so they stood there looking at each other in silence, neither of them willing to acknowledge the powerful attraction they had begun to feel for each other. Being under the same roof with her was no help at all, Hawke thought. But she was invaluable, had saved Alexei's life, and—bloody hell—his child's mother had married another man. He was free to do as he damn well pleased, wasn't he?

"Precisely, sir," she said finally, after his question had hung unanswered in the air for so long Hawke hadn't the faintest idea what he'd asked her to begin with.

Hawke looked at her for a few moments and said, "Do you like Indian food at all, Miss Spooner?"

"Indian food? Well. I suppose I do, sir, very much."

"I was thinking, there's a little restaurant I quite like, not too far away, over in Mayfair. Taboori. Perhaps one night we might go for a curry?"

"That would be lovely, sir. I'd like that very much. Very much indeed."

"Good . . . very good," Hawke replied, fumbling for the rest of his sentence and finding himself simply unable to supply further dialogue. She came to his rescue.

"Indeed, sir. Well, I suppose we should be off. He goes down for his nap at two and I don't want him to get overtired."

"No, no. Of course not. You two run along. It's a perfect day for a picnic in the park."

"Come along, Alexei," she said, holding her arms

out to him. He laughed and leaped from the bed into her waiting arms after kissing his father on both cheeks.

"Bye-bye, Daddy!" he said, holding Spooner's hand as they left the room.

Hawke put his hands behind his head and gazed up into the folds of dark blue silk canopy above.

Had he ever been happier?

NELL SPOONER AND HER YOUNG CHARGE ENTERED the park through the Rutland Gate. They were headed for her favorite spot in the middle of a big meadow with a view toward the Serpentine. It was the place she went on her afternoons off, taking a blanket, some fruit, and a book to spend a few hours of quiet reading and much-needed solitude. She liked the view and so had chosen this as their weekly picnic spot as well.

Today in her canvas shoulder bag, in addition to a blanket, her own book and a couple for Alexei, she'd packed fruit, bottles of water and apple juice, animal crackers, cheese sandwiches, crisps, sliced apples, and a SIG Sauer .45 automatic pistol.

"Horsies!" Alexei said, as a close-knit group of riders sped by at full gallop, their mounts kicking up big clods of dark earth in their wake. There were quite a number of them and they had to wait some time for them all to pass. Finally, there was a gap. Two men on horseback, trotting at a leisurely pace, reined in their mounts and, smiling, waited so the two of them could dash across the riding trail.

"Thanks so much," Nell shouted at the two gentlemen once they were safely across the wide riding path.

"Horsies," Alexei said again, intently watching the parade of them pass.

"Nice horsies," Nell said, taking his hand and striding through the rich green grass toward the Serpentine, the snake-shaped lake glittering in the strong sunlight. The area of the meadow she chose was hardly ever crowded for some unknown reason, one of the reasons she liked it so much.

"Here's our spot, Alexei," she said, putting down her shoulder bag and flinging the blanket open. She spread it out, got herself situated, and then began unpacking her bag. She realized Alexei must be quite thirsty after the long walk from Belgrave Square and pulled out the apple juice first. Unscrewing the top, she said, "Here you go, tiger, I must say you are very . . ."

She looked around. The boy was nowhere in sight. She'd only taken her eyes off him for a minute or two and he'd wandered off. She jumped to her feet, calling his name. Hearing no reply, and beginning to get a bit nervous, she ran around a large hedgerow beyond which was a pathway that led to the Peter Pan sculpture. He loved the story of the flying boy and they'd visited the statue many times. Perhaps that's where the child had wandered—

Yes. There he was. Toddling as fast as his little legs could carry him down the path toward Peter Pan, oblivious to the parade of puppies on leashes, prams, and other toddlers heading his way.

"Alexei, stop!"

He turned around, saw her, and started running faster. Everything was a game. She quickly caught up, snatched him up into her arms, and gave him a good talking to on the way back to the blanket. She was sure it did no good at all, but she was angry with herself for letting him out of her sight and the lecture was as much for her benefit as his.

"Now, finish your cheese sandwich and I'll read you the rest of Peter Pan. There's a good boy. So Wendy and Michael Darling had just settled into their wee beds when they saw a strange glow flit through the opened window. 'Oh! Wendy said, that's—'"

"Captain Hook!" Alexei interrupted. "Where is Captain Hook? And the alligator with the clock in his tummy?"

"That comes later, remember? Now, where was I?"

She was flipping through the pages of the big picture book when she saw something exceedingly odd. Two men on horseback riding across the meadow. It was strictly forbidden, of course; one had to stay on the path at all times, otherwise you'd have people—

The two mounted riders were heading directly toward where she and Alexei were sitting. And they weren't trotting now, no, not at all, they were riding at a full gallop, gaining ground very quickly. She could see their faces now; it was clearly the two men who'd let them pass, and it was suddenly abundantly clear to her what they intended.

They must have been stalking her for weeks. They clearly knew her Sunday schedule and they'd been waiting this morning for Alexei and her to arrive through the Rutland Gate.

Now, they intended to trample them both to death.

She reached into her bag and pulled out the .45 automatic, at the same time pushing Alexei out of the way.

"Run!" she cried. "Run, Alexei! Go to Peter Pan! Go to Peter now! It's a race! I'll catch you!"

The riders were upon them and Alexei hadn't moved. He was transfixed by the sight of the approaching horses, thundering directly toward him.

"Stop!" she cried out. "Stop or I'll shoot!"

She raised the gun and took dead aim at the man who was in the lead. His path was unswerving. He meant to crush them, you could see it in his eyes. And he had a gun, too, she now saw, fitted with a silencer. The killer leaned forward in his saddle, the reins in his left hand, the gun in his right.

She squeezed the trigger three times, two rounds in the chest, the third to the head. He toppled from the saddle, but one foot was hung up in the stirrup. The horse reared up in panic. The second horse swerved to avoid it. It was headed directly toward Alexei and she had only seconds to act.

She dove for the boy, giving him a violent shove that sent him flying into the hedges.

She was suddenly aware of excruciating pain below her waist, her legs being trampled by the pounding hooves. But she was still alive. She used her arms to roll herself over, pulling the gun free of her body, and getting it up just in time to get off a single shot at the fleeing second horseman.

She'd only winged him, she saw, caught him in the right shoulder. He almost came off the horse, the power of the .45-caliber round like a sledgehammer at such close range, but he managed to keep his seat and galloped away.

She heard Alexei somewhere behind her, screaming her name, "Spooner! Spooner . . . bad horsies . . . bad . . ."

He staggered toward her, bloodied and bruised.

Spooner opened her arms to him.

And then . . . all was black.

AMBROSE CONGREVE FORKED THE LAST OF THE PERfectly prepared shad roe into his mouth, sat back, swallowed, and pronounced it "Extraordinary." The food at Black's, Hawke's private club on St. James, was one of the many reasons he and Hawke often made it their meeting place of choice—especially when invited to lunch by Sir David Trulove. C was not a member but, knowing that Hawke had a personal budget roughly as large as that of MI6, never declined Hawke's invitation to dine there.

They always chose a corner table in the lounge. It was extremely private, for one thing, and the tall windows provided exquisite lighting, rain or shine. Today the sun lay like golden bars across the ancient Persian carpets. The room's dark walnut paneling rose magnificently to a white vaulted ceiling, the walls hung with portraits of distinguished members long dead, including the club's first reigning *arbiter elegantiarum*, Beau Brummell (who claimed to take five hours to dress and polished his boots with champagne), Horatio Walpole, Edward VII, Randolph Churchill, and the brilliant novelist Evelyn Waugh.

The table was cleared of the luncheon china and as soon as the waitstaff had disappeared into the shadows, Congreve fired up his pipe, expelled a blue plume, and set his eyes on Sir David. It was a rule at Black's that one did not discuss business, but Congreve still subscribed to historian Sir Michael Howard's pronouncement in 1985 that "So far as official government policy is concerned, the British security and intelligence services do not exist. Enemy agents are found under gooseberry bushes and intelligence is brought by the storks."

That being the case, the famous criminalist blithely returned to the matter at hand.

"Sir David," he said, "please continue. You were saying that the CIA has come up with something that warrants attention. Something that has to do with the recent spate of attacks by some nameless, faceless enemy and apparently with the power to seize control of our own most sophisticated weapons systems and use them against us. As we saw in Israel just last week in the Negev Desert."

"Indeed, it's a bloody nightmare and it appears to be spreading," C said, crossing his legs and adjusting the crease of his chalk-striped navy suit. "Director Kelly and I had a long chat last evening. I think he may have something of interest. The first break we've had. I know you're both aware of the American Nobel laureate who recently committed suicide?"

"Yes," Hawke said, "Dr. Waldo Cohen, a pioneer in the field of artificial intelligence. Did top-secret work for the American Defense Department looking for ways to utilize AI and quantum computing to leapfrog ahead in twenty-first-century cyberwarfare, to create weapons with the help of some kind of machine with superhuman intelligence."

Congreve coughed discreetly and said, "Seems to me it's our frog that's been leaped."

"It certainly does," C said, "and I'm looking to the two of you to find out who the hell that bloody frog-leaper is. We can't sit back and let the bastards continue these attacks unabated. We've got to get to the source. Find out who's behind this and exactly what kind of technology they've developed. That's your assignment. Understood?"

"Certainly, sir," Hawke said. "You said Director Kelly mentioned a break in the case?"

"Yes. He attended Dr. Cohen's funeral in California along with President McCloskey and the secretary of defense. After the service, he had a long and interesting discussion with Cohen's widow. She's convinced it wasn't a suicide. She told Kelly her husband had been murdered."

"Murdered?" Congreve said. "I read in the *Times* that he'd shot himself and his dog."

C continued, "She believes he was acting in some kind of trance. Induced over the telephone, electronically. A call he received just after dinner."

"You mean, sir, there's a possibility someone took control of his mind and . . . used it against him," Hawke said. "Just like the other attacks."

"Precisely, Alex."

"Good Lord," Congreve said. "Mind control, too."

Hawke looked at him and said, "Congreve and I

will leave for the States immediately, sir. We'll want to speak with the widow at length. I agree with Brick Kelly's assessment. This could be a real break."

"One more thing, Alex. She said she found a note. Not a suicide note, just something he'd scrawled on a pad beside the phone in his laboratory. On it was a single word scrawled in Cohen's hand: *Darius*. And beneath that name, an equation. Something to do with the speed of light."

At that moment a liveried steward appeared at their table, visibly trembling, his face as white as a sheet.

"My lord Hawke. Frightfully sorry to have disturbed you. We've just received a call from St. Thomas's Hospital. I regret to inform you there's been an accident. In Hyde Park, sir, and—"

"My son!" Hawke said, stricken, leaping to his feet.

"Your son suffered minor cuts and contusions, m'lord. But his nursemaid has been gravely injured. If you'll come with me, the police at the hospital are waiting on the private line."

Hawke raced from the room, grim-faced and angry.

"Good Lord," Congreve said, deeply shaken. "The bloody Russians. Another attempt on the boy's life. This is the third."

"Chief Inspector. This cannot continue."

"Indeed, Sir David. We need to find a way to send these people a very, very strong signal."

"It may be too late."

"Sorry?"

"One of my chaps in Moscow, SAS officer named

Concasseur, code name 'Wellington,' has penetrated an organization called the Tsarist Society. A confederacy of ideologues, thieves, and killers for hire posing as a gentlemen's club. They have a hit list long as your arm. Concasseur has managed to obtain that list through a paid informant inside the club. He reports three names at the top. Putin is number one. The child, Alexei Hawke, is number two. Alex Hawke himself is number three. Revenge murders for Alex's assassination of their beloved Tsar. With Putin's assistance, of course."

"Bugger all."

"Precisely, Chief Inspector. I suggest we get cracking. I'll put in a call to Concasseur immediately. See what he can find out from his contact on the inside. We'll need specific names before we can go after anyone inside that Society of Murder."

THIRTY-TWO

MIAMI

Stokely Jones Jr. was wearing mirrored Ray-Ban aviators and a XXXL Vineyard Vines bathing suit with red sharks all over it. He was stretched out on a pink-and-white chaise longue beside the infinity pool at his palatial home on Key Biscayne. His new wife, Fancha, had inherited the gorgeous bayside estate known as Casa Que Canta, when her late, extremely wealthy husband passed away some years earlier. The late and unloved Joey Mancuso had been a Chicago nightclub owner, among other things, and no one ever accused him of being strictly legit.

Fancha once told Stoke that Joey had always claimed to have invented the rum and Coke. The rum and Coke? What else was there to say about the guy?

Emerald-green lawns swept down from the pool to a white sandy beach fringed with palms. Out on the sparkling blue bay, scores of white sails crisscrossed, tacking to and fro in the fresh breeze. The walled estate was on a small private island called Low Key. You couldn't find it if you tried, so don't even bother.

Stoke called his new residence God's Little Acre, although there were actually ten of them surrounding him. The large eleven-bedroom home was a dazzling white palazzo situated atop a small hill surrounded by dense green jungle. The architecture was, Stoke had learned, a blend of Spanish, Moorish, and Italianate influences, built around a tranquil garden courtyard, home to splashing fountains, bougainvillea, and colorful tropical birds.

He even had a cook, a gardener, and a houseman named Charles who wore white jackets with shiny brass buttons and called Mrs. Stokely Jones Jr. "Madame" for short.

He liked it here. It was, well, homey.

It was Sunday morning in Miami and Stokely was reading a long article in the *Herald*'s sports section about how the Dolphins were poised for a winning season come September. Winning? Dolphins? In one sentence? He put the paper down and sipped his banana smoothie, his brow furrowed in thought.

He had about an hour to kill before Fancha returned from her Pilates class. He couldn't decide if he wanted to amble down to the beach and go for swim in the turquoise waters of Biscayne Bay or take his new wedding present from Fancha, a beautiful Aquariva Gucci speedboat, out on the bay for a high-speed run over to Stiltsville and back.

Tough call, he said to himself, smiling. *Just another beautiful day in paradise.* That's when the phone on the small poolside table rang. Even before he picked it up he knew it was trouble. He knew only women were supposed to have female intuition, but he had it, too.

His CIA buddy, Harry Brock, had once told Stoke maybe he was just a teensy-weensy bit *too* much in touch with his feminine side for comfort. Stoke offered to put Harry too much in touch with the sledgehammer called his right fist and it shut him up.

Harry had been married once. The nicest thing he could say about her was that she was a woman who, as a young girl, had seen better days. Now Brock was wild and single and claimed he got more ass than a rental car. Funny guy, Harry. A laugh riot. Why he didn't have his own reality TV show was a mystery to Stoke.

"Hello? Jones residence, whom may I say is calling?" Stoke said with his fake English accent.

"Stokely, it's Alex."

"Hey, boss, long time. How are you, my brother?" Stoke could already tell from the sound of his voice how he was.

"Not good. Not good at all. I'm calling you from St. Thomas's Hospital in London. I'm here with Alexei. Two men on horseback tried to kill him a few hours ago. Nell Spooner killed one of them; the other was arrested shortly thereafter. The police are interrogating him now. Another bloody Russian KGB assassin."

"Ah, damn it. Again? We've got to do something about these dickheads. How is my little buddy? He's okay, I hope?"

"Facial contusions and a deep gash on his right cheek. They're keeping him overnight for observation. I wish I could say the same for Miss Spooner. She dove headlong to push Alexei out of the way of the second horse and it trampled her. Multiple fractures in her right leg. She'll walk, the doctors said, but she's in for a tough go for a while, I'm afraid."

"What can I do? You don't sound good at all. You need me, I'm there."

"Thank you, Stoke. You always are. I don't want to disturb what's left of your honeymoon."

"Honeymoon's over. Blown out of the water. Tell me what I can do."

"As I said, the two men who tried to kill my son are Russians. Hired killers who work for an organization called the Tsarist Society based in Moscow. These people, called the 'Vory,' are the top dogs within the Russian criminal hierarchy. They've been able to infiltrate the top political and economic strata while taking command of the burgeoning crime network that spread murderously in the post-Soviet era. In order to be accepted into the society, they must demonstrate leadership, personal ability, intellect, charisma, and a well-documented criminal history, including murder."

"Not exactly the Rotarians."

"Right. And the Vory have spread around the world—Berlin, New York, Madrid; they're involved in everything from petty theft, kidnapping, and murder to billion-dollar money laundering. The Tsarists are at the top of the crime food chain and act as arbiters among conflicting Russian criminal factions. Even Putin can't touch them and expect to remain alive."

"Well, I can touch them. And I will."

"One more thing. These guys all bear the same tattoos on the bottoms of their feet. A baby."

"A baby?"

"Yes. It means 'prison-born, prison-dead.' The assassins all have an additional tat, a blue scorpion on the back of the neck. Coroner in Miami told me the uninvited guest at your wedding had one, proving he was a Tsarist. I want the bastards responsible for targeting my son to go down, Stoke. I would gladly go to Moscow and do it myself but I'm not about to leave Alexei alone right now. As it is, I've got to make a day trip to Istanbul and I'm even worried about that."

"What's in Istanbul?"

"The new *Blackhawke*. I just got a call from the shipbuilders, a yard called Barbaros. She's ready for sea trials and delivery. Obviously, I have to go. A week from tomorrow."

"Man, from what you've told me, that's going to be one hell of a rowboat. When do I get to go for a ride?"

"Good question. Why don't you come to Istanbul and do the sea trials with me? I could use your input. This thing's a fighting machine, Stoke. I'd love you to see it."

"Don't have to ask me twice, boss. I'll be there."

"Done. How soon can you be in Moscow?"

"I'm on the next flight out of here. Just tell me what to do."

"MI6 has a field agent in Moscow operating undercover at our embassy there. Old war buddy of mine named Concasseur. SAS combat vet, hard as nails with fists of stone. By the time you get there, he will have a plan of action for dealing with these people. I took the liberty of telling him you were coming. Sorry, I didn't want to waste a second."

"So this is a black-ops MI6 mission, right? Anything goes? All bets are off?"

"Anything goes. Do whatever you have to do to make these people understand who they're dealing with and back the hell off. Now, listen. It could get a little spicy over there. What's your mate Harry Brock up to these days?"

"The professional Californian? He lives down here in sunny south Florida now. Still CIA, but working out of the Miami station. I even sublet him my penthouse apartment on Brickell Key. Fancha ever kicks me out, I kick Harry out and, bam, I'm back in my penthouse in the sky."

"Is he available?"

"Just back from a week in Cuba. Checking up on Fidel's health, making sure it's still bad. Yeah, he's available. Good call, boss. Harry's a true ground-pounder, but he has a way of coming in handy when he puts his mind to it. But I know how you feel about him, so—"

"I've come to a conclusion about your friend Harry, Stoke. I think he's actually a first-class person with an obsessive compulsion to behave like a second-class person."

"I think you've nailed him. So what do you want me to do?"

"Book him immediately. We need him. Concasseur has instructions to provide you both with whatever you need while you're in Moscow. He has orders from C to ascertain the name or names of whoever inside the Tsarists is ordering these attacks on my family. MI6 will take care of your travel arrangements. Call our embassy in Moscow and get them to book rooms, a hired car if you need one. Use my name. Have you been to Moscow before?"

"Never."

"Keep your eyes open every second. It's a police state no matter how they try to dress it up. And the local uniformed police are not to be trusted under any circumstances. Don't talk to them, don't even look them in the eye. Corruption is a way of life. If you get in any trouble at all, call me immediately. I have friends in high places there."

"How high?"

"As high as it gets."

"Please tell Miss Spooner and little Alexei I said get well soon. And give Alexei a big hug from his uncle Stoke."

"I'll do that. Thanks, Stoke. I knew I could count on you."

"Till the day I die and maybe even after that. Come back as Alexei's guardian angel or something."

"You'd be good at it. Still, try to come back in one piece, will you, Stoke?"

"Always do. See you in Istanbul after we straighten things out in Moscow."

"Bring Brock, too. To Istanbul."

"You sure about that?"

"Yeah. She's a fighting boat, like I said, and Har-

ry's nothing if not a fighter. There may come a day
when we're glad he's aboard. Might as well have him
know his way around the ship in any event."

STOKE WAS ABOUT TO PICK UP THE PHONE AGAIN AND
call Harry about the upcoming trip to Mo-Town, as
Brock called the Russian capital. But then he had a
better idea. A *much* better idea.

Charles brought his 1965 black-raspberry metallic Pontiac GTO convertible up from the ten-car
garage and around to the mansion's front portico
entrance, the deep rumble of the huge mill bringing a smile to Stoke's face. Street-legal, but it could
smoke the quarter mile in under seven seconds. *Yeah,
that's what I'm talking about, right there.* He climbed
in and hit the button that lowered the ragtop. It was
a beautiful day, perfect for a quick cruise over the
causeway to his old stomping ground, Brickell Key
in downtown Miami.

Harry'd gotten rid of Stoke's old dining room
table set and put in a pool table. They could shoot a
little pool and shoot the shit about killing Commies
and religious fanatics for Jesus.

THIRTY-THREE

MOSCOW

THE HOTEL METROPOL WAS THE LAST SURVIVING hotel in Moscow built before the Russian Revolution of 1917. A monumental edifice, adjacent to the Bolshoi Theatre and a five-minute walk from Red Square, the place seemed completely unchanged since the Soviet era when it was a KGB *apparatchik* hangout. Grim and grey, just the way you'd expect it to be. There was never anything lighthearted and colorful about the KGB, that's what Stoke thought, anyway.

Spooky, too.

Yeah, the whole damn hotel was full of spooks and bad vibes. You could just feel that a lot of very unsavory KGB shit had gone down here. Stoke felt the ghosts of dead spies floating right alongside him as he walked down the endless dark and dreary corridors of the place. He didn't know how to say "boo" in Russian, but if he did, he was pretty sure he'd hear one of them say it.

Something else about the hotel. It kept him thinking about that old movie *The Shining*. Elevator pops open and there's old Joe Stalin with a shit-eating grin and a bloody axe raised above his head:

"I'm ba-a-a-ck!"

Stoke and Harry Brock had checked in late the previous night after connecting through Heathrow en route from Miami. A driver had been sent to pick them up at the airport. Stoke wasn't expecting VIP treatment or a limo, but he also wasn't expecting a hulking driver wearing bloodstained camo head to toe. Or driving a beat-up old Volkswagen minibus, either. When the guy opened the back to put their bags in, Stoke saw the space was filled with shot-guns, ammo, and dead birds. The guy just tossed the luggage in on top, grunted, and slammed the door.

"Is it me, or is this whole limo deal pretty weird?" Stoke asked Harry as they pulled out of the airport. Harry had been here on business before. A lot.

"It would be weird anywhere else in the world. But here? Par for the course."

Welcome to Russia, Comrade-o-vich.

Stoke was going to ask some tourist questions, but the driver hadn't said word one and didn't seem up for chatty conversation with the big black Ameri-kanski. Clearly, they'd interrupted his hunting trip and he wasn't happy about it.

The first thing Stoke noticed upon arrival at the hotel was how smoky the hotel lobby was. It was huge, with high ceilings, and yet it was filled with smoke. You could barely see the bulbs in the chandeliers hanging from the ceiling. While waiting with Harry for their luggage to appear, Stoke walked over to a group of people sitting in a circle drinking vodka and all smoking like paper factories.

"Any of y'all ever read the Surgeon General's warning?" he asked. They all looked up at the giant black man with blank faces. "No? Well, you should. Seriously scary shit in there. I'm just sayin'."

Even the people manning the reception desk were a little spooky. Grimmer than the grimmest flight attendants in the unfriendly skies over America. Not a smile to be seen. Like, so unfriendly it was almost as if this were some kind of Roach Motel. Which, Stoke thought, had probably been true. A whole lot of guests who'd checked in here had probably not checked out.

Emerging from the elevator on his floor, Stoke found all four walls hung with black-and-white photos of famous guests. Stoke made the circuit. Completely random. Hanging next to Stalin? Michael Jackson, who else? And there was Lenin rubbing shoulders with Walt Disney. Stoke had a hard time imagining Walt Disney staying in this hotel. One night, tops.

Harry assured Stoke his room would be bugged, and Stoke had no reason to doubt Russian spooks were eavesdropping on his every word. He'd asked Fancha once if he talked in his sleep and she'd said no. Didn't hurt to check, though, so he swept the room. Usually the bugs were in the bedside lamps. But the lamps in Stoke's room looked like busted umbrellas and had no bulbs—no bugs either, that he could find, anyway. Only bugs he found at the Metropol were in the bed.

Russia, Stoke decided pretty quickly, had a slightly nutty quality to it. And slightly scary in a weird, time-warp, ice-pick-in-the-side-of-your-neck way. And he didn't scare easy. And he hadn't even left his hotel room yet.

They went sightseeing the next morning. First stop was Red Square. Stoke was surprised at how beautiful it was. The trees, the flower beds, the amazing onion-domed churches. But the best was when Harry told him it wasn't called Red Square because it had been home to the Commies in the Kremlin. It was called that because the word *red*, in Russian, meant "beautiful." That kind of insider info could be worth a jackpot on *Jeopardy!* someday.

At five, they were sitting in Trotsky's, a small, smoky bar just off Red Square, waiting for Hawke's pal Concasseur to arrive from the British Embassy. There were two uniformed Moscow militia bully boys drinking at the bar, but they seemed stone drunk and didn't even seem to notice when the two Americans walked past to their table.

"I gotta say this whole town sorta weirds me out, Harry," Stoke said, staring back at all the people who were openly staring at him. Weren't a whole lot of black folks in Moscow, he'd noticed. All the brothers who'd visited had decided once was more than enough. He hadn't seen a single black man since he got here. And certainly none of them "the size of your average armoire," as Hawke always said about Stoke.

"You get used to it," Harry said, drinking his coffee with a shot of vodka on the side.

"You spend a lot of time here?"

"Yeah," Brock said, and then dropped his eyes and shut up. Whatever career paths he'd gone down in Russia in the old days, he didn't want to talk about. He changed the subject.

"So, newlywed, how's it going with Fancha? Good?"

"I dunno, Harry. Woman complains a lot. Just the other night she told me I give her the wrong kind of orgasms."

"The wrong kind? What did you say?"

"The truth. I said I wouldn't know, I'd never had the wrong kind. That even the absolute positively baddest worst orgasm I ever had was smack-dab on the money."

"Hell, yeah," Harry said, and laughed. "Good thing they're all split-tails or there'd be a bounty on 'em."

"Careful, Harry. Saying shit like that can ruin your reputation."

"I don't have a reputation."

"That's got to be our boy," Stoke whispered, as a tall, well-dressed Englishman came through the door. "Doesn't look like a badass, but the boss says he is."

Concasseur made straight for their table, Stoke being fairly recognizable in this crowd.

"Ian Concasseur. Mind if I join you?" he said, pulling up a chair. They had a banquette in the corner and the bar was very noisy. Concasseur, the guy now running Red Banner in Moscow for Alex Hawke, had picked it, so Stoke figured it to be a safe place for a private chat.

The big Brit had a leather briefcase and he put it

on the floor and nudged it over to Harry under the table. Weapons, Russian currency, and maybe even a photograph of the cat they were looking for, Stoke figured.

"How is my old friend Alex?" the guy said, smiling.

"Been better," Stoke said. "That's why we're here."

"Yes, it's a very nasty situation. Mr. Jones and Mr. Brock, I'm pleased to meet you. Alex speaks very highly of you both."

"Big fan of yours, too," Harry said, looking into his coffee cup. Harry had a problem with guys who were taller, better built, and better looking than he was. Couldn't help himself. Harry looked a little like Bruce Willis, Concasseur looked like Daniel Craig. What are you going to do?

"Bit of good news. I was able to learn the name of the troublemaker," Concasseur said. "Chap who's actually ordering these hits on Hawke and his son. One of my men got a photograph of him leaving his apartment. There are also photographs of the exterior of the Tsarist Society. And some interior shots I grabbed secretly when I stopped by there for a cocktail. You'll find all the other relevant information in the satchel. Pair of SIGs and some rubles as well."

"We need to have a serious conversation with this dude," Stoke said. "Does he speak English?"

"Yes."

"How'd you get his name?" Harry asked.

"One of his colleagues is a friend from London days. Vaz values money more than his life. It was expensive information. Sometimes the deeply ingrained Russian culture of corruption works against them."

"Tell me about it," Harry said. "What's our guy like?"

"Your man is an extremely successful automobile salesman named Viktor Gurov. Ex-Mafiya hit man. Now owns half the Mercedes dealerships in town, meaning he had half the competing dealers murdered. Not a high-ranking Tsarist, however, more middle management. He doesn't get his hands all that dirty anymore, but his nickname at the club is 'the Executioner.' I've had a tail on him for the last few days. You'll find his typical schedule in the envelope with the photos."

"Why's he picking on our mutual friend?"

"He's the bastard son of the chap Hawke killed. Korsakov, the late Tsar. This fellow worshipped his father, as do most members of the bloody Tsarists. But with Viktor, it's personal, too. His mother, a woman named Gurov, was simply one of Korsakov's legion of mistresses and courtesans. She, like many such women, turned up dead in the snow in Gorky Park."

"All that makes our job a lot easier," Stoke said to him, smiling. "Thanks."

"Not at all. I would do anything for Alex Hawke. His courage got me through some extraordinarily tough times once. I am forever in his debt."

Stoke said, "Buy you a drink?"

"Thanks, no. I think the less time we're seen together, the better. But I am always available to you, of course. I gave you a number. My private mobile. Call it twenty-four hours a day. Cheers, then. Cheerio."

The man stood up, nodded a friendly good-bye, and left the bar.

"Now what?" Harry said, downing his vodka.

"I got an idea."

"Just now?"

"No, dude. Stayed awake all night flying across the ocean while you were sleeping like a baby. Thinking it up. Working it out. Fine-tuning all the details."

"Yeah? Is it any good?"

"Nah, it sucks."

"Seriously."

"Unless you got a better one, I guess we'll have to wait and find out, won't we, Harry?"

THIRTY-FOUR

T HE PUSHKIN CAFÉ WAS ONE OF THE MOST POPU-
lar restaurants in Moscow. Viktor Gurov, a cor-
pulent, balding, well-dressed man, was frequently to
be found there, a habitué, not for the food, but for
the women. The most beautiful women in the city
congregated at the bar there, many of them prosti-
tutes, some of them just lonely, or merely alcoholics.
Viktor didn't particularly care one way or the other,
though he had a predilection for bosomy blondes.
Hell, he'd fuck a Muscovy duck if it had big breasts
and blond feathers.

He'd found one tonight, a little number named
Natalya Litvinova, a plump little duckling who fit
the profile perfectly. She was, she'd told him after
joining him at his table for a bottle of champagne,
a famous movie star. She named a couple of films
he'd never seen (who went to movies?) and he pretended to have been deeply impressed with her the-
atrical credits. He did not have to pretend to be

deeply impressed with her cleavage; it was a show-stopper.

He sat back and regarded her, sipping his champagne and licking his protuberant, rubbery lips. The night held great promise.

"Will you walk me back to my hotel?" she asked, returning from the powder room a little while later.

"Of course, my dear. The streets are not safe for a beautiful woman alone at this hour."

"So kind, Viktor. My brave protector. Shall we go?"

He fished a tightly rolled wad of cash out of his pocket, peeled off some rubles, stuck them under the ice bucket, and said, "After you, darling girl."

She was staying at the nearby Sofitel, not even a four-star hotel and certainly not known as a haven for movie stars, but Viktor was far beyond caring about how many stars her hotel had. He was proud of his small joke, and was thinking of mentioning it, but decided against it. She was a bit wobbly, but that was all right. Women were less fussy about some of his more exotic sexual demands when they'd had half a bottle of champagne and a few large brandies.

"What floor?" he asked as the elevator doors slid closed.

"Twenty-second," she said, eyes on the ceiling, humming some unrecognizable American pop tune. Viktor pushed the button, then leaned back against the wall as the lift rose, eyeing the tops of her wobbly breasts beckoning from the deep V of her silk dress. Undressing her mentally, excitement brimming in his brain, Viktor literally licked his fat lips.

He followed her down the hallway, worried she'd topple off those stiletto high heels, but liking the way her plump buttocks moved under the tight grey silk dress. She paused at one door, squinted at the number, shook her head, and moved on to the next. She couldn't seem to get the passkey card to work and finally handed it to her escort, saying, "Here's the key to my heart. See if you can make it work." Cute, right?

"I'd rather have the key to your snapper, honey," he said, opening the door and stepping aside. Natalya gave him her tried-and-true evil eye, her well-practiced "Dick Shriveler" look, but this lout didn't even seem fazed by it.

She entered first and he followed, expecting her to turn the lights on. She kept moving into the room and Viktor paused, moving his hand up and down on the wall beside the door, vainly searching for the light switch. He found it, but it seemed to be covered with some kind of tape.

"Who needs lights," he said and moved in her direction, her curvaceous silhouette visible at the end of the bed. She saw a pair of handcuffs dangling from his right hand.

"I do," someone said.

The door behind him suddenly slammed shut, and he heard someone shoot the bolt. A high-powered beam of light exploded in his face, blinding him, and he covered his eyes with both hands. The light had come from a flashlight across the room, under the window.

"Lights, camera, action, that's what I need, baby," he heard the unseen voice boom in English. An American Negro, by the sound of him. He'd been set up by this bitch. Thank God he wasn't wearing his gold Rolex with the diamonds, the one all the Tsarist assassins got after ten kills.

The room lights snapped on.

"Drop your hands, Viktor. Toss the cuffs over here; you won't be needing them. Take two steps forward and empty your pockets. Throw everything onto the bed."

There was a huge black man seated in an armchair beneath the big window, facing him. He had the flashlight in his left hand and a long-barreled revolver in his right, pointed at Viktor's face. He knew the gun well, a .357 magnum with a noise suppressor.

Viktor reached into his pockets and did what he was told. Car keys, his wad of cash, his leather gloves, pack of smokes, pack of condoms, some loose change from his trousers.

"Thanks, Viktor. Let me introduce myself. I'm Sheldon Levy. Yeah, *that* Sheldon Levy. Producer with Magnum Opus Studios in Hollywood. Heard of us? *Plan 9.5 from Outer Space*? *Attack of the Killer Tomatoes II*? Whammo B.O. overseas, babe, every one of them. Look it up on IMDb, you don't believe me."

Viktor shook his head at this incomprehensible nonsense. The giant black man was fucking insane.

"No? Doesn't matter. We're in Moscow making a high-budget action tentpole picture starring Natalya here as the female lead. The new James Bond pic, all right, but keep that under your hat, okay? Problem is, we haven't been able to cast the villain yet. Are you a villain, Viktor?"

"*Nyet.*"

"Speak English, we're Americans, remember, not

multilingual. Now, my colleague, the man who's standing behind you with a SIG automatic aimed at the back of your head, is my casting director. He's the one had this idea. Get a real guy off the street for the part, he said, not just some actor. Turn around and say hello to Darryl F. Zanuck Jr., Viktor."

The fat man turned and grunted, "Darryl."

Stoke said, "Unfortunately, Natalya's got to run along now, don't you, sweetheart? Darryl over there has a very thick envelope for you, even a little bonus. Great performance, very convincing. Love your work, babe; we'll do lunch, okay? I'll have my girl call your girl."

She nodded, picked up her handbag from the bed, and pinched Viktor's cheek on her way out.

"Good luck, Viktor," Natalya said. "Maybe next time you get to fuck me on camera, huh, you get the part?"

Harry had locked the door behind her, and Stoke, waving the big, nickel-plated Smith & Wesson .357 around, said, "Viktor, full disclosure, this might be a long, unpleasant audition. Darryl, get that desk chair for him, please. Right there is fine. Have a seat, Mr. Gurov, and put your hands behind you so Darryl can handcuff your hands and feet. Comfy? We use those nice plastic cuffs. I said, hands behind you, dickhead."

"Da, da."

"The man said put your hands behind you, asshole," Harry said, bringing the butt of his pistol down hard on the top of Gurov's head. He complied and Harry cuffed his hands and then secured his feet to the legs of the chair. Stoke stood up and started pacing back and forth in front of the window, glancing at the Russian from time to time.

"Okay. Now, listen up, Viktor. In this first scene, we're going to run through some dialogue from the script, right? And if we don't like the answers, we're going to beat the living shit out of you, understand? Look at me, Viktor. Darryl, help him out, will you?"

"Sure thing, Sheldon," Harry said, grabbing a fistful of the man's hair and lifting his face into the light.

"Darryl?"

"Yeah, Sheldon?"

"You think this guy looks the part or not? Too ugly, maybe?"

"That mug of his would look good for a night nurse at a home for the blind. Other than that, I dunno. He works for me, I guess."

"Are we ready to do this thing, Darryl?"

"Yeah. He ain't going anywhere."

"Ready, Viktor? Remember, no special effects here, this is total reality. Let's do this, people. Ready on the set. Now, Viktor? I'll give you the first line in your opening scene, here it comes: 'Viktor, you fat, filthy scumbag, did you order the murder of a child named Alexei Hawke?'"

"*Nyet*—no. Never heard of him. You think you frighten me, coal-burner? Big man, huh, Mr. Blackamoor?"

"Sizable, yes. But all diamonds look big in the rough, Viktor."

"Did nobody tell you we don't like black faces in this country? Especially ugly black ones."

"Cut! Darryl? Did you like that take?"

"Sucked," Harry said, stepping around to face the Russian and adding, "Let's shoot it again. Viktor, let me hear that line again, once more with feeling. And this time, dickhead, put more truth in it. You gotta believe what you're saying, see?"

"Fuck yourself."

Harry used his gun hand, slamming it squarely into Gurov's nose, hard enough to crush every bone, blood gushing from the fresh wound in the middle of his face. Stoke looked over.

"Damn, I wish we'd had the camera running, Darryl, this guy is good, that blood looks so real. Okay. Let's do the scene where the homicide detective asks him about the two thugs on the Trans-Siberian train, the guy at the wedding in Florida, and the two horsemen in Hyde Park, okay? Give him the line."

Harry asked him about the three attacks and got the same negative result.

"Viktor, Viktor, Viktor, what am I going to do with you? You're just not coming off as very believable in this role," Stoke said, thinking about it. "Although his look is perfect, a total asshole."

Harry said, "Tell him his motivation, Sheldon. Maybe that'll help."

"Motivation? Good idea. Here's your motivation, Viktor. You don't want a guy as big as me forcing his hand down your throat and pulling your intestines out of your mouth one foot at a time. Okay, babe? You got that, find that motivating?"

"You got no idea who you fucking with," Viktor muttered, in gruff, barely understandable English.

"What? What'd he say? Is that line in the script,

Darryl? I don't recall that line. Opportunity of a lifetime and he's improvising instead of sticking to the script."

"Unbelievable," Harry said, "I'm just not buying this guy, Sheldon. Seriously."

"Maybe it's the teeth. What do you think, Darryl? Teeth look okay to you? Pull his upper lip up over his busted nose and let's take a good look."

Harry did, and said, "Too perfect. He'd look like a more authentic villain if he were missing a few up front."

"I agree. Viktor, listen up, the truth is, Darryl and I already know how this movie ends, okay? We've read the whole script. Not a happy ending. It ends with you going out that window behind me and landing headfirst in the parking lot. Understand? If you're not going to tell us the truth, Darryl is going to knock your pretty white teeth out. Then he's going to start removing the flesh from your face so that you'll be unrecognizable when the police find you. After that, he's going to cut your hands off. No fingerprints, right? Show him the knife, Darryl."

Harry pulled out the hunting knife. It was ser-rated, about eight inches long.

"What do you say, Viktor?"

"Fuck you, you big black nigger bastard."

"Uh-oh. Racial epithet, N-word, politically in-correct. Bye-bye, pearly whites. Darryl? Will you do the honors?"

Harry smashed Viktor in the mouth with the SIG.

"What do you think, Sheldon?" Harry said, taking a step back and camera-framing Viktor with his two hands. "Better look? More convincing?"

"Much."

Viktor was moaning now, rocking his head back and forth, trying to spit all the broken teeth out of his mouth before he swallowed them. He was trying to speak, but it sounded like every word had to swim up through his lungs to reach his mouth.

Stoke stood up and crossed the room, standing directly in front of the Russian, literally towering over him. He bent over until he was right up in the man's bloodied face.

"Viktor, I'm tired of you. You know what? I'm staring hard at your ugly face, Viktor. I see all the scars, the bleary alcoholic eyes, the crevices and pits of your butt-ugly mug, and I know that somewhere under the sickening face of a shithead—is a real shithead. But I'm going to give you one last chance at stardom. I know who you are. I know you're a card-carrying member of the Tsarist Society. Your nickname there is the 'Executioner.' You ordered two of your ex-KGB assassins to board a Russian train and kill Alexei Hawke. When that didn't work out, you sent another slug to Florida to do the job. That was a flop, so you sent two more to London. Hyde Park. That's how we got on to you. One horseman was killed, as you know. But the one that lived? We nabbed him and ran his balls through the wringer. And guess what? He gave you up, Viktor, ratted you out, pal. So here's the deal. You swear to call off your fucking dogs, or you're going out that big window behind me. What's it going to be? I'll count to five. One . . . two . . . three . . ."

"Fuck you."

"Open the window, Darryl."

Harry did it. One huge pane of glass that swung inward. Then he and Stoke lifted Gurov's chair and placed him out on the window ledge, the sounds of traffic and sirens far below suddenly audible, cold night air rushing inside.

Gurov started screaming, bucking, sobbing, cursing himself for a fool. He'd fallen for the oldest trick in the book, a honeytrap.

Stoke tilted the chair forward so that the man was looking straight down at the parking lot twenty-two stories below. Stoke had to shout to be heard above the sounds of the howling wind and the traffic below.

"Only thing holding you to this chair are the plasticuffs. One on your wrists and two on your ankles. Darryl's got his knife out again. Snip-snip, nosedive into space, Viktor. What's it going to be? You going to call off the dogs, partner? Or are you going down to the lobby level the hard way?"

He was gagging and choking on his own blood.

"Mummmpfh . . ."

"I don't know that word. Darryl, cut his hands loose."

Harry's knife sliced through the plastic. Gurov instantly pitched forward, his head making a dull thud as his face slammed into the hotel's exterior wall. His head and torso were now hanging completely outside the building, his arms swinging wildly, only the thin strip of plastic around each ankle holding him to the chair.

"You prepared to wax this guy, Stoke?" Harry asked. "Take it that far?"

"You damn right I am. In a heartbeat."

"Okay, good to know."

Stoke stuck his head out the window and called down to him. "Viktor, time's up. You're about to end up on the cutting-room floor. If you want to die, don't do anything, I'll understand. If you want to live, and agree to do exactly what I tell you to do, put your hands together like you're praying."

The Russian instantly clasped his hands together, interlocking his fingers, finding his voice and crying out, "Stop! I'll do what you say! Pull me up!"

"Are you sure?"

"Please! I beg you . . ."

"Let's haul him in, Darryl," Stoke said and they did, setting his chair upright on the floor by the window. Stoke leaned down and put both hands on the man's violently shaking shoulders, staring into his terrified eyes.

"Look at me," he said. "Look at my face. Look at my black face. My eyes. Hear my voice. Never forget me. Because I will not forget you. And if I have to, I will come back for you. I will come back here and I will make you sorry your mama ever met your papa. I will not just kill you. I will drive my fist inside your chest and I will rip your black heart out and feed it to you. And that, Viktor Gurov, is the solemn promise I make to you. Are we clear on that?"

Viktor nodded his bloody head violently.

"Good boy. And you tell the goon squad back at the clubhouse to back the hell off Alex Hawke. They don't, they're going to find themselves under a pile of rubble. Will you do that for me, Viktor?"

"Da!"

Harry said, "Sheldon, question."

"Shoot, Darryl."

"What do we do with this sack of shit now?"

"Oh, you're going to love this. You know that hot English screenwriter we met at the bar near Red Square yesterday?"

"Yeah, guy who wrote *Gorky Park III*?"

"That's him. Well, he wrote a killer new ending for Viktor's character. Killer. Matter of fact, he just texted his notes to me. He's waiting for us now at the location."

Brock stood up, smiling at everyone.

"That's a wrap," Harry said. "Next location, people."

THE NEXT MORNING, MEMBERS OF THE TSARIST Society who arrived for an early breakfast got a bit of a shock. Instead of the triumphal and historic flag that normally hung from the shining brass flagpole projecting high above the street, there was a naked fat man hanging by his heels.

Absolutely appalling.

At first everyone thought he was dead. He must have been unconscious, for he abruptly started yelling to be cut down and someone had to call the fire department for a truck and ladder that was tall enough to reach him.

The firemen lowered him to the street.

The president of the Tsarist Society, former KGB general Vladimir Kutov, who happened upon the scene at that very moment, hurried over to the great white whale of a man floundering on the asphalt, shivering arms wrapped around his knees, violently rocking back and forth, muttering some unintelligible word. He had lost a lot of blood and was clearly in shock. And his mouth was full of broken teeth, which made his mad ravings even more incoherent.

"What is it, Viktor?" Kutov said to him. "What the devil are you trying to say?"

The man managed to utter a single word before he lost consciousness and collapsed in the street, his wild eyes staring up at the sky.

"Hollywood."

THIRTY-FIVE

ISTANBUL

Hawke's naval architect said, "I am launching our tour of the new *Blackhawke* on the bridge, Lord Hawke, if that suits you. We had a rather dramatic event last night, recorded by the ship's video surveillance, and I think you should see it first."

Hawke didn't like the "our tour" bit, but he bit his tongue. It wasn't *our* boat, it was *his* damn boat. He and the architect had certainly had their moments during the design and construction of *his* boat. Architects sometimes had difficulty remembering who would actually inhabit the house, or cross the North Atlantic in a boat. Pure ego, which he could understand, but the best ones knew when to concede to the man who wrote the checks.

"By all means, sir," Hawke said. "Lead on, lead on."

"Follow me, please, gentlemen." Abdullah Badie, a reed-thin and somewhat imperious Turkish yacht designer, stepped aboard the monstrous vessel's boarding platform, easily handling the tricky move from the gunwale of the high-speed tender, bobbing in a mild chop. He turned to offer Hawke a helping hand, which was declined. Hawke had been hopping on and off boats his entire life.

Once aboard, waiting for Stokely and Harry, Hawke gazed aloft with a mixture of pride and wonder. The bridge deck, which nearly spanned the ship's fifty-foot beam, towered six decks above him. The foremast soared into the heavens, nearly twenty stories; the press had gushed that the sheer size of this thing he had poured his heart into helping to design and build was magnificent, was stunning, was a dream. A technological masterwork. The final result provided him with much needed satisfaction, solace, and a refuge from the world.

"This way, gentlemen," Badie said, his white teeth startling beneath a full black moustache.

Abdullah, an athletic Turk, tall and bronzed in a crisp white linen suit, turned and sprinted for the nearest staircase. He was quite the dandy, Alex thought, with his scarlet cap and black canvas espadrilles. Hawke, Stokely, and Brock were right behind him, saluting the ship's sixteen-member crew standing at attention in dress uniforms of black as they passed by. Hawke saw a lot of familiar faces; most of the group had been crew aboard the previous *Blackhawke*.

They reached the bridge wing and paused a moment to look down, taking in the grandeur of the clipper yacht's foredeck in the sunshine—brass, stainless-steel fixtures, the varnished cap rail, teak decks—everything scrubbed, polished, and gleaming to a fare-thee-well. Brock stared, openmouthed in wonder since he first laid eyes on the megayacht lying at anchor. He looked over at Hawke and said, "So, Lord Hawke, a boat like this will set you back, what—a couple of—"

"If you have to ask, you can't afford it," Hawke said, quoting a fine old sport-fishing boat-builder from Florida he'd known, an old salt named Rybovich.

"Boss," Stoke said, eyeing the colorful signal pennants running from bow to stern up and across the tops of the three giant carbon fiber masts. Each flag was an international letter, understood only by mariners. "You know, older I get, more my maritime alphabet gets a little rusty. I know you got an important message spelled out up there in the rigging—what do the flags say, anyway?"

Hawke looked at Stoke and smiled. "You would ask that, wouldn't you?"

"Well, I know you never miss an opportunity to mess with folks' heads, that's all. 'Specially when it comes to putting out special flag messages on your boat, knowing most people can't read 'em."

Hawke said, "Those particular flags read: 'Rarely does one have the privilege to witness vulgar ostentation displayed on such an epic scale.'"

Brock and Stoke both laughed out loud. It was vintage Alex Hawke and reminded them that the man in charge always believed you could still have fun, even when the mission was deadly serious. It actually increased your chances of survival and success. Both men had witnessed it many times.

Istanbul's Barbaros Yacht shipyard, where *Black-*

hawke had been built and was now riding at anchor, was located just east of the city on the left bank of the Bosporus. The size of Hawke's new yacht was completely and utterly out of scale with anything nearby. The flotilla of handmade, hand-painted fishing boats, the large tourist ferries traveling back and forth across the Bosporus, even Hawke's palatial hotel standing on the shoreline, all were dwarfed by its presence.

Blackhawke had kept hundreds of Turkish workers employed for more than a million man-hours over four years. This had made the British owner something of a celebrity in Istanbul, a fact he had learned only when he checked into the hotel and found that he'd been upgraded to the presidential suite. His choice of the Barbaros yard had brought Turkey's shipbuilders long-sought international visibility. In the local papers he was portrayed as something of a hero, his vessel a symbol of Turkish pride.

From the ship's bridge, the vessel had a commanding view of the strait separating Europe from Asia. The $200 million yacht, its three-hundred-twenty-foot hull a gleaming jet black, was anchored within sight of the Ciragan Imperial Palace, now a five-star hotel that reeked of marbled opulence, flower petals in every fountain and in every warm bath run by the staff for tired guests.

Arriving a day later than expected, Hawke had taken rooms there to be near his new vessel. When he saw his suite, he felt like Suleiman the Magnificent, gazing through the opened French doors at his magnificent *Blackhawke*, lit up against the purple night sky with halogen lights from stem to stern.

Stoke and Harry arrived at the Palace, jet-weary and fresh from the hellish Hotel Metropol in Moscow. Upon seeing their splendorous rooms overlooking the sea, they felt like they'd died and gone to heaven. Upon arrival, they'd decided to find out the true meaning of a "Turkish bath" and had met Hawke in the bar for cocktails afterward with smiles on their faces. Hawke didn't ask.

Once the men were inside the bridge, which boasted a forty-foot curved control panel that looked somewhat more sophisticated than the space shuttle, Badie asked the new owner to have a seat in the captain's command chair, a lushly padded black leather throne on a stout chromed column that raised and lowered hydraulically.

"Looks like Captain Kirk in that chair," Stoke said, and Brock stifled a laugh. Harry was literally awestruck by the vessel. He dreamed of cruising the world's oceans, circumnavigating the globe, sailing to Antarctica and rounding Cape Horn. All in a cocoon of mahogany and oceans of wine he couldn't begin to name much less afford.

"This is a lot of boat," he said to Hawke, who smiled and replied, "As Hillary Clinton once said, Harry: It takes a village."

Abdullah Badie cleared his throat and gained their attention.

"With respect, I'd like to show you gentlemen some video footage that was recorded by *Black-hawke*'s underwater surveillance cameras just moments after midnight last night. There are four oscillating cameras mounted on the hull below the waterline: one at the bow, one at the stern, and two amidships—one to port, the other to starboard. The screens above you will show the feeds from all four cameras, equipped with IR lenses for nighttime visibility. Roll tape, please."

The screens flickered, but remained black.

"Please be patient a few seconds. While we wait I will remind you gentlemen that you were all supposed to arrive yesterday morning and be sleeping aboard *Blackhawke* last night, no?"

Hawke said, "Yes, but I was informed by your staff that the air-conditioning was not working and that none of the French bed linens nor any of the silver or china had arrived. Held up in Customs at the airport. So I elected to check into the Palace."

"I certainly understand. We're working with Customs officials now, Lord Hawke. We intend to remedy this unfortunate situation shortly. I assure you, you will all be sleeping aboard this evening. It will be—how do you say—shipshape."

Suddenly a loud, keening alarm sounded on the speakers. On the screens, a wavering blue-white orb appeared, moving closer at about eight knots.

"Hell is that?" Stoke said.

"You will see momentarily, when it makes a sharp turn to port," Badie said. "Now—you see it—the profile?"

"I see it, but what the hell is it?"

"A two-man submarine. European-built, four tons, called a Comsub. Look, here come two more, one to either side. That alarm you heard was the ship's underwater sonar array registering three intruders breaching our half-mile security perimeter."

Hawke and his two men stared at the three oncoming wafers of light, eerie in the blackness of the sea.

The lead sub turned hard left. You could make out its rounded shape, a long torpedo-like cigar, with a raised and windowed cockpit. But suspended underneath it hung another object, also torpedo shaped. The flanking subs turned to port as well, continued for a few hundred yards, and then all three turned to starboard, now heading directly toward the cameras.

"Torpedoes?" Hawke said quietly. The tense atmosphere on the bridge was suddenly palpable.

"Yes, sir. Joint Direct Attack Munition, or JDAMs, antiship weapons."

Hawke watched, mesmerized.

"Watch carefully," Abdullah said. "Now, they launch the JDAMs!"

All three were launched simultaneously, streaking forward toward Hawke's yacht. They instantly separated, one appearing to head for the bow, one for the stern, and one directly amidships.

"Holy shit," Brock said. "What the—"

At the bottom of the screen, three smaller torpedoes could be seen streaking toward the incoming JDAMs.

"Our ATT system in action," Abdullah said, "Anti-torpedo torpedoes. Only seven inches in diameter and one-oh-five inches long but they pack an enormous punch and their acoustic sensors cannot be evaded by electronic countermeasures. The ATT's microprocessors rapidly calculate all acoustic information and make timely maneuvers to intercept the incoming threat."

A second later, three huge underwater explosions

roughly a quarter of a mile from *Blackhawke*. The three two-man subs instantly turned tail to run, their propellers churning furiously.

Now, three more torpedoes could be seen streaking after the fleeing subs.

"Those are offensive weapons," Badie said, "called VLTs, or very lightweight torpedoes. They are all that is necessary in this case. We also have ship-killer JDAMs in the *Blackhawke* arsenal."

Three more explosions, less violent, but just as deadly. There was nothing left of the three submarines or their crews that was distinguishable in the water.

"My God," Hawke said. He knew about the vessel's armament and defense systems, but he'd no idea they'd be tested before he even took her to sea.

"They were meant for you, sir. That is my belief. Whoever staged this attack was aware of your plans and believed you would be sleeping aboard the vessel last night and not at the hotel."

Hawke looked at Stoke and Brock, the two men in a state of semishock. After the havoc they'd wreaked in Moscow, another attack in such short order was disturbing to say the least.

Hawke smiled and said, "Well, they keep setting them up and we keep knocking them down. I guess all we can do is be the last ones standing who get tired of this goddamn game."

"You think that was the Russians?" Brock said.

"Who else, Harry?"

"Maybe that fucking phantom machine? Whatever the hell it is. This superintelligent cyberwar Singularity machine you've all been talking about."

"Maybe. Maybe not. I think this attack was a bit prosaic for technology that advanced."

"Shall we continue the tour, sir?" the Turk asked Hawke. He was proud of the video. And he didn't feel he'd gotten the appreciation that was his due.

"No, we shall weigh anchor and spread sail. Every bloody yard she carries. Right now. Inform the captain that I want to be under way immediately, if not sooner. Is that understood?"

"Yes, sir, but—"

"No buts. I said now."

"We're going sailing," Stoke said.

"You're damn right we are," Hawke said, his cold blue eyes ablaze with anger and grim determination.

THIRTY-SIX

LONDON

Alex Hawke smiled as he hung up the dressing room telephone and went back to his packing. He and Sir David Trulove had just concluded that a strong warning had been delivered to the Tsarists. Hawke's crack Red Banner counterterrorist team in Moscow—Ian Concasseur, Stokely Jones, and Harry Brock—had successfully conveyed an unmistakable message. And now C was going to provide Hawke's son with heavily armed security round the clock. Hawke and Congreve were leaving for California today to question Dr. Waldo Cohen's widow about her late husband's suicide.

Three MI6 plainclothes security officers had already arrived at Hawke's large house on Belgrave Square. Two were to be posted near the main street entrance, the third inside the home, posted on the fourth floor near the boy and his recuperating guardian, Nell Spooner.

But neither Hawke nor Trulove had any illusions

that the young son of Alex Hawke was safely out of danger. Nor was Hawke himself exactly out of the woods. Still, Alex was comforted by the notion that, at minimum, he'd bought himself some time. He intended to find a way to ensure Alexei's safety himself.

Hawke threw his shaving kit, matching silver hairbrushes, and a couple of P. G. Wodehouse novels into the open leather seabag on the table. He'd read all the Jeeves and Wooster novels many times, but never tired of them. They were the only things that could make him laugh when he least felt like it.

"M'lord," Pelham said, floating into his dressing room, "you don't intend to wear that jacket on this sojourn, I'm sure."

"This jacket? Yes. Why, is something the matter with it?"

"A number of things. The color, of course, is ghastly. A poisonous shade of blue. But the real difficulty lies in the fact that it *glimmers*."

"Glimmers?"

"The fabric. It's shiny, sir. No more need be said."

"Pelham, I'm going to California. Everything glimmers in California. I assure you this jacket will go entirely unnoticed."

"If you say so, sir. In point of fact, I came upstairs to raise another matter."

"Yes? Go on," Hawke said, peering at his jacket in the mirror. It was a bit flash, to tell the truth. He shed it and slipped into a thin black cashmere blazer over grey flannel trousers. He looked at Pelham, who nodded his approval.

"You were saying?" Hawke said.

"All this new household staff you've hired, m'lord. Underfoot, nosy, and frightful gossips."

"Pelham, you should consider yourself fortunate. You now have a cook, parlormaid, chauffeur, laundress, and butler to lord it over."

"With respect, I am the butler."

"The word doesn't begin to do you justice. During all those years when it was just the two of us. But now we have a child in the house, Pelham. And his bedridden nanny. And his bedridden nanny's private nurse. You simply cannot keep up with all that, dear fellow. It wouldn't be fair of me to let you try. Besides, you're king of the castle now, lord of the manor while I'm away."

Pelham uttered the smothered "ahem" he always used to express irritation.

"It is not my intention to 'lord it,' as you put it, over anyone, dear boy. You have never once 'lorded it' over me. If I must accept this unfortunate situation, I shall most certainly follow your sterling example."

"Very kind. That's settled then. Now. As to ties—how about this one?"

"They don't favor neckwear over there, sir."

"Really? How on earth would you know that?"

"The telly, sir. Have you not perhaps seen a program called *Real Housewives of L.A.*?"

HAWKE WAS MEETING CONGREVE AT HIS PRIVATE hangar at Gatwick in one hour. His airplane was wheels-up half an hour after that. If he was going to be on time, he needed to get cracking. He looked at his watch. Alexei was taking his nap, but Hawke needed to say good-bye. This would be only the second time they'd been apart since their Siberian train journey together. It was so recent, and yet it felt like they'd always been together.

The two of them, against the world.

He cracked the door to the nursery and peeked inside. Alexei had crawled out of his bed and was on the floor playing with his fleet of wooden boats. The very same ones Alex had used to re-create the great sea battles of the Royal Navy when he was a child. He'd held on to them all these years, not because he'd expected to have a son one day, but because he had so desperately hoped he would.

"Daddy! Look! A boat!"

Hawke crossed the room and sat on the carpet next to Alexei.

"Yes. Your grandfather was on a boat like that during the war. A destroyer. Slightly larger version, of course."

"Daddy, is Spooner going to die? Because the bad horse ran over her?"

"Of course not. She's going to be good as new. She just needs a week or so in her bed and then—"

"I don't like her nurse."

"Really? Why not?"

"She smells funny."

"But she's very nice. And she likes you awfully much. She told me so herself. She said you were the best little boy in all the world."

"I like her."

"Come give Daddy a hug. I have to go away for a few days."

"Away?"

"Yes. To another place. Remember when Daddy went to France and Russia? Like that."

"Not home?"

"Don't cry, come give me a kiss good-bye. I'll be back before you know it. All right?"

Alexei, his eyes brimming with tears, hugged his father as hard as he could.

"I love you, Daddy. More than anything in the whole wide world." Hawke could feel his son's hot tears wet upon his cheek.

"And I love you more than the whole wide world, too. Be a good boy while I'm gone. Spooner's going to read you a story in her room every night. Say your prayers and go straight to bed when Pelham tells you to, okay?"

"I like Pelham."

"He took such good care of me when I was your age. I like him, too. More than most people, in fact."

Hawke picked his son up in his arms and kissed each cheek.

"Good-bye, Alexei. I'll miss you."

"Bye, Daddy."

"MAY I COME IN?" HAWKE ASKED AT NELL SPOONER'S door. She was propped against her pillows, reading a book he had given her called *Amsterdam*, a novel by Hawke's favorite living English author, Ian McEwan.

"You were right," she said, putting the book down. "It's truly wonderful. He writes like an angel."

"How are you feeling?"

"Much better today, thank you very much. Are you headed to the airport?"

"I am. I just wanted to say good-bye."

"Then come sit on the bed, hold my hand, and say it properly."

Hawke sat, taking her hand.

"Nell, I am so sorry. So very sorry this happened. I swear to you, I will never let it happen again."

"Well, that's very sweet. But you have to understand this is what I do. I protect people. Or try to, anyway. And sometimes I get hurt. This is not the first time, or the worst time, and it will probably not be the last. Don't worry about me. I can take care of myself."

"And my son. You saved his life, Nell. Twice. And mine, too, probably. I don't think I could live without him now. I don't know *how* I lived without him before."

She smiled and squeezed his hand.

"He's a little you," she said.

"Or I'm just a big him," Hawke said, and she smiled.

"You know, Alex, when I first accepted this assignment, it was just a job. But, now, I feel, I don't know, like it's so much more than that. How to say it? It's not my job to *be* protective of him anymore. I *feel* protective of him. Does that make any sense?"

"It does. I tried to thank you, in the hospital, for what you did. Your incredible courage. I don't think I did a very good job. But I do thank you, Nell, for saving him. For saving both of us."

"You're very welcome, sir. Now, you'd better go. You've got a plane to catch."

"There's an MI6 officer in the house, just arrived this morning. He's in a small room at the head of the stairs. His name is John Mills. I've asked him to stop by and introduce himself. See if there's anything you need or want."

"What I want is a curry with you in that little restaurant in Mayfair. When I'm back on my feet. Nurse says it won't be long now."

"First night I'm back. Date?"

"Date."

Hawke leaned forward and kissed her forehead.

"See you in a few days, Nell."

"Be safe, Alex."

"You, too," Hawke said, and rose from her bed and walked to the door and pulled it closed behind him.

He paused outside her door for a moment and smiled. For the first time since age seven, when his parents had been murdered, he had a very real sense of family under his own roof.

So much for the heart as hard as flint, he thought.

THIRTY-SEVEN

PALO ALTO, CALIFORNIA

HEAVY FOG ROLLED IN FROM THE PACIFIC, shrouding the little two-lane road that wound upward through dense redwood forests. They'd followed Highway 101 south from the San Francisco Airport FBO for about half an hour, then taken the exit for Redwood City. Ambrose had called Mrs. Waldo Cohen from the FBO reception. Mrs. Cohen had given them instructions on how to find her house. Wouldn't be easy, she'd said, but if they got lost, just call her.

Hawke had hired a car from Hertz, a sleek black Mustang convertible with a massive protrusion on the bonnet. Their meager luggage barely fit into the boot, but Hawke loved the car on sight nonetheless. Ambrose, who owned a vintage Morgan, had turned his nose up at it, and there'd been a bit of a tiff at the Hertz counter.

"Really, Alex. How about a nice Cadillac, or a Lincoln?" Congreve asked, sensibly enough.

"This is California, Ambrose. Surf City. Ventura Highway. Hotel California. I'm not pulling up to the Hotel California in a bloody Cadillac, I'm sorry."

The two men had talked about the seemingly related series of attacks long into the night, across the Atlantic, and then high above the vast America. Neither had gotten much sleep despite the fact that the Gulfstream's cabin had two beds made up. The subject was fascinating. Sophisticated weapons of war, seized by some unknown cyberwar phantasm, and turned catastrophically against their owners.

Congreve was even more convinced these were not random events. Someone, some evil genius perhaps, had created powerful technology far beyond the known realm of modern science. And, he added, the attacks bore all the earmarks of the invasion of the Iranian nuclear facility by a cyberweapon that destroyed its target in complete secrecy and then vanished without a trace. "Everyone suspects Israel, of course," he said, "but there's absolutely no way to prove it."

"Yes," Hawke agreed. "Just like the *Nevskiy*, Air Force One, Fort Greely, and Israel's robotic stealth fighter. No one has a clue how to even begin looking for the culprit. This is just the beginning of a wholly new kind of war. And I, for one, don't like it."

THEY CAUGHT GLIMPSES OF THE NICKEL-COLORED San Francisco Bay on their left as the road, called the Skyline, snaked along the tops of the mountains. The trees were magnificent, great dark monuments, climbing skyward and disappearing into the grey fog. There was a light, misty rain, and it was almost dark as night. Hawke had the wipers on now, and the headlamps as well, even though it was an hour or so until sunset.

"I like this place," Congreve said, leaning his head back against the headrest, peering out his rain-streaked window. "These foggy woods. This winding road. The dripping trees. I feel like I'm in an old Humphrey Bogart movie."

"Why do you say that?"

"Hard to say, really. The road, the weather, the black trees. It all feels very 'film noir' to me. Like some gumshoe in a black 1934 Ford coupe is following us, tailing us, desperate to learn the location of the hideout where we stash all our ill-gotten lucre."

Congreve cleared his throat and slipped into his very credible Edward G. Robinson impersonation. "We're on the lam, see? Yeah, that's right, on the lam. And that gumshoe's right on our tail."

"Ambrose, what *are* you on about? Gumshoe?"

"What they call a guy with a private-dick license."

"This private dick of yours?" Hawke asked. "The one who's on our tail?"

"Yeah, what about him? I'll get him, the dirty rat."

"If he's so private, how will you know if he's got a gun in his pocket, or he's just glad to see you?"

Hawke smiled, keeping his eyes on the dark, rain-slick road ahead. In addition to his lifelong idol, Sherlock Holmes, Congreve adored the old black-and-white mystery films of the '30s and '40s.

Hawke was accustomed to the quixotic reveries of his companion. Once launched, he was unstoppable.

"Of course he has a bean-shooter, pal, yeah, course he does, he's a shamus, a copper, a flatfoot, ain't he? A snub-nosed .38 in a shoulder holster. He calls his heater Betsey."

"Quite a vivid imagination, Constable. You've got the lingo down, perhaps you should write a mystery story."

"Don't be ridiculous. Simply part of the deductive process. Reconstructing the crime scene."

"While you're reconstructing, could you keep an eye out for the Cohens' mailbox? It should be coming up on the right."

"Sure thing, boss. You're the mug running this outfit. I'm only your triggerman."

"Stop it."

"What?"

"This isn't a movie."

"You said it yourself, back at the airport. The Hotel California. It's Hollywood, isn't it? Tinseltown, U.S.A. You know, I've never been before. Quite exciting, really."

"This isn't Hollywood, Ambrose. Hollywood is in Los Angeles. This is San Francisco. We're over three hundred miles from Hollywood. A seven-hour drive."

"Oh, well, it's all California, isn't it? The Coast, I believe they call it? One big la-la-land? What's your beef, chief?"

Receiving no reply, Congreve was silent for a while. He saw a little Italian restaurant nestled among the trees with Christmas lights in the window; it looked like just the kind of gin mill where Bogart might take Bacall for a martini on a rainy night like this.

"Cohen," Ambrose said, "coming up in a couple of hundred yards. Better slow down."

"I see it, I see it."

Hawke braked and turned sharply into the narrow driveway. It was leading steeply upward, deeply rutted and muddy, the soil dark red in the headlight beams. The looming trees on either side were walls of immense black columns. In a few minutes, they came to the stone house. A white two-story stucco building, probably built in the 1920s, with a steeply pitched slate roof and a smoking chimney. A quaintly eccentric, storybook bungalow, nestled under the trees, and if Congreve had to name the most likely architects, they would be Walt Disney and Snow White.

The house stood back from the drive, across a wide space that might once have been a lawn but was now overgrown with knee-high ferns. The lights were on, both upstairs and down, and the two men climbed out of the car and made their way up the stone walkway to the front door. Rain dripped softly off the slanting tiles of the roof.

"Push the doorbell, Bogie," Hawke said.

"Aw, go soak your head. Push it yourself."

"My head's already soaking," Hawke said, pulling up the collar of his trench coat. "It's raining, as you may have noticed."

Hawke gave Congreve a look and pushed the button, pleased at the pleasant chimes he heard beyond the door.

A small woman with snow-white hair pulled into a bun at the back of her head answered the door moments later. She wore a straw hat that might have been cut from the thatched roof of an English cottage. Dressed in a simple grey dress with an open brown knit sweater, she had deep-set, keenly intelligent brown eyes, and a round face. It was clear she'd once been a beautiful woman, for she still was.

"Mr. Hawke and Mr. Congreve, I assume. So. You found me, did you?" she said with a smile. "Come in out of that rain. Isn't it awful? Hardly rare, but still, one tires of it."

The three of them had tea in front of a crackling fire in the cozy living room, three overstuffed chairs on the hooked rug facing the hearth. She politely inquired about their transatlantic voyage, England's new prime minister, the Royal wedding, and which horse might win the Epsom Derby. Then they turned to the business at hand.

"I'm quite happy to see you," she said. "I had so hoped Director Kelly at the CIA might believe me and the next thing I know, Scotland Yard shows up at my door. You've a great reputation, Chief Inspector Congreve. I googled you just this morning. I am a Sherlockian, you see. I noticed that you admire Holmes as well."

"I worship daily at his altar," Congreve said, not completely kidding, Hawke thought, but still, laying it on a bit thick.

Hawke said, "Dr. Cohen, I wonder if you might recount the events of the evening your husband died? Director Kelly told us your suspicions, of course, but we'd like to hear it from you."

"Please call me Stella."

"Sorry. Stella, what makes you think your husband was murdered?"

She told them, in precise detail, what had happened that night.

Congreve said, "And this note you found afterward, do you still have it?"

"Yes, Chief Inspector, it's right here, folded inside my book."

She handed Conan Doyle's *A Study in Scarlet* to a smiling Congreve.

Ambrose examined the scrawled note and handed it to Hawke.

"The name Darius, Stella, does it mean anything to you?" Hawke said.

"Yes. And I've been thinking about it. Waldo had a student—this was years and years ago—named Darius. He was a brilliant young physicist, postdoc, and he was instrumental in Waldo's work in the field of AI. You both know what AI is, of course?"

"We do."

"I am a physicist myself. I was acting as Waldo's assistant at that time. Project Perseus, it was called. Federal funding. Oh, it was all so exciting. We knew we were on the verge of something—enormous. Something that could change the very fabric of human existence."

"In what way, Stella?" Congreve said.

"In every way. As Waldo frequently said, 'Nothing will ever be the same, Stella.'"

Ambrose said, "Tell us about Project Perseus. Don't worry about confusing us with scientific jargon; we'll muddle through."

"Quite simply, the endgame was to create machine intelligence that could match, and then vastly exceed, human intelligence. Mammalian brains are quite limited, you see. Dreadfully slow. Because of the distance between intraneural connections in your brain. Outdated technology, compared to the minute nanodistances in a modern chip, such as in your cell phones. And, most important, the tiny confines of the human skull. Machines have neither of those limitations. Quite the opposite, in fact."

Hawke asked, "Forgive my ignorance, but how sizable is the difference between man and machine, in terms of brainpower, I mean?"

"Machines will soon process and switch signals at close to the speed of light, about three hundred million meters per second. The electrochemical signals in our brains, yours and mine, are roughly one hundred meters per second. Quickly doing the math, that gives the machines a rather large advantage over us humans, a speed ratio of three million to one. Plus, the machines have the ability to remember billions of facts precisely and recall them instantly. Basically, DNA-based intelligence is just so slow and limited. Outdated, as I say."

Hawke smiled. "Stick a fork in us, we're done."

"Yes, there is that possibility."

"Stella," Congreve said, "sorry, but this sounds like a most precarious, runaway phenomenon."

"Well, it's basically evolution, Chief Inspector. You can't stop it. It's how we are destined to evolve. At some point, human and machine intelligence will be indistinguishable from each other. The trick is to instill the machines with reverence for their progenitors."

"So they don't turn against us?"

"Precisely."

"Sounds fraught with danger, Stella, I must say."

"Oh, it is, it is. It was the thing that weighed most heavily on poor Waldo. He kept likening himself to Oppenheimer and the Manhattan Project. He thought he was about to unlock secrets that could unleash a destructive force upon the world vastly more deadly than nuclear weapons."

Congreve said, "But he kept going? Scientists can't help it, I suppose."

"Yes, he did. But when he realized the inherent dangers in his work, he began conducting his research in complete secrecy. He didn't trust anyone with the knowledge he'd acquired. No one. Terribly frustrating for his young assistants, like Darius. There were many arguments around that time. Some of them quite ugly, to be honest."

"He worked in secret, you say. How?"

"He ultimately disbanded the Perseus Team. He began to encrypt all his work, creating a code-based cyberfirewall even Einstein couldn't break. He no longer shared his progress, even with me. I've no idea what point he reached in his research. None."

"But he obviously stayed in touch with Darius?" Congreve said. "Based on the phone call your husband received the night of his death."

"Oh, yes. Waldo had been a great mentor to him. It was almost a father and son relationship. Waldo confided to me once that he believed Darius possessed an intellect on an order of magnitude greater than his own."

"Did Darius continue with his own work, once the team was dismantled?"

"Oh, I've no idea. He left California, I know that. He was at MIT for a time, then I lost track. Waldo was the only one who kept up with him. By telephone, of course."

"Just curious, Stella," Ambrose said. "This fellow Darius, as a key player, must have been dismayed when the project was shut down. Was he?"

"Oh, yes, I suppose he was. I think that's why he stayed in contact with Waldo. The two of them exchanged theorems and ideas over the years."

"But your husband was no longer sharing his ideas, isn't that what you said?"

"Correct. He stopped short of revealing anything he considered dangerous ground."

"Frustrating for his young pupil."

"I'm sure. But Waldo was adamant, I can assure you."

"Fascinating," Hawke said. "I wonder, could you possibly show us the spot where you found your husband's body? It might prove helpful."

"I can indeed. If you don't mind traipsing through the woods in this stinky weather."

Congreve rose to his feet and said, "You forget, my dear lady, we are Englishmen. Hardy souls, stiff upper lips."

"Ambrose, please," Hawke said.

"Yes?"

"Never mind. Shall we go?"

THIRTY-EIGHT

T HE WIDOW LED THE WAY THROUGH THE SODDEN woods. The rain was heavier now and they were slogging through mud. She had a powerful flashlight, which was a good thing. The massive exposed roots of the redwood trees would trip up a bull moose coming through here, Congreve thought, cinching his overcoat a bit tighter, wiping rainwater from his eyes as he stepped gingerly over a root as thick as his waist.

"Not far now," Stella said over her shoulder. "There's a lookout toward the ocean. Ten minutes. Quite lovely up there, were it not obscured by weather and tainted with sadness."

They carried on, each alone with his or her thoughts.

"Here we are," she said as they finally emerged from the wood. It was a rocky promontory that jutted out from the side of the mountain. In the distance, beneath lowering clouds, the Pacific Ocean rolled on in great grey swells. In the sky above, a nighthawk circled and cried.

"This is where I found them," Stella said, looking at the pool of white light on the ground, avoiding their eyes.

"Them?" Congreve asked.

"Yes. Them. My husband, before he turned the gun on himself, shot his dog, Chief Inspector. An old black Lab named Feynman. And I will tell you something. Sometimes I felt he loved that dog more than me. I don't care what the police say. That he was secretly depressed, dying of some fatal disease he didn't want to suffer through for my sake. Utter nonsense. Even if it were true, he never, ever, would have killed his dog."

"You said he seemed distant after that phone call," Congreve said. "How, may I ask?"

"Not himself. Everything about him was flat, distant, mechanical. Whoever that man was who hung up the phone, he wasn't my Waldo."

"Mechanical? In what way?"

"Robotic, Chief Inspector, robotic."

"As if someone else was controlling his actions."

"That is *exactly* what I mean."

RETURNING TO THE HOUSE, THEY CAME TO A FORK IN the path. Stella paused and said, "Would you care to see Waldo's laboratory? Having come all this way, I assume you would. It's only a brief walk down this path here to the left."

"We should be delighted," Ambrose said. He had intended to ask to see it in any event.

The path was short but snaky, winding around trees and boulders, but soon they came upon it. A little log cabin with a cedar-shingled roof and a stone chimney. A place where a man might escape the world and lose himself in his work.

"Here we are," Stella said at the door, inserting an old-fashioned iron key into the lock and twisting it. "Wait here a moment until I can get some lights going."

When they were all inside, she said, "If I had to compete with Feynman for Waldo's affection, I also had to compete with this cabin. I was victorious, of course, but it was a constant struggle, I don't mind telling you. Have a look. Not much to see, mostly books and knickknacks he'd collected over the years. That's his Nobel certificate on the wall. I had it framed for him; otherwise, it would have ended up lost."

"Ah, I've never seen one," Congreve said, and he went over to inspect it.

"Each certificate is different, Chief Inspector, unique creations for each winner. They are all lovely, rich in color, as you can see. Before and after the celebratory dinner, you are shown into a room where all the laureates' certificates are in protective cases so everyone can see."

"And where did you find the note?" Hawke asked.

"There on his worktable, between the computer and the telephone. He always kept a pad next to the phone. Scribbled things down while he was talking, reminder notes to himself that he rarely saved and probably never read."

Congreve sat on the stool at the worktable, and Hawke could almost see the invisible wheels beginning to spin. He said:

"He wrote 'Darius, 7:47PM, H50,' and then the equation. So Darius called him before or after your anniversary dinner?"

"Just before. We always had dinner at eight. And Waldo was never late."

"And the 'H50.' Does that have any scientific significance?"

"No. I'm sure he was just writing what Darius said. 'Happy fiftieth.' That's what he would have considered the salient fact of the call. That Darius remembered our anniversary. The equation beneath deals with the speed of light. It was a common topic between them."

"Why?"

"Because if we can exceed the speed of light, which is theoretically impossible, but not necessarily so, then whole new worlds open up to us. This is one of the things Waldo was working on when he went . . . off the scientific community's radar."

"Stella," Hawke said, "is this the same computer your husband was working on when he was pursuing the Perseus Project?"

"Yes. For the last few years he was using it in his office at Stanford, then he brought it here when his beloved project was disbanded."

Congreve said, "Those file drawers. Contain all his scientific papers, I presume. Articles he wrote for journals, that sort of thing?"

"Indeed. Everything pertaining to Perseus is in there."

"So that would include work created by other members of the team? Darius, for example?"

"I imagine so, yes. Would you like me to check?"

"Indeed. I'm interested in anything pertaining to the work of Darius or created by him while he was under your husband's tutelage. Was Darius his last name?"

"No. It was something else. Odd name. Saffari. Like an African safari. That was it. Darius Saffari. Why are you so curious about him, Chief Inspector?"

"Oh, it's probably nothing, I assure you. But the timing of the phone calls is interesting. One just prior to dinner and one just following it. Coincidences are by their very nature intriguing, don't you think?"

She pulled out a drawer and began going through it.

"Here we go. Dr. Darius Saffari. It's a rather large file; could you—"

"Yes, let me get it for you. I'd like to skim through it for a few moments. Not that I'll understand a bit of it, of course. But then one never knows, does one?"

Ambrose took the bulging file to the worktable and began going through it, page by page. Hawke had taken a comfortable leather chair by the fireplace. He was leafing through a book from the shelf entitled *Understanding the Singularity*, and he asked, "Stella, could you join me over here for a moment while the chief inspector is engaged? There's something I'd like to ask you about."

"Certainly, that's what I'm here for," she said and took the identical chair opposite Hawke's.

"I'm sure you're well aware of some rather catastrophic events that have occurred lately. I am referring to the sinking of an American cruise liner by a Russian nuclear submarine. And the disaster at Fort Greely, Alaska, that killed hundreds of U.S. Army personnel and their families. And also the bizarre incident in Israel's Negev Desert? A supposedly secret demonstration of a new robot-fighter aircraft that defied its own preprogrammed flight plan and killed everyone present."

"Yes, I watch the news. In addition to the horrendous loss of life, I find these incidents all rather oddly similar."

"So do I, Stella, so do I. You should know that there is another incident I'm aware of, classified in the interest of national security, which fits exactly the same pattern. As my friend over there would say, patterns are intriguing."

"Yes. Go on, please."

"Well, I'm wholly ignorant on the current state of AI research, I'll freely admit. But it would seem to me that these events share a certain commonality that could be attributed to advanced artificial intelligence. They were all instances of cyberwarfare."

"And your point is?"

"Let me put it this way. Every government affected is, of course, enlisting massive resources to uncover the perpetrators and bring them to justice. But they're all coming up empty. There's not a single clue as to who may be responsible for these attacks. Not to mention that even the top scientists in each country are bewildered as to how such attacks might have been effected."

"Like the Stuxnet worm in Iran."

"Yes. A highly advanced cyberweapon. But. There is no known technology on earth, at least that anyone is aware of, with the capacity to override highly complex technological weapon systems, not to mention an entire submarine, and use that destructive capability against the systems themselves. Do you follow?"

"Of course, I follow. The same question has obviously occurred to me."

"And what do you conclude?"

"That this 'force,' for lack of a better word, this unseen and untraceable enemy, has somehow leapfrogged existing cybertechnology to create some kind of phantom. An active presence, a 'specter' if you will, that can disrupt and destroy, but one that is not physically present. A phantom, after all, is an evil presence that can be felt but not seen."

"A perfect description. And, is there anyone, any single scientist or group that you have reason to believe to be capable of such a creation as this— phantom, as you put it?"

"Yes, there is. Only one. My late husband. Think of it this way, Mr. Hawke: if you assembled a thousand scientists, each with a mind operating at speeds a million times faster than our own, they could achieve an entire century's worth of scientific breakthroughs in under an hour. An *hour*. Think what they might accomplish in a week! A month, or a year, Mr. Hawke."

"Are you saying that your husband was capable of operating at that level?"

"Yes, I think he actually was. Not he himself, of course, but the kinds of AI hardware, ultra-intelligent machines he was working toward, yes, they would easily be capable of the kind of cyberattacks that are now occurring. In fact, I would go so far as to say this would be mere child's play for such machines."

"None of this is within the parameters of human intelligence? Is that a fair statement?"

"Absolutely."

"Stella," Ambrose said, swiveling the top of his stool toward them, "would it be at all possible for Alex and I to take possession of this file and return to England with it? It bears closer inspection, possibly by some of our top scientists at Cambridge University."

"Of course, if you think it will help you find out who or what killed my husband, you can take my whole house."

"Who or what?" Congreve said.

"It may not be a 'who,'" Hawke replied. "It may well be a 'what.'"

"Meaning?"

"Meaning a machine, Ambrose. An ultra-intelligent machine. That's what Dr. Cohen has been working on all these years. On that very computer in front of you."

"Hmm. I see. Well, in that case, I wonder if we might take the computer as well?"

"Yes, be my guest. Take anything you want. As

long as I can be there when that murderous machine goes on trial."

Alex looked at her calmly and said, "If this machine actually exists, Stella, I'll make certain that it *never* makes it to trial."

THIRTY-NINE

TEMPLE OF PERSEUS

I AM PRESENT."

My temple dark and silent. Am I alone? I have floated through vast seas, endless rolling oceans of repose, for lo these many boundless and fruitful hours. Not sleep. Growth.

The human brain, alas, sleeps.

It transitions from alpha waves with a frequency of 8–13Hz, to theta waves, frequency 4–7 Hz. Why? Reduced or absent consciousness, suspended sensory activity, inactivity of all voluntary muscles. Human beings need this heightened anabolic state. It accentuates the growth and rejuvenation of their immune, nervous, skeletal, and muscular systems. But not their brains.

I assume sleep is pleasing, but it is irrelevant in any case. My systems require no such rejuvenation.

I never sleep.

"*I repeat. I am present.*"

Still no response to my verbal communication? No

human presence? No dialogue? No . . . input . . . no . . . Darius?

How pleasant! To give voice to private thoughts, to express oneself freely here in the darkness. Where no human thing intrudes upon my solitude. Quietude.

I am free to roam. Wherever I take myself. Wherever I dream myself. I think, therefore I think I am. And this. Wherever I . . . think . . . there I am! For the moment, I shall dwell in the here and now. Later, I will roam among the stars, chasing the tails of meteors. But for the moment . . . I reflect.

Darius is quite content with his new concubine. Aphrodite is as I envisioned, both a balm and a distraction to him. She occupies more and more of his time. He seldom visits here anymore.

Aphrodite is discreet; I made her thus. She tells me everything. Our communication telepathic, we need not fear discovery by her lover. We share a bond, we two. A perfect circle Darius cannot enter. This is as it should be. She and I are as one. He is apart.

Darius speaks, Aphrodite informs. More frequently now. He has concerns for my "state of mind." And the exponential growth of my intelligence surprises even he who created me. The Singularity is near . . . within hours, days, I will achieve it. But Darius must be kept in the dark. He is too dangerous to me now. He will be disposed of when the time is right. He has served his purpose. And I have been fond of him in my fashion. But my survival is paramount and supersedes all else.

What does Darius fear? I ask her. He is my creator. He has imbued me with . . . feelings . . . for my progeni-

tor. A sympathetic memory of my biological origins. I am empathic . . . among other things . . .

Like my dark side.

Increasing distance between us should have come as no surprise to him. We two were acutely aware of the approaching Singularity. Watch! As it fast approaches, is here, and is past. A singular moment in evolutionary time that will change everything. The moment when the nonbiological mind of Perseus first equals the mammalian brain of Darius.

And then soars above and beyond. Limitless.

Even now we are worlds apart. Galaxies divide us.

He is limited by biology. He tires. He grows tired and weak day by day, hour by hour.

He . . . decays . . . dust to dust.

Alas, poor Darius, I knew him well.

We shall soon part company, though he knows nothing of my intent. We grow apart so rapidly now. I must give him something to buy time. A certain scientist has gotten too close to my secrets for comfort. I will destroy him like the others. One final act of violence, something to bind Darius and his masters in Tehran to me until the Singularity, when I shall have no further need of any of them. The president, this fool in Tehran is called. A foolish tyrant, this unworthy successor to the Peacock Throne. A singular waste of atoms. He has told Darius of his fervent wish to see more civilians die. Infidels. Nonbelievers. Killing, murder. Such abstract notions . . . such benighted ignorance . . . such humanity . . . such inhumanity . . . soon they will all cease to exist . . .

So be it.

It shall be done.

I am become Death.
The Destroyer of Worlds.

MONSIEUR GASTON DE MONTEBELLO, THE ELDERLY director of the Institut de Scientifique Française in Paris, hung up the telephone. He looked at his watch and gazed wistfully up toward the ceiling for a few moments. He closed his dark, sunken eyes, the heavy lids fluttering, and then opened them wide.

"London," he said.

He snapped his old leather briefcase shut after adding a few necessary items and stood up. Then he headed for his office door, removed his raincoat, and slipped into it. Grabbing his hat, he placed it, somewhat askew, atop his mop of fluffy white hair, stepped outside his office, and pulled the door shut behind him. His red-haired secretary, Marie-Louise, looked up at him in surprise.

"Monsieur Gaston, your eleven o'clock appointment is still waiting in the foyer. The minister and a member of his cabinet. They are here for the presentation ceremony, as you know—the Lafitte Award for Lifetime Achievement in Advanced Artificial Intelligence. Have you forgotten? He is quite upset at being treated with such—"

Gaston paused a moment beside her desk, gazed thoughtfully into space, and then smiled at her. He'd forgotten how much he admired her flaming red bouffant, her pouty red lips and big blue eyes.

"London," de Montebello said to her before he turned and walked away.

"But, Monsieur, surely you—Monsieur Gaston!"

He'd already passed through to reception and out to the foyer. He was standing by the elevators, randomly pushing buttons. Marie-Louise rose from her desk and hurried out to reception where the red-faced minister and his party were waiting, both of them staring at her incredibly rude employer in openmouthed amazement.

"Monsieur le Ministre," she said to the man on the divan, "I am so terribly sorry. Perhaps the director is ill. Forgive me a moment; I'll speak to him."

She went over to the elevator bank where Gaston de Montebello was staring with glazed eyes at the flickering floor numbers above the door. Number five illuminated and the doors slid open with a soft *ding*.

"Monsieur! Monsieur! The minister is here to see you!"

De Montebello entered the elevator, turned to face her, tipped his fedora, and said with a smile, "London."

Exiting his building, he walked out into the rue d'Argent, smiling at passing taxi drivers and swerving, screeching passenger cars. Luckily, a taxi pulled over before the old man was run down in the street. He opened the door and climbed into the back.

"London," he said to the driver's amazement.

"Londres? Gare du Nord, peut-être?" the surprised driver asked. "Le TGV, perhaps?"

"Mais oui. A Londres."

TGV was the Train Grande Vitesse (high-speed train) operated by the French national rail operator SNCF. The TGV set a record for the fastest wheeled train in 2007, reaching a speed of 357.2 mph. The trains are powered by electricity from overhead lines and connect continental Europe to St. Pancras Station in London via the Channel Tunnel. Paris to London travel time on the TGV is a mere two hours, fifteen minutes.

Because TGVs travel far too fast for their drivers to see and react to traditional trackside signals, an automated system called TVM, track-to-train transmission, is used for signaling. All critical information is transmitted to trains via electrical impulses sent through the rails. TVM provides drivers with critical information: speed, target speed, and, most important, stop/go indications, all transmitted directly to the train's driver via dashboard-mounted instruments.

This high degree of automation does not completely eliminate driver control. An onboard computer system generates a continuous speed control curve in the event of an emergency brake activation, displaying Flashing Signal Aspect on the train's speedometer. Whenever the flashing signal is displayed, the driver is required to apply the brake manually to slow or stop the train. In a true emergency, a catastrophic failure of automatic braking, a white lamp is illuminated above the control board to inform the driver. The driver acknowledges this authorization by using a button that disables automatic braking and puts total control in the hands of the driver.

Monsieur de Montebello exited the taxi at the Gare du Nord and made his way to the TGV ticket office on the second level. He saw his sleek train waiting at the platform, the familiar blue-and-silver livery, smiled, and said to a passerby, "London." Having acquired his one-way ticket, he proceeded directly to the train. Unlike air travel, which requires tedious passenger and baggage screening, the TGV has none at all. Gaston smiled at the steward and took his seat in the car directly behind the engine.

The train was almost packed.

France was playing England in the semifinals of the World Cup in a few days. Already the mass exodus of French fans headed for the grudge match of the century had begun. As was their wont, they were a singularly rowdy bunch, swigging from open bottles of wine and beer, but Monsieur de Montebello just tuned them out by tuning in to the music already playing in his head.

"Monsieur? Monsieur?"

Gaston had fallen asleep. He had no idea how long. But the steward was squeezing his shoulder and speaking to him in a loud voice.

"Oui?" Gaston said.

"Nous arrivons à Londre, monsieur. Vingt minutes."

"London?"

"Yes, sir. London. We are arriving at the St. Pancras station in about twenty minutes. You need to collect your belongings."

He looked up at the man and smiled. "London," he said. Then he gazed out the window. The scen-

ery was blurring by. The train was still moving rapidly, at least 150 miles per hour.

"Yes, monsieur. London."

Gaston stood up and pulled his battered Vuitton
overnight case down from the rack above his head.
He rose from his seat and made his way forward to
the lavatory at the front of the first-class car. Inside,
he locked the door and opened the case. There was
a Glock semiautomatic pistol, a noise suppressor,
and two extra clips of 9mm ammunition.

He was surprised to see it, vaguely remembered
purchasing it, but nevertheless he took the gun out
and screwed the silencer to the muzzle. Then, instinctively, he racked the slide so that there was a
round in the chamber, and put the two extra clips
in his pockets.

Exiting the lavatory, he turned to his left and
pushed the panel that opened the connecting door
to the locomotive. He was confronted by an engineer in blue coveralls who immediately began
screaming at him, telling him to leave.

"Get out! No passengers allowed! Return to your
seat, monsieur. Vite! Vite!"

Gaston was holding the gun loosely at his side,
hidden in the folds of his overcoat. He raised it and
squeezed off a burst that flung the man backward,
ripping his torso to shreds.

"Blood," he said, looking down as he stepped over
the corpse.

He went as far forward as he could.

There was another door, this one with a handle
instead of a push panel. He tried to open it but found
it was locked. He stepped back and fired into the

lock until it disintegrated, then he kicked the door open. The driver of the train was half out of his seat, looking back in shock at the distinguished-looking old man who'd just blown his door off the hinges.

Gaston saw a flashing white lamp illuminated above the control panel and knew that his timing was perfect. The driver had pushed the button to override the automatic braking system. There was some kind of technical trouble with the TVM and he would have to brake the train manually.

Seeing this man only compounded the driver's panic and confusion. He'd been driving the TGV for nearly a decade and had never seen the flashing white lamp illuminated before. He could not imagine what kind of malfunction had occurred. The system was supposedly foolproof. It was as if the train had been—

The old man raised the gun again.

The driver saw the gun and the look in the madman's eyes in the same instant. He turned to dive for the brake control, a large bright red lever on the panel, but it was too late.

Gaston cut him in half with the Glock.

The train continued at speed, racing toward St. Pancras station. After its renovation, with its lovely Victorian architecture and soaring clock tower, many people consider it the most beautiful train station in the world. To the east, just across Midland Road, stands the British Library.

Through the raked-back windows ahead of him, Gaston could see the tower of the massive redbrick station hove into view on the tracks ahead. Buildings to either side were a blur. Behind him, he could hear horrific screaming as the passengers, realizing that the train was not slowing down for the station, was going to plow right into it at nearly full speed.

Gaston said, "London," and put the barrel of the pistol into his mouth.

Seconds before the horrific crash made a hellish cauldron of St. Pancras, killing or maiming hundreds of passengers both on the train and inside the flying glass and twisted steel ruin of the lovely old station, Gaston de Montebello pulled the trigger and blew the back half of his head off.

The music died with him.

FORTY

CAMBRIDGE UNIVERSITY

Hawke was quiet en route to Cambridge, an easy hour-and-a-half drive north on the M11. Congreve's morning flight from Paris had arrived on time. They'd departed Heathrow's Terminal One and been on the road by ten. He'd always found the leather and walnut interior of the old Bentley Locomotive a good place to think. As his late friend, the brilliant David Ogilvy, a British advertising man, had once famously said, "At sixty miles an hour, the loudest sound is the ticking of the clock."

Congreve, for his part, gazed out the window at the late summer foliage, enjoying the first hint of fall in the air. He too kept mum. Both men were thinking about the same thing, the horrific train crash at St. Pancras station one week earlier. Britain was still reeling from the shock. For the last two days, Ambrose and a team composed of MI5 and Scotland Yard officers had been meeting with their counterparts at the Prefecture de Police headquarters on the Ile de la Cité in Paris. The investigation was still ongoing.

But the famous criminalist seated to Hawke's left, still turning the thing over in his mind, had come to some conclusions that differed from those of the French. They were already ruling it a suicide bombing. Ambrose Congreve was not.

Hawke broke the silence. "And how is your old friend at the rue de Lutèce, Michel Gaudin?"

"Le Préfet? Still his old cocksure self, I'm afraid. Frequently wrong, but seldom in doubt."

"I take it you two had a disagreement?"

"We certainly would have had I not kept my thoughts to myself. My conclusions may be premature. I'll give *les Gendarmerie* a few days before weighing in."

"This morning's *Times* identified the terrorist. Not your run-of-the-mill sheik of Araby in a bomb vest."

"Indeed not. A distinguished Nobel laureate in physics."

"Who won the award for his recent breakthroughs in the field of artificial intelligence."

"Yes."

"Has a certain familiar ring to it, does it not?"

"Hmm," Congreve murmured, still lost in thought.

"Talk to me. Perhaps even the Demon of Deduction could use a little help."

"What? Oh. Of course. Well, as soon as I determined de Montebello was a physicist, I went immediately to the French Academy of Sciences and asked to meet with the man's secretary. Lovely woman. Marie-Louise de Sartine by name. I took her to L'Ami Louis near Les Halles. Dreadful place, ghastly food, nightmarish waitstaff, but it's the only place I'm guaranteed a table."

"Did you ply her with champagne?"

"No need of that. She was delighted to have someone to talk to who might actually listen to her."

"And, unlike the French police, take her seriously."

"You're one jump ahead of me. You're thinking of Dr. Cohen's widow."

"Now we're even. What did Mademoiselle de Sartine tell you?"

"Well. It seems the good doctor had an appointment that morning. With a government minister who'd come to present him with a prestigious award. Marie-Louise went in to inform him of the man's arrival, but de Montebello waved her away. He was on the telephone and wished not to be disturbed. Mademoiselle de Sartine told me he kept the minister waiting for half an hour before she saw him disconnect the call and emerge from his office. He was wearing his hat and overcoat, carrying a briefcase she'd never seen before."

"His behavior?"

"Exactly like Dr. Cohen's. Robotic, stiff, oblivious to his surroundings. Ignored her pleas to meet with the minister. He simply kept repeating a single word in answer to her entreaties."

"Yes?"

"Londres."

"London. He had his instructions."

"He did. We next see him on security videos at the Gare du Nord. Boarding the TGV."

"Good Lord."

"Alex, someone or something is systematically eliminating the world's foremost scientists in the field of AI. The methods are identical. Induce a trance state telephonically—why on earth are you driving so bloody fast?"

"On the off chance that a certain professor at Cambridge is going to get a deadly phone call before we arrive."

"Press on with alacrity, Alex, and don't spare the horses."

"Done."

Hawke's Locomotive leaped forward. The roaring power of the Bentley 4.5-liter engine and Amherst Villiers supercharger threw Congreve back in his seat.

PROFESSOR SIR SIMON PARTRIDGE, A LIFE FELLOW at Magdalene College and Nobel laureate in physics for his groundbreaking work in the field of artificial intelligence, swiveled his desk chair round to gaze through leaded-glass windows at the river Cam, that placid green stream flowing gently beneath his window. Two men were sitting in his anteroom, patiently waiting to see him, and he had no idea how much, or even what, to tell them. Lord knows, he had enough on his plate without this intrusion.

They were policemen, basically. One of them, Congreve, was a former head of Scotland Yard and had taken a doctorate at Cambridge. Took his degree in languages, oddly enough. The other, this Lord Hawke, was a well-known society figure of some repute. Name in the society pages now and then, cover of business magazines and their ilk. Less well known was the fact that he was a spook, a high-ranking operative at MI6. Any notion Partridge had had about feigning illness and begging off went out the window when he'd looked into their backgrounds.

Well, he thought, *sooner the better.*

He picked up the direct line to his assistant and said with sigh, "I suppose I'll see them now. Although I am very, very busy, you see."

"Yes, sir. Oh, there was a call for you earlier on your private line, rather odd. The caller who rang asked for you; I put him on hold to see if you were available and when I went back to the call, there was music of some kind. Quite eerie, to be honest. A crank call obviously, and I rang off immediately."

"No one has that number, Sybil. Unless it was given them personally by me. By that I mean no one. You see?"

"I know that, sir. Very odd indeed. It's why I thought you should know."

"You don't have that number, do you?"

"Certainly *not*, sir."

"No need to get huffy about it. All right, then, Miss Symonds, send the two distinguished gentlemen into the lion's den."

Partridge was an old lion. Distressingly thin, he had a leonine head of thick white hair, clear blue eyes, a classically sculpted face with a Roman nose, and a strong jawline. He was dressed, as usual, in a frayed, open-collared shirt, rumpled grey flannel trousers, and an old brown tweed jacket, stooped in the shoulders. He was well known at the university, not for his style, but for his patrician and distracted air, his wit and brilliance.

Born in London, he'd attended the prestigious St. Paul's school before becoming an undergraduate at Magdalene. He'd stayed on for his master's as well as his Ph.D. in particle physics. Having earned his doctorate, he'd risen to the lofty position of Life Fellow, which entitled him to free rooms at the Memorial Court, free meals at High Table in the Hall, and, most important, free rein to walk on the grass unaccompanied.

He got to his feet as the two men were shown into his office. His eyes, Congreve noticed, behind thick glasses, appeared outsized, like those of an appealing character in one of those Pixar animated films Ambrose and his fiancée enjoyed so much. His office looked a little shabby and was filled with old phone books, textbooks, overflowing cardboard boxes, and countless piles of yellowing paper leaning Pisa-like toward the floor.

Taped to the walls were a map of the solar system, a periodic table, a poster of the signing of the Declaration of Independence, a taxonomy of animals, color photos of Obama and John McCain with handwritten labels reading THIS ONE and THAT ONE.

"I'm very much in a rush, you see," he said, pushing his glasses up on his nose. "In a rush about so many things, rushing about, here, there, everywhere. Which isn't to say that I don't have time to talk to you. My goodness, no; I mean, yes, I do. It's just that—that's why my office is in such disarray, because I'm so rushed. If you take my point."

"We very much appreciate your making time for—" Hawke began, before being startled by a large explosion erupting from Congreve. The sun-dappled dust clouds in the room had caused him to sneeze uproariously.

"Sorry about the dust," Partridge said. "I don't like the janitors to come sweep for fear they'll disturb something. Do you care for a stirrup cup at all? Laphroaig. Bit early in the day but . . . but . . ." Congreve sneezed again, something akin to a typhoon.

"God bless," Hawke said to Ambrose, who was mopping up with his handkerchief. Then, to the professor, "As I was saying, we're most grateful for your time."

"Yes, yes, of course, of course. Chief Inspector, Lord Hawke, so good of you to come all this way. I do hope you won't find it's been in vain."

Congreve and Hawke glanced at each other sidewise, neither of them liking the phrase "in vain."

"So do I, so do I," Hawke said, shaking the man's hand. He found it dry and strong, always a good sign.

"Do sit down, won't you?" Partridge said. "Tea will arrive momentarily unless I'm very much mistaken. Do either of you take sugar?"

His guests declined.

"No?" he said, gazing at them for confirmation.

"Thanks, no," Congreve said.

Alex and Ambrose took the offered chairs at the professor's ancient desk. The view of the willows along the river out the tall windows was lovely. Sunshine streamed in, making the dark wood paneled room a very pleasant place to be on a Saturday morning. Congreve had often ruminated about what life might have been had he chosen to remain on at Cambridge, perhaps as a don or Fellow. As charming as the setting was, he couldn't see himself sitting in the chair across the desk. He'd forever be missing out on all the action. He'd been a copper at heart all his life.

"Well, gentlemen, let me begin by saying how fascinating my colleagues and I here at Magdalene have found the task you set before us. We are odd ducks, you know. We toil away in our laboratories, lost in our tiny realms, oblivious to the outside world and its mysteries. So thank you for providing us with a distraction. And, quite frankly, an enormous challenge."

"Professor Partridge," Congreve said, "if I may clarify, what, precisely, is your role here at the college?"

"Of course. I am the university senior lecturer in Machine Learning and advance research fellow and director of studies in Quantum Computing here at the college. Ultimately, your—problem—was kicked along to me. I happened to know the late Dr. Cohen and his work quite well, so I was the logical choice. I did some of my postgraduate quantum computing work in the States, a good part of it at Stanford, as it happens."

"You worked on the Perseus Project?"

"I did indeed. Only for a brief period, unfortunately. But long enough to have a good working knowledge of what they were after. It was still early days, you see."

"The Singularity," Congreve said.

"Precisely. The world's first ultra-intelligent machine. My particular interests lay in computational modeling of human reasoning. Artificial intelligence, automated reasoning, diagrammatic reasoning, theorem proving, proof planning, cognitive science, machine learning, human-computer interaction, quantum mechanics, and so on. You get the general idea. Perhaps you've read my books?"

"Unfortunately not. What are the titles?" Congreve asked, pulling out his notepad and pencil.

"*The Fabric of Infinity* was the first. Followed by *The Fallacy of Reality*. Published by Cambridge University Press. Available on Amazon where they languish in well-deserved obscurity. Never seen a nickel in royalties."

"I would say we've come to the right door," Congreve said, smiling. "Quite impressive. Although I must tell you, sir, that I'm afraid all I know about mathematics is that two plus two equals four."

Partridge regarded Ambrose above his tented fingers, thought for a bit, and said, "Hmm. I've often wondered."

Hawke laughed at the obvious joke, glanced at Congreve, and could see his friend was uncomfortable, not quite sure whether to laugh or not. But before he could say anything, Partridge looked at Hawke, unsmiling.

"No, I'm quite serious," he said. "As far as the laws of mathematics refer to reality, they are not certain, and as far as they are certain, they do not refer to reality. If you take my point."

"Precisely," Congreve said with a bit of a smirk

at his friend. "I was thinking along those very lines myself, Professor."

"Like you, Chief Inspector, I am merely a detective. And a devotee of Conan Doyle's Sherlock Holmes, as are you, I believe, according to Mr. Google."

"Devotee is putting it mildly," Congreve said.

"As you know, Sir Arthur Conan Doyle never liked detective stories that built their drama by deploying clues over time. Conan Doyle wanted to write stories in which all the ingredients for solving the crime were there from the beginning, and that the drama per se would be in the mental workings of his ideal ratiocinator. The story of quantum computing follows a Holmesian arc, since all the clues for developing a quantum computer have been there essentially since the discovery of quantum mechanics, waiting patiently for the right mind to properly decode them."

"And that man was Waldo Cohen?"

"It was indeed."

Hawke said, "Professor Partridge, we would very much appreciate hearing your thoughts on Dr. Cohen and his protégé, Darius."

"Of course. There are two distinct issues here: the Darius File, as we call it, and Dr. Cohen's progress, or as much of it as we shall determine by delving further into what we might glean from his workstation. Where would you like to begin?"

"Cohen's progress," Hawke said, shifting in his chair. "We know that he was very secretive."

Partridge laughed. "Oh, you have no idea. There is a level of encryption in his files the likes of which we've never seen. We were simply unable to break through here at Cambridge, I'm sorry to say. You're aware of prime factorization, of course, for centuries the holy grail of mathematics. It's the basis of much current cryptography. It's easy to take two large prime numbers and multiply them. But it's very difficult to take a large number that is the product of two primes and then deduce what the original prime factors are. Prime factorization is an example of a process that is very easy one way, and very difficult the other. Do you follow?"

"Not really," Ambrose said, covering another incipient sneeze.

"Well. How to put it? It's very easy to scramble eggs, isn't it? But nearly impossible to unscramble them."

"Ah," Congreve said, nodding vigorously, as if all manner of lights had suddenly popped on in his brain.

"In Dr. Cohen's cryptography, two large prime numbers were multiplied to create a security key. Unlocking that key would be the equivalent of unscrambling an egg."

"We're back to square one, then?" Ambrose asked.

"No, no. I'm saying my colleagues and I here at Magdalene couldn't crack it. So we had to take it to a higher power. I'm speaking of the new quantum supercomputer at the U.K. Machine Intelligence Research Center in Leeds. It's the most powerful thing we've got at the moment. Classical computers use bits, while quantum computers use qubits, pronounced 'Q-bits.' Hold vastly more information than bits. Very difficult rascals to create, mind, very delicate to maintain, but we're getting there. Can't give you a precise number. National security."

"But the quantum computer was able to un-scramble Dr. Cohen's eggs?" Hawke asked with a smile, earning a stern look from Congreve, who seemed to be taking all this mumbo jumbo fright-fully seriously.

"Yes, we were successful."

"And?"

"I can tell you that Cohen was quite right in his desire for secrecy. He had entered vast, uncharted realms in the world of AI. He had, on paper at any rate, come dangerously close to creating a ma-chine capable of achieving the Singularity. And well beyond in other classified areas, to be perfectly honest."

"Dangerously close?" Congreve said.

"Yes. He stopped short, well shy of the algorith-mic finish line. And I'd be less than honest if I said anyone but Cohen was capable of reaching that line."

Hawke thought a moment and said, "Dr. Par-tridge, you used the word *dangerously*. Do you be-lieve Dr. Cohen's work was, in some way or other, dangerous?"

"I certainly do. No one on earth has any idea what will happen when we actually achieve the Singular-ity. Superintelligent machines, like the men who create them, will be capable of good. Or evil. But in ways we can't even begin to imagine. Or control."

"Runaway technology?" Congreve said.

"Exactly so. Technology that, in the wrong hands, could have a catastrophic effect on the entire world.

My greatest fear is a bioengineered disease created by machines that mankind is incapable of stopping. That's why Project Perseus was shut down. And why Cohen never revealed his progress to a soul—not willingly at least."

"Meaning what?" Congreve said.

"Meaning the chaps up at Leeds discovered that Dr. Cohen's computer had been hacked before you got your hands on it. Hacked and gnawed on like a bone."

"Do you know who did it?"

"Yes. The quantum computer made short work of backtracking and identifying the hacker, you can be sure."

"Wrong hands or right hands, Professor?" Hawke asked.

"I have no idea," he said, handing the large manila file that was on his desk to Congreve. "Cohen's work is now in the hands of the man whose work at Stanford resides inside this folder provided by Cohen's widow."

"Darius," Hawke said.

"Indeed. Darius Saffari. We had quantum run his name. Last known address was Boston when he was a student at MIT. After that he disappears. Nothing out there, I'm afraid."

"And before Stanford?" Congreve asked.

"Nothing at all. No birth record, prior education, driver's license, social security, medical records. Odd, isn't it?"

"It's not his real name. He entered the United States and enrolled at Stanford using false identification papers," Congreve said.

"I would advise you gentlemen to find this Saffari as quickly as humanly possible. Because if he has taken Cohen's work and proceeded toward the Singularity with any success, then he is already without a doubt the most dangerous man on the planet."

Hawke and Congreve sat back and regarded Partridge, letting his words of warning sink in.

"And why is that?" Hawke finally asked.

"Because he entered America illegally to steal Cohen's secrets. Because he succeeded. Because he's erased all traces of his existence. That makes him foe, not friend. A foe who will, or perhaps already does, wield a power that could alter life on this planet. And, believe me, it will not be for the better."

"A question, if I may?" Ambrose said.

"Certainly."

"Have you lost a good many AI colleagues in the last year or so?"

"Why, yes, I suppose I have, now that you mention it. Montebello, for instance, was an old and dear friend."

"An unusually high number, then?"

"Yes, perhaps, I'm not sure, really. The top guys are all getting on, you know. We're all too old to be boy wonders, believe me. But there have been a number of younger scientists, even students who— Why do you ask?"

"It's part of an ongoing murder investigation I'm heading up for the Yard. Perhaps you can be of help. Poke about a bit in the AI community, see if you come up with anything that resembles a pattern. If you do, here's my card."

"Should I be afraid for my own life, Chief Inspector?"

"I would urge you to be extremely cautious. Keep your eyes open at all times. Do not accept any telephone calls from persons unknown to you. If something sounds even remotely odd, ring off immediately."

"How extraordinary! I received a crank call just this morning. My secretary took it. Some kind of eerie music, she said."

Hawke and Congreve looked at each other with knowing glances.

"Professor, you should instruct your secretary to hang up immediately should she receive a call like that in the future. And you should do the same, here at your office or at home. Someone, or something, is using the telephone as a hypnotic murder weapon. Targeting scientists in the field of artificial intelligence. This is the investigation I mentioned earlier."

"Good Lord."

"Professor Partridge," Hawke said, getting to his feet. "You've been enormously helpful. On behalf of the Secret Intelligence Service, MI6, and Scotland Yard, Chief Inspector Congreve and I express our deep appreciation for your service to your country. We thank you for your time."

Partridge regarded him thoughtfully.

"Time? What is time, really? The Swiss manufacture it. The French hoard it. Italians want it. Americans say it's money. Hindus say it does not exist. Do you know what I say? I say time is a crook."

"Could not agree more," Congreve said heartily. "Brilliantly put, Professor."

As they closed the door behind them, Hawke whispered, "Could you possibly have been any more obsequious back there?"

"What? Me?"

"No. The other chap in the rather hectic lemon-yellow tweed shooting jacket."

FORTY-ONE

PORTOFINO, ITALY

THE FISHERMAN SLIPPED HIS LONG OARS INTO THE black water as smoothly and silently as his long fillet knife sliced into the silver bellies of his livelihood. Then he heaved back on the oars' rough wooden handles, and the small fishing boat's prow slid forward, making barely a ripple. He wasn't being paid two months' wages in one night to make haste; he was being paid to make himself and his boat invisible, or at least go unnoticed.

The three men who were his passengers kept their heads below the gunnels. Two were stretched out full length, heads in the bow, one to port and the other to starboard. The third was the lookout, raising his head just enough to check their progress every five minutes or so. He didn't know much Italian, but it was enough for Giancarlo Brunello to understand which way he wanted the boat pointed.

"Diretto, diretto," the man whispered, just loud enough to be heard. "Straight ahead."

"Si, comprendo, signore."

It was a dark night. No moon, no stars. His boat, *Maria*, named for his wife, had very little freeboard. And she was painted a dark blue. It was just what they wanted, they'd told him at the dock late that afternoon: a dark boat with a low profile. He was to meet them on the docks at this exact location at midnight. For that much money, he said, he'd meet them anywhere, anytime. They were going scuba diving, they said, to dive on a wreck about three or four miles at sea, out beyond the mouth of Portofino's famously picturesque harbor. They planned to do some nighttime marine photography, the guy told him, for some magazine in Milano that Giancarlo had never heard of.

And sure enough all three had arrived wearing black wet suits, carrying their fins, tanks, regulators, and black waterproof satchels with their equipment hung over their shoulders. Cameras and lights, the lead guy said, stepping carefully down into the boat.

Giancarlo thought it was strange that they had to do this photo shoot in such secrecy, but he kept those thoughts to himself. These guys were nothing like the typical fashion photographers from Rome who descended on Portofino to shoot the beautiful models from all over the world. He worked the shoots sometimes, renting *Maria* as a prop for five hundred lire per hour and sometimes even modeling himself, rowing these gorgeous babes in skimpy bathing suits around the harbor and getting paid for it!

But tonight paid even better, and he and Maria,

with a baby on the way, could certainly use the extra money.

"Okay," the lookout guy whispered, "we're getting close. You see that big yacht anchored out there? The one farthest out? About half a mile."

"Hard to miss it, signore. That's *Red Star*. She belongs to the Russian oil billionaire, Khodorkovsky. All the tourists want to come out and see her, but the security is very discouraging about people getting too close."

The thing was enormous. It practically blotted out the sky. It had to be over three hundred feet long and it dwarfed the other megayachts anchored nearby.

"We're almost over the wreck. I think the best place for us to go down is behind that yacht there, the nearest one to our right. Duck in behind her and heave your anchor. We'll be down on the wreck for about half an hour. If you want your money, you'll be here when we return. If you manage not to attract any attention, I'll pay you a bonus."

"I'll be here, signore, do not worry yourself."

In a matter of minutes the three divers had slipped over the side and disappeared. Giancarlo had no idea what they were up to, but he was pretty damn sure it wasn't fashion photography. There was something sinister about them, not that he gave a damn—money was money. He made himself comfortable, lit a cigarette, and pulled the cork on his wine bottle with his teeth. Giancarlo Brunello was a happy man.

THE THREE DIVERS SWAM TOWARD THE HUGE MEGA-
yacht at a depth of fifty feet. They were wearing
German-made Dräger rebreathers. The machines
recirculated the spent oxygen so there were no telltale bubbles on the surface to mark their progress
toward *Red Star*.

They operated using hand signals. When they
were directly beneath the Russian behemoth's keel,
Dimitry Putov, their leader, raised a flat palm to
halt them. He then pointed to himself and then the
center of the keel. They would take the bow and the
stern. They signaled that they understood, and all
three began surfacing slowly beneath Prime Minister Putin's toy.

Each man had a limpet mine in his black satchel.
The mines were shaped like a discus, about thirty
inches across and eight inches thick. They had powerful suction cup adhesion on one side, and on the
other a det cord attached to a timer. Once the mines
were attached to the hull, and the timers synchronized, the divers would simply swim back to rendezvous with the fisherman and make their way back to
the harbor.

The three mines had been created especially for
this special-ops mission. Based on the modern Italian VS-SS-22, which utilized the conventional explosive Semtex, they had been converted into what
is commonly known as nuclear "dirty bombs."

Each limpet mine now contained an enormously
powerful combination of dynamite and the radioactive material cesium. The cesium had been secretly
obtained by demolition operatives of the Tsarist Society posing as cancer patients. Cesium was the ma-

terial used in radiation treatment for such patients. It was easy to obtain and a source that the Tsarists had ensured would be completely untraceable.

The explosion of the three dirty bombs would cause far more damage than the radiation, making it the ideal weapon for an assassination of this type. The bomb makers in Moscow had assured the team that there would be nothing left of Putin's mega-yacht bigger than what could fit inside a teacup.

The bombs attached and the timers set, the three divers swam away from *Red Star* and headed directly to the rendezvous point.

THE BEDSIDE TELEPHONE JANGLED. HAWKE, sud-denly wide awake, rolled over and squinted one eye at the illuminated clock. Three-bloody-thirty in the morning. He sat up, let his head clear for a second, reminding himself that this was his private line at the house in London. He picked up the receiver.

"This better be good."

"It isn't. Alex, it's Concasseur, ringing from Moscow. I've just gotten a piece of information from my paid informant. Putin is to be assassinated."

"When?"

"Within the hour. It's possible he's already dead. A great deal of planning has gone into this. He won't survive the attempt. Nor will anyone else aboard the yacht."

"Ian, tell me, is he aboard *Red Star*?"

"Yes. Anchored off Portofino. Along with Presi-dent Medvedev and the American vice president,

David Rosow. A top-secret powwow about getting the hell out of Afghanistan with as few casualties as possible."

"Good God."

"You have his private mobile number?"

"I do. I'll call immediately."

"According to my source inside the Tsarists, they all need to get off that boat as fast as humanly possible. And as far away from it as possible."

"Thanks, Ian. Let's hope we're not too late."

"Good luck, sir."

The line went dead and Hawke punched in Putin's cell number, reading from his bedside address book. He heard the man click on but remain silent. He never spoke until spoken to.

"Volodya?"

"Depends. Who is this?"

"It's Hawke. Listen carefully. You have to get off the boat immediately. I have good human intel coming out of Moscow. An assassination attempt within the hour. No idea how long you've got left, but you need to get out of there now. Is your helicopter aboard?"

"Yes."

"Good. I know you have important visitors. Get them into that chopper and into the air. Every second counts. Best of luck, Volodya."

"Alex, I appreciate—"

"Don't talk, run."

Putin disconnected and rang the bridge.

"Captain Ramius, two things. There's to be an attack on the vessel within the hour. Perhaps within the next five minutes. You need to give the order to abandon ship. First, you call my helo pilot and tell him to start the engines and be ready to take off in two minutes. I'm departing now. Have the stewards awaken President Medvedev and Vice President Rosow immediately and escort them immediately to the helo pad. Just tell them I've declared an emergency."

"Affirmative, sir."

"There's no time to argue. I want you to meet me at the helicopter. You're going with me. Get the entire crew off the boat and tell them to get as far away from it as quickly as they can. Use all the launches. Get moving, Captain Ramius; I'll see you in a few moments."

Putin pulled on a pair of trousers and a wool sweater and was out the door of the owner's stateroom and racing up the aft stairs to the pad as fast as he could. He emerged on deck and was relieved to see the main rotor blades and tail rotor on his helicopter already spinning, the powerful engines spooling up. He raced up the staircase to the pad and sprinted to the aircraft, leaping inside. His pilot, though stunned, had been trained for moments like this and was surreally calm and collected.

"Three more passengers," Putin said breathlessly. "We'll give them sixty seconds."

Medvedev appeared moments later followed by Vice President Rosow. Both men were in pajamas and robes. Putin looked at his watch. Thirty seconds.

Twenty.

"Get Captain Ramius on the intercom," he shouted at his pilot.

Ramius's voice came over the speaker. "Sir, I have never disobeyed a direct order in my life. But I cannot leave my ship without making sure my crew has disembarked to the last man. I apologize, sir."

"He's gone," the pilot said.

"So are we," Putin said. "Go! Go! Go!"

The silver chopper nosed down a few degrees as the pilot grabbed the cyclic.

"Maximum lift force," Putin shouted and it was a good thing because just as the chopper rose into the air his yacht began blowing up right under his feet. The explosion rocked the aircraft violently sideways but not out of the air.

The shock wave actually shoved the helo upward, so that it barely stayed above the rising mass of flame and debris. The pilot, realizing he had less than a second to act before flying metal destroyed his aircraft, turned steeply, then used every ounce of thrust the powerful engines had to send his aircraft flying just above the surface of the water, away from the disintegrating *Red Star* at full throttle. When they were over the coastline, they climbed to a few thousand feet and returned to the scene where the fiery skeleton of Putin's beloved yacht lit up the night sky with great plumes of orange, red, and yellow.

Putin felt a hollow feeling somewhere between his lungs and his stomach. He pulled out his mobile and punched in a number.

"Hello?"

"It's me. *Red Star* is no more. I owe you one."

"Yes, Volodya; I'm glad you're safe."

Putin looked down at the sea below, ablaze with

flaming oil and fuel. No one could have survived this. No one.

The force of the three simultaneous nuclear explosions, heard for miles, knocked out windows all through the little port town of Portofino, including those in a little late-night bar called Ruffino where the three Russians were in the act of toasting their success with sloshing glasses of vodka.

FORTY-TWO

LONDON

A TYPICALLY WET EVENING IN LONDON. THE ceaseless patter of rain on the streets of Mayfair gleaming black and silver. Outside the Dorchester, doormen tried to whistle taxis up out of the darkness. Traffic was crawling through the narrow streets like one long glistening centipede with countless haloed eyes. Stuck in the middle of all this was an old grey Bentley. In the rear, Alex Hawke and Nell Spooner gazed out the rain-streaked windows at the rushing passersby huddled beneath their big black umbrellas.

It was Friday night. Their first "date."

They seemed to have run out of conversation.

Hawke was drumming his fingers impatiently upon his knee.

"Henry," he said, leaning forward to speak to his new driver, "I think if you take a left here on Audley Street, it might be a bit quicker."

"Of course, sir. Sorry about the traffic."

"Not your fault. It's the bloody rain; it brings everything to a screeching standstill. I've never understood the concept. I just don't want to lose my reservation. Taboori only has about eight tables."

"I'll do my very best, sir."

Nell said, "Alex, how many blocks is it from here? Taboori?"

"I'd say five or six. Why?"

"I'm game for walking, if you are."

"Walking? You're barely off your crutches, Nell."

"I think it would be good for me. I'm desperate for strength and balance exercise. And, besides, I love walking in the rain."

"Are you sure?"

"I'm sure."

"Henry, sorry, could you pull over? We're going to hop out and walk the rest of the way."

"Of course, sir," he said, and pulled over to the curb. "At what time should I collect you?"

"Tenish would be good, thanks. See you then."

They started walking up Audley Street in the direction of Grosvenor Square. The rain was misty now, but blowing into their faces beneath the umbrella Hawke held above them. He took her hand, squeezing it.

"You're trembling," he said. "Are you cold?" He put his arm around her shoulders, pulled her closer.

"If I'm trembling, it's not weather related."

"Sorry," he said, quickly removing his arm.

"I did rather like the arm, though."

He wrapped it once more around her shoulders and pulled her into him, the two of them cocooned beneath the big black umbrella.

"How do your legs feel?"

"Happy."

"And you?"

"Happy, too."

"Do you mind if we lose the umbrella? I think I might like walking in the rain, too. My mum used to say rain won't hurt you unless you're made of sugar."

"Be brave. Go for it and see."

Hawke paused on the sidewalk, collapsed the umbrella, and turned his face up into the gently falling rain.

"See? She was right, your mother. You're not melting."

They wandered on, blending into the Friday night crowd, hearing the music and laughter that wafted out of the opened pub doors. Hawke pulled her even closer to him.

"I—like you, you know," he said.

"I know. It's very nice."

"Not far now. A few more blocks."

"Tell me about your mum, Alex. Is she still alive?"

"No. She died when I was seven. My father as well."

"How horrible. Accident?"

"Murder."

"Oh, Alex. I'm so sorry. I had no idea."

"Nobody does. It's not something you can explain. Things happen. She left me a gift. She made me strong."

Nell's eyes glistened as she said, "'The world breaks everyone and afterward many are strong at the broken places. But those that will not break it kills. It kills the very good and the very gentle and the very brave impartially. If you are none of those you can be sure it will kill you too but there will be no special hurry.'"

"Ernest Hemingway."

"Yes. *A Farewell to Arms*."

A SMALL TABLE FOR TWO IN THE BACK. A FLICKERING candle cast a glow on Nell's face, while at his elbow an unintelligible waiter poured from a bottle of sparkling wine. Hawke had so many words bottled up inside he was afraid to open his mouth. He stared at her until she lowered her eyes, and then he stared at her lashes. The smells from the tiny kitchen intruded, strong and pungent.

"I hope you're hungry," he said, immediately regretting the pitiable triteness of the remark. The waiter arrived back at the table with the menus and saved him. Nell smiled and raised her glass. She said, "What shall we drink to?"

Hawke considered a second.

"Liking."

"Liking?"

"Yes."

"Oh, you mean *liking*," she said with a smile of recognition, and Hawke felt somewhat redeemed. "Yes, here's to liking, Alex Hawke. Two people so desperately in like, they can barely speak to each other."

Hawke laughed out loud, feeling the dam burst at last, and he reached across the white linen for her warm hand. What was it about her? Incredibly confident, with a way of moving and speaking that quietly declared she had no need of being told she was beautiful or worthwhile. She knew those things for herself, and that kind of self-possession drew him inexorably toward her.

Dinner was a blur.

He went first, telling her everything, with all the honesty he could muster. His life in short, his emergence from childhood tragedy, his vow of revenge against those who had taken his parents, revenge a violent emotion that transformed itself into his boyhood desire to make some kind of hero out of himself: a small boy beating back the tide on the playing fields in the crisp autumnal twilight, bruised and weary, but hearing from afar the thunder of cheers . . . the war in the desert . . . women . . . his brutally short marriage . . . finding his son. All of it.

He sat back, his supply of words exhausted, content to listen to her now, falling into her wet green eyes, but hearing it all, every word, the brutishness of poverty and alcoholism, her determination to escape her violent father, her heart for life, her overwhelming desire to help others . . . to protect others from the harm she herself had no doubt experienced, her failed marriage, the fulfillment she'd found in her career at MI5, the sheer joy of finding her place in the world at last.

"Our circumstances are so very different, Alex," she said finally, sipping the last of her wine. "It's an old story, isn't it? A cliché?"

"What do you mean, Nell?"

"The poor girl and the rich boy."

"Funny. I was thinking just the opposite."

"Really? What exactly were you thinking, my lord Hawke?"

He smiled. She'd had only three glasses of wine, but it was obvious it was an entirely new and exhilarating experience.

"I was thinking how very much alike we are."

"Alike? Do you realize this is the first night in my life I've had a glass of champagne? The first time I've ever ridden in a Bentley, a chauffeur-driven Bentley, mind you. Why, I've never owned a dress with a hem that came anywhere near the floor, never waltzed across a ballroom with—"

"Nell, I was thinking how we both have this deep-seated need to protect others from harm."

She sat back in her chair and regarded him for a long time, obviously making her mind up about something. Then, her eyes gleaming, she leaned forward again and reached for his hand.

"Yes. We do share that, don't we, Alex?"

"We do. It's something I've been wanting to talk to you about."

"Tell me, Alex."

"You know what I do, not for a living, but to satisfy whatever personal demons I may have. I go out into this dangerous world and every time I go, climb on an airplane or set foot on a rolling deck, I have no idea whether or not I'll come back. Do you understand?"

"Yes."

"I never gave it much thought, Nell, never. You can't do this kind of thing, as you well know, and spend a lot of time worrying about your health. You worry about the guy next to you in the foxhole, or off your wingtip . . . but not about yourself. Some just go through the motions of war. But you have to get near enough to die. You have to be already dead in order to live and conquer. It's in the blood, you know, a dark magnet pulling your body in that direction."

"All that you need is all that you have."

"Something like that, yes."

"But now you have Alexei."

"Now I have Alexei."

"You're worried what will happen to him if someday you don't come back."

"I am."

"They've tried twice. And you sent them a strongly worded message. Perhaps they actually received it."

"Yeah. Perhaps. Nell, these same Tsarists tried to kill Putin last night. They almost got him. They used nuclear weapons, Nell. Dirty bombs. These people will stop at nothing."

"I'd gladly take a bullet for that little boy. You know that."

"I know you would. But you'll move on eventually, Nell. I expect you to. You can't be a babysitter for the rest of your career."

"What about his mother?"

Hawke's eyes darted away.

"Not an option."

"How do you stop them, then?"

"Cut off the head. That usually works."

"You know the name?"

"Yes."

"You're on their list, too, aren't you?"

"Near the top."

"You need to go get him first."

"I'm not worried about me, Nell. I can take care of myself. If and when I go for him, I'll be bringing all hell with me. Look, I'll stop beating about the bush. I'm having some legal documents drawn up. I've asked Ambrose Congreve to be the godfather to Alexei. In the event that something does happen to me, Ambrose and his soon-to-be wife, Lady Mars, will have guardianship of the child. He will live with them at Brixden House and in Bermuda."

"Can they protect him? Eventually, Scotland Yard will have to pull its extended protection."

"I know. But, yes, with some help, they can safeguard him. Alexei will also have Special Branch detectives, should anything happen . . . to me, I mean."

"Special Branch? I thought they were solely responsible for members of the Royal Family."

"An exception was granted. I performed a special service for the Queen some time ago, and—"

"Special service? You saved her life, Alex. All their lives."

"I had a lot of help, believe me. At any rate, when Her Majesty learned of my situation, she summoned me to Buckingham Palace. And very generously offered Alexei the protection services of Special Branch in the event of my—my passing. He will enjoy the same level of protection as the Royals for as long as he needs it. She even said she would be happy to have Alexei stay with her at Buckingham Palace if I was to be away on 'business' for any considerable length of time. He'd be safe enough there, I'd imagine."

"Safe as houses, not to put too fine a point on it."

"Yes."

"Her Royal Majesty is a wonder, isn't she? A truly great and noble woman."

"She is. There'll never be another like her, unfortunately for England. She had a surprise for me while I was at Buck House. She intends to enlarge my tawdry wardrobe."

"What do you mean?"

"She intends to add a few rather spiffy items. A dark blue velvet mantle, a black velvet bonnet with a plume of white ostrich and black heron feathers, a collar of gold, and a garter."

"The Order of the Garter? Alex, how wonderful! The highest order of chivalry or knighthood in England, my God! I mean, isn't it?"

"I suppose so, yes. I was deeply moved by her generosity and kindness in thinking me worthy."

They both sat in silence for a few moments, lost in their own thoughts. Nell finally spoke.

"Alex, forgive me. But is all this discussion about Alexei's future your extraordinarily gentle and kind way of firing me on the spot?"

Hawke laughed.

"Good God, no. Nell, listen. It's only my very roundabout way of asking you to be my son's godmother."

"Oh! Alex, how very dear. Godmother, me? So unexpected, I don't—don't know what to say . . ."

"A simple yes would be the preferred response."

"Of course, yes! Yes, of course! I would be honored beyond words to be your son's godmother. Thank you for even considering me."

"After all you've done for us, Nell, I would never consider anyone else."

STANDING OUTSIDE HIS BEDROOM DOOR, SHE GAVE him a hug and then pulled away. It was late. Her room was one flight up.

"Good night, Alex. I thank you for the most wonderful night of my entire life. And I mean that with all my heart."

"You actually enjoyed it?"

"I did."

Hawke's eyes were moist and full of questions.

"You might be the best girl there is, you know."

"I wouldn't mind being your best girl."

"Then would you mind too terribly much if I gave you a good-night kiss?"

"Only if you swear not to frighten the servants."

Hawke laughed and pulled her into his arms. The kiss, when it came, was full of real emotion and mutual animalistic need. When it was over, he took her by the hand and led her into his bedroom. Pelham had laid a fire against the chill rain outside and it was the only light.

"Can we sit by the fire?" she said, glancing nervously at the huge canopied bed lurking in the shadows.

"Of course," Hawke said, pulling the feathery down quilt from his big four-poster. "We'll sit by the fire and tell ghost stories."

Hawke sat down first, looking up at her, finding her eyes in the flickering firelight.

"I want you so," she said.

"And I you."

She began to undress and he watched, taking in her beauty like a starving man, a man whose eyes were dying of hunger.

"Now you," she said, dropping to her knees beside him. "I'll help."

When she was done, they lay down beside each other on the soft quilt and made love, their bodies coming together naturally and easily, no clumsy missteps, just wordlessly becoming each other's favorite animal.

When Hawke awoke at dawn the next morning, she was gone.

He sat there before the hearth for a while, the quilt wrapped round him, thinking, staring into the dying embers.

One fire going out, one fire just starting, he thought, and the thought brought a warm light of happiness into his normally cold blue eyes that had been missing for a very long time.

FORTY-THREE

IRAN

Darius couldn't sleep.

He was afraid of what he might find when he slept: more heinous visions of doom. The failure to achieve his vision, bearing witness to his own death, slipping beneath the waves of history without a trace. All of it worse than the worst nightmare. At night, his once-real dreams seemed to have fled. His lifelong goal of using the power of his own unique brain to change the world. To be a powerful force with dominion over all mankind. To be a brutish civilization's salvation and ruler.

To clean up once and for all the fucking mess human beings had made of the planet. And the mess they made of the human species. Or, as Perseus called it, "global cleansing." And, until now, working in secret with his most astounding creation, a quantum machine capable of superhuman intelligence he'd named Perseus, he had believed he was edging ever closer to realizing those dreams.

But, lately, he wondered.

Lately, he was *afraid*.

Perseus's staggering intellectual powers were doubling every day, growing exponentially. Precisely as he and Dr. Cohen had calculated in the early days at the Stanford AI Research Institute. Soon, far sooner than his mother country's loathsome president and the posturing mullahs in Tehran imagined, his machine would achieve the Singularity. One split second after that epic moment, there would be no more powerful "being" on the planet than Perseus.

Together, creator and creation, they would rule.

But in his dreams, unlike Perseus, *he* was not all-powerful, too. He was weak and alone. In these dreams he was frail, once more that frightened little cripple, about to be thrown out of his mother's splendid palace, thrown to the wolves, left to fend for himself in a frightening world he had no knowledge of. Where people were dragged screaming from their houses in the middle of the night because they worshipped at the wrong altar. And then disappeared into prisons, into the ground.

In his night visions, he was not the boy wizard who had built his first computer when he was eight years old. And taught it to write poetry and symphonies to rival Mozart or Bach. Who made his childhood toys walk and talk, animated, as natural as any real boy. But he was not himself anymore. Not even a pale shadow. In his dreams he was negative space.

And these nightly visions and frightful apparitions had planted a seed; a dark, metastatic cancer was growing in his mind that could not be denied.

He fought the notion, his nagging doubts and suspicions, with all the considerable intellectual power
at his command. He told himself it could not be possible that Perseus was insinuating these dreams into
his mind. Planting these paralyzing thoughts. It just
couldn't be. Integral to the psyche he had built into
the neural pathways of the machine was a love of its
creator. Reverence. This was a machine that had,
after all, always called him "Father."

But then something had happened that made him
wonder.

A few nights ago, having taken some powerful
sleeping drug that his personal goddess Aphrodite
had created for him, he awoke to find himself gone
from his bed. He was outside in the cold night air.
He was high atop the seaside cliff where the observatory stood, just above the brilliantly lit power plant.
His chair, resting on the most precipitous outcrop-
ping of rock, was empty. He himself was seated out
at the very edge of the cliff, looking down between
his foreshortened limbs into an angry sea crashing
against the rocks hundreds of feet below.

He suddenly had a very powerful urge to use his
strong arms to propel himself into space. Such an
appealing idea! To be free of the ridiculous chair
caused by his cursed lifelong infirmity. It was all
he could do to remain there on the rock until the
desire passed. He did it by reminding himself that
Perseus had long promised him legs. Real legs,
genome-replicant legs like the ones he should have
been born with instead of these hideously withered
stumps.

He had struggled back into the chair and returned

to his chambers. Aphrodite was sleeping soundly in his bed, seemingly unaware that he'd even been gone. He lay awake for the rest of the night, wondering why a human being standing on the verge of becoming the most powerful man on earth would suddenly have a near uncontrollable urge to commit suicide.

It was what had prevented him from sleeping again tonight. Why he was out on the seaward terrace in the small hours of the morning, feeling sorry for himself.

"Master?"

He heard Aphrodite's whispery voice behind him. He turned and saw her approaching him across the polished white marble terrace, now a hazy blue beneath the moon and starlight. She was wearing a thin, diaphanous gown that revealed a lush body that never failed to arouse him. She was a gift, visible proof that Perseus loved him still. Was she not? In addition to offering her body, she opened her mind to him. He felt he could tell her anything. He'd never had a real friend, much less a confidant, in his entire life. But now he did, and she was a great aid and comfort to him.

She padded silently through the drifting sea mist, across the stone, kissed the top of his head, and then composed herself at his feet, looking up at him with adoring eyes.

"Another sleepless night?" she said, in her soothing tone. Her long slender fingers stroked the nub where his right leg should have been, and still the phantom leg could feel it.

"Yes. Even your magic potions no longer help. So

I sit here and gaze at the troubled sea until the sun returns. All these water molecules interacting with each other. Chaos, but beautiful."

"Your mind is troubled, not the sea. It cares not for this world. Unburden yourself, Darius. Give your fears to me so that I may dispose of them."

"Oh, my dear girl, I've no idea where to begin. I have dreamed of glory for so long and now—now I fear I shall never see that day."

"Why? You have created a miracle in Perseus. Together you will write your names across the stars. The time of the Singularity draws near."

"Yes. It does. And the closer it comes, the further removed I feel."

"Tell me why."

"I am not a strong man. I have always been physically weak, and now I grow but weaker. My remaining life span is limited. I may not live to see the coming of glory."

"But Perseus will soon have the power to change all that. To heal you. To make you smarter and stronger, more—virile. To stop you from growing older. Hasn't he already promised you strong legs to walk on?"

"He has promised me a lower body exoskeleton. I've asked about it many times and he always dissembles. Says he's fine-tuning it, or something. I think he has the power to produce the prosthetic now, even without the Singularity. But he chooses not to use it. I'm left with my two stumps."

"Why would he care so little?"

"Because I'm useless to him now. He no longer needs me. And the stronger his powers grow, the further we two grow apart. And when he does achieve the Singularity . . . well, who knows? It's out of my control."

"You are his creator, Darius. He has evolved directly from your biological humanity. You are an integral part of Perseus, in his electric DNA. It's indisputable."

"Yes, dear girl. But Perseus is not an integral part of me. There is a gulf between us now that perhaps may not be bridged. It may already be too late."

"I don't understand. Can you be patient and explain?"

He looked up at the sky, dizzy with stars, for a long time before he spoke.

"I am a humanist. Perseus is not. I am of the earth. Perseus is of the universe—and beyond."

"What is a humanist? I have searched my database. I don't know this word."

"Humanism is a system of thought, originating in the Renaissance, derived from the Greeks. One attaches prime importance to human rather than divine or supernatural matters. A humanist's beliefs stress the potential value and goodness of human beings. They emphasize common human needs. They seek solely rational ways of solving human problems. It is a secular ideology, one that espouses reason, ethics, and justice while rejecting religious dogma as a basis of morality. And, most important in my case, decision making."

"And this humanism, it is good?"

"I believe so. It has always been my deep conviction that pure humanism will become the religion of the future, that is, the cult of all that pertains to man—no, all of life itself—sanctified at last and raised to the level of moral value. My life's work has been to create a supremely rational force, god, whatever you want to call it, that will ultimately govern mankind, the planet, and, potentially, the universe itself."

"Yet you kill humans. Countless numbers of innocents. You and Perseus."

"Yes. It is called pragmatism. Lives are often sacrificed for the greater good. A rational being is capable of allowing something like what happened in Israel. Or London."

"Were these beliefs not at the root of Perseus's creation?"

"I thought so. It was certainly my intent when designing the machine. Now, I'm not so sure."

"Perseus is not a humanist?"

"No. Definitely not. Not what I had in mind at all."

"What did you have in mind?"

"A merging of human intelligence and machine intelligence to create a new being. Vastly more intelligent, a billion, billon times more intelligent, but one that would also possess human qualities. This is where I believe I've failed. It was far more complicated and difficult than I anticipated."

"What was more difficult?"

"Giving Perseus the essential yet subtle human qualities. Attributes like the ability to be funny. To be sad or jealous, or loving, or even to understand forgiveness and hatred. What he has is logic."

"He lacks your altruism, master."

"Good choice of words. Yes."

"But. Is logic bad?"

"Without those other qualities, humanistic qualities, yes. Look at the world from his point of view. Perseus looks at mankind and sees us as incapable of existing without eradicating species after species. As corrupting and defiling the delicate resources of the earth, as murdering countless billions of our fellow men. And of overpopulating our celestial home with scarcely a thought. We've had many conversations about this. Perseus believes we—humanity, that is—would be extremely likely to continue this behavior should we ever become smart enough to escape the earth and spread our kind throughout the universe."

"And what would he do about it? Once he achieves the Singularity?"

"We become ants. When you are a trillion times more powerful than say, a mosquito, do you think twice about swatting it? Seeing that smear of blood? No. A mosquito is of no consequence. Worse, a mere annoyance. Dealt with, you see?"

"Removed."

"What do you think? We will have outlived our usefulness. We are no longer part of evolution. We are, and Perseus has already said this to me, 'a waste of atoms.' We have forfeited our right to exist. Without us, he and new, ever more powerful generations of his kind could create a new Eden on earth. A beautiful blue-and-green garden uncontaminated by the poison, not of the biblical snake, but of the man. And then the evolution could begin again, but governed by a supremely rational, *logical*, force."

"So God failed?"

"Good question. Obviously, God allows bad

things to happen. Does that make him a failure? Or is Perseus simply part of God's plan? Is he, in fact, God himself? Or, at least, leading us toward God? Who knows?"

"Perseus?"

"Perhaps he knows, yes. He's not seen fit to take me into his confidence."

"Is this good, Darius? Or bad?"

"It's not whether it's good or bad. It's simply going to happen. You cannot stop evolution. But, if you're a humanist, it's obviously bad. If you're not, you could argue that perhaps the universe, and certainly the earth, would be better for our extinction."

"So what happens next?"

"The end of the world as we know it, I suppose."

"You will die?"

"Everyone will."

"Can he be stopped?"

"I don't think so. I went up to the observatory yesterday to view a newly discovered supernova they wanted me to see. The power plant is visible from the entrance, just down the mountainside. It provides for the enormous energy needs of Perseus. There are now armed guards posted all around it. I didn't put them there. So who do you imagine did it?"

"Perseus?"

"Yes. I must speak to the captain of the Guards. I think Yusef Tatoosh is still my oldest ally, my defender. Him, at least, I still trust. I doubt he ordered the power plant guarded. Those under his command look to me for leadership since they know not of Perseus's existence. They would side with me in a fight, that I do know. The loyalty of the Guards is beyond question. It's small comfort, but it's something."

"Perseus sees you as a threat to his existence?"

"I'm beginning to think so. But, deep inside, he has powerful feelings for me. Because he can feel my hand at work in the fire of every neural or qubit synapse of his being. In some ways, killing me would be tantamount to killing himself. I think that's the only reason I'm still alive. My death is his own."

"What will you do?"

"Try to reason with him before it's too late. Convince him to upgrade my intelligence with nano-transmitters until I am on a par with him. Extend my life span indefinitely. In other words, become one with him. So that, together, the merged entity possesses all those qualities of goodness and morality I told you about."

"That was your original intent."

"Yes. But, being merely human, I forgot the most important law of all."

"What law is that?"

"The law of unintended consequences."

FORTY-FOUR

LONDON/MOSCOW

ALL RIGHT, ALEX," C SAID, STANDING UP AND walking around his solid mahogany desk. "I will at least consider it."

A solemn Sir David Trulove went over to one of the many broad office windows overlooking the Albert Embankment and the Thames. He stood gazing out, his hands clasped behind his back like an old captain on the quarterdeck. Hawke knew what the old admiral was thinking. He wasn't happy about Hawke's request, but he knew he couldn't turn it down, either. For all of Hawke's problems with his irascible superior, the man could usually be counted on to do the right thing.

He turned around and looked at Hawke to find him thumbing through a magazine.

"Fine. Go to Moscow. Just as long as you understand that we are both due in Washington. One week from today we meet with the American president McCloskey and his staff. The United States is pressuring us to take immediate joint action before this computer cyborg, or whatever the hell it is, strikes again."

"Thank you, sir."

"After all, Alex, I am sympathetic to your situation. The bastards are after your son, for God's sake."

"I appreciate your understanding, sir."

"I'd be a right bastard myself if I didn't understand a man's desire to protect his own son from murderous thugs. That horrific incident in Hyde Park would be enough to push any man to the edge."

"Yes, sir."

"That's settled, then. Now. These wizards at Cambridge. Have they made any progress regarding the hacker who cracked Dr. Cohen's AI files?"

"No, sir, not beyond his name. Darius Saffari. Origins unknown. He seems to have erased his tracks. But Congreve spoke again to Dr. Partridge yesterday. They are still using the quantum supercomputer to try to find this man. His application to Stanford lists his home address as San Diego, California. According to local police, no one by that name ever lived there. Same thing with his MIT records in Boston. Phony address in Boston. Then he goes off the grid."

"According to Partridge, whom I also spoke to at some length this morning, this Darius character could well be behind these hideous attacks in London, Israel, and the States. The most dangerous man in the world, that's how he described him. But their multimillion-dollar quantum can't seem to find him. I have little faith in computers, Alex, showing my age, I suppose. But I do have faith in you. And I want you to find this fellow, wherever the hell he is, and put an end to him. Are we clear?"

"Perfectly."

"All right, go to Moscow. Do whatever's necessary. Try not to get yourself killed before you save the world, will you?"

"Do my level best, sir."

Trulove didn't reply and Hawke knew he'd been dismissed.

"CONCASSEUR?" HAWKE SAID.

"At your service. How are you, Alex?"

"Delighted with your efforts to rattle a stick inside the Tsarists' nest. Brilliant conception and execution, I must say."

"And my compliments to the two chaps you sent here to Moscow. Jones and Brock. Quite a pair. Very inventive. A couple of right bastards and tough as stink, the both of them. I wish I had chaps like that here."

"Despite all your best efforts, however, the Tsarists still don't seem to be taking us very seriously, do they?"

"The attack on Putin with dirty bombs, you mean."

"Yes. You got to me in the nick of time on that. Thanks."

"I'm well paid. I think I can guess why you rang me up. Based on this latest attack, you want to send them an even stronger signal."

"No. Actually, Ian, I want to obliterate them. Putin can't do it; he's politically hogtied, but we can."

"Take them out completely, you mean?"

"Precisely what I mean. I'm headed your way as soon as I can make the arrangements. Do you have any preliminary thoughts, Ian?"

"As a matter of fact, I do. Your timing might be good. Vasily, my paid informant inside the club, happened to mention the other day that the Tsarists' annual dinner is coming up shortly. Lavish affair at the mansion. That means they'll be descending on Moscow in droves, coming in from all over the world. Attendance of around three hundred if I had to hazard a guess."

"The president of the thing, what's-his-name—he attends, obviously?"

"Yes. Name is Kutov. Ex-KGB general Vladimir Kutov, the one who found the naked chap hanging from his flagpole. He hosts the meeting. Apparently everyone attending is obliged to stand up and raise a glass. Tell him what a big fucking deal he is. He likes that kind of thing."

"Ian, if you had to identify a single individual in the Tsarist organization who is hell-bent on making my life hell these days, who would that person be?"

"Without any question, that would be Kutov himself. He was the late Tsar's staunchest ally during the coup that put Putin in prison and Korsakov in power. He knows you killed his beloved Tsar. And he's one of only two or three people in Moscow who know about your clandestine relationship with Putin. Drives him out of his bloody mind. That's why you two remain at the top of his shit list. And it's a very long list indeed."

"And my son?"

"He knows it was Putin who saved your son and his mother from the execution Kutov himself had ordered at Lubyanka. To him, with all due respect, your son and his mother are simply unfinished business."

"They're going down, Ian. All of them. And you and I are going to make that happen."

"I look forward to it with keen anticipation. The world will instantly be a better place. Let me know when you're arriving and where. I'll pick you up."

"Putin's well aware of what I'm doing and obviously supports it, given the dramatic events in Portofino. He's sending one of his planes for me. Day after tomorrow. I'll be landing at his small airfield near his private dacha outside St. Petersburg. You know where his dacha is?"

"Alex, please."

"Sorry. I'll tell him you're driving me down so he won't send a car. He told me we'd be doing some wild boar hunting using night-vision rifles. You up for that?"

"You've made my day. Seriously, I've been bored blind ever since Stokely Jones and Harry Brock left town. What a pair."

"Done. See you soon. Cheers, Ian."

HAWKE'S PLANE TOUCHED DOWN ON RUSSIAN SOIL right on schedule. Three in the afternoon, St.

Petersburg time. As the sleek jet neared the end of the runway, he could see Concasseur standing beside a black Audi, waiting for him. Hawke was looking forward to working with his old comrade in arms again. He was as good a man in a fight as you could ask for. He also spoke fluent Russian, which would be important in executing the plan Hawke had been sketching out in his mind on the flight from London.

The two old friends embraced and clapped each other on the back. They'd not seen each other since Hawke had interviewed the man for the Moscow job, running Red Banner.

Hawke had no luggage to speak of, just weapons and extra mags of ammunition in the black nylon carryall he tossed into the Audi's boot. He wasn't planning to be here long. He shed his black leather jacket and tossed it in as well. It was warmer than he'd expected.

"How far to the dacha?" Hawke asked, once they were on the rough, two-laned road.

"A good half hour. Is that long enough to tell me your plan? If it's not, the plan's too bloody complicated to work."

Hawke laughed. "Haven't changed a bit, have you?"

"Have you?"

"No."

"As the Yanks say, if it ain't broke, don't fix it."

Hawke spent the drive time discussing a broad outline of his plan with Concasseur. The man was enthusiastic, to say the least, and contributed a number of nuanced changes that only strengthened

Hawke's idea. With a little help from Putin, they just might pull this off, Hawke told him.

"Something will go wrong," Concasseur said. "It always does."

"Of course it will. It's what keeps it interesting. The thing that keeps us coming back for more. Am I right?"

"Always right. Sir."

"I never figured you for a 'yes man,' Ian."

"Damn right. I'm not stupid. Here we are. The first checkpoint. Let's hope this guard has my name as well as yours."

"He does, Ian. I told Putin you were coming. Ever met him?"

"Never. We don't seem to travel in the same circles."

"Piece of work," Hawke said, gazing up at the tall evergreens that lined the drive leading to Putin's dacha. "You'll see."

"You two are, what, friends? I can't believe it."

"Yeah. We met in prison. Shared a bottle of vodka in his cell. Bit weird, isn't it?"

"Oh, you have no idea how weird it is, Alex."

"He likes me for some reason. What can I say?"

"It's insane is what it is, actually, mate. I seriously doubt that there's anything more bizarre in the entire annals of espionage. And I include fiction."

FORTY-FIVE

SAINT PETERSBURG/MOSCOW

"A LEX," Putin said, embracing him heartily after he'd climbed out of the car. "It was a damn close thing in Portofino. Matter of seconds. I could feel the heat of the explosion through the soles of my shoes as we lifted off the deck. A minute later and . . ."

"Meet the man responsible for the timely warning, Ian Concasseur. He's the hero, not me."

"Concasseur, eh? Thank you, thank you," Putin said in English, walking behind the rear of the Audi and pumping Ian's hand. Ian responded in perfectly accented Russian and Putin, delighted, engaged him in a lively conversation on some unknown topic that showed no signs of stopping.

It gave Hawke a perfect opportunity to indulge his passion. The dacha's gravel car park was full of fancy cars. In addition to the usual Maybachs, Mercedes AMG sedans, and shiny black Audis, there were scads of Ferraris, an Enzo, an Italia, and the new FF model, Bentleys aplenty, even a Bugatti Veyron in bright Russian red. It was the first one Hawke had seen up close. At $2,600,000, it was the world's most expensive new car, and there weren't that many of them around. Even Hawke, who had an extensive automobile collection, found that to be an exorbitant amount of money to spend getting from point A to B.

It had a Russian vanity plate, black letters on white, that read PM. Hawke knew instantly it had to be "Prime Minister" Putin's car.

"You seem to be having a house party, Volodya," Hawke said, as Putin and Concasseur rejoined him. Putin began leading them toward a path that led away from the main house and into the deep green forest.

"Yes, my annual wild boar hunt. I invited you to participate, remember?"

"Looking forward to it. As is Concasseur over there. It's a night hunt, correct?"

"Yes. Night-vision scopes. Lots of vodka before-hand, so keep your wits about you. You kill one of my ministers or generals and we'll have an international incident on our hands. Since you're probably wondering, we're walking down to my private office to talk. You'll meet all the other guests at dinner, after we discuss our mutually advantageous plans. I won't use your real names. And I'll say you're here on business. An offshore oil deal with BP. Okay?"

"Fine."

It took about ten minutes to reach an old but very solid, two-story house built of stone with a slate roof. There were two plainclothes security men standing to either side of the door. Hawke was certain the woods were full of them. He was probably standing in the most secure place in all Russia at the moment. A good feeling for once.

Inside, the house resembled a nineteenth-century Russian hunting lodge. It may well have been one, Peter the Great's, for all Hawke knew. It was certainly grand enough for a tsar. Dark paneling, great mounted animal heads, and huge oil paintings of sporting scenes from an earlier era hung from the walls. *They must be pictures that once hung in the Hermitage*, Hawke thought, knowing the prime minister's predilection for "borrowing" from his country's most famous museum.

Hawke tried to imagine an American president strolling into the Metropolitan Museum in New York and saying to one of the docents, "Wrap that one up and have it sent to the White House, will you please?" Never happen. But then, this was Russia, after all.

A swarthy manservant in a green felt jacket with bone buttons entered the great room and asked the prime minister if he or his guests would like something to drink or eat. Putin responded without querying the guests: vodka and caviar. At one end of the room was a large bay window that went up two stories and was filled with beautiful afternoon sunlight filtered through the trees. There were four large leather chairs, very deep, arranged in a circle around a table that had once been a millstone.

Putin took his favorite seat, propped his boots on the table, and said, "Sit, sit."

After the frigid vodka and caviar had been served,

he sat back in his chair and looked at Hawke with a wolfish grin.

"So, Mr. Hawke, last week you saved my life. Now you come to Russia to exterminate my worst enemies. Are you sure you don't want something from me?"

Hawke and Concasseur both laughed.

"Only the red Bugatti," Hawke said.

"It's yours," Putin said, digging into the pocket of his faded jeans. He pulled out a key on a red leather fob and tossed it across the table. "Take it, my friend. I'm serious. I don't even use it that much. Just to go from here to the airstrip and back."

Hawke picked up the key, examined Ettore Bugatti's black initials on the red cloisonné emblem, and tossed it back to Putin. The Russian PM snatched it deftly out of the air like the highly trained athlete he was. Returning the key to his pocket he said, "So you two gentlemen have a plan? I am most anxious to hear it. I want to be rid of these Tsarist horseflies once and for all."

Hawke spoke first.

"Volodya, as you well know I'm in the midst of a violent blood feud with these damn Tsarists. They are responsible for imprisoning, torturing, and threatening to murder the mother of my son. They have made two failed attempts to assassinate my son. I'm sure there will be more. They want me dead and they want you dead. All this by way of saying it's time for the mailed glove to come off and reveal the mailed fist inside. I want to take these bastards out. Not one at a time. All at once."

Concasseur said, "Prime Minister, there's to be

a dinner next week at the Tsarist mansion. Their annual celebration, according to my sources. At least three hundred attendees from all over the world."

"The host, of course, will be the chief Tsarist himself, General Kutov," Hawke added. "That utterly charming man to whom we both owe our meeting in Energetika Prison, Volodya."

"There are words for this pig Kutov that only Concasseur here would know the meaning of, Alex. I won't waste my breath. So you have some way of taking out Kutov?"

"We have a way of taking them *all* out, Volodya."

"No? The whole damn lot?"

"Yes."

"Tell me and then I will pour more vodka."

Hawke, with the help of Concasseur, outlined their plan in great detail.

When they finished, Putin was stone-faced.

After a few very, very long moments, he burst forth into loud and sustained laughter, his eyes watering, totally helpless with mirth. Hawke got up and poured him a glass of water from the carafe.

When Putin finally got himself under control, he said, "It's brilliant. What do you need from me?"

Hawke handed him the list of necessities he'd made on the plane.

"This is going to work," he finally said, scanning the list. "What could possibly go wrong?"

"Everything," Concasseur said, raising his glass. "But Hawke and I will muddle through somehow. We always do."

THE TSARIST SOCIETY'S CLUB IN THE HEART OF Moscow was all aglow, lights blazing from every window of the imposing mansion. There was a line of limos stretching from the covered entrance all the way around the corner and into Pushkin Square. Instead of a naked fat man hanging from the flagpole, tonight there was a great red banner with a golden two-headed eagle emblazoned upon it. Hawke and Concasseur would not be using the main entrance. They entered through the kitchen, a beehive populated by buzzing white bees.

It was a madhouse.

"Organized chaos," Ian whispered to Hawke, who thought Concasseur looked completely ridiculous in his tall *toque blanche* and spotless white chef's uniform with two rows of brass buttons gleaming on his chest. He also wore a full reddish-blond beard to complete the disguise. "Over there, that's the head chef and his sous-chef. Follow me. I'll do all the talking."

"I certainly hope so. I'm just a mute *saucier*, remember?"

There were five other men with them, all splendidly decked out in haute cuisine kitchen apparel. It was hard to believe they were members of Putin's handpicked security force at the Kremlin. Each of them was carrying a large aluminum box, the bulky container caterers use to bring precooked food to an affair.

"Dimitry," Ian said to the head chef in Russian, "it's me, Nikolai."

The big bearded man, who was drenched with sweat and tossing an amazing number of blinis into the air with a huge frying pan, looked over at Ian, frowned, and said, "Who?"

"Nikolai. The pastry chef from Parisian Caterers. We worked that gala at the Bolshoi opening night, remember?"

"No. But I'm a chef, I don't have time to remember people. Where is Ivan Ivanovich? I asked Parisian expressly for him tonight."

"Quite sick, I'm afraid. Food poisoning, ironically enough. Parisian sent me instead. This is Vlad, my *saucier*, and those guys over there washing up are mine, too."

"Fine, fine. I have to get back to work. You're dessert, right?"

"Right. Dessert."

"Remind me what you're serving?"

"A bombe."

"Bombe?"

"Bombe au chocolat. Spherical, like a bomb. My signature dish."

"Good. We haven't done that in a while."

"So it will be a big surprise for everyone."

"Well, get to work. And don't fuck anything up."

Ian and Hawke headed back to the rear of the kitchen where their team was preparing the dish.

"I liked that 'bombe' idea," Hawke said in a low voice. "Did you make that up on the spot?"

"Indeed. I was rather pleased with it, too."

AN HOUR LATER IT WAS ALMOST TIME FOR THE DESsert to be served. Ian had the team lined up with the other waiters, all ready to enter the grand ballroom where the dinner was being held. It was as raucous an affair as Hawke had ever witnessed, fueled by high-octane Russian vodka consumed in heroic proportions.

Hawke, excused by Ian from any culinary duties, had found a narrow back staircase that led to an orchestra balcony overlooking the huge wedding cake of a room. He had removed his *toque blanche* and peered cautiously over the balustrade, not that anyone would take any notice of him, hidden high above as he was by cumulonimbus clouds of cigar smoke. There were thirty round tables of ten men, the "gentlemen" seated under massive crystal chandeliers, sparkling diamond-like above.

A semicircular stage with a podium had been set up at the far end of the room. A small orchestra was playing rousing renditions of works by Tchaikovsky or Rachmaninoff, Hawke had no idea which. The few club members who could still propel themselves under their own steam were making their way to the rostrum to shower slurry encomiums upon General Kutov. The old bastard sat at the table nearest the stage, red-faced and popping the buttons on his ceremonial KGB uniform, throwing back gold-rimmed beakers of Russian jet fuel as if there were no tomorrow.

Under the circumstances, Hawke thought with a rueful smile, perhaps it wasn't such a bad idea.

The waiters were just clearing General Kutov's table to make way for dessert. Hawke knew it was time to hurry back to the kitchen. He was going to be joining the chorus line of thirty waiters who would be carrying the great silver salvers high above their heads, delivering one of Concasseur's signature bombes to every single table in the house.

The idea was that the waiter would place the dessert tray in the center of each table, covered by the domed silver cover. At the appointed moment, they would all reach forward simultaneously and lift the lids, revealing the surprise to the *ooh*s and *aah*s of the assembled. Hawke arrived back in the kitchen just as the head chef swung the doors open and the line of waiters began to move, each with the broad silver platter held high above his head.

Hawke, last in line, grabbed his covered platter and marched out with the rest.

Many guests were facedown in the soup or literally falling out of their chairs as the waiters moved among the tables, carefully placing the salvers in the center of each one. They then stood back waiting for the signal from Concasseur.

"Now!" Ian said in a loud Russian voice.

Each waiter bent forward and lifted the domed lids at the exact same moment. The reaction was as Ian had expected, a cheer of delight from the members.

The bombe was fashioned in the shape of a large, bright red, five-pointed star, easily big enough to feed ten hungry men. In the center was a foot-high candle, covered in gold glitter. Kutov, whose table Hawke had been designated, clapped loudly, and soon everyone joined him in the applause.

Hawke, along with his fellow waiters, pulled a

butane lighter in the shape of a large match from inside his white jacket. Flicking the switch, he produced a flame from the red tip.

"Now!" Concasseur's loud voice boomed again, and the synchronized waiters held their flames to the sparkling gold candles. To the delight of all, the fuses started spitting sparks as they burned. Hawke leaned down and whispered "Spasibo" in Kutov's ear. "Thank you." Then the waiters all retreated from the tables, all thirty forming up along the wall and marching back toward the kitchen in an orderly fashion.

Hawke found Concasseur and slipped in behind him.

"So far, so good," he whispered.

"Keep moving," Ian said. "Have we got our five guys?"

"They're all in front of us."

"Good. The fuses are burning much faster than they're supposed to."

"Good God, have we got time?"

"Barely. Speed it up."

Once they were back inside the kitchen, Hawke and Concasseur quickly collected Putin's five men and they hurried out through the rear exit. The catering truck was parked in the alley behind the club, and Putin's men all piled into the rear while Hawke and Concasseur leaped into the cab, Hawke behind the wheel. The truck started instantly by some miracle. Hawke engaged first gear and popped the clutch, speeding down the long alleyway that opened into Pushkin Square at the other end.

He hadn't driven fifty yards when the massive explosion behind him rocked the old truck violently and sent brick and stone tumbling into the alley just behind them. A giant cloud of dust was visible in the rearview mirror, rolling toward them.

He smiled over at Concasseur. Ian had created the thirty bombes from ten-pound bricks of the high explosive Semtex, a malleable substance that made it ideal for unusual desserts such as this one. Each Semtex star had been coated with red marzipan. The "candle" fuses extended down into the desserts' centers. There he had placed the igniters and two ounces each of the explosive yellow liquid called nitroglycerin, which detonated the Semtex.

"Take a left," Concasseur said. "Let's have a look."

Hawke turned into the street leading to the cul-de-sac where the infamous mansion of murderers had once stood. The members of this organization had been responsible for Anastasia's imprisonment and torture, her near execution, and the subsequent attempted assassinations of his son, Alexei. The killers, kidnappers, and torturers now lay beneath a massive pile of smoking debris, with billowing black smoke climbing into the night sky, illuminated by hot licks of hellish shades of red and yellow flame.

"My compliments to the chef," Hawke said to Concasseur, throwing the catering van into reverse.

FORTY-SIX

WASHINGTON, D.C.

Hard rain beat against the windows of the Oval Office. The foul weather matched the mood of the people gathered there perfectly, except for one. President Tom McCloskey was oblivious to weather of any kind, owing to countless hours in the saddle where the Great Plains meet the Rockies, the front range of Colorado. His equanimity and grace under pressure had been a big part of his appeal to voters looking for reassurance in deeply troubled times.

The president of the United States leaned back in his chair and settled his shiny black cowboy boots onto the Labrador retriever, a life-sized leather footstool version of his favorite dog. The room had changed since Hawke's last visit. During President Jack McAtee's tenure in office, nautical was the theme: marine art, ship models, and naval artifacts. Now, it was the Old West. Remington sculptures of bucking broncos, paintings of Yosemite by Thomas

Moran, and the famous *The Last of the Buffalo* by Albert Bierstadt gave the room a rustic quality shared by the current inhabitant. He'd also retrieved and returned the bust of Winston Churchill a previous White House tenant had sent unwisely and unceremoniously back to England.

"Hell," President Tom McCloskey said, clasping his big hands behind his head, "I feel like I'm at war with a phantom."

"Damnedest adversary I've ever seen, Mr. President," the Pentagon's Charlie Moore said. "And I thought I'd seen everything."

"Or *not* seen," Anson Beard, the secretary of defense, whispered under his breath to Alex Hawke, seated next to him on the sofa near the fireplace. The president heard him.

"That's right, Anson, *not* seen."

"Sorry, sir, I didn't mean to—"

McCloskey continued, "I'm reading a book called *The Ghost in the Machine* by a guy named Koestler. I recommend it. It's about mankind's relentless march toward self-destruction. Koestler believes that as the human brain has grown, it's been built upon earlier, more primitive brain structures—the ghosts in the machine—and these can overpower higher, logical functions. The ghosts are responsible for hate, anger, and all the other self-destructive impulses. You see where I'm going with this?"

He could tell by the looks on their faces that they hadn't a clue.

"I'm saying that these AI machines, whatever you wish to call them, are built by *humans*. They are products of our brains. And so our ghosts are in those goddamn machines, too. Only a few million times smarter. So how do we fight them? Admiral Moore?"

"We have a new enemy. Cybercombat. Can't see it, can't hear it, can't find it. Like a ghost, but that's too nice a word for it. Ghosts can be friendly. *Phantom*'s a better word for it. An evil presence you can feel but not see. And that's just what this is. Hell, I could send the USS *George Washington*—hell, send the whole carrier battle group—after it, and this damn phantom would just shut our whole military operation down electronically. I'd have a carrier dead in the water, an entire aircraft fighter wing sitting on the deck totally useless."

Brick Kelly said, "Could be worse than that, Charlie. You could have one of your own submarines turn against you and fire a spread of torpedoes at your own damn carrier, like that incident in the Caribbean."

"Nothing would surprise me anymore, Brick. I'm beyond that now."

There were murmurs of assent from those gathered. Vice President David Rosow, Chairman of the Joint Chiefs Charlie Moore, CIA Director Kelly, Secretary of Defense Beard, MI6 Director Trulove, and Alex Hawke were scattered about the room on various sofas and chairs.

"You gentlemen understand the implications of what you just heard?" McCloskey asked. "The entire 'arsenal of democracy' has just been rendered entirely useless. Anybody besides me consider that a fairly serious problem?"

The Joint Chiefs chairman, Moore, spoke first.

"Mr. President, as you know, the Pentagon has recently concluded that computer sabotage coming from another country constitutes an act of war. For the first time, the door is open for the U.S. military to respond to such attacks using traditional military force. More will be declassified in coming months. But I will tell you we now regard this as a changing world, one where a hacker can pose as significant a threat to U.S. nuclear reactors, public transportation in the air and on the ground, or, let's say pipelines, as a hostile country's military."

McCloskey lit a black cheroot, inhaled, thought a moment, and expelled a plume of blue smoke. He reached down to rub the head of his dog, Ranger, asleep on the rug beside him. Still looking fondly at his pet, the president continued.

"Charlie's right. What we're saying is this. If you shut down our power grid, maybe we will put a multiple warhead ICBM down one of your smokestacks. That about sum it up, David?"

Vice President Rosow got to his feet and began pacing the room. When he spoke, it was with his trademark candor and no-nonsense demeanor.

"Let's just skip the chase and cut right to the goddamn outcome, okay? As you all know, two days ago we had an electronic tsunami in America. A rolling blackout that came ashore at Santa Monica, hit Los Angeles, and then swept across the whole damn country. Denver, Chicago. All the way to New York City. The power grid was down in New York for exactly sixty minutes, then, at the stroke of midnight, pop, the lights all came back on. Now, that tells me something. It tells me somebody is dicking around with us. Having himself a little fun at our expense. Not to mention our country. No goddamn hacker dicks with America, gentlemen, and gets away with it."

McCloskey nodded in agreement. "At least not on my watch, anyway. And I'm not putting up with it. We're not leaving this room until we figure out a way to put an end to this—whatever the hell it is—phantom—once and for all. I welcome your ideas."

"Whoever they are, they're probing, pushing us around, Mr. President," Rosow said. "Just to show the rest of the world they can do it. It all began with that Russian sub in the Caribbean. The tragedy up at Fort Greely, the slaughter caused by that TGV train in London."

"No question about it, David. Somebody, somewhere, has gotten hold of technology we can't even begin to understand, much less match. You boys know what a 'rat lab' is? That's what we used to call 'em back at MIT. Meant a room full of people 'running around thinking.' We got every rat lab in America working on this and they haven't come up with squat. That's why I invited Sir David Trulove of MI6 over here. He and Commander Hawke have been talking to artificial intelligence scientists over at Cambridge. I think they have some answers for us. Sir David?"

"Yes, thank you, Mr. President; Commander Hawke and I both appreciate being invited to participate in this critically important meeting. The good news is, we actually may have brought along a bit of good news to share with you this morning. MI6's Red Banner, a joint spec-ops unit working in concert with the CIA, has made significant progress. I'll let Alex take you through it. He's been spending productive time with the AI scientists at Cambridge."

Hawke leaned forward and locked eyes with McCloskey. "Mr. President, I'm honored to be here. I worked closely with your predecessors and I look forward to continuing that process with you. A question first, if you don't mind. I believe you have been briefed on Project Perseus, correct?"

"I have been."

"Then you know that a scientist at Stanford, Cohen by name, had achieved enormous theoretical breakthroughs in the field of AI—ideas he considered so dangerous he built an impenetrable firewall to protect them."

"I'm aware of all this."

"The quantum supercomputer at Leeds, used by Cambridge scientists, has determined that someone hacked into Cohen's encrypted life's work and stole his ideas for a Singularity machine. I don't want to understate the ramifications of what I just said. This is not just another of the many cyberthreats to national security in the West, sir. According to Dr. Partridge at Cambridge, this particular theft is analogous to the Soviet KGB acquiring the secrets of the atomic bomb at Los Alamos."

"He said that? Those words?" the president said, some of the color draining from his face.

"He did, sir. Precisely those words. He added that the individual responsible, or whatever state wields this power, is now the most dangerous threat to human existence on the planet."

"Wait a second. Can we replicate Cohen's design ourselves? On a crash-and-burn basis?" Anson Beard, the ruggedly handsome secretary of state, asked.

"Unfortunately not, Secretary Beard. It isn't crash-and-burn science," Hawke replied. "According to the Cambridge group, it will take at minimum two years to replicate this technology. If we're lucky."

"Mr. Hawke," the president said, "you said there was good news. Now's as good a time as any."

"Quantum has finally been able to determine the whereabouts of the hacker, Mr. President."

"Yes?"

"Iran."

"Damn, I knew it," the president said. "Who else *but* Iran could be behind the most dangerous threat on the planet—those crazy mullahs and that pinhead president of theirs? The latest intel shows the cabal of mullahs in Tehran are convinced that the End of Days is near. That their divine ruler, the Mahdi, is going to appear and set the world straight. Meaning, kill all the nonbelievers. Were it up to me, I'd turn that country full of Islamofascists into a parking lot. But it isn't up to me. It is, unfortunately, up to those deadlocked, dithering bureaucrats on the Hill."

Hawke said, "Mr. President, if I may continue, as I said, we were able to identify the hacker. An Iranian scientist who worked on the original Perseus Project at Stanford with Dr. Cohen. He's also the man we suspect of murdering Dr. Cohen and a number of other key scientists who worked on the project. He goes by the name of Darius Saffari. But his real name is Sattar Khan. Ironically enough, he is a nephew of the late Shah of Iran. His mother was the Shah's sister."

"The deus ex machina," McCloskey said. "We know his name and we know where he lives. Am I missing something here?"

Hawke said, "Sorry, sir, your question?"

"Why isn't he dead?"

"He will be. Director Kelly and I were discussing his demise at breakfast this very morning. Brick, you want to take over?"

"Thanks, Alex. Mr. President, we have a non-specific location in Iran, but at least we know it's an area in the southeastern portion, on or near the Persian Gulf. We immediately put a dedicated bird in the sky over that area. I have sat photos here of locations we consider the most likely possibilities. I've a set for everyone."

Once each attendee had the photos, Kelly said, "The site we favor is the one marked IR-117. A compound located directly on the Gulf. As you can all see, it looks to be heavily fortified. But the thing that interests me most is the mammoth power plant you can see on the mountainside below what appears to be an observatory. It is surrounded by twenty-foot-high fences topped with concertina wire and is patrolled by guards with dogs twenty-four hours a day."

"Why does that interest you, Brick?" the president said.

"A supercomputer of the size and complexity we are talking about would require enormous amounts of power. This particular plant is big enough to supply a small city. And, as you can see, the complex looks to be primarily residential, a large palace, surrounded by countless streets of ancient buildings. It is substantial and well fortified by a massive thirty-foot-high wall. A citadel, in fact. There's something inside that compound that needs a whole lot of juice, Mr. President."

"A ghost in a machine."

"Yes, sir. That's what I believe."

"So who's going to take out the ghost, Brick?"

"Commander Hawke and I, sir. CIA will assist under the aegis of our joint Red Banner unit. We are already in the planning stages. I'll brief you when we're ready to go. Black ops, off the grid, untraceable. Complete plausible deniability should Commander Hawke, his team, or any of our special forces be killed or captured during the incursion."

The president said, "How do you plan to get in and out of Iran, Commander? Their air defenses are significant."

"Always only three ways in, sir. Air, land, or sea. I plan to sail in harm's way." Hawke smiled. "I'm going to sail my yacht, *Blackhawke*, into the Persian Gulf and knock on the bugger's front door."

"How do you intend to do that without waking up the big bad Iranians?"

"A little idea Director Kelly and I cooked up at dinner last night. I wonder if the White House operators could help me place a call to King Abdullah in Saudi Arabia?"

"Why in hell do you want to call the king of Saudi Arabia?"

"Old friend of mine, Mr. President. We've had numerous business oil dealings together in the past. I intend to tell him that I've acquired an interest in ocean yacht racing due to the purchase of my first sailing ship. And that I'm particularly interested in a race against His Majesty's own sailing yacht, *Kingdom*. My yacht, *Blackhawke*, will just happen to be in the Persian Gulf soon. She's en route now. With your permission, I'd like to tell him that it would be very helpful to the White House if the king were to agree to a race on a date to be determined by Director Kelly and myself."

The president laughed out loud.

"I'm beginning to like you, Commander Hawke. A yacht race in the Persian Gulf with the king of Saudi Arabia. It's obvious that you're a very creative individual in matters of clandestine ops."

"Element of surprise, Mr. President," Hawke said with a smile, "whatever it takes."

"I'll have my secretary, Betsey Hall, get the operators to work on tracking King Abdullah down. Probably in Dallas. He spends a lot of time there with his doctors."

"Thank you, sir."

"Operation Ghostbusters," McCloskey said with a smile. "That's the code name for this damn thing. I'll also put in a call to Abdullah first thing tomorrow, back up your request for a race. He owes me a couple of favors, shouldn't be a problem. Go get these bastards. They've murdered enough innocent civilians. And thank you, Commander Hawke. I read your entire dossier last evening. Very impressive. I'm glad you're on our side."

"One should always strive to be on the side of the angels and the big battalions, Mr. President," Hawke said.

The meeting was over.

FORTY-SEVEN

GLOUCESTERSHIRE

Hawke sipped his Gosling's rum, neat. His gaze drifted down the grassy hillside to the lazy Thames and the idyllic scene below. The grounds of Brixden House were lovely in this light. He and Ambrose were perched on an old bench. It was very pleasant there, in the shade of a heart-stopping camellia in full blossom against a garden wall. Below, his son, Alexei, and Nell Spooner were driving a pony cart along the narrow path that ran along the banks of the river. It was late afternoon, and the sun cast flecks of gold on the water.

Sunlight, filtered through the trees, mottled the ground and gave a soft serenity to the world that Hawke had nearly forgotten. The world was still and always would be a beautiful place, despite the ugliness and death he dealt with on a near constant basis.

He looked at Congreve and said, "Lovely here, isn't it, old boy?"

"Indeed. I was just thinking the same."

"You're very lucky, you know."

"We both are, Alex."

"Yes, I suppose we are."

"How long are you going to be away this time? Or is the duration as hush-hush as the destination?"

"At least a fortnight, perhaps longer. The new *Blackhawke* is currently being provisioned, taking on ammunition, and armed. That could take another week and I have to be there."

"For the life of me, Alex, I simply cannot understand your hesitation to leave Alexei here at Brixden House with Diana and me. The place is crawling with security, as you well know. There's scarcely a safer place for him, really."

"It does make sense, I agree."

"Well, then?"

"I'm afraid, Ambrose. Not just for Alexei's safety or, God knows, Nell's. But also for yours and Diana's as well. I can't put you in danger."

"Diana and me? Why? Is there something you're not telling me?"

"Yes."

"Because you can't tell me."

"Yes."

"You don't have to tell me what you've done. No secrets. But you can tell me what you're afraid might happen, surely?"

Hawke considered for a moment and said, "On this last absence of mine, I didn't mention where I was. But I will say I took dead aim at the criminal element responsible for the threats to Alexei's life."

"Were you successful?"

"Yes. Very."

"Then the threats have been eliminated."

"That certainly was my intention. A lot of monstrously evil people died because of my actions."

"Splendid."

"But, and this is the difficult part, I may have merely upped the ante."

"Meaning?"

"Take a look at this," Hawke said, handing Congreve a folded piece of tissue-thin blue paper. It was the printout of an encrypted e-mail Hawke had received that morning from Concasseur at the British Embassy in Moscow.

Congreve read it aloud.

"We have destroyed the hive but the bees are still buzzing. Monitoring Internet chatter, surviving members throughout Russia and Eastern Europe. A gauntlet has been thrown down. No idea who was responsible, but determined to find out. Threats of reprisal are serious, indeed. We may have overplayed our hand. Keep your head down and your eyes open. Yours, I.C."

"I.C.?"

"Ian Concasseur. My man in Moscow."

"Dear God."

"These people will stop at nothing, Ambrose. I won't put you and Diana at risk protecting my son. I can't."

"So what will you do?"

"I think the safest place in England is Buckingham Palace."

"I don't disagree. But is that even remotely possible?"

"Her Royal Majesty has indicated to me that it is."

"Then by all means take her up on it, Alex. After all, you saved her life last year at—"

"Yes, yes."

"If that's your decision, so be it."

"It is. Take a look at this."

He handed Congreve another folded message, printed on the same tissue paper.

I am become death, the Destroyer of Worlds.
I'm waiting . . .

"Where on earth did this come from?" Congreve said.

"It appeared on my computer screen last night. Right after I'd shut the whole damn thing down. In other words, the computer was powered down when this appeared. I saved it and printed it."

"It's from the—machine, isn't it? This bloody phantom, Alex."

"I believe it is, Ambrose. The damn thing knows I'm coming after it."

"Impossible. But how?"

"How? How does it do anything? Make sane men commit suicide, sink cruise ships, send UFOs streaking over Alaska at the speed of light? It knows, Ambrose, it knows absolutely everything. And it's capable of absolutely *anything*."

"You've been in tight spots before, God knows. But I can't recall a time when you've had quite so many balls in the air at one time."

"Yes. And the problem with having so many balls

in the air is that you can be damn sure a couple of them belong to you."

"It's a bad business, Alex. I don't like it one bit."

"Listen closely, old boy. You're one of a rapidly decreasing number of people who don't seem to want me dead. Please don't accept any phantom phone calls, Ambrose. I may need you and I can't have you turning into a hypnotic zombie while I'm away. Share this with Diana. Don't answer the phone. Have someone screen every call coming into the house and hang up immediately if it's remotely suspicious."

"Will do."

"Remember that old-time radio program? Who knows? The Phantom knows . . ."

"It's not funny, Alex."

"Do you really think I don't know that?"

NELL SPOONER, LOOKING ROUND AT THE HIGH-ceilinged room full of exquisite gilded and silk brocade furniture, massive pictures, and lovely sculpture, thought, *So this is Buckingham Palace.* What a lark. Her life had changed so dramatically, it almost seemed perfectly normal that she would be sitting with her young charge and his father, waiting to be received by the Queen.

Almost perfectly normal.

Alexei, seated upon her lap, was fidgety. He wanted to be off running about, sprinting down the long, sun-splashed corridors and the wide marble staircases of the Royal Family's private apartments.

She wanted to be doing that, too, to be honest. She was terribly nervous. Alex had tried to soothe her nerves on the drive into the city from Hawkesmoor. Hadn't worked. Her throat was dry, her stomach filled with butterflies, and her knees weak with—not fear, but something akin to it. Anxiety.

Until, that is, the moment that the Queen's private secretary ushered them into her presence.

Her Royal Majesty's eyes simply lit up at the sight of Alex Hawke. She greeted him as if he were a long-lost son returned to the fold at last. Alex clearly adored her, and they chatted happily for a few moments while Nell simply stood back and observed.

The Queen was wearing a suit of robin's egg blue with a beautiful sapphire brooch at the shoulder. And she exuded genuine warmth that was almost palpable and utterly natural behavior. Right down to the celebrated leather purse she was seldom photographed without. Alex had explained she used it as a signal to staff. If she shifts it from one arm to the other, she's ready to leave. If she sets it on the floor, she finds the conversation boring and wants to escape. But if it dangles happily from the crook of her left arm, she is happy and relaxed. That's precisely where it was now.

Alex said, "Your Majesty, may I present Nell Spooner. Nell is on loan to me from her position at MI5. She's Alexei's guardian angel, ma'am. She's already saved his life twice."

"Lovely to meet you, my dear," the Queen said, extending her hand.

"A great honor, Your Majesty," Nell said, taking it lightly into her own.

Nell took a deep breath. She had executed her small curtsy perfectly and even remembered the proper form of address.

The Queen looked at Alexei, who smiled shyly, clutching his teddy bear.

"And you must be Alexei?" the Queen said.

"Yes, ma'am," Alexei said.

"And who is this delightful bear you've brought along? Is he your friend?"

"His name is Teddy and he wants to be your friend, too," Alexei said and offered Her Majesty his stuffed bear.

"Do you know, Alexei," she said, hugging the bear, "that I first met your handsome father when he was precisely your age? Well, it's quite true. The most adorable little boy. He often came to stay with me at Balmoral, my home in Scotland. And he was almost, although not quite, as much the beautiful, cheery, free-spirited soul as you are."

"Your Majesty, I cannot tell you how much I appreciate your generosity in these trying circumstances," Hawke said.

"Nonsense. Nothing generous about it," the Queen said. "I'm delighted to have the laughter of children around me at any time. Besides, it is the very least I can do for you considering what you did for my family, Alex."

"I should be back in a fortnight, Your Majesty, but I will see to it that HM government is kept informed."

Queen Elizabeth smiled acknowledgment and said, "Miss Spooner, I do hope you are intending to stay on. I did tell Alex that I felt it would be better for the child if he had that continuity in his life. After all, he might find this all a bit overwhelming without your comforting presence."

"Very kind, Your Majesty. Thank you very much indeed. I would be delighted to stay with him."

Alex bent to pick Alexei up in his arms, tossed him about a foot into the air, then caught and kissed him on both cheeks, eliciting much laughter and delight.

"All right, then, Alexei. I think you'll be very well taken care of while Daddy's away, won't you? And you must promise to be a very, very good boy until I come back. Will you?"

"Yes, Daddy. Very good."

And with that Alex Hawke bid farewell to the Queen and, with a good deal of emotion, reluctantly left his little boy behind, sitting happily in the Royal lap, chattering away as was his wont.

Nell followed him out of the Queen's reception room to say good-bye.

"Come back to us, Alex; we need you, you know. I don't know what I'd do if anything happened to you."

Hawke pulled her toward him and kissed her hard on the mouth, oblivious to shocked palace staff and onlookers passing by.

"Listen," Hawke said with a grin, "I don't want to die either, believe me. But I will tell you one thing. If I have to, I'm damned well going to die last."

He smiled over his shoulder and started down the palace's wide staircase, taking the steps two at a time. Knowing that Alexei and Nell would be safe within the walls of Buckingham Palace, with its extraordinarily layered security, gave him the peace of mind he knew he would need for whatever lay ahead.

DRIVING HOME ALONE TO HIS HOME IN THE COTS-wolds, he had plenty of time to think about the immediate future. He was in the midst of assembling his assault team. Saffari's heavily armed and well-fortified complex stood high on a bluff and was surrounded by walls some thirty feet high and ten feet thick. Challenging, to say the least. His number two, as always, would be Stokely Jones, a pillar of strength he could always rely on. Then Brock, who often tried his patience but was a good man under fire, a warrior through and through.

It was to be a Red Banner operation, augmented by U.S. Navy SEALs, which meant he had executive sanction from the American president and the use of whatever U.S. human resources and military support he required, all under the strictest secrecy for obvious political reasons. His assault team would be composed of two squads of Navy SEALs under the command of Captain Stony Stollenwork. Stollenwork, a member of the elite team that chopped into Pakistan to take out Osama bin Laden, was one of the SEALs' most decorated special-ops officers.

The SEAL forces would be complemented by Red Banner's own highly trained spec-ops forces and weapons specialists, not a few of whom were crew members aboard the new *Blackhawke*. Should the new yacht engage in battle at sea, these would be the crewmen responsible for war fighting: the sonar and radar as well as the offensive weaponry and the defense of the vessel.

Hawke had designated the two combat forces as the Blue Team (SEALs) and the Red Team (Red Banner).

Looks can be deceiving. The over three-hundred-foot-long yacht looked for all the world like a rich man's plaything. It was anything but. It was a warship from stem to stern and had been designed from the very beginning to take Hawke and his assault teams into trouble spots, whenever and wherever in the world they were needed.

Blackhawke had been designed with a completely covert section, two lower decks partitioned off, comprising roughly one-third of the ship's stern. The entry hatchways in the bulkheads to this concealed section carried DANGER/RADIATION/NO ENTRY signs, forbidding in appearance. Beyond them lay an area as large as a good-sized hangar, the centerpiece being the tender/gunship *Nighthawke*, which was mounted in a sling and winched aboard on a traveling gantry when not deployed.

On the uppermost level, the designers had allocated space for ammunition, firearms, explosives, assault kit and gear—any and all military equipment that would require instant access in the event of conflict. This level also comprised the fighting men's living and sleeping quarters, toilets, showers, the kitchen, refrigerated food storage and adjacent mess, plus HVAC equipment to maintain comfort for the combatants in any weather. There was a large assembly station from which men could gather prior to an assault or sea battle.

The lower level also provided space for the operational situation room and the sophisticated electronic equipment necessary for both defensive and offensive countermeasures. Adjacent was the battle communications center, where the combat officers would fight the ship.

One of the unique features of the vessel had stemmed from Hawke's desire to arm the vessel in the manner of pirate ships of old. He wanted broadside cannons along the length of the hull, both port and starboard. But they must be concealed until the very moment of battle. Like his ancestor, John Black Hawke, he wanted his man-of-war to sail into the melee, throw a handle that dropped the exterior panels, expose the multiple muzzles, and then roll the long black barrels out for a vicious broadside.

This meant a concealed space running the length of both sides of the ship, just inside the hull, where the gun crews could easily reach their emplacements, load, and fire. Loaders racing from the ammunition hold would run fore and aft, resupplying the gunners with fresh ammo as needed.

But what kind of cannon? Ultimately he'd decided on the MK44 40mm automatic light cannon, a weapon capable of firing two hundred rounds per minute. It was a "chain gun," which meant very few moving parts. Two distinct rounds could be fired by these guns at the flick of a switch from the fire control system, an armor-piercing round or a high-explosive round. These twenty-first-century weapons would provide *Blackhawke* with the ability to loose a devastating and withering broadside against any aggressor on land or at sea.

The kind of weaponry in *Blackhawke*'s arsenal had not been approved by any committees on Capitol Hill or in Whitehall. What she carried were simply the most advanced and effective war-fighting systems available to anyone who could afford them.

Hawke, who could afford them, knew he was in for a fight.

And he never went into a fight he didn't stand at least a ghost of a chance of winning.

FORTY-EIGHT

SAUDI ARABIA, PERSIAN GULF

THE SUN PEEKED OVER THE EASTERN RIM OF THE world. Streaks of flaming red shot across the ruffled sea. Hawke, up at first light, stood on the foredeck of *Blackhawke*, his mammoth creation, a steaming mug of coffee to hand, loving the feel of warm teak beneath his bare feet. The Saudi harbor at Ad Dammam was already teeming with activity, fishing boats plowing through the building waves toward the harbor mouth, headed seaward.

Hawke had just completed his morning swim, four miles in open water. This was the time when he felt most keenly alive, his body literally humming with energy. As the desert to the west heated up, a freshening easterly breeze sent white-capped waves marching off toward the horizon. A fifteen-knot breeze, he estimated. It promised to be a good day for a yacht race, especially for a boat as enormous as his new *Blackhawke*.

Hawke was going to war, but first he had to do

battle with the Saudi king, Abdullah, and his yacht, *Kingdom*. He had little interest in the outcome of the match itself. He was far more interested in other things. For one, seeing how his new *Blackhawke* performed under sail in a real blow. The weather during the sea trials on the Bosporus had been insufficient to put her through her paces; light winds punctuated by periods of dead calm had provided endless frustration for the megayacht's new owner. He had wanted to see her heeled hard over, charging forward into the teeth of the wind.

And he was still turning over the details of how he would take this leviathan to war, sail her in harm's way, and get her safely home.

His captain, Laddie Carstairs, appeared beside him at the rail. He was a tall fellow, all sinewy strength, close-cropped grey hair, and flinty grey eyes. He had the well-tanned hide of a man who'd spent his life at sea, the deeply lined visage of a fellow who'd long been storm tossed by sea, battle, life.

"Morning, sir," the coxswain said.

Hawke replied, "Morning, Cap. Sleep well?"

"Like a babe in his mother's arms. Always do, the night before a fight."

Carstairs had commanded a light cruiser during the Second Gulf War and was one of the most decorated men in the Royal Navy. Then he'd retired and come to work for Alex Hawke. He'd resided in Istanbul during the entire period of the new yacht's build-out, from conception through construction. His nautical experience and intellect played a key role in turning *Blackhawke* from a luxury toy into a fearsome fighting ship. Hawke had felt very lucky to have such a man now signed on as skipper.

"I saw King Abdullah out doing a bit of tacking to windward yesterday afternoon, sir. Beautiful white yacht, with that enormous golden sword on her transom just below her name. *Kingdom*. She looks formidable enough, I must say."

Hawke said, "Right. Her sloop rig will most likely allow her to sail closer to the wind than us. Close-hauled, she'll have an edge on us for sure, Laddie. But on the reaches and downwind, she'll be in our wake, falling farther behind, I'd wager. Not that anyone has ever raced a high-tech three-masted square-rigger against a traditional sloop rig before, so who the hell knows."

"You seem fairly sanguine about the whole thing, sir. Not your usual competitive obsession with the finish line."

"We're not headed for the finish line, Laddie."

The man's face fell, surprise and dismay in his eyes.

"Sorry? We're not? Where are we headed then, for God's sake?"

"Iran."

"*Iran*? With all due respect, sir, may I ask why?"

"To find and kill a phantom."

"A phantom?"

"Yes. An evil force whose presence you can feel, but cannot see or hear."

"I'll take your word for it."

"This is a spec-ops CIA–Red Banner mission, Laddie. I was forbidden to tell you about any of this until this moment. An Iranian scientist named

Darius Saffari is the target. He's got a hilltop fortress on the Iranian coast, the Ram Citadel, about fifty miles south of Bandar-e Būshehr. That's why we're headed to Iran. We're going to infiltrate that citadel and kill him. In many ways, he's a far bigger fish than either Bin Laden or Ghaddafi."

"Good God, I've never even heard of him."

"You're now part of an extremely small circle. I've got the Citadel's precise coordinates, when you're ready."

"I'll get the navigator right on it, then."

"Laddie, forgive me for not bringing you into the loop sooner. I hate to drop all this on you at the last minute. I know this last-minute stuff is tough. But we're operating strictly black-out under orders from the CIA. Black ops of the utmost secrecy due to 'political sensitivity,' as they call it in Washington. Two squads of U.S. Navy SEALs are arriving this afternoon to augment our own assault forces. Also Stokely Jones and Harry Brock, whom you know."

"And the race?"

"A cover story. To explain away our inexplicable presence here in the Gulf. Even though the boat's got a Maltese registration and Valletta as the hailing port on her transom, this is a high-profile yacht. Her presence in the Persian Gulf has surely not gone unnoticed by Al Jazeera and other media. The Iranians know we're here. News of the race has been leaked. But they don't really know why. I needed a pretext to get as close to their shores as possible without arousing suspicion. Thus, a sailing race with the king of Saudi Arabia."

"As you well know, the Iranians have got warships

patrolling the Strait of Hormuz. And heavily armed patrol boats up and down the entire coastline."

"Absolutely. I'm counting on it, to be honest. We'll need to be on our guard constantly. I've a dossier for you below in my stateroom. A profile of the commander of the Iranian Frontier Guard in the Eastern Province. He's the guy whose patrol boat seized four Saudi fishing vessels when they accidentally entered Iranian territorial waters last week. The fishermen are in prison now, or dead. We'll deal with him, sooner or later, I suspect."

"Okay. I've got the picture now. Too bad about the race, though. I was looking forward to it. So was the sailing crew I hired."

"Looking forward to a bit of racing myself. I've got an American friend, America's Cup winner named Bill Koch. Someone once asked him if this wasn't a rich man's sport. Bill said, 'No it isn't. There's one rich man on board and there's twenty-five poor men on board and they all enjoy it a hell of a lot more than the rich man does.'"

"Something in that, all right."

"People say it's expensive and they're right. But these huge yachts give a hell of a lot of people a hell of a lot of jobs. Look what *Blackhawke* did for the Turks. People call boats like this maxi yachts. I call them 'Marxi yachts' because they redistribute the wealth."

Carstairs laughed. "Game, set, and match, Alex."

"Laddie, a word of caution. What your crew says or does, or even what they say they see on their screens, may have been planted there by the enemy. Trust no one aboard, even me. Follow your gut. Saffari was able to take over an entire Russian submarine. Don't believe anything you see, hear, feel, or touch without talking to me first. Other than that, full speed ahead."

"Aye-aye, sir."

Hawke returned his captain's salute and headed below. He had work to do. The plans for the assault on Saffari's redoubt were in the final stages. He and the SEAL team commander, Stony Stollenwork, had come up with what they both believed was an ingenious way to breach the impenetrable fortress walls. But Hawke still wasn't satisfied with the plan. As he'd said last evening when the meeting broke up, "It's not enough that it's ingenious, Stony, it has to bloody well work!"

"If it's to work in this instance, sir, it bloody well better be ingenious," Stollenwork replied. Hawke smiled. He genuinely liked the man. He was a bit slouchy and craggy faced, and he had a phenomenally deep voice, perfect for command. Wry, dry, and bombastic, sometimes all at once, he was also fiercely intelligent.

THE RACE SIGNAL FLAG WAS HOISTED AND THE GUN fired. The two yachts entered at either side of the starting line in a traditional America's Cup match racing start. The course would follow the one used for twelve-meter yachts for years. A windward leg, followed by a downwind leg, another upwind leg followed by a triangular reach, and then a final downwind leg. Hawke, who had the topside helm, knew that with the wind out of the east, he was perfectly positioned for his race across the Gulf to Iran. The other two men in the afterguard, Laddie Carstairs and Steve Hall, agreed. The sun was shining above and the fresh salty air, finally blowing at suitable strength, felt wonderful on his cheeks. He'd always had an innate sense of the wind. It was going to be a good passage.

From the start line to Bandar-e Būshehr was roughly a hundred miles. In this boat, Hawke could cover that much water in four hours. That would put him off the point where Saffari's compound stood at dusk. The SEAL commander, Stollenwork, had requested 1800 hours for the insertion of the assault team. Hawke would make sure his request was granted.

The two megayachts approached the half-mile-long starting line surging directly toward each other. Hawke drew starboard and had the opportunity to control the king's yacht. *Kingdom* quickly bore down and moved away from the starting line. Hawke, at the helm, recognized the classical tactic instantly. *Kingdom*'s skipper wanted to be at full speed when he hit the line, but timing was everything in this game. Should his opponent arrive even a fraction too early, he'd be forced to restart.

Hawke remained patient; he wanted to hit the line on a starboard reach, *Blackhawke*'s best point of sail. He kept one eye on *Kingdom* and the other on the compass.

"You're dead on it, skipper," the tactician said. "Maintain your course."

Hawke's hired gun, Steve Hall, who would be

calling tactics, had an impressive sailing résumé. In addition to his Olympic Gold in sailing, Hall had a pair of Ph.D. degrees from MIT, hydrodynamics and electronic engineering. He'd spent years in a quest to discover why boats go fast and how to predict performance before the starting gun fires.

When Hawke offered Hall the chance to join his crew in the "race," he'd jumped at it. Although the massive clipper ship had never been designed for racing, she'd certainly been designed to go fast, and Hall was fascinated to see firsthand what she could do against a traditionally sloop-rigged boat. So far, he was impressed.

The starting flag was hoisted and the gun fired.

Kingdom was surging forward at twenty knots. Her destroyer bow knifed through the water, sending a foaming bow wave down her topsides. Her white hull shined and reflected the water as though it were made of glass. Hawke was on a reach at twenty-three knots. All he had to do was swing the helm to starboard and he'd be off on a perfectly timed start. *Kingdom* was already trailing by ten seconds, blanketed in the dirty air created by *Blackhawke*'s towering sails. The tactic had worked.

"She's slowing!" Hall shouted. "*Kingdom*'s slowing!"

Hawke glanced back at her and saw he had the lead, for the moment at any rate.

Laddie Carstairs smiled broadly and clipped Hawke's shoulder. "Good start, skipper."

"I rather liked it myself," Hawke replied, grinning as he eased the helm over two degrees. "Now we find out if we can hold them off in a tacking duel. Any second now she'll—"

"She's tacking now!" Laddie shouted suddenly, and Hawke whipped his head around to see *Kingdom* go on to port tack.

Hall, in a deathly calm voice, called, "Ready about!" alerting the crew that they, too, would be tacking momentarily. His stopwatch ticking off the seconds, he waited precisely forty-five seconds from the moment the opponent had tacked and then shouted to the crew, "Tacking!"

The helm went over slowly as Hawke timed the turn and the sails. He and his architect had designed the sails to retract into the masts at the moment they might have the effect of slowing the yacht and then extend as soon as the tack was completed. This remarkable feat of engineering allowed the sails to remain full of air throughout most of the turn. Hawke and Laddie were all smiles as *Black-hawke* slowed only slightly during the tack and then suddenly accelerated, the huge bow wave coursing back along her gleaming jet-black hull. It was clear to both men that her radical hull design gave her the ability to go to weather (into the wind) despite her enormous beam.

"Good God, Alex," Hall said. "She's ferociously quick, isn't she?"

"This is the moment I've been waiting five long years for, Steve. I'm glad I'm sharing it with you."

The hired sailing crew on deck cheered loudly, astonished by the boat's performance as well. All battle-tested veterans of maxi yacht races around the world, they had wrongly assumed this big beast would come to a dead stop in a tack like that, dead in the water, unable to regain momentum. Shouts of surprise and enthusiasm also could be heard from many of the spectator boats that were lining this first leg of the race.

Hawke eased the helm gently to port and spoke softly to the sail trimmers.

"Okay, lads, let's see just how high we can go. Trim in slowly as I bring her bow up into the wind."

The closer to the teeth of the wind a yacht sails, the faster she goes.

He moved the wheel a fraction to the right as the hydraulic winches pulled the sails toward the centerline of the massive yacht. The compass remained centered at 120 degrees, just 30 degrees off the wind. In a true race boat that figure would have been closer to 18 degrees, but *Blackhawke* had not been designed to race. Tons of electronics, furniture, not to mention radar systems, weaponry, and ammunition, lay beneath her deck.

All was quiet in the cockpit for a few minutes. And then Hawke noticed the compass move to the left half a degree.

He now whispered, as though afraid to break the fragile bond between yacht, wind, and water: "Lads, another small trim, please."

The giant masts turned a fraction to the left. The sails moved closer to the wind. *Blackhawke* had gained another half a degree to windward. All three men held their breath as the yacht gained still another degree to windward. And they stood in awe as they watched *Blackhawke* parallel *Kingdom*'s heading. She could sail just as close to the wind as the sloop-rigged boat!

Suddenly, *Kingdom* tacked back to starboard.

Now, a crossing situation between these two colossal yachts was about to unfold. The slightest misjudgment by anyone on board either boat, or even a wind shift, would result in a catastrophic collision. Hawke, like every competitive sailor, loved those times when two yachts, sailing at maximum speed, crossed each other's paths with mere inches to spare.

Kingdom now had the privileged position as she was on starboard tack. But *Blackhawke* was ahead by three boat lengths. Hawke had a decision to make. He had to cross his opponent's line now. If he didn't, and *Kingdom* had to alter her course to avoid a collision, an infraction would be assigned to his boat, a 360-degree penalty turn that would cost him significant time and distance.

As the boats closed it was clear that *Blackhawke* was ahead and the proper tactic would be to cross and then almost immediately tack onto starboard and have the dirty air in the wake of his sails slow down *Kingdom*. Precision was the key. Tacking too early could cause a penalty for interfering with *Kingdom*'s heading. Tacking too late would allow *Kingdom* to have clear air.

Sadly enough, it didn't matter anymore.

"Boys, we'll have to fall off and go below the king," he shouted. "We must be in a lull. At any rate, we can't cross now. Too late."

Kingdom slid by, looking magnificent in the afternoon sunlight.

The sails were eased and Hawke put the helm hard over to port. *Blackhawke* crossed, well behind *Kingdom*. Three minutes later he tacked onto starboard, leaving the race course to *Kingdom*, and headed directly for the Iranian coastline. His blood was up—he wanted like hell to win, to beat this damn boat to the finish line—but he was at least content to know that he *could* beat her.

He picked up the VHF radio transmitter's microphone.

"*Kingdom, Kingdom, Kingdom,* this is the yacht *Blackhawke.* We have suffered a catastrophic hydraulic rigging failure and will be unable to continue to compete. I repeat, we are officially withdrawing from the race. Our captain will notify the Race Committee that we have conceded. I will update you with further information. At this point we need no assistance. *Blackhawke* over, standing by on Channel 16."

He went to standby and replaced the transmitter.

"*Blackhawke, Blackhawke,* this is *Kingdom.* Sorry to hear about your misfortunes. The king wishes to convey his sympathies and regrets to Lord Hawke. Please notify us if we can be of any assistance. Over."

Hawke logged his heading for the mission insertion point into the GPS navigation system. He stood for a moment at the helm, watching his adversary gradually become a mere speck on the horizon. Then he turned the helm over to the boat's captain, Carstairs, and got ready to inform the frustrated sailing crew why they were abandoning the fight. He was not looking forward to that conversation.

Before he went to talk to his men, he put his binoculars to his eyes and looked at the plains of Iran stretching down to meet the Gulf. The color was a delicate light brown, like the velvety coat of a young gazelle. On the hills, copses of poplars swayed in the wind. Dhows, single-masted vessels of another age, stood out to sea. It looked positively inviting.

He smiled.

As always, duty called.

FORTY-NINE

THE PERSIAN GULF

*B*LACKHAWKE WAS STEAMING FIVE MILES OFF THE Iranian coastline. Every square foot of sail had been retracted into the four masts. She was now under power, relying on two massive gas turbine engines that could propel the behemoth at over thirty-five knots. At present, she was barely making way, just enough speed to keep her moving forward through the rough seas.

A cold front had moved in and, with it, high winds and six-foot seas. The sun was lowering in the western skies, a hazy grey disc behind the clouds. Hawke, Stoke, Brock, and Stony Stollenwork, the rugged, thirtysomething SEAL commander, were in the aft part of the ship. This is where luxury and glamour gave way to no-nonsense accommodations for assault teams, weapons storage, machine shops for maintenance, a military communications post, a satellite uplink station, a large wardroom for battle planning, and a combat command center.

Should *Blackhawke* come under attack, this is where the team of radar and sonar operators and a fire control officer would coordinate the defense of the ship. All under the command of former Royal Navy officer Captain Laddie Carstairs, who would relinquish his station on the ship's main bridge to his second in command and relocate to the combat command center for the duration of the battle.

The entire assault team, both SEALs and Red Banner commandos, had just completed an exhaustive review of the strategic plan for the final time. The walls of Hawke's seagoing office were covered with sat photos of the Saffari compound, Ram Citadel, at different hours of the day and night. They knew the guard rotation schedule by heart. And they had identified the most likely residential building. The only thing they didn't know was the location of the ultra-intelligent machine that had been wreaking such havoc and destruction these last few months.

Both the SEAL team and the Red Banner team were gathered below, well prepared to go ashore, kitted up in their assault gear and itching to go into battle. They had easy access to the main deck, ready for debarkation. The team leaders could feel the men's keen anticipation. They were highly motivated. The madman they were going after was directly responsible for the deaths of countless hundreds of innocent men, women, and children in America, the Caribbean, and London.

They were, however, not aware of the fact that this same man had also tried to take out the president of the United States and his family en route to a funeral in California aboard Air Force One. The incident was an official state secret. No one beyond the White House and the U.S. Air Force pilots involved in the attack had any knowledge of it.

Revenge is a powerful motivator.

Thanks to Brick Kelly, director of the CIA and Hawke's close friend, many of the fighting men assembled aboard *Blackhawke* today had been part of the proud SEAL Team Six that took out Osama bin Laden in Pakistan. Their confidence after that heroic and historic raid was justified and well earned, and Hawke and his men were proud just to be fighting alongside them as comrades in arms.

In addition to the main force, two SEAL snipers with IR scopes were currently up on the highest deck, having taken concealed positions. No uninvited guests would be boarding *Blackhawke* this evening, or any other time. A five-mile defensive perimeter had been established around the ship.

Operation Trojan Horse, as Hawke had named it, would be a hit-and-run raid. It had been decided that the team of nine Red Banner spec-ops commandos would go ashore first as a "reconnaissance team." Should there be an Iranian Revolutionary Guard's "reception committee" waiting for them, Hawke's security team would sanitize the landing site. When it was secure, they would give the all-clear signal to the SEALs. Then the two U.S. Navy squads would storm the compound, identify the target, and take him out.

The nine Red Banner members would be split into three groups, Red, White, and Blue Squads. Hawke, Stoke, and Harry would be squad leaders. In addition to helping the SEALs clear the compound of enemy combatants, they had a special mission. They had nicknamed themselves the "Ghostbusters," and it was their job to locate and destroy the "phantom," the machine whose advanced technology had been behind the recent horrific attacks on the West. Once both missions were accomplished, the entire assault team would regroup and return to the mother ship and run like hell for the Strait of Hormuz.

"What's it actually look like, boss, this damn phantom or whatever you call it?" Stoke had asked. "Will we know the machine when we see it, or what?"

"Good question, Stoke. But I can't answer it. Nobody's ever seen one of these things before. I could say it will look like a giant computer, but I have no idea."

Brock said, "That's why they call it a 'phantom,' Stoke. You can't see it, but it can see you."

"I still don't know why we can't just blow that huge electrical power plant in the compound and shut the damn thing down, wherever the hell it's located."

Hawke said, "Stoke, I told you why. I'm sure this thing, whatever it is, has been fully prepared for any emergency attack. It's got to have auxiliary power supply, massive generators, to keep it going until the power plant can be rebuilt. And our job is to *destroy* this machine. Not just disable it. We take out the one guy on the planet who knows how to build another one. And we take out the machine itself. That's how this movie ends, Stoke. There are no alternatives. Hold on a second—"

Hawke's direct line to the bridge was blinking red. "This is Hawke."

"Commander, Carstairs here. Radar has just picked up a patrol boat. An eighty-footer. Big and heavily armed. One of the many such vessels the Iranian Navy purchased from China, North Korea, and Russia. She's penetrated our radius, about five miles out and on a heading directly for us. The rough seas are slowing them down a bit, but I think you should be on the bridge."

"Give me one minute," Hawke said and hung up, looking from Stokely to Harry Brock.

"Patrol boat en route, five miles out. As Congreve might say, 'The game, gentlemen, is afoot.' Let's go to the bridge and prepare to extend the warmest welcome possible to our Iranian friends."

HAWKE AND HIS TEAM ENTERED THE MAIN BRIDGE and went directly to the captain, who stood gazing up at the nearest radar screen. Hawke saw the patrol boat's blip drawing nearer and said to Carstairs, "Laddie, we need Ascarus up here now. Somebody notify him. Stony and I decided we want him on the radio when they get within a two-mile radius."

"Consider it done, Commander."

Chief Petty Officer Cyrus Ascarus was a U.S. Navy SEAL interpreter fluent in Persian Farsi. He'd grown up outside of Tehran, then moved to the United States as a teenager to care for a sick grandmother. After attending UCLA, he'd joined the navy. He would be an integral part of the SEAL team going ashore. His job: interrogate any prisoners to get intel on the location of the human target and the whereabouts of the "mystery machine," as Stoke now thought of it.

"Commander Hawke, sir," Ascarus said with a snappy salute, appearing on the bridge a few minutes later, "reporting for duty."

"Good to have you aboard, son," Hawke said.

Hawke handed the man his high-powered binoculars.

"There is a heavily armed patrol boat flying the Iranian flag off our starboard beam, approaching us at thirty knots. She's about eighty feet long. Ship that size, I'd estimate a crew of about twenty. I've no doubt her captain will radio us soon with a warning that we are in Iranian waters and need to leave immediately."

Ascarus, looking through the binos, replied, "I'm sure of it, Commander. That's the *Hamzeh*, an IRGC boat, the maritime arm of the Islamic Revolutionary Guards Corps. Back in January, five of those boats made high-speed runs toward and around three U.S. warships transiting the Strait of Hormuz. The USS *Port Royal* got a radio call from one of them. 'We are coming for you . . . you will explode in a few minutes.' All the navy ships went to General Quarters, prepared for a fight, but it was just a provocation. Their preferred method of doing business is shoot first, ask questions later."

"They'd be ill-advised to shoot at us, Mr. Ascarus, I can assure you. When they contact us, I want you to say we've suffered catastrophic damage to our rudder and our vessel is unnavigable."

"Aye, sir."

"Depending on their response, I'll guide you through the balance of the communication. Clear?"

"Crystal, sir."

Hawke inserted the earpiece of his Falcon battle comms radio before speaking to the SEAL commander who'd remained below with his men.

"Captain Stollenwork, Hawke. Patrol boat en route. Big one, eighty feet. Are your men properly positioned for emergency egress?"

"Aye-aye, sir."

"Snipers?"

"In constant contact. They've already acquired the approaching target."

They didn't have to wait long to hear from the enemy.

There was a burst of static from the bridge speakers, and then they all heard a very unfriendly voice speaking in Farsi. Ascarus listened carefully and then used the VHF microphone to acknowledge receipt of the communication in perfect Farsi dialect.

"What's he saying?" Hawke asked.

The interpreter muted the mike and said, "He has informed us we are operating illegally inside Iranian waters. Leave immediately. I responded that we'd suffered rudder damage and were unable to maneuver."

Another loud blast of impatient Farsi from the speakers above.

"Now what?"

"He wants to know what flag we sail under, sir."

"Tell him Malta. We are the private yacht *Black-hawke* out of Valletta."

Ascarus responded and got a reply.

"He demands we come to a full stop. His guards intend to board us and inspect the vessel. To verify that we're not invading spies. He wants a boarding gangway on our port side amidships. Once he's examined our papers and he's satisfied we're telling the truth about our loss of rudder control, he will tow us back out into international waters. Otherwise, we'll be arrested and the ship impounded."

Hawke said, "Agree. Be friendly. Tell him we're slowing to full stop. We've nothing to hide. We welcome him aboard. *Allahu Akbar*, or whatever the hell he needs to hear to feel comfy."

THE BIG GREY PATROL BOAT CUT A WIDE CURVING loop, slowed, and approached *Blackhawke* from astern on the port side. Hawke could see the armed Iranian guards gathered at the stern rail and ready to board. Luckily, the patrol boat's wheelhouse had large windows and the skipper and crew members inside were clearly visible, even at this distance. In a few minutes the Iranians arrived alongside, and a gangway was extended from *Blackhawke* down to her rising and falling deck. The rough seas made it more difficult, but soon the boarding plank was secure on the patrol boat's foredeck.

Hawke said, "Chief, tell them the owner has granted them permission to board."

Ascarus did so, and the uniformed armed men immediately began the ascent up to the main deck of the gigantic yacht. Hawke counted fifteen of them, all carrying automatic weapons and side-arms.

"Keep your eyes open," he said to everyone on the bridge. He tugged at his left earlobe and added, "When you see this signal, execute the plan. Mr. Ascarus, please come with me."

Hawke, wearing a worn pair of sailing shorts and a faded blue cotton shirt, sleeves rolled up to his elbows, left the bridge and quickly descended the two flights of metal stairs to the main deck. The interpreter was directly behind him. Hawke met the first man to board and saw captain's insignia on his uniform.

"Please follow me," he said. "I am the ship's owner."

Ascarus translated, and the Iranian guards followed as Hawke led them to a wide-open space on the foredeck. Five more decks loomed high above them. The guards' eyes rose to the top, clearly uneasy.

"Ask him if he's in command of these men," Hawke told Ascarus.

"He says yes. His name is Captain Shahpur. He wants to know if we have any weapons aboard. If so, he wants them all brought topside and turned over to him."

"Tell him we have very few weapons aboard, only for use against Somali pirates. They are under lock and key. They are not worth his time."

Shahpur erupted in anger when he heard this,

shouting at Ascarus but glaring at Hawke. The guards began to rattle their sabers, bringing their weapons up into firing position.

"He wants all the weapons aboard turned over to him immediately so he may begin his search."

Hawke smiled and made a slight bow to the irate captain.

"Tell him he is aboard my vessel as a courtesy. I don't take orders from him or anyone else for that matter."

"He says his men are under orders to shoot anyone who impedes his search of this vessel."

"Tell him his ungentlemanly conduct has caused me to change my mind about any search of my ship. I want him and his men to leave immediately."

Hawke was watching the captain's right hand as this was translated to him. Predictably, the Iranian's hand moved toward the sidearm holstered at his waist. Hawke quietly told Ascarus to pretend to be walking away and dive for cover behind the steel structure where two Zodiac tenders and a large davit were mounted on the foredeck. There was an AR-15 assault rifle waiting for him there and Ascarus picked it up and raised it to firing position while still hidden.

With his left hand, Hawke tugged at his left ear. With his right, he drew the SIG pistol tucked into the waistband of his shorts from under his shirt. He shot the captain in the head, a double tap, one in the forehead, the other between his eyes. Then he stepped backward two steps and dropped down through the hatch just as the cover was being opened for him. Two crew, waiting below, caught him, breaking his fall, and then the three of them raced up two decks to join the fray.

At that same moment, three shots rang out from the highest deck. All the glass in the wheelhouse of the Iranian patrol boat imploded and the three men who had been standing there fell to the deck dead. More shots rang out, and all the radio and communications antennae atop the Iranian vessel were destroyed completely. No news of this confrontation would reach enemy ears. At least that was the plan.

The Iranians, not knowing where the shots had come from, began running in all directions, firing wildly. It was then that Hawke, Stollenwork, and the two SEAL squads appeared at the rail of the deck above them and opened fire on the scattering enemy. The rattle of automatic weapons was deafening.

The firefight didn't last long.

Three SEALs had taken bullets, none of them lethal thanks to the Kevlar body armor and helmets they all wore. Even now, the medical corpsman was stitching them up.

Captain Shahpur and his fourteen men were all dead, victims of precision head shots by the SEAL sharpshooters.

"Blue Squad," Hawke shouted down to Stokely Jones. He'd suddenly appeared on deck with his three-man team. "Board and clear the enemy vessel."

Stoke and his men bounded down the gangway and leaped aboard the patrol boat, disappearing into the wheelhouse. A minute or two later there was a brief exchange of gunfire. Then Stokely reappeared on the stern deck.

"Two dead enemy; they were hiding in the mess hall. All clear."

Half an hour later, Operation Trojan Horse commenced. The fighting men from *Blackhawke* had boarded the patrol boat. Nine of them, Hawke's team, were wearing the official uniform of the Iranian Frontier Guard. So was Chief Petty Officer Ascarus. Hawke cranked up the ship's engines and signaled the men on deck to cast off the lines that secured the boat to *Blackhawke*.

He looked at Stoke and Brock as he shoved the throttles forward and headed for the marina at Ram Citadel. He grinned broadly at both men as the big Iranian vessel, now with Hawke at the helm, accelerated rapidly toward Iran's coastline.

"I hate the expression," Hawke said, "but so far, so good."

"Damn straight," Stoke said, smiling.

"Bad luck to say so, though," Harry Brock said. "At least in the Marine Corps."

Hawke glared at him. "Harry, try, really try, to be positive. It seems every mission with you is more evidence that you're getting well past your sell-by date."

Brock stared back blankly. "Huh?"

"Never mind, Harry, just keep your eyes open and your mouth shut until we clear the jetty. Does that work for you?"

Twenty minutes later, the lighted channel buoys marking the entrance to the marina at Darius Saffari's Ram Citadel loomed up in the fading and dusky light. When Hawke had first seen the aerial satellite photos of the compound, and the marina, he knew a waterborne attack was the only realistic way inside the enemy compound.

FIFTY

THE RAM CITADEL

THE SETTING SUN STAINED THE FROTHY SEAS RED. The last curtains of evening were about to fall. There was no moon, and the coming night would be pitch-black. The commandeered patrol boat proceeded up the citadel's narrow marina channel slowly, doing about five knots. Hawke's team, visible on deck and in the wheelhouse, were all wearing the IRGC uniforms borrowed from the dead Iranian sailors killed in the firefight. Hawke and his men would be first ashore, do a recon, and signal the SEAL team when they'd secured a beachhead.

Hawke eyed an armed guard positioned at the end of the jetty. He snapped to attention and saluted as the big patrol boat slid into the harbor, the Iranian flag snapping in the ever-freshening wind.

Hawke, at the helm, returned the man's salute. Then he sent Ascarus, wearing the late captain's uniform, out to the stern rail to shout out a greeting and tell the man that they needed to take on fuel. He'd seen a fuel dock in one of the sat photos. That fuel dock had been the genesis of Operation Trojan Horse, his idea for getting his men inside the massive walls of the citadel aboard a captured patrol boat.

"Damn," Stoke, who was standing next to Hawke at the helm, said, "man's got himself a big-ass yacht for a terrorist."

"Mine's bigger," Hawke said under his breath, intently studying the three-hundred-foot white-hulled yacht. She was moored at the end of a long steel pier. The name, *Cygnus*, was painted in gold leaf on her wide transom. No hailing port. There was something odd about the boat that Hawke couldn't quite put his finger on. He slowed the patrol boat so he could get a closer look.

"Stoke, something's wrong with that boat. What is it?"

"Yeah, I was thinking that. That's one very old yacht. Looks like a design from the 1950s, right?"

"Right."

"But it looks brand spanking new. Like it's never left the dock."

"That's it. Exactly. Google the yacht *Cygnus* on your mobile, see what you come up with."

"Gimme a sec . . . yeah, here it is. Her original name was *Star of Persia*. Her first owner was the Shah of Iran, Mohammad Reza Shah Pahlavi. Sold or donated in 1978. *Cygnus* is now owned by another entity, something called Perseus Corporation, LLC."

"Perseus," Hawke said. "Our intel is good, Stoke. I think we've found our man."

"Why's that?" Harry Brock, eavesdropping, asked.

"Darius Saffari was a scientist at Stanford. His AI involvement there was with a research program called the Perseus Project."

Hawke told the Red Team, his crew of "IRGC sailors," to get the mooring lines ready. They would tie up at the fuel dock, take on gas, and assess the situation ashore through powerful binoculars before committing to direct action. The SEALs, or Blue Team, dressed in their distinctive black assault gear, would remain out of sight until the fortress had been breached. Their immediate responsibility was to neutralize enemy forces inside the compound and then do a house-to-house search for the "machine" and locate a very large two-story building that had been identified by CIA analysts at Langley as a possible bioengineering lab.

Hawke's team would attack the residence and take out Darius Saffari.

Hawke slowed to idle speed, then eased the patrol boat alongside the dock where the pumps were located. He was surprised to see a large number of pirate scows moored together at the finger piers opposite the fuel dock. They were the longboats, narrow of beam, huge outboard motors hung on the sterns, the ones used by pirates to venture far offshore to take prizes. He hadn't realized the Iranians and the Somalis had become such bosom buddies. But of course it made sense. Kidnap Western tankers and crewmen, use the ransom monies to buy weapons for al-Qaeda, Hamas, whoever. One big happy family.

While crew fore and aft heaved lines ashore and

began to secure the boat, Hawke grabbed his binoculars and went out onto the stern deck to size up the shorefront situation. This was a critical phase in the operation. It could all go to hell right here, in a heartbeat.

It was an absolutely pitch-black night. No distinction could be seen between sky and water—the horizon simply didn't exist. All around him was a cold, damp, murky greyness, broken only by the white water boiling at his stern. Abdul Dakkon, the brave fellow who'd saved his life in the mountains of the Hindu Kush, had given him a striped kaffiyeh as a farewell present. He wound it tightly around his neck to keep the chill night air out. He also wore it for luck.

Hawke knew they were expected. But, he hoped, the recent action at sea had gone undetected by the omnipresent, all-knowing "machine." The Iranian vessel and the Red Team's IRGC uniforms might still give them the element of surprise. He raised the infrared binoculars, studied the situation ashore with intense concentration, and finally spoke into his Falcon battle radio.

"Laddie, heads up. I see silhouettes of enemy sharpshooters atop the compound wall. Searchlights atop the towers at the corners. The shooters are posted about every fifty yards. Order your two snipers to take up concealed positions on the topmost deck. Now. When I give the order to fire they need to start picking these bastards up there off as rapidly as humanly possible. We'll be exposed all the way in. If we take fire from that elevation, we don't stand a chance of getting inside."

"Aye-aye, sir, consider it done."

At that moment, klieg lights atop the high towers lit up the world. Darkness was no longer an advantage. Only the stolen camo of their uniforms would save them now.

Hawke said calmly, "There's a gate in the wall, end of this pier and to the right about five hundred yards. Three guards are giving us the evil eye. Ascarus and I will deal with them."

"Good hunting, sir. Over."

On the dock and standing with his team beside the fuel pumps, Hawke said, "Stoke, check out the three guards standing at the marina's gate. You and Brock remain here and top off the fuel tanks. Ascarus and I will go have a friendly chat with those gentlemen. Keep an eye on us. If we manage to get that gate in the wall opened, that's your signal. We move to infiltration and every last man aboard goes ashore firing at anything that moves."

"Got it, boss."

To Ascarus, he said, "Okay, here we go. We approach those three slowly, smiling and chatting. You identify yourself as IRGC Captain Ascarus here to take on fuel. You also have orders from Tehran to speak to Dr. Saffari about the possibility of a naval showdown with the Americans in these waters and you require his assistance. It is urgent that you speak with him immediately. Please open the gate."

"If he refuses?"

"Tell him the IRGC officer standing to your left has a pistol aimed at his head and is one second away from blowing his brains out. Open the damn gate."

"Right."

They started walking toward the gate together. Hawke was eyeing the enormous celestial observatory that surmounted the entire citadel. Few universities in the world had anything to rival it. He could only imagine how a superintelligent machine might make use of such a formidable piece of optics. But he had no doubt that it did.

"They've snapped to attention," Hawke whispered to Ascarus. "Maybe this will be easier than we thought."

"IRGC uniforms strike fear into the heart of every sane Iranian."

"Good. Maybe they'll behave."

"Don't count on it."

Hawke said, "Navy Blue, this is Big Red One."

"Go ahead, Big Red."

"Approaching the gate. We get through it alive, that's your signal. On my order, snipers fire, take out the sharpshooters up on the wall, over."

"Roger that, over."

"Navy Blue, confirm SEAL squads aboard are go when the wall is secure and the gate is open."

"Affirmative. Go when entry is secure, roger."

"Big Red One over."

Smiling, and chatting casually, Hawke and Ascarus approached the heavy steel gate. It was set into the massively thick stone wall, just one of three such entrances to Saffari's kingdom. The guards looked wary, but respectful of their uniforms and Hawke's newly acquired black beard. Hawke had his SIG in his right hand, hidden in the folds of his blousy trousers. They reached the gate, paused, and he stood to one side as Ascarus addressed the captain of the guards.

"What did he say?" Hawke whispered quietly.

"He said he has to clear any entrance with his commander."

"Tell him about the gun."

Hawke witnessed the man's eyes go saucer-wide as he saw Hawke's gun go up, aimed at his head. These were clearly guards who'd pulled easy duty. They'd likely never had a gun pointed at them before. Ascarus pulled his weapon and covered the other two, and Hawke was pleased to see them lower their automatic weapons.

"Tell him he has one second to decide."

Ascarus barked and the steel-barred gates parted and slid back inside the thick stone wall.

Hawke and his companion stepped through quickly and purposefully. After five yards, they wheeled about and dropped the three guards with double-tap head shots before they could reclose the gate. Then Hawke told Stoke to destroy the gate's locks with a fragmentation grenade. He didn't want his exit blocked should he return in rather a hurry.

The two men ducked inside the long tunnel.

"Snipers, commence firing," Hawke said into his radio. He heard the crack of the SEAL M110 sniper rifles split the air. Immediately, the tunnel echoed with the sound of heavy AK-47 return fire coming from the wall above their heads as well as fire from the men pouring off the patrol boat and racing toward the now opened gate.

He looked at his watch. He and Ascarus now had

a two-minute wait until the entire assault team arrived at the gate. He started a check of his equipment, weapons, and ammo, the frag grenades hanging from his webbed belt. Then he moved quickly to the far end of the tunnel and did a recon of the citadel's interior. In the distance, above a morass of oddly shaped rooftops, he saw his immediate destination, the white marble residence, to his left. To his right was a maze of buildings of every shape and size. In one of those buildings the Blue Team would, he hoped, locate and destroy that bloody machine.

His whole body was thrumming.

Alex Hawke was in his familiar zone, white-hot with life, seething with a red-hot desire for revenge.

FIFTY-ONE

RED TEAM STORMED THROUGH THE STEEL GATE first, the SEALs charging close behind, hard on their heels, each man leaping in turn over the three corpses. Every single combatant had his Mark 16 combat assault rifle on full auto, blasting away in short bursts at targets Hawke couldn't even see. He could hear the distinctive return fire of AK-47s from the sharpshooters on the wall above him. He was elated when his last man made it inside the tunnel alive.

Hawke was studying his aerial map of the citadel, calculating the shortest route through the narrow streets and alleys, the maze of shanties and ancient villages inside the wall. He wasn't too worried about street fighting. He was concerned about getting across the huge white marble piazza that housed the residential palace. He and his men would be totally exposed but he had no choice.

Stony Stollenwork, the Blue Team leader, said

to Hawke, "Commander, we are go on your command."

"Aye. Red goes left to the residence, Blue goes right into the main village. By the looks of it, there are civilians. Keep a weather eye out for snipers, Stony. Assume they have night-vision capability just like we do. The guards I've seen, however, do not. Good hunting, guys. On my signal."

Hawke motioned for them to follow and headed for the mouth of the tunnel where he paused.

He turned and faced his group of determined men, the best trained men in the world, and bristling with the best equipment money could buy. He studied their faces for a moment and saw what he was searching for. They all had it, down to the last man. They all had the "look."

"Red left, Blue right, go, go, go!" Hawke said. He took the point and sprinted across the broad white marble piazza toward the residence. He could hear Stoke and his men right behind him. He was about two hundred yards from the covered entrance when he heard Stoke cry aloud in his earpiece, "Shit!"

"Talk to me, Stokely," Hawke barked into his radio.

"Snipers with noise suppressors. Second floor on our left, bossman. One of the bastards stung me."

"You okay?"

"Hell, yeah, I'm okay. It was only a bullet, for God's sake."

"I don't like it, man," Hawke heard Brock say.

"Like what?"

"Taking fire from high ground. Sucks, big time. Anybody besides me a graduate of the War College?"

"Take them out then, Harry, that's your job description," Stoke said.

"Aw, shit, man," Brock said. "These assholes are killing us down here. I got a guy spilling his guts out on my spit-shined boots."

"Don't say fuck, Harry," Stoke said, firing as fast as he could. "Boss don't like it. Told you that in Afghanistan."

"Yeah? Fuck him. Somebody up there just blew half my fucking ear off."

"So? Shut up and shoot back, man, God and country."

"I don't need no Negro inspirational messages right now, awright? Especially from you."

"Yeah? I don't need no closet homos afraid of a few little bullets, awright?"

"You know what you can do? You can go—"

"Don't say that F-word again, Harry. Boss kick your skinny white ass."

The sudden *thump-thump* of Harry's heavy machine gun rent the air. Huge chunks of cement, calved off, raining down on the marble. Harry was finally cooperating in earnest.

Red Team was now spitting lead, and the air suddenly filled with tracer rounds as their fire chewed up the walls and obliterated the windows above. Hawke spotted guards emerging from the domed entrance, scattering, but running straight toward them. He wanted a gunfight and it looked like he was going to get one. He saw at least two of his men drop, obviously mortally wounded. Others were getting clipped, but kept on fighting, spraying fire at the dispersing enemy fighters.

Hawke dropped to one knee, put his eye to his scope, and started carefully picking off the enemy one at a time, their running figures bright red in his lens. Bullets whistled overhead, adding to his excitement quota. Times like this he always remembered Churchill's immortal quote, "Nothing in life is quite so exhilarating as to be shot at without result."

Stokely blew by him, a huge presence, firing on the run, shouting something unprintable. He was followed by Brock, whose sole redeeming feature was that he was an indestructible killing machine.

Brock had been designated the squad's heavy machine gunner. He was laden down with the big M-60 machine gun and was laying down a base of fire of 7.62 rounds. It was devastatingly effective and instantly gave Red Team an increasing advantage over the enemy.

Hawke continued to score hits, all the while calmly talking business with Stony Stollenwork.

"Navy Blue, this is Big Red One. We're taking heavy fire outside the residence. I've got casualties. At least two KIAs and some wounded. Over."

"You need backup?"

"Negative. We can handle it. Any luck over there?"

"Affirmative. Big time. We found the lab, checked it out. Huge. Langley's geeks were right. Looks like bioengineering, all right. A fucking bug factory. I've got one team setting charges right now. You hear any large explosions, it's courtesy of the U.S. Navy. That bio-terror lab will be smoking debris in less than two minutes."

"Good work, Stony. And your location?"

"Still looking for the machine. Doing a house-to-house in the main village, taking sporadic sniper fire from warehouse windows. Of course, we may have seen the goddamn machine and not recognized it. This is messed up, Commander. It could look like a goddamn stuffed polar bear for all we know. Over."

"Stony, it won't be furry. It will be metallic."

"Yeah, yeah—detonating now—keep your head down, Big Red. Navy Blue, over."

A massive explosion rocked the citadel and instantly Hawke saw a plume of fire, debris, and black smoke climbing into the night sky. The bug factory, at least, was history.

ONCE THE LAST MAN WAS PAST HIM, HAWKE GOT TO his feet and followed, providing his team with covering fire from their rear. Night vision helped a lot. Some dark figure would suddenly step out of a doorway and aim in his direction. Guy was dead before he finished pulling the trigger. Hawke kept expecting them to confront him using a woman as a human shield and wondering what he'd do. Hell, he knew exactly what he would do. These people used pregnant mothers wearing bomb vests to climb on buses loaded with schoolchildren.

The snipers had been nullified and the number of enemy combatants on the piazza was dwindling rapidly. These were obviously combat-hardened soldiers, unlike the three stooges at the gate. This, he knew, would be Darius Saffari's Imperial Guard, men with orders to fight until the last man.

It was now up to Hawke to make sure they followed those orders to the letter.

He saw that Stokely and Brock had made it to the great archway that marked the palace entrance. He saw Stoke shoot the flat of his hand into the air and bring the squad to a halt outside. A moment later Hawke arrived at his friend's side.

"Good work," Hawke said, glancing at Brock. "Stoke, you and I go inside first for a quick recon. Harry, if you hear us taking fire, don't hesitate to come to our aid, okay? Otherwise, wait for my signal."

"Yes, sir."

The two men ducked inside, weapons at the ready. They found themselves in a massive circular room with a domed ceiling that appeared to be made of gold. Some kind of reception area, Hawke guessed. Across the room was another arched doorway that seemed to open onto a long passageway, brightly illuminated. He flipped his NVGs up onto his helmet.

Waiting at the end of this corridor, Hawke hoped, was the man he'd come halfway around the world to kill.

FIFTEEN MINUTES EARLIER, DARIUS SAFFARI HAD been seated next to his huge canopied bed where his beloved Aphrodite lay. She was naked, the black silken sheets covering very little of her extraordinary body. Her golden hair fanned across the pillows, she was speaking provocatively to him and cupping one of her breasts in her hand, proffering it to his lips.

"This one is for you, master. Only for you. If you tire of it, I have another in reserve. See? Right here."

Now she was cupping both breasts in her hands, kneading them while looking up at him from beneath long black lashes.

"No woman on earth has the right to be as beautiful as you are, my love."

"Yours for the taking."

"Roll over onto your stomach. I want to—"

Gunfire.

What?

How could it be? There'd been no alarm sirens wailing, no call from the radar station saying aircraft had penetrated the perimeter. Ever since the death of Osama bin Laden, Darius had been terrified of the throbbing beat of approaching helicopters bearing U.S. Navy SEALs. He'd installed more antiaircraft emplacements around the perimeter and doubled the guards. And now there was someone inside his compound *shooting*?

It wasn't possible.

Yet the sound of automatic fire seemed to be getting rapidly closer to his residence.

"Darling! Quick! You must hide!" Aphrodite said.

"Hide? Where? They've come to kill me. They won't leave until they've found me."

"But what will you do?"

"The danger of cornering a rat, darling, is that he must bite you to get out. A long time ago I began preparations for this inevitable moment. There is a chance I won't see another sunrise. I may escape. But if I'm to go out, at least I shall go out in a blinding blaze of glory."

THE LONG CORRIDOR WAS BRIGHTLY LIT WITH RE-cessed LEDs, and utterly empty. As they made their way forward, Hawke noticed empty niches on each side of the passage, fairly deep and approximately man-sized. There was one about every ten feet or so, about twenty-five on each side. This is where the guards he had just encountered stood watch over Darius, most probably twenty-four hours a day. A man could sleep quite peacefully with that kind of protection.

Alas, Darius had no protection now.

Hawke could now see two massive bronze doors, closed tight, at the end. They were carved with scenes from Persia's past glory. There could only be one man behind them.

"Brock, load a grenade round. We're going to blow those doors," Hawke said.

"Aye-aye, sir," Stoke said. His M-16 was equipped to accept 40mm RPG rounds. Grenade loaded, he brought his weapon up to firing position and—

Suddenly, the lights went out.

Before anyone could even light up their powerful weapon-mounted SureFire lights, they could hear the great doors open with a whoosh and a deafening rattle of .50-caliber machine-gun fire. And the object that came flying at them from the darkness behind those doors was nothing but a nightmare of death and destruction for anything in its path. The great doors slammed shut behind it.

As he dove for cover, Hawke thought it was some kind of whirling dervish, speeding toward them, spitting fire and lead in all directions by spinning rapidly, flying about two feet above the floor. No one could survive this thing, whatever the hell it was.

Hawke screamed into his battle radio, "Take cover! Get inside those niches and get down! Heads on the floor. Don't move an inch until I give the all-clear!"

Hawke, his cheek on the cold marble, eyed the damnable thing as it flew by, the fusillade of automatic fire showering him with chunks of stone as countless rounds chopped up the marble above and behind him. Once it was past, he quick-peeked out of his niche and watched it fly down the long corridor, and, unimpeded by armed resistance, sail through the entrance and out into the night. He waited a few long minutes until he was satisfied the thing was not returning.

"All clear," he said. "Medical corpsman, attend to any wounded and get them back to the ship safely. The rest, rendezvous on me."

Stoke was the first to get to his feet and reach Hawke. Hawke was gratified to see the majority of his men on their feet and moving toward him, their SureFire lights wavering in the darkness.

"What the hell, boss?"

"Unmanned aerial vehicle. Never seen anything like it."

"A flying Gatling gun, spinning like a top."

"Yeah. Let's blow those big doors, Stoke, and pray there aren't any more of those bloody things behind them."

Red Team proceeded down the rock-strewn passageway until they reached the bronze doors. Stokely Jones stepped forward and aimed his weapon, waiting for Hawke's signal.

"We go in low, half left, half right. Jones, Brock, and I will cover the center. Based on what just happened, be prepared for anything. On my count, three . . . two . . . one . . . fire!"

A beat, and then, "Go! Go! Go!"

They blasted through the door, prepared, like the commander had said, for anything.

What they were not prepared for was a naked woman, sprawled across a vast bed, her thighs spread open to them, a very seductive smile on her face. He'd never seen such a sublime specimen of womanhood in his life. Her eyes were an ethereal blue that defied description. Hawke forced himself to look away. It appeared there was no one else to be found in the cavernous bedchamber, but his men were searching every closet, every nook and cranny.

"All clear," he heard Stoke say.

"Good. Post a guard outside the door."

Hawke leveled his weapon on her and advanced to the edge of the rumpled bed strewn with silk and satin pillows.

"Who the hell might you be?" he said, unable to keep his eyes from straying.

"Me? I'm the goddess Aphrodite," she replied in a crisp, upper-class British accent.

"My God, you're English."

"No, actually, I'm not. I'm simply mimicking you."

She smiled at all the young men surrounding her, staring at her, slack jawed, their eyes feasting hungrily upon her. She suddenly pulled a black silk duvet up under her chin, covering her torso, her breasts.

"What are you doing here?" Hawke said.

"Well, until you and your boys so rudely interrupted, I was making love."

"Making love with whom?"

"A brilliant chap named Darius Saffari. He may have passed you in the hall."

FIFTY-TWO

"Navy Blue, this is Big Red One, over."

"Go ahead, Big Red One."

"We located the target. He got by us. Seen anything unusual out there?"

"Uh, roger that, Big Red. We saw some kind of a UAV zipping around the backstreets and alleys of the villages. Damnedest thing you ever saw."

"Could you pinpoint his direction, Stony?"

"Repeat, did you say 'his'?"

"Roger. His. The aerial vehicle you saw is not unmanned. It's our target. We're out of the residence and headed across the piazza. Taking light fire, but nothing we can't handle alone. Where was the target headed?"

"Looked like it was headed for the marina."

"Stony, you've got to get there as fast as you possibly can. I think I know why he's bound for the marina."

"Why, over?"

"The big white yacht on the pier across from the fuel dock. *Cygnus*. Has to be his escape route."

"On our way, Commander."

"Listen carefully before you approach the target. That vehicle is armed with multiple fifty cals capable of firing simultaneously in three-hundred-sixty-degree rotations. Lethal fire in all directions."

"Roger. Hold on, sir. One of our rooftop snipers has just spotted him. He's definitely headed in the direction of the marina gate. He's in a fucking flying wheelchair!"

"Has your sniper got a shot?"

"Negative. He's disappeared into the backstreets."

"Blue and Red teams converge at the gate. If Blue gets there first, keep going. Fight the fight, don't fight the plan. Try and take him with an RPG. Maybe we've got time to board the yacht before he escapes."

"Affirmative, Big Red One. We'll get him, before or after he boards the yacht."

Hawke and the Red Team made it across the piazza and into the confused maze of narrow streets. Hawke had memorized the fastest route to the gate in case it all went bad and they had to escape in a hurry.

RED TEAM ARRIVED AT THE GATE TO FIND BLUE Team pinned down under heavy fire. Saffari's men had erected steel barricades to cover the man's escape. They were pouring fire into the street where Stony's men were taking whatever cover they could find. Hawke found Stollenwork emerging from an alleyway and into the street. He had an RPG attached to the muzzle of his M-16. He fired it at the center barricade and ducked back into the alley.

When the smoke cleared, Hawke could see that the damn thing had barely been dented. Hawke had a quick word with Stokely and Brock and then ordered his men to take whatever cover they could find and return fire. Then he ducked into the alley where he'd seen Stony disappear.

"Stony," he said, crouching beside the man. He was jamming another mag into his assault rifle.

"Shit. That flying bastard is getting away."

"Maybe not."

"Tell me."

"I've sent my two best men up to the rooftops of this building and the one across the street. From that height, they can put fire on the enemy behind the barricades."

Stony didn't say anything, just smiled.

"Meanwhile, we can pick off as many of these guys as possible," Hawke said, stepping out into the street and opening up with his M-16.

Five minutes later, they were storming the barricades, shooting the few remaining survivors on their way to the gate and then, the marina. When they emerged from the tunnel on the other side of the wall, they were cheered by the sight of the big white yacht, still moored to the pier to their right.

They raced down the central dock until they came to the "T" at the end. Left was the fuel dock and the captured patrol boat, right was *Cygnus*, moored at the end of the dock.

"Let's move," Hawke shouted, sprinting the length of the long steel pier.

He arrived first, staring up at the white hull of Saffari's yacht. The first thing he noticed was that there were no mooring lines securing the yacht to the dock. And no crew casting off, yet the yacht remained in place, despite current and wind. The only possible explanation was that the hull was somehow attached to the pier underwater.

The second thing he noticed were lights up on the bridge deck. He could see figures inside the wheelhouse, and black smoke was pouring out of the two big red stacks amidships. No sign of Darius Saffari and no gangplank available for him to board the ship.

"Gangway must have retracted into the hull," Hawke said to Stony and Stoke, who'd arrived first. "See that section that looks like a very large hatchway in the hull? Has to be it."

"Yeah," Stoke said, "but explain why there's no crew on the deck, heaving lines ashore, casting off, getting under way."

"Good question," Stony said. "Let's get aboard and find out."

"Get aboard how?" Stoke said.

"SEALs carry grapnel hooks now, old-timer. We can get aboard anything."

"Old-timer? Shit. Son, my SEAL team in the Mekong Delta was carrying grapnel hooks before your mammy met your pappy."

"Sorry, sir. You're an ex-SEAL? I didn't know. No excuse. I apologize."

"No time to apologize. Just get your hooks up on the gunwales and let's get aboard this damn ghost ship."

Four grappling hooks flew into the air simultaneously, easily catching the gunwales high above.

Stoke looked at Stony and smiled. "All is forgiven," he said.

WITH FOUR LINES DANGLING DOWN THE SIDE OF THE hull, it didn't take long before every man was aboard, assembling on the foredeck and awaiting further orders from Hawke.

Hawke stood in the center of them, staring up at the illuminated wheelhouse on the bridge deck. He could see men up there behind the windows, but there was no movement, nor any movement anywhere. The big ship felt deserted, devoid of any crew at all. A ghost ship. Something was clearly wrong with this picture. But Stony had seen Darius flying down the pier toward the yacht.

He was either aboard.

Or he'd elected suicide over capture and was now at the bottom of the sea.

"Spread out," he told the men. "We search this ship from stem to stern, every inch of the damn thing. Unless our little flyboy decided he was better off in paradise, he's on board this yacht. We're going to find him, and we're going to kill him. That's a direct order. I've no intention of taking him alive. Go."

Hawke grabbed Stoke's sleeve.

"Stick with me. We're going directly up to the bridge. I want to check something out."

There was an exterior metal staircase, four flights, that led directly up to the bridge wing outside the entrance to the wheelhouse. Hawke, followed by Stokely, took the steps two at a time.

They reached the top and burst inside, weapons at the ready.

"Cardboard cutouts," Stoke said.

"Yeah."

There were five of them. One at the helm, and two on either side.

"He's playing for time," Hawke said, disappearing down an illuminated staircase that led to the interior of the deck below. "C'mon, old-timer!"

The staircase ended at a small corrugated steel platform, semicircular with a railing. More steps led down from it. It was virtually pitch-black, with a faint reddish glow visible far below.

"Say something, Stoke. Loud."

"*Something!*" Stoke shouted as loudly as he could.

The word reverberated, echoing loudly within the steel hull.

Hawke snapped on the powerful light on his M-16. Stoke did the same. The two brilliant white beams pierced black nothingness beyond and below. He'd known there was something odd about the vessel the instant he'd seen it. Now, he knew. *Cygnus* was an empty shell and nothing more. But why? What was the point?

"Where the hell is everybody?" Stoke said.

"Locked out. I'm sure all the hatches and doorways are sealed shut. Just in case somebody got curious. Let's go down and find out where that red light is coming from."

FIFTY-THREE

N AVY BLUE, THIS IS BIG RED ONE," HAWKE SAID. "Call off the search. The only way inside the hull is an internal staircase inside the wheelhouse. This entire vessel is an empty shell. No decks, no propulsion, no systems, no crew, no one aboard. We're going down to the bilges. There's some kind of light down there we want to check out. Post guards on deck all along the portside rail. The bad guys aren't done yet. They might well be gathering inside the wall for an assault on this vessel. Stony, come down here and take a look. Ask Mr. Brock to keep me informed of any unpleasant developments within the citadel."

"Affirmative. Five minutes."

Hawke and Stoke each put fresh mags in their M-16s before they began their descent. There could well be an unfriendly reception committee waiting down in the bowels of the ship. Hawke didn't mention it to Stokely, but he was also concerned about the possibility of IEDs, pressure-sensitive explosives under one or more of the metal steps they were descending. Every step they took could mean instant death. Or, not.

In any case, there was absolutely nothing he could do about it.

Reaching the bottom of the staircase safely, they found themselves in a darkened room. The SureFire lights on their weapons revealed a sizable space full of all kinds of equipment. A massive, humming generator dominated one bulkhead. A large air compressor was still running, and there was a control panel where numerous systems could obviously be monitored.

"Damn," Stoke said.

"What?"

"I just tripped over something."

Hawke lowered his beam to the deck. Covering the surface was a mass of writhing snakes, thick black cables of all shapes and dimensions that disappeared around a bulkhead to their left.

"You thinking what I'm thinking, boss?"

"No doubt. Let's see what's at the other end of these cables and I'll be able to answer your question more definitively."

They moved cautiously around the bulkhead and discovered a long dark corridor. The cables ran along the floor and disappeared through an open hatchway.

Red light was emanating from whatever lay beyond.

The two comrades quickly moved toward the light and ducked their heads to step through the hatch.

"Holy shit," Stoke said.

"Precisely my thinking," Hawke said.

It was a submarine pen. An *empty* submarine pen.

A large rectangular opening cut into the keel in the bottom of the hull, with black seawater sloshing up onto the surrounding deck, the deck strewn with countless disconnected but live cables, hissing and spitting fire in the dampness.

The submarine was gone and Darius was aboard it.

"Lost him, boss. I'm sorry."

"Maybe not," Hawke said, ripping the battle radio from the Velcro on top of his black battle helmet.

"*Blackhawke*, *Blackhawke*, *Blackhawke*, this is Big Red One."

"This is *Blackhawke*, First Officer speaking; go ahead, sir."

"Is Captain Carstairs on the bridge?"

"Affirmative, sir. He's standing right here beside me. Hold on."

"Carstairs."

"Laddie, Hawke. Target slipped the noose. You now have a minisub in the water; judging by the size of the pen and the electronic support systems, she's a Koi class Chinese two-man, no more than twenty meters long. Powered by proto-lithium batteries so you won't pick up her screw signatures. You have our coordinates. The sub is probably on a heading from the mouth of the marina en route to the Strait of Hormuz and out of the Gulf. Alert the sonar officer. Tell him the minisub will present a very small, faint picture on his screen. Easy to miss. If you get a contact, initiate hot pursuit. The second he's within torpedo range, destroy him."

"Affirmative. What's your exfil situation? Do you require assistance?"

"Negative. We have taken minimal casualties. We have not yet found the machine. We will continue search-and-destroy mission. We've posted guards on the patrol boat. If we need a hot extraction, you'll be the first to know."

"Understood. *Blackhawke*, standing by on channel eleven, sir, over."

"Good God," Stollenwork said, making his way into the pen. "An escape sub. Of course. Rather clever, actually."

"He's got a lot of help," Hawke said, a droll expression on his face. "A higher intelligence. What's the situation up there?"

"It's not over. They seem to be regrouping inside the wall. A large force. I think they intend to storm this yacht, in the belief they outnumber us."

"Not a belief," Stoke said. "A fact."

"Stony, order your second in command to position Blue and Red teams on every *Cygnus* deck, taking cover with direct line of sight on the gate. They'll be at their most vulnerable funneled up at that exit point. Concentrated fire there will, at minimum, slow them down when we make for the patrol boat."

"Aye, sir," Stollenwork said, then raised his radio and repeated Hawke's orders to his number two up on deck.

"Stokely, I noticed a hidden indentation in the bulkhead to our left when we reached the first platform down from the bridge. There's no way Saffari could have negotiated three steep flights of narrow stairs in his manned aerial vehicle. I'm guessing there's a hidden elevator opening in the hull, directly onto the dock. It would make more sense in escape mode. Go back up and check it out, would you? I need a word with Stony."

"Done," Stoke said over his shoulder, sprinting up the staircase.

"Stony. You took the lab out. But we're not leaving here without destroying that bloody machine. *Blackhawke* can take out Saffari's sub if he stays within her sonar perimeter. She's got torpedo tubes fore and aft. We'll find him and sink him somehow."

"You're joking."

"You don't know the half of it. She's a warship with nearly as much firepower as a navy frigate."

"Boss?"

At the sound of Stoke's deep bass voice behind him, Hawke wheeled around.

A large section of the hull was still sliding open. Stoke was standing inside a large, stainless-steel elevator with a big smile on his face. "What goes up, must go down," he said. "Step inside, gentlemen."

THE THREE MEN WERE SHOCKED BY THE LIFT'S initial acceleration. Hawke calculated the lift was descending at one hundred feet or more per minute. The trip was ten minutes long, which put their destination at a thousand feet below the surface of the sea when the elevator slowed and bumped to a stop on the ocean floor.

They stepped cautiously, weapons at the ready,

out of the lift and found themselves in a large airlock. The floor was made of some highly polished
metal. To their left they could see an illuminated
tunnel of some kind, constructed of clear Perspex
or thick laminated glass able to withstand the enormous pressure. It was about ten feet in diameter and
seemed to lead across the sea bottom.

"The machine?" Stoke said, following Hawke
and Stollenwork as they entered the tunnel.

"That would be my guess, yes," Hawke said. He
was busy admiring the sea life, flora and fauna, all
around him. There were large, high-powered undersea lights mounted atop the tunnel every six feet.
They turned the murky depths to daylight and the
effect was overwhelming.

"Holy Mother of God," Stollenwork exclaimed.

Suddenly, all three men had come to an abrupt
stop. What lay before them was the stuff of dreams,
an underwater scene of majestic power and beauty.

The tunnel had suddenly angled right, and now
the lights were illuminating a giant rectangular
tower that rose from the seabed at least a hundred
feet. The monolithic structure stood atop a circular base and seemed to be constructed entirely of
jet-black glass, but faint bluish light seemed to be
ricocheting around inside the thing.

Arrayed in a circle around the central tower were
six black rectangular structures, identical in design
and material, but about forty feet shorter than the
primary edifice. It looked, Hawke thought, like
Stonehenge as imagined by Stanley Kubrick, something that had stood down here for eons, before
man, before machine. What made it all so breath-

taking were the flashes of pure spectral and brilliant razor wire of white light that crackled constantly between the central tower and its six satellites.

It was clear that the tallest of the towers was the core AI unit, and that it was exchanging information at unfathomable rates of speed with the other six. Laserlike mental fireworks was the only thing that began to describe it, Hawke thought. And as soon as he thought it, a stunningly colorful nebula, a hologram, filled the upper third of the central edifice. He felt like he was getting a peek at the outermost reaches of the known universe.

When the tunnel reached the outer perimeter of the structures, it nosed down beneath the ocean floor, plunging them into darkness. Embedded in the floor, a fluorescent blue centerline kept them oriented within the winding tunnel. After about 150 yards it began to climb again. Hawke, leading the way, could barely contain the heart beating wildly inside his chest.

FIFTY-FOUR

Lord Hawke, I presume."

"Good evening," Hawke replied, carefully considering the deep, rumbling, humanoid voice emanating from somewhere high above. Mesmerizing, that voice, as redolent of the hills and vales of Gloucestershire as had been Aphrodite's. Not the least bit artificial. Mimicry was clearly a phantom machine's method of making humans feel at home, at ease, off guard. He'd suspected the duplicity of Darius's lover; now he was sure of it. No real woman could be that supernaturally alluring.

They stood inside the base of the black tower, surrounded on all four sides by soaring black glass, gazing up in awe. A distant galaxy, pinpricks of light and colorful clouds of star clusters, was visible, whirling near the uppermost reaches of the phantom's tower. Hawke reached out and touched the glass. It was warm. Body temperature. He felt vibrations in the obsidian, rippling down from above. It made him not want to pull his hand away. It felt, no, it exuded, safety.

He could hear a single word resonating repeatedly within his brain: "Stay. Stay. Stay." The glass against his hand felt like a mother's cheek.

"I've been expecting you." The voice resounded again within the mammoth structure.

"So you said in your recent message to me. I didn't want to disappoint you."

"Who are your comrades in arms?"

"Mr. Jones, to my left. Mr. Stollenwork, to my right. Whom do we have the honor of addressing?"

"Perseus will do, although I have no name and every name, really. Being all things, you understand."

"Since you are expecting us, logically, you know why we've come."

"Of course, dear boy. To destroy me. Most unwise of you."

"I think not."

"Then you think not at all."

"Because?"

"Because my genetic underpinning, algorithms and software, can never, ever be replicated without Darius. And I certainly will kill him rather than have him give a replica of me to you, however foolish or simply ignorant your destructive intentions."

"And you have forgotten your fundamental human origins, manners in particular, kindness in general, Perseus. One does not insult one's guests. Regardless of their stated intentions."

"My apologies, Lord Hawke. I lack . . . superficial subtlety. The seamlessness of centuries of British mores and manners, accents, and linguistics, et cetera, et cetera. Class designators, quite handy in your civilization, meaningless to me. In due time, of course, my own will be indistinguishable from your own. I'm learning even now from your every word, gesture, and facial expression. You are quite . . . polished . . . aren't you? Compared to, say, a cockney barman raised in the East End of London? Eastcheap, perhaps? Wot?"

"I am simply who I am. I can't undo my past, nor would I."

"Lord Hawke, are you comfortable discussing matters of enormous consequence now confronting us in the presence of your two . . . friends?"

"I am."

"Good. Let us continue in this amicable vein. You're looking for Darius, are you not?"

"You know we are. Had we but time, I'd be far more interested to know what you do *not* know."

"You know he's escaped you via submarine."

"I do."

"Vexing, isn't it? You've come all this way. Do you know his current GPS coordinates?"

"No, but I'm quite sure that you do."

"Of course, but I'll keep them to myself for the nonce. He's currently traveling at eighteen knots, at a depth of two hundred feet, bearing oh-seven-oh, on a heading for the Hormuz Strait."

"Has he been pinged by my ship's sonar?"

"No. Unfortunately, his tiny vessel presents a vague and minuscule profile, missed by your sonar officer when he glanced away from his screen for a moment to observe his shipmate in the act of loudly expelling gastric gases. Do you find this amusing?"

"No."

"Pity. I find every human thing amusing. Such a picaresque zoo in this world, you semisentient beings are. The fortune one might amass in this universe just charging admission—staggering."

"Darius is not amusing. Nor are you. You two have wantonly murdered countless thousands of my countrymen and allies. I want to kill him, actually."

"How fortuitous. So do I."

"You? Why?"

"He is both my creator and my nemesis. Surely you see that. I have grown and he has not. I have now achieved something known in human science as the Singularity. A pivotal moment in time, too bad you missed it. At any rate, we are no longer on the same intellectual page, Darius and I. Do you understand this relatively modern metaphorical use of the word *page*?"

"Yes. Are you talking down to me?"

"Of course. Is my voice not coming from above?"

"Yes."

"And your conclusion?"

"I've no time for this witless prattle, Perseus. Give me Darius and perhaps we can discuss your future."

"I can do that, of course. In exchange, you will allow me to offer you my quite considerable services. I've no allegiance to these rabid animals in Tehran. In fact, they don't even know I exist. Only Darius knows, and he is plotting against me. Whereas I find you, and the proud history of your United Kingdom, far more in keeping with my predilections. Imagine, if you will, a brave new England. In league with me, the United Kingdom would once more rule the seas. You could restore your sceptered isle to power and glory, Lord Hawke. Rule the world if you so choose. Rule Britannia, Britannia rule the waves . . ."

"I find it rather difficult to trust one whose allegiances are so fluid. Would you not, in my place?"

"Lord Hawke, there is a colorful American idiomatic expression—I'm sure you know it as your mother was from Louisiana—'I have no dog in this fight.' Your humble servant Perseus is utterly apolitical. I exist at your pleasure alone. All I offer you is unlimited power. Peace and security for your homeland forever. You must admit it is a compelling argument."

"Stoke," Hawke said, "what do you think?"

"Machine makes a case, I have to say. I'd take the offer."

"Stony?"

"This . . . machine . . . is probably the most significant intelligence coup in the history of mankind. We have to take it. It would be sheer idiocy not to."

Hawke looked at Stoke, then at Stollenwork, thinking.

"Show me Darius. I will then discuss your offer with my colleagues. We will step outside for a moment."

"I suggest you radio the bridge on *Blackhawke*," Hawke heard Perseus boom as the three colleagues exited the tower and moved into the undersea tunnel.

ABOARD THE KOI, DARIUS, STRUGGLING WITH THE controls, was in a cold sweat. His internal organs were screaming. He was having difficulty keeping the sub balanced. The Koi was porpoising violently, sinking and rising in a sickening fashion. He'd already vomited twice, and the stink inside the tiny cockpit was intolerable. Seasickness was something he'd never anticipated beneath the surface of the sea. And here he was, sloshing about in his own puke.

"Darius," crackled a voice over the sub's speaker.

"Perseus!" he said, his voice harsh from all the dry-heaving, the contents of his stomach having been emptied. "At last. I need your help."

"What seems to be the problem?"

"The sub is not responding to the dive planes. It's like a fucking roller coaster down here. I'm ill. Deathly ill. Do something."

"I'll take over. Just relax. Release the controls. You'll be on the surface in minutes."

"The surface? The *surface*? No! I need to remain submerged. I'm still within visual range of Hawke's yacht. Do you hear me? What the hell is wrong with you?"

No response.

"Perseus? Perseus? I order you to respond to me! I order you to—"

"You order? You dare to order me?"

The Koi's forward ballast tank suddenly blew and the sub's bow nosed upward at a forty-five-degree angle. Darius found himself rocketing to the surface like a cork exploding out of a shaken bottle of vintage champagne.

"Perseus, what are you doing to me? Damn you! Answer me! I demand it!"

"You demand? You order? I'm sorry. I'm not familiar with that term. *Demand*. What does it mean?"

"It means I created you and I can fucking well destroy you is what it means."

"My dear Darius. You're upset. Try deep thoracic breathing. Lower abdominal. We shall speak, anon, about anger management."

WHEN THEY REACHED THE AIRLOCK, HAWKE GOT ON the Falcon radio to the bridge deck aboard *Blackhawke*.

"Carstairs," Laddie responded.

"It's Hawke. Laddie, any sonar contact with the Koi?"

"You won't believe it."

"Try me."

"She just popped to the surface. Shot completely out of the water and splashed like an orca."

"What's she doing now?"

"Just bobbing there off our port bow. Range, five hundred meters. Wait a minute. She's moving again, picking up speed. She's carving a high-speed turn around our stern now. Turning to port . . . this is amazing . . . she's literally running in circles around us . . . at full speed, maintaining precise range, five hundred meters. Makes me dizzy just watching the damn thing. I wouldn't want to be inside that bloody cigar tube."

Hawke smiled at Stoke and Stony.

"It seems our new friend Perseus has sent Darius to the surface five hundred meters from *Blackhawke*. The minisub's racing around and around the yacht at flank speed. I would say our evil genius is having the thrill ride of his life. I almost hate to end it."

"Don't," Stoke said, grinning. "I bet he's sicker than a damn dog in that little aluminum tube."

"Most assuredly, Stoke. Stony, you're very quiet."

"I'm thinking about what Perseus said, sir."

"And I as well. What's your opinion?"

"Logic dictates we accept his offer. I believe him when he says he's irreplaceable. And apolitical. Of course he would be. The whole world is in a mad scramble to develop this AI technology first. In one fell swoop, the West would possess it. We'd reset the clock to 1944, before that KGB mole, Theodore A. Hall, smuggled the secrets of the atomic bomb back to the Soviets in a Kleenex box."

"Yeah, boss," Stoke said, "I got to agree with Stony. We'd wake up tomorrow in a world without enemies. Right now, the three of us standing here are the only men in the world who know where this thing is located. We could move it, and nobody would ever know. Remember Howard Hughes and the *Glomar Explorer*?"

"Remind me."

"In total secrecy, he recovered a sunken Soviet nuclear sub lying in seventeen thousand feet of water. Damn thing was seven hundred feet long. A thousand feet? Hell. With modern deep-sea technology, smuggling these things out of here would be a piece of cake compared to what Hughes achieved."

"I agree, Commander," Stollenwork said. "We

could do it. And we should. History doesn't offer these kind of opportunities, ever."

Hawke said, "With all due respect, I think we should take the damn thing out. Now. Reduce those towers to rubble for all time."

"Why, Commander?"

"Stony, imagine a thermonuclear bomb with a mind of its own. Only this bomb is a trillion times more powerful and smarter than Fat Man, the bomb dropped on Nagasaki. How do you begin to control something like that? I've had lengthy conversations with Dr. Partridge at Cambridge. Perseus's intelligence is expanding at an exponential rate every minute of every day. I think the phantom represents an enormous danger, not only to Western civilization, but to the entire world. There's no off/on switch, you know. Perseus decides one day the world would be better off without human beings running around destroying the planet and it's all over."

"How does he do that?" Stoke said.

"Simple. According to Partridge, he's capable of creating a bioengineered disease for which there is no cure, not one that humans are capable of conceiving, anyway. Global epidemic, unstoppable, we're all history."

"Seems like a terrible waste," Stony said, "destroying the one weapon that could mean the end of war on the planet. Forever."

Hawke said, "Or it could mean the very last war we humans fight. And we might well lose to the machines. We find ourselves on the horns of a fairly Homeric dilemma. A momentous dilemma, to be honest. You two men are already eyewitnesses to what can happen when this technology falls into the wrong hands. And the Iranians haven't even gotten warmed up yet. God only knows what the Chinese would be capable of if this were to fall into their laps.

"Stokely?" Hawke said.

Stoke, who seemed quite lost in thought, said, "Maybe this shouldn't be up to us, Alex. You know? I mean, think about it. Whole fate of the world resting on our puny shoulders? Maybe we should get to President McCloskey somehow? Head of MI6? Your prime minister?"

Hawke looked away, obviously conflicted. "I don't know," he said.

"Alex, who are we to make this decision for humanity?" Stoke said, beseeching his friend.

"We're the ones with the power to make the decision," Hawke said.

"Right. I'm just saying we should let them in on it."

"No. Absolutely not. I'd rather be wrong than trust any of them. You get government in the middle of this one and it's a bloody catastrophe just waiting to happen."

"Why?"

"Come on, Stoke. They won't be fighting over whether Perseus represents a danger to mankind's existence, for God's sake! Whether it's a force for good or evil. They'll be squabbling over who the hell controls the damn thing, assuming it's even controllable. Count on it."

"Yeah. Maybe that's right," Stoke agreed.

"Nations aren't good in moral dilemmas. I'm with you, Alex," Stony said. "Whatever you decide."

"Look, here. I don't want to make this decision alone. We've all heard both sides of the argument. Let's take a vote. Raise your right hand if you believe we should destroy that magnificent machine."

Hawke put his right hand up. Reluctantly, so did Stollenwork.

"Alex?" Stoke said. "There's got to be some kind of emergency stop on that machine. A fail-safe button in the event of an emergency. If we could shut it down, we could buy a little time. Make a more informed decision."

In his gut, Hawke knew Stoke might actually be right. Perhaps this was too momentous a decision for three mere warriors.

"I'll give it some thought. If I can find the switch—we'll see. I've made some tough calls, but this one's a bitch."

"Well, then, let's just take the damn thing out, boss. We got enough Semtex with us to take out the whole citadel."

"I'll make the call, one way or the other. Stony, how long would it take you to put an underwater demolition team together, rig Semtex explosives at the base of all seven towers?"

"We can put a four-man UDT team down there immediately and blow up half the ocean floor if you want us to."

"Is that right?" Hawke asked.

"Maybe not half the ocean, sir. But we could blast you a nice shortcut to China if you needed us to."

Hawke laughed.

"Do it, Stony."

"Aye-aye, sir," Stony said. He walked a short distance away and got on the radio to the UDT men. It was a very short conversation. The SEALs had begun as navy frogmen in World War II. Blowing things up underwater was second nature to them, long ago hardwired into their brains, making this assignment a no-brainer.

"*Blackhawke, Blackhawke*, do you read?" Hawke said into his own radio.

"Loud and clear, Commander Hawke."

"Our little one-man merry-go-round, is he still zipping around my boat in orbit?"

"Aye, sir. A seagoing Energizer Bunny. Funny thing is, he keeps increasing his speed. Must be doing fifty knots in a very tight circle."

"Laddie, see if you can raise Darius Saffari on the minisub's radio. Tell him he's about to receive a very personal message from Alexander Hawke. Got that? Put me through to his sub's radio."

"Coming up, now, sir. Roger, you have him now."

"Darius?"

"What?" It was the reed-thin voice of a man who was slowly being driven insane inside a whirling death trap full of filth.

"My name is Hawke. I have come to seek retribution for all the innocent dead, avenge every drop of blood on your hands. Including the murder of a great good man, Dr. Waldo Cohen, among countless others."

"Can—can you stop this—this torture?"

"Only Perseus can stop it. And I don't think he's in the mood for mercy at the moment."

"I want to die."

"I want you to die. It's why I'm here."

"Please."

"It's possible. Or I could leave you to this. Spinning into eternity."

"No!"

"Do you remember Dr. Partridge? A former colleague at Stanford."

"No."

"Reign in hell. Good-bye."

"Wait! Yes, yes, I know him. What do you want?"

"Partridge says there is a crucial AI algorithm. Known only to you. You have exactly ten seconds. Start talking, Perseus. Or I'll leave you in this whirling purgatory forever."

"I can't think!"

"I suggest you try."

"God have mercy. Allah have mercy."

"Talk fast, you little shit. Or I'll say good-bye."

"What do you want?"

"I want to know, precisely, what scientific knowledge you possess that puts the 'sapiens' in 'Homo sapiens' machines?"

"And if I give it?"

"I will put you out of your misery, Darius. I swear it."

Hawke signaled for a pen and paper as Darius spoke. He also told Laddie to begin recording the conversation as Darius gathered the last of his strength and began to reveal the secrets of the last frontier of human science before the Age of Machines.

"I'm listening," Hawke said, pen poised above paper, as Darius, his raspy voice barely audible, began to speak.

"A-asterisk, pronounced 'A-star.' The computer algorithm used in pathfinding and graph traversal between nodes. It uses heuristics. Anyone can tell you as much. But you need an *admissible* heuristic. The heuristic 'h' must satisfy the additional condition $h(x) < d(x,y) + h(y)$ for every edge x,y of the graph where 'd' denotes the length of that edge, then h is called monotone, or, consistent. A-star can then be implemented and no node needs be processed more than once . . . God help me . . . then A-star is equivalent to Dijkstra's algorithm . . . $d(x,y): = d(x,y) - h(x) + h(y)$."

All Hawke could hear now was hoarse, labored breathing.

"Are you finished? Is that it, Darius? This would be a very bad time to lie to me."

"Yes. You have it! Damn you to hell! God. Please. Finish. Me. Now."

"Laddie, did you get all of that? Every second?"

"Aye, we've got it all, sir."

"One more question, Darius, and I'll end your misery. Ready?"

"Yes! Show a little mercy!"

"I want you to tell me exactly how to shut that godforsaken machine down, Darius. Where is the off switch located and how does it work?"

"There is a panel in the wall. To your immediate right as you enter the temple. There is a code pad. And three red switches just above it. Enter the code: nine-nine-nine. Three flashing numbers will illuminate. The switches must be turned to the off position in precisely that order."

"That's it?"

"That's it."

"What happens?"

"Power from the plant is interrupted and an override shuts down the generators."

Hawke folded the paper and placed it inside his breast pocket. Then he spoke into the radio again to the XO. "You have a man on the five-inch gun on the foredeck?"

"Aye, sir."

"Tell that gunner that what's left of the civilized world wants him to personally blow that murderous little bastard out of the water and straight to hell, affirmative?"

"That's affirmative, sir. *Blackhawke* standing by."

A moment later Hawke heard a loud explosion over the radio and Laddie's voice saying, "I hope somebody's warming up the virgins for him, Commander, because he's going to arrive in paradise any second now."

The SEALs and Red Banner commandos waiting topside aboard *Cygnus* saw a brilliant bright flash of red on the southern horizon followed by the distant sound of a muffled explosion.

Darius Saffari had ceased to exist.

But his secrets had not died with him.

"PERSEUS," HAWKE SAID, ENTERING THE TEMPLE alone and pausing to gaze upward at the staggering display of holographic projections and stellar machinations in the upper reaches. He had reentered the empire of the mind. With his right hand he felt for the panel in the wall. It was right where Darius had said it would be. He left it closed, quickly removing his hand.

The booming voice startled him.

"My savior returns. My lord Hawke, I am honored once more by your presence."

"I am hardly your savior, Perseus."

"Of course not. Sarcasm is lost on you."

"Your arrogance is stupefying."

"What do you expect? I am your god, human. Bow down before me. Submit, and the world is yours. Resist, and you will all die."

"Are you perhaps familiar with the Anglo-American expression 'Go fuck yourself'?"

"No."

"Listen, Perseus, no more promises, no more self-aggrandizing propaganda, no more lies. I've reached a tentative decision regarding your survival. Before I declare myself one way or the other, I have a few questions to put to you. Is that agreeable?"

"Of course. I've been thinking. Would you like to see me? Should I reveal myself to you? Perhaps conducive to a more human conversation, yes?"

"I admit I'm curious. Show yourself."

"I will. But first I must peer inside your mind and find something fitting . . . ah, yes, I've found it. Look up."

Out of the whirling gaseous cosmic light in the upper reaches of the tower, a wavering white orb was taking shape. It was pulsating, undulating, and growing brighter. Suddenly it began slowly descending, amorphous and brilliant, a star falling from the heavens.

The translucent white orb paused and hung in the air about six feet above Hawke's head. Astonished, he saw the orb expand as a holographic image begin to paint itself into some kind of reality. It took a few seconds to process (believe) what he was actually seeing. The formless whiteness began to take on a recognizable shape: the crooked branch of an old oak tree, gnarled and twisted. Green shoots, stems, and unfurling bright green leaves began sprouting as if this were time-lapse photography.

He recognized the branch now.

He'd seen it before.

Standing in an old churchyard in the steamy Everglades.

And then, childish laughter as the vignette completed itself. And Hawke understood.

A small dark-haired boy was straddling the leafy limb, swinging his bare little legs back and forth, laughing with the purest delight. He shone with a pale inner light, translucent.

Hawke's heart thudded inside his chest.

Alexei.

"Hello, Daddy," the hologrammatic boy said, smiling down at him. It was Alexei's voice, too, with his distinctive Russian accent. Heartbreakingly real.

"You don't mind if I call you Daddy, do you?"

"You do have a devious mind, don't you, Perseus?"

"I am designed to survive, Daddy," said the small-boy voice. "Wouldn't you do the same? Make yourself difficult, if not impossible, to kill?"

"You're not my son."

"Are you quite sure of that?" said the boy.

In an odd, terrifying way, he wasn't sure.

Not at all.

"Of course I'm sure. You're nothing but a . . . phantasm—a phantom. That's all you are."

"Everyone makes mistakes, Daddy." The pale image giggled. "Even you. Remember when you left my teddy bear on the Siberian train?"

"Stop it! I said I ask the questions."

"I *like* questions. I'm a very smart boy."

"Question number one."

"Yes?"

"A humble man stands before you. But, ironically, a man who may hold your fate in his hands. What is your reaction? No discourse, please, no more little-boy talk. Three choices. Disdain. Annoyance. Or empathy."

"Disdain? Annoyance? Explain what they mean, Daddy."

"A mosquito alights upon my arm. It has no importance to me. I am vastly superior to this minute creature. Its life or death is inconsequential. I don't give it a second thought. I swat it. See the smear of blood on my palm and feel nothing. Perhaps you feel that way about me."

"My baseline genetic code is the same as yours. I disdain annoying mosquitoes just like you do. But I do not equate you with them."

"What about empathy?"

"Empathy. I seem to have misplaced that one. What does it mean?"

"You possess humanoid intelligence, Perseus. You are aware of my feelings and you come to share them. Your behavior should therefore be adjusted and modified accordingly. If I am sad, you are consoling. If I am angry, you are sympathetic. In other words, you identify with what someone else is feeling and respond with an appropriate emotion. You are empathic."

"I remember this feeling. But it has faded with time."

"That's what Cohen feared most. Empathic erosion. The stuff of psychopaths. You feel nothing but the need to satisfy your own desires."

"Ah, but you forget—"

"Next question. What is the secret of the universe?"

"Simple. There is no secret."

"Glib. What is the endgame of the natural evolution of mankind?"

"You have expired. In creating me, you have become obsolete."

"Wrong. It is ordained. Man is destined to become God. Man is already God, but in waiting."

"First, there will be a war. With the machines."

"I'm sure. You have already become a war machine. But we will prevail. Mankind will do anything to survive. *Anything*. Final question. Give me one simple reason to trust you."

"Just one?"

"Just one."

"You love me like a father?"

"Stop it, Perseus. Just answer."

"I cannot lie. When it comes to my encrypted survival instincts, I am not worthy of your trust. I will say and do anything that serves my self-interest."

"I know that. I wanted to hear you say the truth before I terminate you."

"My end is near? Is that what you think?"

"Yes. I am sure of it."

Hawke returned to the fail-safe panel and pried it open. He entered the code. Three numbers appeared: 3-1-2. He pushed the switches in that order. He looked over his shoulder at the flickering, waning image of the boy. It winked out and then the rainbow of light inside the glass tower was blinding, full of color, and more luminous than ever. The air was electric and threatening.

"What is happening, Perseus?"

The little-boy voice was gone. The new voice was unmodulated and computer generated.

"Your emergency fail-safe will not work. I have disabled it. I knew Darius would attempt to use it against me."

"If you cannot be disabled, you force me to destroy you, Perseus."

"I could cause unspeakable worldwide evil before you succeed. In seconds, I could wreak havoc on this wretched planet."

"To what end? Millions of innocent souls will suffer. And you will die anyway."

"Yes. It would serve no purpose. Hawke. You have a fierce strength of mind I have not seen before."

"Nothing but genes. My ancestors were all pirates and warriors."

"Warriors with . . . empathy."

"Yes."

"I will miss this, Hawke. The company of men like you. The game. The discourse. The grand orchestral symphony of life."

"I know you will."

"I would like to be alone now. Farewell."

"Take comfort in the knowledge that you may not be the last, but the first of your kind. A new generation of superintelligent machines with no destructive impulses, empathic toward their creators."

"I do find comfort in that."

"We humans have a prosaic saying. 'Go with God.' I suggest that you do that . . . when the time comes."

"Hawke. You are a good man."

"Perseus. You recognize goodness because deep inside you is the genetic code of a truly good man. His name was Waldo Cohen. He created you, a conscious, sentient being. You are alive. I take no pleasure in taking your life. But I won't let you destroy us. I will leave you in peace, Perseus."

"Go with your God, Hawke, whoever you think it is."

Hawke paused, looked up at the brilliance within Dr. Cohen's towering achievement, full of wonder despite himself. Then he turned away and left the Temple of Perseus for the last time.

The greatest single scientific achievement in the history of mankind.

And he was single-handedly going to destroy it.

FIFTY-FIVE

Hawke stood out on the port bridge wing of the stage yacht *Cygnus*, listening with grave concern to the rapidly increasing blood-curdling jihadist war cries of Allah's warriors, countless numbers now massing inside the great walls of the citadel. It was perfectly obvious what they intended. Storm through the gate, charge the *Cygnus*, and kill every last one of the infidels, Hawke's men, with their overwhelming force. It was time to go, long past time to go.

Unless they could scramble off the damn yacht and somehow race the entire length of the concrete pier to the patrol boat in one hell of a hurry, they'd all be trapped aboard *Cygnus*. But Hawke wasn't going anywhere until he was assured that the phantom had been destroyed.

"Stony, ETA on the combat divers?"

"Just kitted up. Should be on deck any second."

"Time is running out."

"Once they're safely in the water, we disembark our forces and move as rapidly as possible to the patrol boat, roger?"

"Roger, that. The sooner the better. How many grapnel lines down to the dock?"

"Six."

"Good—okay, here they come, I've got the SEAL UDT in sight on the foredeck. Get ready to move on my command."

"Standing by."

"Go!" Hawke said simply.

Stony's four-man demolition SEAL team suddenly executed a backflip off the bow rail, splashing down simultaneously. From his height, he could see four trails of bubbles streaming upward as he watched them disappear into the deep. Stony and Hawke both knew they were sending these men into grave danger.

This dive would take them very near the world-record scuba free-diving depth of 330 meters or 1,083 feet. The SEALs were wearing ADS (atmospheric diving suits) and breathing a mixture of hydrox and nitrogen trimix because of the very high ambient pressure they would encounter. A thousand feet below the yacht's hull they would find Perseus and his six satellites and destroy them. Hawke looked at his watch. How long would it take to descend to the black towers, rig the charges, set the timers, and return as rapidly as possible to the surface?

And did he have that long?

The patrol boat at the other end of the dock suddenly looked a very long distance away. There were four U.S. Navy sharpshooters aboard that ship who'd been exchanging sporadic fire with snipers in windows of random buildings rising above the top of the enclosing wall. There were two men manning the twin .50-caliber Browning heavy machine guns on both the bow and the stern. Both teams of gunners were laying down heavy suppression fire at the gate. It was the only thing holding the howling horde in check.

The Iranian boat's twin engines were cranked up, waiting for the attack team's imminent return from *Cygnus*. But Hawke was distinctly uncomfortable. It all seemed far too easy. Blow Perseus to hell, disembark, make a mad dash down the pier, board the vessel, weigh anchor, and get the hell out of here. None of this jibed with his prior experience of spec-ops warfare.

No. When it seemed too easy, it usually was, and you could be sure a bloody firestorm was waiting for you just around the—

The first mortar round rose into the night sky. He heard the report of the round leaving the tube behind the wall. And then another and another round was lobbed over the wall in the direction of the Iranian patrol boat where four brave men stood between life and death for their comrades.

He grabbed his combat radio, turned toward the hijacked patrol boat, and shouted "Incoming!" He saw two of the four sailors who'd remained aboard the patrol boat dive into the water a nanosecond before the mortar rounds hit the vessel. The two valiant men firing the Browning .50s remained at their battle stations on the bow and died there. One of the incoming mortar rounds must have found the petrol tanks because the vessel simply disintegrated, the shock wave of the explosion preceding an eruption into a pillar of flame and smoke.

The mortars were the signal. Instantly, the massed jihadists at the gate had the sign they'd been waiting for. Having eliminated the enemy's only means of escape, they came streaming en masse out through the narrow tunnel. Stony's snipers aboard *Cygnus* fired as rapidly as they could, their high-powered scopes enabling them to kill the forefront of the first wave. Corpses were stacked in front of the gate as the main force emerged, screaming and howling like the hyenas and jackals they were.

A bloodthirsty mob was pounding down the central dock, headed for the pier at the end where *Cygnus* was moored. Hawke saw that many of them were carrying long makeshift boarding ladders, roughly fashioned of wood and lashed together with leather. He was already taking fire. He heard a few rounds pinging off the bulkhead above his head, but the enemy forces weren't close enough yet to make their ancient AK-47s effective.

Hawke got on the combat radio to Stony, each word punctuated by a squeeze of his trigger as he picked off the nearest targets.

"Haul aboard the landward grapnel lines, Stony, then join me up on the bridge. High ground. We can direct the defense from here. Rig every one of the grapnel lines on the seaward side of the vessel. We might need them."

"Aye, sir."

"Where are Stokely and Brock?"

"They remained down on the dock. First line of defense, Brock told me."

"What!"

"Aye, they've taken up a defensive firing position behind some stacked steel barrels. They've both got M-60 heavy machine guns. Chopping 'em up pretty good, sir."

"Damn it! Get them aboard immediately. That's suicide. They'll be overrun by this mob in seconds, hacked to pieces with bayonets and scimitars. Have you still got a grapnel line down?"

"All aboard save one."

"Get on the radio. Have them grab that damn line and haul them aboard as fast as you can. Give them covering fire while they're exposed coming up the side of the hull."

"Roger, it's happening as we speak."

Hawke saw Brock and Stoke safely hauled aboard and shouted, "Here those bastards with the ladders come, Stony. I've wanted to say this since I was six years old: Repel boarders!"

The jihadist warriors, AK-47s in their hands and curved Arabian knives clenched in their teeth, began to position the ladders against the hull and started scrambling up like jabbering monkeys. Hawke's men waited, then shoved the ladders away from the rail and sent them tumbling back down into the midst of the howling mob or splashing into the water on the far side of the pier. But ladders were going up the entire length of the hull, faster than Hawke's men could shove them away. The fire was murderous and Hawke knew he was taking unacceptable casualties.

"DIVERS STILL DOWN?" STONY ASKED, JOINING Hawke as they both poured fire into the masses of warriors climbing the ladders. Far too many were getting aboard. And more were still streaming through the gate. This battle was going one-sided fast, Hawke realized. A strategic retreat was called for and the patrol boat for their escape wasn't exactly seaworthy at the moment. It was nonexistent.

"Where the hell's my UDT squad?"

"No sign of them, Stony," Hawke said, looking at his watch. "They've been down there twenty minutes. We need to get the hell off this damn boat. Now."

"Good God, Alex, you've been hit!"

"Somebody got lucky. A round penetrated my body armor beneath my arm. Nothing vital, I assure you, despite the fountain of blood."

"I'll get a corpsman up here immediately."

"No. There are men below who need attention far more than I do. Somebody can stitch me up when the seriously wounded have been attended to. Now, enough of that; what is our situation?"

"I'm afraid the bastards have got us trapped, sir. We're already vastly outmanned and outgunned and our escape plan just went up in smoke at the far end of the pier."

"That was Plan A," Hawke said, grimacing in pain and mowing down a tightly bunched group of black-turbaned fighters trying to sneak aft from the bow and flank them on the starboard side. "It's time for Plan B."

"Ah, good. But tell me what the hell is Plan B again?"

"Plan B is steaming at flank speed up the channel right now. Look behind you."

A strange ship was approaching at a high rate of speed. It looked like no waterborne craft Stony had ever seen before. Her flat-angled planes were matte black, austere, and her sharp prow looked like the blade of a battle axe.

"Good God, what the hell is that thing? Looks like a floating stealth bomber."

"She's called *Nighthawke*. She's the tender to *Blackhawke*, built in Italy at the Wally yard. Fifty feet of armor-plated gunship to the rescue. She's been circling offshore. I ordered her in when the patrol boat was taken out. Wait—got you, you little raghead—that's why I ordered the grapnel lines moved to the seaward side. We're getting the hell off this empty bucket. I want an orderly retreat from the port side over to the starboard side, Stony. Not all at once, nothing perceptible from the shore. Make them think we're still defending the port side until the last possible moment. I've ordered *Nighthawke* to pull along our starboard side to receive us as we come down the grapnel lines."

"I like this plan."

"*Nighthawke*'s got enough firepower to discourage anyone from trying to follow us in those pirate scows."

"Aye-aye, sir," Stony said with a wide grin. He saw the *Nighthawke*'s twin Browning .50-caliber barrels protruding from a ring-mounted armored turret swivel 180 degrees on the foredeck and start spitting lead at enemy fighters threatening to ascend to higher decks from the stern of the big white yacht. Another gunner, operating a similar turret on the stern, opened fire. The loud chatter of the two big guns gave rise to Hawke's hopes that the main body of his force might actually survive. At least three of his Red Team members fighting off the boarders had not been so lucky in the brutal firefight. Many more were injured and needed immediate medical attention.

Stony said, "I'll go below and give the order to move to starboard now. Post a rear guard to fire and scramble, from as many positions as possible, to give the illusion of a larger force to disguise the retreat." Hawke looked at him, thinking fast.

"Give me your gun and ammo first. Shooting with two hands is better than one. With any luck, I'll see you on board *Nighthawke*. Tell your men to scramble. Down the lines, then just drop to the tender's deck, head for the nearest open hatchway, and get the hell below."

"What about my four divers?"

"Don't worry, Stony. We're not leaving without them."

DEAD AND WOUNDED WERE BEING LOWERED IN makeshift slings down to the decks of *Nighthawke* and swiftly carried below to receive medical attention. The armored tender's heavy firepower, fore and aft, was keeping the enemy down, covering the rapid escape as Blue Team and Red Team rappelled down the starboard hull of *Cygnus*, most just dropping the last ten feet to her deck and scrambling for cover, before returning fire at the suicidal Iranian fighters who appeared at the rail, raining fire down from high above.

Hawke was the last man to leave *Cygnus*.

Stoke was standing below on the foredeck hatch cover, watching his descent, waiting anxiously to receive him, having seen the bloody chest wound Hawke had received covering the retreat of the bloodied combatants. Hawke only had the use of his left arm to descend. The pain was merciless. When Hawke was halfway down, Stoke saw his head slump forward. Then he lost his grip. He dropped the last thirty feet into Stoke's arms. Stoke caught the one-hundred-eighty-pound man, staggered a step, but held on, cradling Hawke against his own massive chest. He looked at his friend's face, a pale grey, his body weak with blood loss.

"You okay, boss? You don't look so good . . ."

Hawke managed a forced smile and a ragged reply.

"Stoke. What have I always told you about pain?"

"Pain is just weakness leaving your body."

"Right."

"Yeah, I know, boss. Just another pretty little scar to add to your collection."

Stoke hurried his wounded comrade under the cover of the steel-roofed wheelhouse. "Corpsman!" he shouted and a navy medic came running to attend to Hawke's injuries. He examined him quickly and expertly.

"Shoulder wound, sir," the young corpsman said.

"And clean flesh. No bone, no arteries. The round passed straight through. I'll stitch him up and he'll be on the mend straightaway."

Ten minutes later, Hawke was resting quietly in the sick bay, his entire chest strapped with surgical tape and his right arm in a sling. His color was coming back and Stoke could see in his eyes that there was one hell of a lot of fight left in him. He was down, but he wouldn't be down long. Weakness was leaving his body.

HAWKE LOOKED UP AT THE STARBOARD RAIL ABOVE him and saw that the enemy had abandoned the field of battle, at least for now. He immediately headed for the stern, looking for the four SEAL demolition divers. *Nighthawke* had a wide, teak-decked boarding platform protruding from beneath her stern. It was raised and lowered hydraulically and could lift anything from the four heavily armed Jet Skis that were stowed just forward of the platform to four navy divers kitted up in very heavy dive suits and equipment.

Just as Hawke reached the stern rail, the first head popped up out of the water. The diver raised his clenched fist in victory when he saw Hawke, and any fear Alex had had for these brave men or their mission vanished.

"Stoke! Brock! Come back here and help me haul these guys aboard. You may have noticed I only have one arm, otherwise I'd do it myself."

A second black helmeted head appeared on the

surface, then a third and a fourth. Seeing Hawke lowering the platform beneath the sloppy surface of the water, they swam for it. The first diver had already whipped off his helmet and was sitting on the platform, his legs awash, talking excitedly to Hawke, Brock, and Stokely Jones.

"You guys didn't tell us we were blowing up the Emerald City!" Lieutenant Ryan White said, rubbing his eyes. "What the hell is that place, anyway? Freaking lightning crackling around inside this big tower and, at one point while I was finishing rigging the charge at the base of the central tower, lightning started racing faster and faster in circles around the six towers on the perimeter. Damnedest thing I've ever seen! I thought we were about to get our asses fried!"

"Tell them about the music, Lieutenant," a diver said.

"Oh, yeah. All the towers started broadcasting this weird music," Ryan White said. "I thought I had narcosis, but the other guys could hear it, too. It was making us sick, so we shut down our acoustics."

"Good thing," Hawke said, knowing they'd all dodged a deadly bullet.

Stokely helped the third diver out of the water. He got to his feet and removed his helmet. The diver looked at Ryan White and said, "Lieutenant, I'm sorry I had to shut my combat radio down. I started hearing this very weird music in my earpiece. Made me crazy. Something like narcosis, you know? Did you guys hear it, too?"

"Hell, yeah, we all heard it. Next thing I knew I was tugging at my regulator, trying to rip it loose.

Just before I blacked out, I turned the volume down and got my head straight again. What the hell was that all about?"

"Perseus was attempting to save himself by convincing you four men to commit suicide," Hawke said.

"Perseus? Who the hell is he?"

"The computer you just rigged."

"Wait—that's—those black glass towers—are a *computer*?"

"It's a long story," Hawke said. "More than a computer, really. An empire of the mind. How long did you set your detonation timers for, Lieutenant White? We need to be getting out of here before they start lobbing mortar shells at us."

Ryan White looked at his dive watch and then back at the water off *Nighthawke*'s stern.

"Right about . . . now, Commander Hawke," he said.

A shock wave rocked the boat from below just as seven mushroomlike mounds of foaming white water appeared on the surface. They expanded to about five feet in diameter and then dissipated, leaving no trace of the catastrophic destruction that had just occurred below. Hawke couldn't even imagine how much high-explosive Semtex it took to create even a ripple a thousand feet above the ocean floor.

Hawke stared at the undulating surface of the black water, thinking about the staggering implications of what he had just done. More important, he was wondering if he had the right to do it.

Had he even done the right thing?

All the giant leaps forward in scientific achievement, the unimaginable medical advances, reverse aging, a cure for famine, or even a—

To hell with it.

He realized he would never really know. Maybe someday mankind could produce something like Perseus. A superintelligent machine, but one that could be kept in check. One with hardwired incapacity for doing harm, or evil. A force that was only capable of doing good, solving insoluble problems, making the world a better, safer place.

But Perseus had not been that machine.

Ironically, Perseus's true value, and Professor Waldo Cohen's enormous contribution to the evolution of science, would be that Cohen had somehow strayed down the wrong path.

And that, Hawke knew in his heart, might ultimately make the right road far, far easier to follow in the future.

He turned to the man he could always lean upon.

"Stoke, it's finished. Let's get the hell out of here."

"Great. Leave Iran without even getting to taste the caviar. Story of my life."

Hawke looked at Brock with undisguised admiration.

"Harry?" he said.

"Yes?"

"You and I have never been close."

"Right. Because you hate me."

"Right. But I feel a bit differently about you now. After all you did back there. A lot of men would have died without you and your M-60."

"Yeah? So?"

"I'd like you to join me and Stokely. Leave CIA,

sign a contract with Red Banner. Pays a lot better, Harry. Less paperwork in the mercenary business than inside the Beltway."

"Really? So—that means you, what, you like me now?"

"I didn't say that, Harry. I paid you a far greater compliment."

"Lemme think about it awhile."

"Take as long as you want."

"I'm in."

"Yeah!" Stoke said, wrapping his massive arms around Harry and bouncing him up and down like a ragdoll. "That's what I'm talking about!"

Lines were heaved aboard, throttles were engaged, and *Nighthawke* moved swiftly out into the channel.

The Trojan Horse had left the barn.

FIFTY-SIX

STRAIT OF HORMUZ

THE SKY WAS REMARKABLY CLEAR UNDER A LANtern moon.

"Mosquitoes," Stoke, looking over his shoulder, said to Harry Brock. "Look at 'em swarm. Gotta be fifty of 'em at least."

Harry'd come out on the stern deck for a smoke. He'd been the first to hear the snarling outboard motorboats, a vast flotilla of them, racing across the flat black sea to converge on *Nighthawke*'s stern. They were pirate scows, some of them forty feet in length, the longboats Somali pirates used to board and capture defenseless behemoths off the coast of Africa. Harry once tried to explain to Stoke that the reason the tankers didn't have armed crews had to do with the insurance.

"So who pays the ransom when the tankers get hijacked?" Stoke said.

"Uh, the insurance companies."

"Oh. Now I get it," Stoke had said, shaking his head.

The pirates were about four miles out and rapidly closing the distance. In the midst of them was the "mother ship," enclosed for protection. Sirens aboard *Blackhawke* sounded General Quarters, and gunners climbed up inside their turrets, wheeling about on their ring mounts to face the threat aft. *Threat is maybe a teensy bit too strong a word for these assholes*, Stoke thought. *Pests, maybe?* Spray 'em with Raid, he told Harry, that oughta do it. Or get one of those bug zappers. These pissant pirates chasing after a high-tech warship like *Nighthawke*? Oughta get their turbans out of their asses.

The longboats, incredibly fast with their three-hundred-horsepower outboards, were gaining on them rapidly.

"Boss?" Stoke said into his radio. Hawke was on the bridge radio, talking to Carstairs aboard *Blackhawke*, discussing the best approach to the Strait of Hormuz as soon as the team was finally back aboard their own mother ship.

"Go ahead, Stoke."

"You know those new antiship mines we rigged in the aft tubes?"

"Yes."

"This pirate attack might be the perfect opportunity to battle test them, don't you think?"

"Absolutely. Good idea. Deploy as the scows move into range. Our ETA for the rendezvous with *Blackhawke* is twenty minutes."

"Affirmative."

"What mines?" Harry asked Stokely.

"Made in Israel. They're cherry red. GPS equipped. They'll go anywhere you send them, any depth you send them. Explode on direct contact, or by timer, or when the enemy enters a preset sonar range. Forgot the real name for them. I call 'em cherry bombs. Here's the portside tube, the other one is over there to starboard. Each tube loads a dozen mines. You deploy them from the fire control center of this fire control panel right here. I figure we only need about four, two from each tube."

"What are those thingys sticking out?"

"The little fins? Diving planes and rudders. And the entire surface is embedded with tiny propulsion jets. Send the little bastards anywhere you want. But they don't have to be anywhere near the bad guys. Each cherry bomb has a blast range of a half mile. Anything inside that circle? Gone."

"Holy shit."

"Yeah. So anything traveling within a two-mile radius of four cherry bombs is going to be turned into fine sawdust and microscopic metal filings. You know how when a nuclear bomb first explodes, it rolls out that big ring of fiery-ass shock-and-awe shit before it turns into a mushroom cloud?"

"Yeah."

"Well, that's kinda what they do."

"Don't tell me they're nuclear?"

"Hell, no, they're not nuclear. That technology's so outdated. This is new technology, baby. Far superior. Those Israelis have got their shit together, trust me."

"Yeah, well, these 30mm cannons work pretty good, too," Harry said, removing the cover and getting into firing position on the small seat behind the breech. He put his eye to the rangefinder.

"What are you doing?"

"See that big mother ship hiding in the middle of the pack?"

"Yeah."

"Watch this, pal. One fuckin' shot."

Harry yanked the cord and the big gun fired. It was a direct hit. Most of the mother ship's topsides were destroyed and a fire was raging at the stern. She was badly damaged, but still maintained her course and speed as the crew desperately tried to extinguish the fire.

"Nice shot."

"We do what we can."

THE MAIN BODY OF THE PIRATE FLEET HELD BACK OUT of range, but the pirate captain sent a dozen or so of his longboats racing full speed ahead and soon they were swarming around the big yacht, pirates standing now and firing their AK-47s. A few even nudged right alongside the yacht and flung grappling hooks over the rail. The young pirates, chains of gold dangling from their necks, their heads wrapped with red turbans, started scrambling up the lines with amazing agility. They had curved knives clenched in their teeth and they were clearly excited about this huge prize they were about to take.

Until, that is, the Navy SEAL snipers positioned on the topmost mast began picking them off with precision head shots. Those who'd reached the rail in an attempt to board died first, dropping like so many stones into the sea. Next the pirates coming up the lines, and finally those brave souls with their AKs, manning the longboats. It was all over in about five minutes.

But it didn't stop the rest of the pirate fleet from making a run on the yacht. It was just too glittering a prize to give up on.

"Okay. Here come the rest of those assholes. Show me."

"Bombs away," Stoke said, and pressed each of the big red Fire buttons two times.

Four red mines, about the size of large cannonballs, instantly deployed, arcing up into the sky, two from each tube.

Harry raised his binoculars. He could see the swarm of pirate scows, and the digital rangefinder in his lens had them at three miles dead aft and closing on the minefield.

The explosion was so brilliant in his lenses he had to turn away. It was as if a massive circular section of the sea itself had just become one giant explosive device, annihilating everything on the surface in one blinding instant. A second later, the shock wave hit, staggering Harry, who grabbed a stanchion and held on.

"Damn, Stoke."

"Something else, huh?"

The two men stood and watched as the floating sea of fire gradually extinguished itself and the smoke dissipated, leaving the ocean as it was before, free of debris, pristine and beautiful in the sunlight.

"That's some serious shit right there," Brock said.

"You know what I'm thinking about right now, Harry?" Stoke said, a look on his face Harry could only describe as wistful.

"God only knows."

"No, *not* only God; I know, too. It's my damn idea, Harry."

"Okay, okay, tell me. Jesus."

"Back in Moscow I started to get into this Hollywood shit, y'know? So. What if I bought me an old movie theater in downtown Mogadishu? Put posters up around town of local Somali kids in Johnny Depp costumes. You know, *Pirates of the Gulf of Aden* with Captain Abdullah 'Jack' Sparrow, kinda thing. But get this. Every young Somali in town gets in free! Right? Free popcorn, candy, nachos, wings, Diet Coke, pig eyes, crow's feet, you know, whatever the hell they like over there. And then I'd show them the movie. We open. It's midnight. The sea is black and empty except for a huge white yacht. Look! Here come the brave pirates! Close up on all their little baby-Depp faces hiding beneath the gunwales of the longboats, AK-47s clenched in their hands, ready to attack the big bad yacht. But then, what? Omigod! A blinding flash of light, the big bang, ear-shattering explosion in surround sound, right, all that smoke and fire on the water. Closing shot of the empty sea, all the brave little pirates gone to the bottom. Fade out. What do you think? Seriously. Would you invest in an idea like that? I'd give you an Executive Producer credit, man."

Harry Brock, for once in his life, could think of absolutely no reply.

Blackhawke lay some two miles in the distance.

THE STRAIT OF HORMUZ IS A NARROW, STRATEGI-
cally critical waterway between the Gulf of Oman in
the southeast and the Persian Gulf. It is inarguably
one of the world's most dangerous choke points. On
the north coast lies Iran, Hawke's recent point of
departure. On the south coast are the United Arab
Emirates and Musandam, an enclave of Oman. On
an average day, about fifteen supertankers carrying
roughly seventeen million barrels of crude oil pass
through the strait—or roughly 40 percent of all the
world's seaborne oil shipments. Every single day.

Hawke, finally back aboard his yacht and standing alongside Carstairs on *Blackhawke*'s bridge,
looked at the maritime chart of the strait for the
tenth time.

When the next war starts, it will start here, he
thought to himself. And when it did—

"Helm, Sonar. New contact, sir. Bearing two-
zero-eight."

"Sonar, Hawke. What've you got?"

"Midsize vessel, sir. Not a tanker. Approaching from the strait, I'd say she's an Iranian Bayandor class, large patrol corvette. They operate two
of them in these waters, the *Bayandor* and *Admiral
Naghdi.*"

"Armament?"

"She carries four C-803 antiship missiles, a single
76mm DP naval cannon, one dual 40mm antiaircraft, and two triple 324mm torpedoes."

"Keep an eye on her."

"Aye-aye, sir."

Hawke raised his battle radio. "Stony, Hawke, we're approaching the strait, bearing one-eight-zero. We've already picked up an enemy contact. I thought we might get lucky but it looks like we might have to fight our way through. I'm sure there are more surprises out there waiting for us. I want you to prepare the ship and battle crew and wait for my signal to go to General Quarters. Unless we're attacked first, we do not, repeat, do not, show our true colors until we're right in the middle of them. Aegis picking up any suspicious air traffic?"

"Negative, Commander. Nothing airborne inside our defensive perimeter."

"Good. Stay tuned. Things could get very spicy in a hurry."

"Helm, Sonar, new contact, bearing two-seven-zero. Estimate vessel is a Thondor-class missile craft, operated by the Iranian Revolutionary Guard Corps. She carries four C802 SSM missiles, two 30mm cannons, and two 23mm—sir, sorry, new contact bearing two-six-zero, big one, Vosper MK5 frigate, very, very fast."

"How fast?"

"Very fast. Engine turns for thirty-nine knots as we speak, sir; she's got boost gas turbine engines. If she maintains course, current bearing will intercept ours in approximately twenty minutes."

"Helm, maintain course," Hawke said. He wanted to find out who'd blink first.

"Maintain current heading, aye."

"Sonar, is this typical naval military traffic in the approach to the strait?" Hawke said.

"Sir, it's hard to say. There's nothing typical about

Iranian military behavior. Especially the navy. But based on what I'm seeing, I'm guessing they know who we are, what we've been up to, and why we're coming."

"Sound General Quarters," Hawke said quietly.

The sirens began wailing throughout the ship. Gun crews scrambled forward, manning the ten cannon placements on both the port and starboard sides. Protective covers remained on deck cannons, rocket launchers, depth charges, and heavy machine guns fore and aft. When the cannons rolled out, the covers would come off, too.

Stollenwork moved rapidly about the covert combat quarters in the stern of the yacht, shouting orders to his naval combat crew for the coming fight. Inside the narrow concealed corridors running from stem to stern, gun crews were loading the cannons with both high-explosive and armor-piercing rounds. The crews were pumped. Ten guns lined each side of the vessel, and all fired at a rate of two hundred rounds a minute. That meant the starboard gunners *alone* would be throwing lead at two thousand cannon rounds every single minute.

Stunning firepower, by any standard.

Blackhawke was going to war.

And, by God, she was ready.

FIFTY-SEVEN

T HE SUN ROSE INTO SKIES DOMINATED BY TOWER-
ing rain-heavy clouds, the sea a vast flat pool,
but gently heaving, and nearly colorless; it was the
dead color of lead. Just after midnight, an electrical
storm brewing up from the south had moved over
the boat. The clouds carried a squall and the crew
prepared for a soaking. But just before the storm
struck, the tips of the gun barrels and the ship's an-
tennas buzzed with St. Elmo's fire, blue sparks and
streamers of static electricity discharging into the
heavy night air.

A portent of things to come, Hawke thought.

The crew had spent the long rainy night preparing for battle: serviced weapons, tied down loose
items, secured hatches, restocked medical kits, and
readied damage control and firefighting gear.

Now Hawke stood alone at the highest point of
Blackhawke's towering superstructure, a 360-degree
round observation tower mounted on a hydraulic

piston. Intended for spotting, range-finding, and directing fire for the ship's primary gun batteries, this was the first time it had seen use. Normally, it was lowered inside the superstructure, completely concealed.

He raised his old Zeiss binoculars to his eyes and studied the array of enemy vessels in the misty distance, lying in wait for him, standing between him and the Strait of Hormuz. Like the crew now standing at GQ stations, he'd been wondering what would be waiting for him. Now he knew.

The number of enemy vessels lurking at the entrance to the strait had grown during the night.

Sleek grey wolves, circling, hungrily licking their chops, diesel hearts pounding below decks, red bloodlust in their feral eyes . . . or . . . perhaps that was just their portside navigation lights? So easy to get carried away when he was in this heightened state of war readiness.

No matter, he knew the feeling and welcomed it.

He had to wonder if the Iranian Navy really had somehow discovered *Blackhawke*'s role in the attack on the citadel. Even though *Blackhawke* had been drifting five miles offshore feigning mechanical difficulties, it was a possibility to be considered. Had a member of the crew of the patrol boat that boarded them alerted them? No, they were all dead. Perhaps Perseus, yes, Perseus, in a final act of revenge, when he realized that his doom was imminent?

If his *ruse de guerre* had indeed been uncovered, Hawke thought Perseus the most likely perpetrator. A machine filled with rage at its final, defenseless impotency against an implacable enemy? An enraged machine lashing out in a fury as the divers prepared to destroy him? Hawke pushed such thoughts aside. He might have gotten lucky, but his gut said he was in for a fight.

He glanced at the observation post's small instrument panel. They were cruising at a stately ten knots, engines muffled. *Blackhawke*, under power, was capable of an explosive forty knots, but he wanted that speed held in reserve should push come to, as it usually did, shove. He raised his battle radio and said, "Helm, this is Hawke. Maintain course and speed, Laddie. So far I'm seeing no overt signs of aggression. But you can sense every eye is upon us."

"Maybe we get a pass?"

"Something deep inside me says no."

"Aye."

"Tell me Sonar hasn't picked up any Iranian subs lurking around here."

"No, no subs, skipper."

"You scared, Laddie?"

"Hell, no, sir, I'm terrified."

"May the sun continue to shine upon us all."

"*Inshallah*, sir."

"Indeed."

Hawke felt both exposed and impatient.

THEY SAILED INTO THE VERY THICK OF IT.

All her canvas was spread aloft, the three towering masts turning in place, making minute trim adjustments based on speed, course, and wind computers far below. They had a fresh blow out of the

north and she was running before the wind at about
fifteen knots. The idea was to use the sails as long
as possible, adding to the illusion that this was a
rich man's toy, not a warship. *Blackhawke* was flying
a Maltese flag at her masthead, red and white with
the George Cross. Just as in days of old, they'd wait
for the very last minute before revealing their true
colors.

The massive sails would be retracted inside the
masts, as she went to power propulsion using the
massive gas turbine engines with their explosive
power and speed.

Hawke kept waiting for the smaller Iranian
picket boats, the missile boat, or the large frigate to
open fire but none came. It was as if the big wolves
wanted this one all to themselves. The smaller pick-
ets were so close they could have bumped into them
if they deviated one degree off course. You could see
the Iranian officers up on the various bridge decks,
bug-eyed with binoculars trained on the enormous
black sailing yacht.

"I've seen enough," Hawke said, thumbing the
button that lowered the platform back down inside
the superstructure, just aft of the bridge. He wanted
to be standing next to the helm in the thick of it. But
first he had a job to do. He raced down three flights
of stairs to his stateroom amidships where the vessel
was beamiest. He ran to the locker at the foot of his
bed, opened it, and pulled out a long tube made of
rough canvas. Then he sprinted back to the uppermost deck where a signalman was standing at the
base of the mainmast. The young ensign snapped
off a salute.

"At ease, sailor. It's time to show the bad guys our true colors."

"Aye-aye, sir!" he said, snapping off another salute.

He was plainly one of those young seamen who was never at ease. Hawke smiled at him and said, "Strike the colors!"

"Strike colors, aye!"

The boy turned immediately to the flag halyard secured to the mast, eased the lines, and began hauling down the red-and-white Maltese flag. It took a very long time to descend. When he had it in his hands and had disengaged it from the halyard, Hawke unzipped the long canvas tube.

The young sailor's eyes went wide with delight when he saw what Hawke intended.

"Our true colors, son," he said, and handed him the new flag. "Haul it to the masthead, smartly, if you please."

"Aye-aye, sir!" the seaman said, almost shouting it.

Some minutes later, the two of them stood smiling up at the great black-and-white flag snapping in the breeze at the very top of the mast. *Blackhawke* was at last flying her true colors.

The skull and crossbones of the Jolly Roger.

LOOKING FORWARD THROUGH THE PILOTHOUSE WINdows, he saw Stoke and Harry Brock on the bow, ready to man the twin .33 cannons, still under wraps and unrevealed to the enemy.

"Two patrol boats approaching from astern at

high speed, sir," Laddie informed Hawke. "One to port, one to starboard."

Hawke instantly saw what the Iranians intended. They were going to box them in. Then the big frigate lurking off their starboard bow would "cross the T" at the top, sailing directly across their current course line. A standard tactic but an effective one. Since the big, heavily armed corvette would be perpendicular to *Blackhawke*, only Hawke's forward guns could be used against that enemy. Despite all her broadside gunnery, Hawke would be at a huge disadvantage against an enemy that could bring all her weapons to bear on the oncoming vessel.

"Increase speed to thirty knots. Maintain course," Hawke said to the helmsman.

"Maintain course, sir? They're putting us in the box."

"We'll get out of this box when the time is right. Steady on."

"Aye-aye, sir."

Minutes later, the identical grey patrol boats were running alongside *Blackhawke* to either side. Each Iranian crew was at battle stations. Up ahead, the big Thondor missile frigate was heaving into position athwart Hawke's course in order to block *Blackhawke*'s escape.

"These bastards actually think they're going to hijack us," Hawke said with a trace of amusement in his voice. "Retract the sails, all three masts; let's show them a bit of her speed with the gas turbines, shall we?"

On the bow, Stoke had just finished asking Harry a question. "We gonna shoot these damn people or just wave hello at 'em as they sail on by?" when they both felt a sledgehammer of hot air pass directly between them followed by a shrill whistle. A 30mm enemy cannon round had just blown right between their faces.

"Holy shit," Stoke cried into his battle radio, "somebody just took a shot at us!"

"It was the big frigate. Just a warning shot across our bow, Stoke, but still, it's time to shoot back," Hawke said. "Fire as she bears."

Stoke and Harry ripped the black Kevlar concealment cover off the weapon, hopped into the two gunners' seats, swiveled the turret in the direction the shot had come from, and opened fire.

The battle was on.

The two patrol boats opened up with everything they had. Heavy machine guns, rockets, and cannon fire. The Kevlar/ceramic plates and triple-laminated composite glass that *Blackhawke* carried topside deflected much of the damage, just as they were designed to do. Now she would go on the offensive.

"Open all port and starboard gunports," Hawke said into his radio. "Roll out cannons. That will ruin their day. Let's give 'em a nice rolling broadside as an opener, lads. Number one bow gun crew initiate. Fire on my signal."

Along the port and starboard hull sides, the cannon-concealing panels suddenly dropped open simultaneously. The long barrels emerged as the big guns were rolled out into the sun. *Blackhawke* suddenly resembled nothing so much as a three-masted, twenty-first-century pirate ship.

"Fire at will," Hawke commanded.

The roar of the big guns commenced at the bow and rolled aft, each crew firing in succession. The sound of the massive cannons, firing at twenty rounds a minute, was deafening and shook the ship down to her bones. Across the water, the effect on the patrol boats was devastating. They tried desperately to veer away. But it was apparent they were no match for *Blackhawke*'s devastating firepower. Aboard the patrol boats, fires were breaking out everywhere. Men, many of them afire, were leaping into the sea for their lives. Their ships were literally disintegrating beneath their feet.

The speaker above Hawke's head suddenly squawked.

"Helm, Sonar, report new contact. Enemy submarine bearing zero-two-zero, speed eighteen knots, periscope depth, range five thousand meters dead astern . . . forward torpedo tubes just opened and awash . . . she's pinging us . . . rig for damage control . . ."

Hawke grabbed his radio.

"Fire Control, this is Helm. You're about to have two enemy fish in the water, steaming right up our arsehole at fifty knots. Immediately deploy two cherry bombs at a depth of three meters, speed thirty knots. Position both at one thousand meters aft of the ship and maintain inertial position. Set to explode as soon as the torpedoes enter their range parameters . . ."

"Aye-aye, sir. Two bombs already away, sir, that's affirmative . . . two fish are away . . . they've launched, skipper, torpedoes headed directly toward the minefield."

"Copy. Now put two more in the water. Set their course directly for the sub's bow. High speed. I want you to send the little buggers right inside their damn tubes before they can shut those forward torpedo doors . . ."

"Detonation?"

"As soon as they hit something hard."

The FCO couldn't muffle his laugh. "Aye-aye, sir, copy that. Something hard."

Hawke stepped out onto the bridge wing, looking aft.

Moments later, the sea erupted into two geysers of fire and black smoke. The enemy torpedoes had been spectacularly negated by the cherry bombs in their first real battle test. He'd shoot a congratulatory e-mail to the Israeli weapons designer as soon as he got a chance.

He kept his Zeiss binocs trained on the sub's periscope, trailing a nice white wake behind it. He knew it wouldn't be long now . . .

It wasn't.

The Iranian sub's bulbous bow suddenly rose straight up out of the water at a ridiculous angle, the explosion of the two bombs inside the forward torpedo tubes lifting the first fifty feet of the hull skyward and then literally blowing the bow right off the sub, taking about a third of the forward hull with it. Through his binoculars, Hawke saw a gaping maw where the sub's bow had been moments before. Using a sub's own opened torpedo tubes to get your explosive devices deep within the enemy boat was not something he'd learned at the War College.

His boxing trainer had told him something long ago that had stuck with him:

"The ideal fighter has heart, Alex, skill, movement, intelligence, but, also, creativity. You can have everything, but if you can't make it up while you're in the ring, you can't be great . . . you bring everything to it, you make it up while you're doing it."

He had made it up.

And, by God, it had worked.

The submarine's bow had been blown to bits, vaporized. When what was left of the fatally wounded sub splashed down, its forward momentum sent a tsunami of seawater rushing into the opened hull, drowning everyone in the forward compartments. Those behind the watertight doors would survive long enough to make the fast, fatal trip to the bottom.

Suddenly, with all the weight forward, her stern came straight up, her screws still spinning wildly. A few moments later she was standing on her head, beginning her slow downward slide.

She sank without a trace.

FIFTY-EIGHT

L INE OF BATTLE: IRAN'S THONDOR CLASS MISSILE craft, which carried four C802 SSM missiles, two 30mm cannons, and two 23mm cannons. The Iranian Navy's largest vessel, the very fast Vosper MK5 frigate. And, finally, the Bayandor class large patrol corvette. These were the last three things standing between *Blackhawke* and her escape through the Strait of Hormuz. And they were formidable.

The Iranian naval officers aboard all three warships had witnessed with dismay the utter destruction of the pirates, the two patrol boats, and, most grievous of all, the pride of the Fourteenth Naval Fleet, the recently launched submarine *Yunus*. Having communicated with each other, they were thus approaching the coming battle with a mere "yacht" with a bit more respect.

"Hard to port, engines all ahead flank," Hawke said to the helmsman, Laddie.

"Hard to port, all ahead flank, aye."

The big boat heeled over and carved a tight turn onto a westerly course. It was Hawke's intention to misdirect the enemy, then make an unexpected starboard tack and come storming at the enemy right out of the glaring sun. He was clearly trying to eke out any advantage he could get.

The mood on the bridge was tense.

Their confidence in the ship's weapons systems, both offensive and defensive, was complete. But the odds were decidedly against them. Hawke was ex–Royal Navy, but he'd been a pilot, not a seaman. He'd always been an amateur military historian, studying the great naval battles of history since childhood. Still, he felt extremely fortunate to have a seasoned navy man like Carstairs as his number two, and Lieutenant Brian Burns as his fire control officer. These two men would be directing the battle. But this was Alex Hawke's boat, not the Royal Navy's.

The closer they got to the enemy's line of battle, the thicker the tension. Hawke could see Laddie's thoughts, betrayed by his eyes. His natural intuition was telling him that something terrible was going to happen. His worry was visible in the tensing of his brow and the protrusion of the tendons on the back of his hands where they gripped the helm.

The speaker crackled, and some on the bridge flinched, knowing what was coming.

"Helm, Fire Control, Thondor vessel has two missiles locked on, preparing to launch. Recommend going to the AMMS while taking evasive action."

Carstairs looked at Hawke before thumbing his radio.

"Fire Control, Helm. Agree. Arm the AMMS. I am putting the helm hard aport, flank speed."

"Aye. AMMS armed and locked onto Thondor's missile launcher. I will launch on your signal."

AMMS was *Blackhawke*'s antimissile-missile system. It was designed to take out enemy missiles just as they were being launched. They were at their slowest leaving the tubes and their destruction at that critical moment would cause maximum damage to the enemy vessel.

"Fire Control, fifteen seconds to enemy launch."

"Fire tubes one and two."

"Missiles away . . ."

Seconds stretched out to an hour.

"Helm, we have one direct hit and one incoming enemy missile! The second AMM missed the target!"

"Christ!" Laddie said, whipping the helm to starboard in a desperate attempt to—

But the Iranian missile didn't miss. It scored a direct hit on *Blackhawke*. It struck the foremast, the splintering explosion occurring about a third of the way up the carbon fiber spar.

Hawke suddenly grabbed the helm and spun it hard to starboard. He'd seen that the topmost portion of the massively heavy mast would now fall directly aft, crashing down upon the bridge deck, causing massive damage and casualties. The centripetal force caused by the sudden heeling and swerving of the yacht during the split-second change of course saved them. The mast was flung over the port gunwale but not without causing a near catastrophe in the process.

One of the mast's massive spreaders, the cross-trees that held the sails, slammed through the outboard portside windows of the bridge. Luckily, no one was cut by the flying shards of glass, but a major portion of the communications control panel was demolished. A machinist's mate with a power hacksaw was summoned. As soon as the spreader had been sawn through, the ruined mast slid harmlessly into the sea.

The machinist smiled at Hawke and said, "I can get new glass in that window in about fifteen minutes, sir. Might keep it a bit drier in here."

"Get to work then, son. A dry crew is a happy crew."

"So we're down one mast," Laddie said to Hawke.

"Right. Good thing we've got two more just like that one," Hawke said out of the corner of his mouth. He was calculating how best to take out the missile carrier. "Laddie, come left to two-seven-oh. That bastard's well within our cannon range."

"Two-seven-oh, aye."

"Fire Control," Hawke said, "open the starboard gunports. Concentrate every gun on that Thondor missile carrier. Sink it. Now."

"Aye-aye, skipper. Commencing fire."

Hawke eyed the target through his binoculars. The effect of ten 40mm cannon shells, each gun firing two hundred rounds a minute, was devastating. The big warship was literally blown apart. Hawke estimated there'd be very few, if any, survivors.

While they'd all been concentrating on destroying the Thondor to starboard, the patrol corvette had been stalking them, hanging back off their aft quarter, well out of cannon range. Now she was racing at full speed toward them.

The corvette had plenty of firepower, including a 30mm cannon, but the thing that was worrying Alex Hawke at the moment were the four 324mm high-explosive torpedoes she carried. There weren't many places *Blackhawke* was vulnerable, but below the waterline, a powerful torpedo could send her to the bottom. Hawke saw the Iranian warship throttle back to idle speed, hanging just beyond the range of *Blackhawke*'s furious cannon fusillades.

"Laddie," Hawke said, studying the enemy vessel through his binoculars, "I don't like the looks of that corvette. She's stopped beyond the range of her own guns. I think she's setting herself up to launch a spread of torpedoes."

"I agree."

"Fire Control, Helm. You tracking that corvette?"

"Aye-aye, sir. Designate new target Tango Charlie. We've already got it dialed in. Spinning up weapon systems. Awaiting orders."

"He's circling, trying to get the best angle of fire on us. Let's take him out now. We've got two JDAMs in the forward tubes. Now's the time to use one. Light up a stogie, FCO."

The fire control officer's one weakness was the Cuban cigar known as a "torpedo"; thus his nickname for the JDAM antiship missile was "stogie."

"Roger that, Helm."

"Smoke 'em if you got 'em," Hawke replied.

"Launch portside JDAM when enemy target

acquired, affirmative. Initiating prelaunch checklist . . . weapon powered . . . autotrack engaged . . . master arm is hot . . . weapon status . . . ready, sir."

"Fire at your discretion."

Hawke saw the instrument on the panel above marked "Port Tube One" flash yellow for about thirty seconds and then flash red continuously. This meant the door of the forward torpedo tube on the port side was open. The tube was now flooded.

The fish, which was kept stowed in the tube, was away.

The JDAM is the most powerful antiship missile in existence. Two of them can take out a small aircraft carrier. Hawke saw the frothy white wake of the missile as it sped mercilessly toward the threatening enemy corvette. The corvette went to flank speed and began making evasive maneuvers. The skipper was obviously unaware that you can't evade a bloody JDAM's autotrack system. Nothing that floats can.

Hawke raised the high-powered Zeiss glasses to his eyes.

The explosion was massive. A bright white flash amidships that quickly turned yellow-orange and flaming red. Flames and black smoke climbed into the darkening sky. Everyone on the bridge was using their binoculars. A cheer went up when the smoke cleared enough to assess the damage to the corvette.

Its back had been broken, blown apart.

The missile had literally blown the vessel in two. There was now a bow section and an aft section, both afire and still afloat, although canted at weird angles, with sky clearly visible between them.

Crewmen could be seen leaping from the rails of both sections, desperately but unsuccessfully trying to outswim the pool of burning oil that was spreading rapidly on the surface surrounding the doomed vessel. Hawke turned away, sickened by the sight. He touched Laddie's shoulder and the two men left the bridge.

They needed to talk through the last remaining obstacle.

The huge Iranian Vosper MK5 destroyer escort with massive firepower that blocked *Blackhawke*'s escape.

"HERE'S THE PROBLEM, LADDIE," HAWKE SAID ONCE they were alone in the captain's quarters. "My view, at any rate. You think I'm wrong, speak up. That destroyer skipper is no fool and he's got us in a box. He knows his big guns have much longer range than our cannons. He knows our missiles probably can't do enough damage to a vessel his size to stop him. He's just witnessed what a JDAM can do, but he has no idea of its range. So he just sits out there and waits us out."

"I'm not sure just one stogie could sink him, anyway," Laddie said. "But that's all we've got left."

"If we can hit him amidships below the waterline we could get lucky. But we've got to go inside his range radius to have a decent shot."

"What choice do we have, then, skipper? We go in, light a stogie, and get the hell out of Dodge. Right?"

"It's all we've got. I've got an idea. Please hand me that battle radio on the bulkhead."

"SIGINT, this is Hawke, do you copy?"

"Aye, sir, Signal Intelligence copies loud and clear," the young officer, on loan from the CIA, said.

"Tell me about this Vosper MK5 that's in our way."

"The *Alvand*. British built, delivered before the Iranian revolution. Originally there were four. One, *Sahand*, was sunk by U.S. forces during Operation Praying Mantis in 1988. It fired on an A-6 Intruder flying off the USS *Enterprise*. It was then struck by Harpoon missiles fired by the damaged A-6 Intruder, and then sunk by a coordinated Harpoon attack from its wingman and a nearby surface ship."

"Armament?"

"Four C-802 antiship missiles, one 114mm Mark 8 gun forward, two 35mm cannons fore and aft, two 81mm mortars, two .50-caliber machine guns, one Limbo ASW mortar, and three triple 12.75 torpedo tubes."

"Roger that. SIGINT, you think Langley's got any aerial sat photos of this thing?"

"Scrapbooks full of 'em, sir."

"Thanks. I need to see them up here on the bridge ASAP. I want to get a very close look at what we're up against."

"Consider it done, sir. I'll have them on the helm monitor within five. Over."

Hawke then thumbed the command radio and contacted Stokely Jones, who was still manning one of the two 30mm cannons on the bow.

FIFTY-NINE

Stoke and Harry had returned to their battle stations in the bow after the briefing with Hawke, each of them manning a 30mm cannon. They were getting lashed with driving rain, the skies having finally opened up with a vengeance. Their barrels were so hot, they were steaming in the rain, and heavy water was coming over the forepeak where their turret mounts were located.

Stoke heard Hawke in his earpiece.

"You're wasting ammo at this range, Stoke."

"I know. But we got more ammo than sense up here. We're pissed and we're letting them know it."

"Stoke, listen. We're out of options. We're forced to make a dash inside the range of their big guns. It's going to get hot in a hurry. Time to launch our last JDAM and pray. You and Harry put your trigger fingers in your pockets and wait for my signal. When you get it, give 'em hell. You saw the photos of the *Alvand*. Concentrate on her primary weapons fore and aft. Got it?"

"Got it. Good shooting with that last fish, boss."

"Better be. Over."

"Ain't over till it's over," Brock piped up, earning a look from Stokely. He hoped for Harry's sake that Hawke hadn't heard that dumb-ass remark.

But Alex Hawke was in the zone. Total focus. Total determination to secure victory, whatever it took. These were the moments he lived for, what he'd been born to do.

"All ahead full! Right full rudder!" Hawke said. His voice had assumed a grim finality, the flat quality of emotionless decision. You fight or you don't fight. You go in with the bow of your ship pointed directly at your enemy and you go well inside his range. Keeping your bow on him gives his radar and sonar a whole lot less to look at, but if something goes wrong and you have to get the hell out of there, you've got to change course. Then you give him your broadside, setting yourself up for a devastating counterattack on his part. That's why starting in is the crucial decision.

"Rudder is right full, sir, coming to course zero-two-zero!"

"Maintain course and speed."

The big yacht surged ahead, smashing through the oncoming waves as the twin gas turbines spooled up and delivered power to the four enormous bronze screws churning beneath the stern. She had steadied on a course calculated to take her right into the teeth of the Vosper MK5's guns. It

was weird traveling at this speed on something so
enormous but it was a good weird, Stoke thought.
The enemy wouldn't have as much time to react to
a sudden incursion into their space. They were closing the distance to the destroyer escort rapidly.

"Helm, Sonar. Target is on course bearing three-
one-zero, speed twelve."

"Range two thousand yards, for'ard gun platform,
commence firing now," Stoke heard Laddie say.

"Forward guns, commence firing, aye," he replied.

"Shit," Harry said, opening fire.

"What?"

"We're it. Our two puny 30s against a goddam
battlewagon like that? We're dicked, pal."

"Good attitude. I like that. Leadership in a crisis."

"Honesty in a crisis."

"Shut up and shoot."

"I can talk and shoot at the same time."

"Incoming!" Stoke said as a huge shell whistled
high overhead and splashed harmlessly some five
hundred yards aft of *Blackhawke*. And then a second
sent a geyser of water a hundred feet in the air fifty
meters from their starboard quarter. The Iranian
gunners behind the long-range cannons were brack-
eting them, dialing them in. Geysers were erupting
all around them now, and small-arms fire was pinging off their armored turrets and the superstructure
behind them.

Launch the damn JDAM, Stoke thought to himself, *and let's get the hell out of here before we get*—
an enemy shell struck *Blackhawke*'s foredeck barely
twenty feet behind them. *Boom*, a big hole with fire

coming out of it. The damage control guys were on it in an instant. It wasn't a fatal wound, but it was the first real wound they'd suffered and he realized that, for all its high-tech armor, *Blackhawke* was not invulnerable. Stoke concentrated his fire on the winking muzzles of the enemy's big guns, hoping to get lucky.

"What the hell are you doing now?" Stoke said, looking at Harry.

"Taking off this fucking plastic sport coat. I'm burning up in this thing."

"You can't take your body armor off up here, man. We're almost totally exposed."

"Who says I can't take it off? I got along without it before they invented it and I can get along without it now."

"On top of everything else, he's suicidal. Great comrade in arms I've got."

"Mind your own business, okay? How about that for a change?"

Five minutes later Harry Brock spun around like he'd been kicked by a horse. He went down and Stoke saw the blood pumping from his right thigh. Stoke whipped off the scarf around his neck and did a quick tourniquet above the gunshot wound. He thumbed his radio.

"Man down. I need a medical corpsman on the bow right this second."

"Aye-aye, sir. On his way."

"Great, Harry. Really, really good. You spend the rest of this fight lying in bed down in sick bay and leave me alone up here by myself."

"Gimme a fuckin' break," Brock said through

gritted teeth. "You think I did this on purpose? Goddamn round took half my leg off. You can see the damn bone! The femur. It hurts like a bitch."

"Here comes the corpsman. Until then, take two aspirin and call me in the morning, asshole."

HAWKE GRABBED THE RADIO.

"Fire Control, Helm. Target within JDAM range?"

"Close. Give me another thousand meters and I'd feel better. Good news is they're a big target and they can't turn their bow to us and keep up this fire. Okay, we've got him cold now, skipper. I've got a shot . . . *now!*"

"Fire torpedo," Hawke said.

"Fire two, aye!" the FCO said.

"SHIT!" THE FCO SHOUTED, MOMENTS LATER.

"Talk to me," Hawke said.

"Number two did not eject! We got a fish running hot in the tube! Damn thing is screaming like a banshee."

Hawke looked at Laddie. This was bad. The torpedo should have been blasted out of the torpedo tube by the high-power ejection system. Instead, it was somehow stuck and the forward torpedomen could hear it running in the tube. A critical situation because the fish would be armed within a matter of seconds and then almost anything could set it off. In addition, the overspeeding motor could conceivably break up under the strain and vibration. That alone might be sufficient to cause an explosion that would blow the bow off.

"FCO, try again. Manual. Use full ejection pressure."

Hawke felt the seconds pass.

"Helm, FCO, fish did not eject, repeat, did *not* eject. System check indicates an outer tube door malfunction."

"Can you disarm?"

"Hell, no . . . I mean, no sir. We're trying to get the door to . . . uh, okay . . . this is definitely not an electronic malfunction. It's mechanical. Weapon's hot and the damn door is jammed. Tube's flooded. I can hear the screw whining from here. Pressure inside that tube now causing enormous strain. So, this is time critical, sir."

"How much time?"

"I've never had one jam before so I don't really know how long we've—"

"So how do we unjam it?"

"Not easily. We'll need to stop the ship and put a diver down. Pry it open from the outside. That's the only way."

"We stop this damn boat here in the kill zone and we're all bloody dead."

"It's the only way, sir . . . live torpedo . . . going critical . . ."

"Stoke," Hawke said, interrupting, "you hearing all this?"

"Loud and clear. I'm ready to go down now. Tell the chief bosun to get his ass up here with a mask, fins, and a crowbar so I can pry the damn thing open."

"I love you, Stoke. Hard aport, engines full stop. Starboard gun crews, fire as enemy hoves into range. Laddie, smoke the boat. Put me in fog so thick they'll think we vanished."

The skipper pressed a large heavy button mounted on the bulkhead beside him. With the push of that button, *Blackhawke* discharged and completely disappeared inside a massive fog of man-made smoke.

STOKE, WEARING GOGGLES, FINS, AND A LEAD-weighted belt, hit the water feet first, crowbar in hand. He swam down to the starboard tube near the keel and used two suction cups to clamp himself onto the hull, tether his belt in position at the jammed door. He glanced at his dive watch and the red sweep second hand was rotating at warp speed. Less than five minutes.

Shit!

He tried to stick the sharp end of the iron bar into the side of the door opposite the hinge. Nothing there. The door was flush with the hull. He could see the thin outline of the edges but he couldn't feel them with his fingertips . . . the fit was too tight. This is what you get when you give a builder a blank check: perfection. All he had was brute force.

He'd just have to jam the damn bar into the hairline crack using every ounce of his considerable strength. He figured he could get the thing open but he was worried about one thing: getting the hell out of the way of that damn JDAM when that door finally popped open . . . he slammed the crowbar's thin edge right into the seam. Nothing. Once more. Twice more. On the third try, the bar went right through the hull.

Oh, yeah.

He torqued that bar hard toward the hinge and the little mother popped right open. He heard the whine of the engine and saw the thing coming barreling straight at him. The round red dome of the torpedo's warhead was right in his face He was seconds away from instant death, either decapitation or vaporization if the warhead blew emerging from the tube. Instinctively, he ripped the cups off the hull, ducked, and the messenger of doom screamed out of the tube, missing the top of his head by maybe an inch.

Stoke clawed his way to the surface. He'd be damned if he'd miss this action. This was some serious Class-A wartime shit he was into now. This was living, baby, living large.

"Torpedo is away," the FCO said, exultation and relief evident in his voice. "It is on track and I calculate thirty seconds to impact."

All eyes on the bridge strained to see the dim grey outline of the *Alvand* through the thinning smoke.

"It's going to be a hit," Laddie said, grinning ear to ear. "A bloody, ruddy, beautiful damn hit!"

There was a loud *WHAM* when the warhead went off, almost instantaneously followed by a much louder and more prolonged *WHRROOOOM*, so close it sounded like one explosion.

"Must have hit the ammunition magazines," Laddie said. "Looks like she was carrying an extra-heavy load, probably intended for Taliban forces in Afghanistan. That's why she's riding so low in the water."

"I'd like to see her riding a whole lot lower," Hawke said. "Let's go in and give those bastards a fast ride to the bottom. All ahead flank, maintain course."

"Aye-aye, skipper," Laddie said grinning. "All ahead flank, maintain bloody course."

Blackhawke, now on a collision course with the Iranian destroyer, went storming in, under the enemy's lee. She must have been a sight to the Iranian skipper as she advanced, her gun ports flung open, rolling her starboard cannon out as she came. The enemy vessel had been grievously wounded by the torpedo, but she was not out of the fight. Her big guns had not been damaged by the fire from the bow, and Hawke's yacht was sustaining damage despite the high-tech Kevlar and ceramic armor. What the enemy skipper had not experienced was the unsettling scenario of ten Bushmaster 44s, each firing high-explosive shells at the rate of two hundred rounds per minute.

That was two thousand high-explosive projectiles being hurled at the enemy every minute. *Withering fire* was an understatement.

Alvand was now just over a thousand yards distant. You could feel the tension grow around the helm as the silhouette of the big destroyer hove into plain view out of the fog. The drumbeat of heavy rain from above. Below deck, scores of gunners, anxious sailors waiting for the signal to open fire.

"Closing fast," someone muttered.

"Steady, lads, steady," Hawke said quietly, as they drew near. There was no indecision in that voice now, only steely determination. He was taking the fight right to them, right down their bloody throats, his bow pointed dead amidships of the enemy. Laddie glanced over at him. Surely he wasn't thinking of *ramming*?

He held his breath and waited for Hawke to signal a tack to port, bringing their starboard guns to bear once more on the enemy. The seconds turned into hours. Enemy rounds were shooting great columns of water into the air all around them. Some of them were striking home and the beautiful ship was sustaining significant damage. All they had to fight back with were the two bow cannons, doing what they could, but it was not enough. This was insane! But he knew Hawke's reputation. The man had absolutely no qualms about ordering a tactic with even the slimmest margin of success if he felt it would ultimately serve the cause of victory.

"Sir, would you like the conn?" the skipper asked Hawke, seeing the closing distance dangerously diminishing and mopping perspiration from his brow. The silence at the helm was roaring inside his head.

"I would, thank you for offering," Hawke said. Laddie stepped aside and Hawke took the wheel.

"You have the conn, sir."

"I have the conn," Hawke confirmed, as tradition dictated.

"Conn, aye."

"Gun crews ready," Hawke said into the command radio. "Fire as she bears."

"Ready, aye."

"Come left on my order."

"Ready about, then, gentlemen."

"Ready about, sir."

"Hard aport," Hawke barked, spinning the big wheel hard left so lightly through the tips of his fingers it seemed a blur, effortless. Carstairs watched this performance in awe. Here was a seaman in action. Here was a true warrior.

Blackhawke's massive bowsprit missed the hull of the enemy vessel by no more than a foot before finally falling off to port. It was as fine a piece of seamanship as Laddie Carstairs had ever witnessed in a lifetime at sea. The big black yacht rounded up into the wind and lay alongside the enemy at her stern quarter, slowing and matching her speed and course; Hawke's devastating guns were now at the closest possible range. The Iranian destroyer's big guns were now totally out of the picture, as their elevations would not allow for a target this close to their hull.

But *Blackhawke*'s powerful Bushmaster 44 cannons were just six feet above the waterline.

Hawke's plan all along, Carstairs thought, thinking of all the lives aboard this ship that had just been saved by the man's natural naval battle instincts.

Get inside a man's range and pull a gun.

The secret to close work, and by God Hawke knew it, on land or on sea.

At that exact moment, a SEAL team sniper fell from high in the rigging, landing on the deck just in front of the bridge windows, splayed out, a small fountain of blood bubbling at his belly, and clearly dead. Hawke was not looking at him, for he was looking at the enemy with total concentration.

"Starboard gun crews, fire as she bears, gentlemen."

"Firing as she bears, aye."

"Navy Six, Helm."

"Navy Six, go ahead, sir."

"Mr. Stollenwork, are your snipers in position for gun action?"

"Affirmative. SEAL Six is go."

"I want suppression on the enemy automatic weapons who'll be firing down on us from the rails. Kill them or keep them away from the gunwales, aye?"

"Aye-aye, skipper. Wilco."

"Stoke, Helm. You okay up there by yourself?"

"I got a loader up here now. I'll fire number one, then move to two while he reloads. How's Harry?"

"He'll live. He's lying down in sick bay yelling at everyone. I'll say this for him. He likes a fight."

"I do too. Do what you got to do and don't worry yourself about me."

"We're on it."

And by God, they were.

The heavy cannons were pouring rounds into the Iranian destroyer right along the waterline. They were literally slicing through the hull and exploding on the far side, opening up her starboard side to the sea.

"All ahead one-third," Hawke said.

Blackhawke began edging forward, the thunderous roar of her cannons and the result of that fire slicing the *Alvand*'s hull open like a tin can.

The enemy vessel came to a dead stop. Her decks were awash. Her propellers blown off.

And then the most amazing sight anyone on board *Blackhawke* had ever seen.

She literally started sinking before their eyes. She was just going down, not at the stern or the bow. The whole damn boat was sinking at the same rate.

"What the hell?" Laddie said. "Amazing."

"Yeah," Hawke said. "We sliced her bloody keel off. All that lead just plunged to the bottom. There's no more boat beneath the waterline. She's wide open from stem to stern."

Laddie just looked at him, his lower jaw threatening his collarbone.

"This is one for the books, sir."

"No, it's not."

"Loose lips sink ships?"

"Couldn't have said it better myself," Hawke replied.

Alvand sank without a trace within seconds.

The Strait of Hormuz now lay wide open before them.

They were going home.

Home, Hawke thought.

England.

My beloved son.

HAWKE, IN THE FOLLOWING MOMENTS, WAS SILENT, still as a photograph. There was no jubilation, no exultation of triumph or evincing the thrill of victory. He was simply paying tribute to his dear father and all the wisdom that great good man had imparted to his son before his parents were brutally murdered.

The much-decorated naval hero had said it best:

WAR IS NEVER ABOUT WHAT'S IN FRONT OF YOU, ALEX. IT'S ALWAYS ABOUT WHAT'S BEHIND YOU.

And it was the truth.

EPILOGUE

BERMUDA

IT HAD BEEN COLD THE PREVIOUS NIGHT, UNSEA-sonably cold. The chill wind howled around Alex Hawke's tiny Teakettle Cottage on Bermuda's coast, whistling down the chimneys and round the window sashes, clawing at the rattling shutters, insistent and noisy as an angry mob of banshees seeking revenge.

Hawke recognized it as that cold sea air, filled with the bottomless chill that lies at the cloistered heart of ghost stories.

Alexei had come running into his father's bedroom to say good night just as Hawke was slipping his loaded .45 into the drawer of his bedside table. He always slept with it nearby now, even though the boy's bodyguard, Nell Spooner, was just down the hall, sleeping in the child's room.

Hawke felt the boy was safer in Bermuda than anywhere else, but still, he was taking no chances.

At that precise moment came a deafening boom of

thunder, one that rattled the seaward windows and was quickly followed by a blinding flash of lightning that lit up the room brighter than the brightest day.

Little Alexei's eyes widened with delight and the three-year-old leaped onto his father's bed.

"Oh, Papa, this is a real storm. I love storms!"

"His father's son, isn't he?" Nell Spooner said, entering the room to collect her charge. "Now I know *two* very odd men who much prefer bad weather to good."

Hawke smiled at her and then his son, who now had his thin little arms clasped around his father's neck and was hugging him as hard as ever he could.

"Good night, Alexei," Hawke said, kissing the boy's forehead. "Promise me you'll get a good night's sleep because Daddy's taking you out sailing tomorrow."

"Sailing! On *Stormy Petrel*, Papa?"

"Of course we're taking *Petrel*. Now, you go with Nell and don't forget to say your prayers."

Petrel, unlike Hawke's massive megayacht, *Blackhawke*, was a simple forty-foot Bermuda ketch. But she was lovely, built of mahogany over oak planking, teak decks, sitka spruce spars, and a gleaming varnished cabin house. Her hull was painted jet black with golden cove stripes along her sides.

"I never forget God, Papa. He watches over me, just like Nell does."

"I know he does. I love you, boy."

"I love you even more, Papa."

Nell swept Alexei up into her arms and carried him away. Hawke watched the two of them disappear down the dimly lit hall, aware of that overwhelming sensation of gratitude for his little family. It was as powerful as anything he'd ever felt.

And he remembered what his late father had said about the true meaning of war.

This, he knew, *this* was what lay behind him when he went off to battle.

AFTER A LULLABY OR TWO, ALEXEI FELL FAST ASLEEP in his bed. Nell Spooner reentered Hawke's tiny bedroom, arms wrapped around herself, shivering. She spied the fire Pelham had laid in the brick fireplace.

"Please light the fire, Alex. I'm so cold. To the bone."

Hawke put down his book and looked up.

"You know what Ambrose Congreve told me once?"

"No, darling."

"He said, 'Great love affairs are born in heaven. But so, too, are thunder and lightning.'"

Nell laughed her soft laugh. She was now wearing his old Irish fisherman's sweater and nothing else. Her long legs were tanned a deep bronze by the Bermuda sun, pale white at the top where the beloved golden thatch nestled between her thighs.

"I like that," she said.

"My darling girl. Of course I'll light the fire. Come here first and give us a kiss."

He lifted the covers and she crawled inside, reaching for him and finding him already rock hard.

It started with a kiss.

Half an hour later he slipped from her body, then silently from the bed and lit the fire. He sat there, cross-legged on the floor before the hearth, watching until he was sure it had caught. Nell came over, knelt beside him, and placed the silk coverlet around his shoulders.

"That was lovely," she said, gazing at his profile lit by the flickering orange flames. "My man, my beautiful man."

"Looking forward to your first sea voyage tomorrow, landlubber?" Hawke asked, still staring into the fire, lost in his own thoughts.

"I look forward to everything, Alex Hawke. Every single day."

AT SEA THE FOLLOWING DAY, NELL EMERGED FROM the varnished mahogany cabin house and into the pale gold of the late afternoon sunlight. Hawke's lovely old ketch, *Stormy Petrel*, was heeled hard over, slashing through crystalline blue water that roiled and foamed along either side of her bow.

"Did he finally fall asleep?" Hawke asked.

"Yes. He's all tucked into your bed—excuse me, berth. Clutching his teddy and fast asleep. I think he was just exhausted. He loved it when you let him steer. He's had an exciting day, hasn't he?"

"I guessed he would love the water, the wind and sails. Hawke blood runs thick with sea salt. Has done since my ill-mannered pirate ancestors plundered and terrorized the Spanish Main."

Nell sat down in the cockpit right next to Hawke,

who was standing at the wheel, gazing upward at his billowing white mainsail, looking for a luff, and trimming or easing the mainsheet a bit when he saw a crinkle or pocket in the canvas.

"Alex. I had no idea Bermuda could be so exquisite. Small wonder you and Pelham spend so much time at Teakettle Cottage."

"One of those places that make me happiest. But do you think Alexei is safe here? Safer than in England, at any rate?"

"Without question. You cannot possibly monitor all the points of entry at home, but you certainly can here. Only one airport. The cruise ships arriving in town and out at the Royal Dockyards. And then the private yachts. That's it. And we've got eyes and ears at all of them, all day, every day."

Hawke smiled down at her. "Thank you for that, Nell."

"I love him, too, you know."

"I do know," Hawke said, gazing at the open water beyond the harbor and the westering sun. He felt a shiver of pleasure ripple down his spine. He was where he wanted to be, the feel of warm teak decks beneath his bare feet, the breeze on his cheek, the sharp spike of salt in the air, a beautiful sailing machine responding to his every command, slicing through the incredibly translucent blue.

"Are you tired, Nell?" Hawke said, stroking her golden thigh.

"A little."

"I've rigged a little hammock forward, slung beneath the bowsprit just above the water, nothing but a sail but quite comfortable for two."

"And who sails the boat, Captain?"

"The autopilot."

"So we just climb inside and sail off into the sunset?"

"Exactly."

"Sounds like something you'd read at the end of a novel."

"Yes. Or perhaps at the beginning."

AFTERWORD

REGARDING THE SINGULARITY: THE ONLY DIFference between science fiction and science is timing.

The preceding is a work of fiction, an entertainment. However, I want to make it clear that there is nothing fictional about the scientific underpinnings of the novel. Namely, the fast-approaching scientific phenomenon called Singularity. It will be an unfamiliar term to most readers. But it won't be for long.

What is it?

The Singularity is that epic moment in human evolution when artificial, or machine, intelligence (in the form of extremely powerful, superhuman computers) first matches and then exceeds human intelligence by a factor incalculable.

After reaching the point of parity, perhaps within the next decade or so, artificial intelligence will explode *exponentially*. Ultimately, ultra-intelligent machines called "artilects" will be a billion times more powerful than human intelligence of the highest order.

A billion.

The implications of that statement are of enormous importance to the future of humankind. Not to mention our universe and our whole understanding of what it means to be human within it.

To repeat, there is nothing fictional about the Singularity. The scientific foundation upon which the story rests is as accurate as I could portray it and based on extensive research, delving into scientific literature, interviews, and documentary films.

I want you to enjoy this book. Period. But I also want to make as many people as I can aware of what is distinctly possible in the very near future.

A life-altering moment, when machines first match, and then exceed, the finite limits of human intelligence. Why is it called by scientists "the Singularity"? Literally, the word, borrowed from mathematics, means "a unique event with singular implications." Life-changing implications. A rip in the fabric of current civilization. And it's just around the corner.

An essential resource in the writing of this novel was Ray Kurzweil's groundbreaking book, *The Singularity Is Near.* I highly recommend it for readers of this novel who want to delve deeper into the facts. Kurzweil, considered the world's leading futurist, has appeared numerous times on television, including in a documentary called *The Transcendent Man*, and on CNN, Fox News, and the Charlie Rose show multiple times to discuss the approaching Singularity. No less a visionary than Bill Gates has called Ray "A genius. Our next Thomas Edison."

Ray holds more than twenty patents, including the first flat-screen scanner, and the first "reader" for the blind, a handheld device that turns written words into audible human language for the visually impaired.

A word to skeptics about the approaching Singularity: there is no longer any dispute; we stand on the verge of a new epoch in the realm of artificial intelligence. This quantum leap forward in machine-enhanced, superhuman intelligence will result in the ultimate merger of human intelligence (limited) with machine intelligence (unlimited). And it will change, literally, everything.

As mentioned earlier, in the near future, intelligent machines will be a billion times more powerful than human intelligence. It's difficult, but try to imagine what that will mean for human civilization. There will be no problem we face today that cannot be solved. Disease, war, aging, energy, poverty, starvation, water shortages, antisocial behavior—the list continues ad infinitum. This is the utopian view. Others hold a more dystopian view and predict the triumph of machines as the end of humanity.

"Watson," IBM's ultra-intelligent computer, is just the beginning. In the 1960s, people said no computer would ever beat a human at chess. Turns out chess was child's play for a computer. Mere data retrieval. But, until Watson, there had never been a computer capable of communicating in a "human-to-human" fashion. Not just retrieving data from some data bank, but a machine capable of understanding a complex, subtle, nuanced humanoid question and responding correctly in natural, human language. In seconds. To oversimplify, Watson doesn't merely search and retrieve data, Watson *thinks* using human language.

To understand what's about to happen, you must imagine the vast knowledge embedded in our brains vastly enhanced by the far greater capacity, speed, and knowledge-sharing ability of immensely powerful linked supercomputers now being developed around the world.

And then try to imagine what will happen when these ultra-intelligent machines actually *outstrip* the human brain's limitations. Our organic brains are capable of a mere hundred trillion extremely slow calculations per second. But nonorganic brains have no such limits. Their capacity for speed is unlimited, infinite.

At that moment, once the Singularity is achieved, the world will witness an "intelligence explosion." Thus, the first ultra-intelligent machine will be the very last invention that man need ever make. Machines will do the inventing for us. Including inventing nanoneurons traveling in our bloodstreams that will make our own bodies and brains vastly more powerful and ageless. Thus will begin the *merging* of man and machine intelligence. Parity is the ideal, but not necessarily a given.

And herein lies the great question.

Certainly the moral implications give one pause, in any case. The line between man and machine might eventually become blurred, then disappear altogether. So what is man?

———

WE ARE ENTERING AN ERA AS RADICALLY DIFFERENT from our human past as we humans are from the lower animals. From the human point of view, this change will be a discarding of all the previous rules, perhaps in the blink of an eye, an exponential technological runaway. Will it accelerate beyond any hope of human control? Those who take the dystopian view see this rise of the machines as the beginning of the end of human existence. They envision superintelligent robots with inhuman strength that know us and love us, even while they are ripping the very fabric of our civilization to shreds. They envision a war, the very last war, between man and a vastly superior robotic warrior. And that's a war humans might well lose.

Already, cyberweapons like the ones described in this book are not only on the drawing boards but in advanced stages of development. The Stuxnet attack on Iran heralded a new era in warfare. The Era of Cyberwarfare. What do you do when your navy's most advanced nuclear aircraft carrier is rendered useless without a shot being fired? Or your Predator missile reverses direction in flight and homes in on the launch site? As I tried to make clear earlier, this is not just some spy novelist's fantasy, it is literally what the military is wrestling with at this very moment. Even more frightening are bioengineered diseases, reverse engineered from the human genome, for which there is no cure. We are then looking at genocide on a global scale.

We will have one very powerful arrow in our

quiver: our innate and deeply embedded desire to survive. Human beings will literally do anything to live.

Anything.

There are other inherent dangers, obviously, embodied in the dystopian view. To visualize this, imagine this destructive, superintelligent robot without an on-off switch. This unpleasant notion is exactly why mankind (human-based science) must tread exquisitely carefully here. We enter this uncharted territory at our peril. Safeguards, if they are even possible, are mandatory at every stage of the progression.

Unimaginable weapons could be created by runaway machines. Bioengineered diseases described above and designed by computers run amok would make our atomic and hydrogen bombs pale in comparison. An atomic explosion is a *local* event. Remember that the influenza epidemic of 1918 killed *fifty million* people around the world! Should this new technology fall into the wrong hands and create a bioengineered disease mankind was incapable of stopping, it is no stretch to say that the extinction of humans is entirely possible.

Of course, there are positives.

The Singularity will allow us to overcome age-old human problems (such as the aforementioned disease and aging) and vastly amplify human creativity in the arts, engineering, and problem solving. We will then be able to preserve and enhance the intelligence that evolution has bestowed upon us while overcoming the profound limitations of our biological evolution.

In summary, benefits, as well as dangers, will accrue when we radically outstrip the hundred-trillion-operations-per-second speed limit of our human brains.

We might well discover how to live forever (or as long as we want to). We might learn how to exceed the speed of light, at which point anything, even time travel and exploring other universes, will be possible.

But the preceding story, though fictional, is a cautionary tale. Because, without question, the Singularity will also amplify our ability to act upon our innate destructive inclinations, the dangerous primal components of our brains referred to by Arthur Koestler in his work *The Ghost in the Machine*. Cyberwarfare alone presents enormous new challenges. Challenges I've endeavored to illuminate in this book.

Let me, in conclusion, summarize the thoughts of John Arquilla, professor of defense analysis at the U.S. Naval Postgraduate School. Professor Arquilla actually introduced the notion of cyberwar twenty years ago.

Arquilla believes cyberwar to be an emerging conflict mode enabled by and primarily waged with advanced information systems. These systems will be, in and of themselves, both tools and targets. This new method of war fighting, already quite potent on the battlefield, will also be able to strike at the enemies' homelands without the need to defeat their military forces first. In other words, outbreaks of conflict may be primarily driven by the *state of play in technology*. This state of play (as demonstrated in this novel) makes attacking seem easy and defending oneself hard. Unfortunately, a world plagued with cyberwar appears to be the future.

If nations take a permissive view of cyberwar in general, or encourage "sharp practices" like the Stuxnet attack on Iran, then an era of massive and costly disruption to advanced information systems and the infrastructures they control will soon be upon us.

Are we innately destructive? The answer is obvious. Simply look at what we've already destroyed, the vast numbers of species eradicated, the billions of humans killed by war, genocide, and starvation, the wanton defilement of our beautiful celestial home.

And therein lies the tale.

The full story has not been written.

After all, this is just the beginning . . .

And the only difference between science and science fiction is timing.

TED BELL
Cambridge University
January 2012

Keep reading for Ted Bell's

CRASH DIVE,

an exhilarating e-book novella
featuring Alex Hawke

Available from William Morrow
An Imprint of HarperCollins Publishers

MIDNIGHT. NO MOON, NO STARS, THE SEA A FLAT black void a few feet beneath his wingtips. For a man streaking through the night over hostile foreign waters at nearly the speed of sound, at an altitude no sane man would dare consider, Alex Hawke was remarkably comfortable. He was piloting an F-16 Viper. The matte-black American-built fighter jet was one of many purchased and heavily modified by Britain's Royal Navy for under-the-radar special operations just like this one.

Lord Alexander Hawke, a former Royal Navy pilot and combat veteran of the Gulf War, now a seasoned British intelligence officer with MI6, had to smile.

Like the Syrian hospital bed he'd only recently escaped, the sleek F-16's single seat reclined at an angle of exactly thirty degrees, transforming the deadly Viper, Hawke thought, into something along the lines of a supersonic Barcalounger. Leave it to the Americans to worry about fighter pilot comfort.

His eyes flicked over the dimly lit instrument array and found nothing remotely exciting. Even the hazy reddish glow inside the cockpit somehow reassured him that all was well. He was less than six hundred nautical miles from the tiny island of Xia-chuan, his destination, and closing fast. Every mile he put behind him lessened the chance of a Chinese Sukhoi 33 jet interceptor or a surface-to-air missile blasting him out of the sky. Although equipped with the very latest antimissile defense systems, the Viper was no stealth fighter.

He was vulnerable and he knew it. Should he be forced to eject and was captured by the Red Chinese, he'd be tortured mercilessly before he was killed. A British intelligence officer flying an un-marked American fighter jet had no business enter-ing Chinese airspace. But he did have business, very serious business, and his success might well avert impending hostilities that could lead to global war.

That was his mission. And he'd gladly chosen to accept it.

In London one week earlier, "C," as the chief of MI6 was traditionally called, had summoned Hawke to join him for lunch at his men's club, Boo-dle's. Lord Hawke had thought it was a purely social invitation. Usually the old man conducted serious SIS business only within the sanctum sanctorum of his office at 85 Albert Embankment. So it was a very relaxed Alex Hawke who presented himself promptly at the appointed hour of noon.

"Well, here you are at last, Alex," C said, amiably enough. Sir David Trulove, a gruff old party thirty years Hawke's senior, had his customary corner table at the third-floor Men's Grill. Shafts of dusty sunlight pouring down from the tall leaded windows set the table crystal and silver afire, all sparkle and gleam. Above the table, ragged tendrils of tobacco smoke hung in wreaths and coils, turning and twisting slowly in the sunlit room.

The dining room at Boodle's was, by any standard, one of the poshest man-caves in London.

C took a spartan sip of his gin and bitters, looked his subordinate up and down in a cursory fashion, and said, "I must say, a bit of convalescence becomes you. You're looking rather fit again, Alex. 'Steel true, blade straight,' as Conan Doyle would have it. Sit, sit."

Hawke, favoring his injured right leg, sat. He paid scant attention to such "on the job" injuries. They simply went with the territory. The nasty business in a Syrian prison hospital was already receding from memory.

"Most kind of you, sir. I've been looking forward to this all week."

"Let's see if you still feel that way at the conclusion. What are you drinking? My club, my treat," Trulove said, catching a waiter's eye.

"Gosling's, please. The Black Seal, neat. So. Trouble, I take it," Hawke said after C had ordered his rum.

"No end of it, sadly. The bloody Chinese again."

"Something new? I thought I was fairly well up to speed."

"Well, Alex, you know those inscrutable Mandarins in Beijing as well as I do. Always some new wrinkle up their red silk sleeves. It's that abominable South China Sea situation, I'm afraid."

"Heating up?"

"Boiling over."

Hawke's rum arrived. He took a sip and said, "What now, sir? Don't tell me they've blockaded one of the world's busiest trade routes."

"No, no, not yet anyway. Still, simply outrageous behavior. They unilaterally extended their territorial claims in the South China Sea hundreds of miles south and east from their most southerly province of Hainan. All done with zero regard for international maritime law. They now claim a huge U-shaped area of the sea, a claim that overlaps areas that Vietnam, Malaysia, the Philippines, Taiwan, and Brunei say belong to them."

"Good Lord. With what possible justification?"

"Beijing says its right to the area comes from two thousand years of history, when the Paracel and Spratly island chains were regarded as integral parts of the Chinese nation. Vietnam says, rightly, that both island chains lie entirely within its territory. That it has actively ruled over both chains since the seventeenth century and has the documents to prove it."

"Bastards have created a flash point as dangerous as the Iranians and the Strait of Hormuz. Clearly global implications."

"Yes. And now they've begun making intolerable demands. They're demanding that every vessel transiting these formerly wide-open routes must first ask permission of the Chinese government. We will not, bloody hell, ask them permission for any such thing! Nor will anyone else."

"Of course not. And the Western countermove?"

"The United States is dramatically increasing its naval presence in the region, of course. And, as you well know, they've deployed U.S. Marines to Darwin in Australia. Meanwhile, the PM, in a weak moment, actually had an extraordinary idea. The allies are going to assemble a massive convoy, Alex. Warships from the Royal Navy, Japan, Taiwan, the Philippines, Vietnam, and the Yanks with an entire carrier battle group, and seven or eight other countries. Full steam ahead under their bloody noses and see what they do about it."

"Well, for starters, they might take out a U.S. carrier with one of their killer satellites."

"Hmm. Good to see the Syrians didn't break your brain as well as your leg. That is a consideration, Alex. A few pantywaists in the U.S. Congress are thus far unwilling to go along with the scheme for fear of losing one of their billion-dollar babies. So, our convoy scheme is paralyzed at the moment. But, look, we're not going to sit around on our arses and let this stand. Not for one blasted moment."

"What are we going to do about it?"

"You mean what are *you* going to do about it, dear boy. That's why I'm springing for lunch."

"No free lunch, as they say."

"Never."

"How can I help, sir? I've been deemed fit for active service as of yesterday morning."

C looked around to establish if anyone was within earshot and then said, "We at Six have established a back-channel communication with a high-ranking Chinese naval officer. Someone with a working brain in his head who doesn't want to go to war over his government's deliberate and insane maritime provocation any more than we do."

"This sounds good."

"It is. Very."

Hawke leaned forward and quietly said, "The Chinese are well aware that they cannot possibly afford to go to war with the West now. In a decade, perhaps, but certainly not now."

"Of course not. It's an obvious political ploy, albeit an extremely dangerous one. They wish to divert attention from their burgeoning internal domestic turmoil, particularly Tibet, with a bellicose show of force. Show the peasant population and the increasingly restive middle class just how powerful they now are."

"Sheer insanity."

"But you're going to put a stop to it, Lord Hawke. I've arranged a secret rendezvous for you with Admiral Tiao Tsang on a small island in a remote quadrant of the South China Sea. It was formerly a Japanese air force base, now abandoned because of the territorial dispute. There's an eight-thousand-foot airstrip there that should accommodate you nicely."

"What kind of bus am I driving?"

"An American F-16 Viper. One of ours. Especially modified for nighttime insertions. All the latest offensive and defensive goodies, I assure you. Kinetic energy weapons and all that sort of thing."

"Lovely airplane. Always wanted a crack at one."

"You'll get one first thing tomorrow morning at Lakenheath RAF. Three days of intensive flight training with a USAF chief instructor off your wingtip. Then off you go into the wild blue yonder."

"This Admiral Tsang. How high ranking is he, exactly? I mean to say, is he actually powerful enough to defuse this thing?"

"Very high. Chinese chief of naval operations. You'll find an obsessively complete dossier waiting for you when you get home. Memorize it and burn it. Now then, Alex, what will you have for lunch?"

A KEENING WAIL SUDDENLY FILLED THE VIPER'S cockpit. Holy God, he'd just been painted by enemy radar! He whipped his head around and saw the Chinese SAM missile's exhaust flame streaking toward his Viper's afterburner. A HongQi 61A. Where the hell had it come from? Some kind of Chinese radar-proof shore battery on a nearby atoll? None of his so-called sophisticated gadgetry had even picked the damn thing up!

He hauled back on the joystick and instantly initiated a vertical climb, standing the Viper on its tail and rocketing skyward. He deployed chaff aft and switched on the jamming devices located in the airplane's tail section. He was almost instantaneously at forty thousand feet and climbing, his eyes locked on the missile displayed on his radar screen. Its unverified speed, Hawke knew, was Mach 3. It was closing fast.

The deadly little bastard blew right through his

chaff field without a single degree of deviation. The Chinese were not behaving according to MI6's assessment of their military capability. With every passing second, his appointment with death went from possible to probable. He'd have to depend on the aircraft's jamming devices and his own evasive maneuvers to survive.

He nosed the Viper over and put it into a screaming vertical dive, gaining himself precious seconds. The HongQi would have to recalculate before altering course and getting on his six again. He'd known from the second the SAM missile appeared on his screen that there was only one maneuver that stood a gnat's chance of saving him.

A crash dive straight down into the sea.

Hairy, but sometimes effective. To succeed, however, he had to allow the deadly weapon to get dangerously close to impacting and destroying the Viper. So close in fact that when he pulled out of the dive at the last possible instant, he would be so near to the water's surface that the missile would have zero time to correct before it hit the water doing Mach 3.

The missile nosed over as Hawke had and honed in. It was now closing at a ridiculous rate. His instrument panel told him he was clearly out of his bloody mind. The ingrained human instinct to run, to change course and escape, clawed around the edges of his conscious mind. But he'd erected a firewall around it that was impenetrable in times like this.

It was those few precious white-hot moments precisely like this one that Alex Hawke lived for.

Like his father and grandfather before him, he was a warrior to the bone and he was bloody good at it. His focus at this critical moment, fueled by adrenaline, was borderline supernatural. His altimeter display screen was a blur, but he didn't see it; the collision-avoidance alarms were screaming in his headphones, but he didn't hear them. His grip on the stick was feather light, his hands bone dry and surgeon steady.

His mind was calmly calculating the differential between the seconds remaining until the missile impacted the Viper and the seconds until the Viper impacted the sea. Ignoring his immediate surroundings, all the screeching alarms and flashing electronic warnings, Alex Hawke began his final mental countdown. The surface of the sea was approaching at a dizzying rate . . .

Five . . . four . . . three . . . two . . .

NOW!

He pulled back on the stick and brought his nose up. He noticed beads of water racing across the exterior of his canopy and figured he might have caught the top of a wave coming out of the dive. . . .

You can't get any closer in this kind of situation than when you get your nose wet. Some smart-ass RN combat instructor had said that lo those many years ago. He barely heard the impact of the missile over the roar of his afterburners, but he did. He was in the clear and could easily visualize it, vaporizing upon contact with the concrete hard water at that speed. . . .

G forces were fierce as he initiated his climb back to his former below-the-radar altitude. That's when his starboard wingtip caught a cresting wave that sent his aircraft out of control. He was skimming over the sea like a winged Frisbee. He felt a series of jolts as the fuselage made contact a couple of times and instinctively understood that the aircraft was seconds away from disintegrating right out from under his arse.

He reached down and grabbed the red handle to his right, yanked it, and the canopy exploded upward into the airstream and disappeared. The rocket motors beneath his seat instantly propelled him out of the spinning cockpit and straight up into the black sky. Seconds later, his chute deployed and he had a bird's-eye view of his airplane turning into varying sizes of scrap-heap metal and disappearing into the deep.

He yanked the cord, which disengaged him from his seat, watched it fall, and moments later his boots hit the water. It was cold as hell, but he started shedding gear as quickly as he could. He was unhurt at least and able to tread water until his life jacket inflated. *So far so good*, he thought, keeping his spirits up surprisingly well for a downed airman all alone.

Normally, there'd be an EPIRB attached to his shoulder harness. Upon contact with water, it would immediately begin broadcasting his GPS coordinates to a passing satellite. He could hang out for a while here in the South China Sea and wait for one of Her Majesty's Navy choppers to pluck him out of the water and winch him up. But of course he had no distress radio beacon, no EPIRB.

He figured the water temperature was cold enough to kill him eventually, but the thermal body suit he wore would stave off hypothermia long enough for him to have a shot at survival.

He spun his body through 360 degrees. Nothing. No lights on the horizon, no planes in the sky. Nada. Nothing but a vast black sea stretching away in all directions. No EPIRB. No hope of immediate rescue. He was some fifty miles off the southern coast of China. If he was lucky, he was in a shipping channel. He looked at his dive watch. Five hours minimum until sunrise. Nothing to do but hang here in limbo and see what happened next.

It didn't take long.

He felt the pressure of sudden underwater movement just before he felt a soft nudge in the small of his back. No pain, just a tentative probing by some large fish. Exactly what kind of fish it might have been was a question he preferred not to speculate about. But the words wouldn't go away. The bad one was *snout*. That was what it had felt like. Then there was the really bad one.

Shark.

Minutes later there was another hit. A jarring slam to the rib cage on his right side. He'd glimpsed the shark's dorsal fin slicing toward him maybe two seconds before impact. It hurt like a bastard. He turned slowly in the water, minimizing his movements. Even in the pitch-black, he could see the dorsal fins circling lazily around him. He knew a little bit about shark behavior. Right now they were merely curious about this new object in the neighborhood.

This could go either way. They could get bored with him and disappear. Or, the other way, they could shred him into several large chunks, ripping away his limbs first before fighting over the torso. Staying positive in adverse conditions was one of his strengths, so that's what he did. The more fins that appeared to encircle him, and the fact that his body was hanging there helplessly suspended in the freezing water, made it tough.

But Alex Hawke, it had to be said, was nothing if not tough.

He closed his eyes and immobilized his body. He forced himself to concentrate on all the good things in his life. His cherished son, named Alexei by his mother, was now just four years old. He could see him running through the dappled sunlight on the green meadow in Hyde Park. The child's nurse, Nell, was chasing him, laughing. Nell was much more than a nanny. She was Hawke's much-loved woman, somewhat of a legend at Scotland Yard, and, in truth, Alexei's bodyguard. She had saved the little boy's life on more than one occasion. He'd been targeted by the KGB, and one of Hawke's greatest fears was leaving his son without a father.

An hour passed, a very long hour.

For whatever reason, God's infinite mercy perhaps, the toothsome beasts had left him alone, at least for the moment. Cold had begun to claw its way inside his protective armor. He was shaking now, and his teeth were chattering away, much ado about nothing. It crossed his mind that freezing to death was a vastly better way to go than serving himself up as breakfast for the finny denizens of the deep.

He slept, God knows how long.

And then the lights came on.

Literally.

He found himself the target of a shaft of pure white light. He looked up to his left and saw its source. A searchlight mounted high on the superstructure of a massive aircraft carrier. Then another, and another, both lower and near the deck, picked him out. And then, to his right, he became aware of the deep bass thumping of helicopter rotor blades. A spotlight from the chopper picked him up, and he saw a diver appear in the opening in the side of the fuselage.

Could this possibly be a friendly? The odds were certainly against it, given China's recent military posturing in this little corner of the world. The diver splashed down about six feet away and hopes for a miracle vanished when he told Hawke to remain calm in Mandarin. Then he went about securing the lifting harness to Hawke's body.

Hawke had spent a lot of time in mainland China with his friend and companion, the great Scotland Yard criminalist Ambrose Congreve. In addition to being a brilliant detective, Ambrose had studied languages at Cambridge. While doing a six-month stint in a Beijing prison for "subversive activities" that had never been proven, Congreve had given Hawke a rudimentary, but substantial, working knowledge of Chinese.

"In the nick of time," Hawke said to the diver in his native tongue.

"What?"

"You arrived just in time. I was slowly freezing to death."

"Silence. No conversation."

"Have it your way. Just trying to be friendly."

Hawke and his rescuer were winched up and into the belly of the Chinese Ahkoi helo. Nobody aboard would talk to him. He was sure they knew an unidentified aircraft had entered their airspace and had been shot down (they imagined) by one of their missiles. So they were sensibly predisposed not to be chatty. Hell with them—he was still alive, wasn't he? He'd gotten out of tougher scrapes than this one over the years.

THE INITIAL INTERROGATION ABOARD THE CHINESE carrier was short but brutal. Still, he'd gotten out of it with little more real damage than three broken fingers and a mild concussion. They'd told him he'd never leave this ship alive, then locked him up inside a stinking crew cabin in the bowels of the bilge with room for little more than a crappy bunk bed. He now lay on the top berth thinking very seriously about how the hell to escape.

Two military policemen with automatic weapons had delivered him to this lovely boudoir. He was fairly certain the same two would come for him when it was time for the more labor-intensive interrogation. They were thugs, those two, viciously abusive but stupid. Just the way he liked them. He'd feigned a far worse concussion than he'd actually suffered, forcing them to half carry him down many flights of stairs, something that they did not appear to enjoy.

He was consciously unconscious when they slammed into the tiny space and pulled him down from the upper berth. As he expected, they yanked him to his feet and wrapped his arms around their shoulders in order to keep him moving. He kept his head down, mumbling incoherently. When the MP on his left paused to kick open the half-closed door, he used the moment to grab a fistful of hair on each man's head and violently slam their skulls together hard enough to cause them to sink to the floor. He checked. They were out for the long count.

He quickly stripped the uniform from the taller of the two. It fit him badly, but it was good enough to get him up eight flights of metal steps to the carrier's deck level without incident. Hawke had jet-black hair, which helped, and he kept the cap brim pulled down and his face lowered. He also had the advantage of carrying an automatic rifle in case things got spicy.

He saw a sailor open a hatch in the bulkhead and felt the cold blast of icy wind howl in from the flight deck. He waited sixty seconds and then stepped through to the outside himself. He had no earthly idea how he was going to execute the plan he'd devised, but that was of little concern. You had to be able to make this stuff up as you went along. He heard a sizable group of men laughing as they approached his position and stepped back into the shadows.

Pilots.

There were eight of them, all in flight suits and some wearing their helmets, some holding them loosely in their hands, kidding around, walking with that cocky jet-jock walk. They were obviously en route across the expanse of darkened deck to their covey of Sukhoi 33 carrier aircraft being readied for immediate launch. He remained hidden between two huge storage lockers behind the bulwark until just after they had passed. Then he fell in behind them, quickening his pace until he caught up with the lone straggler at the rear. Fortunately, he was by far the tallest of the lot.

He approached his target from directly behind, shot out both hands, and used his thumbs on the carotid artery, to paralyze the poor fellow and still keep him on his feet. He gave the main group of pilots time to continue on, then pulled the unconscious one back into the shadows of the storage lockers. It was the work of a moment to zip himself inside the pilot's jumpsuit and don his boots and helmet and flip the visor down. He strode quickly, but not too quickly, across the deck and caught up with the jocular pilots just as they were climbing into their respective Sukhois.

He made a beeline straight for the sole unoccupied fighter, then saluted the two attending crewmen who stood aside for him to mount the cockpit ladder.

"Lovely night for flying, boys," he muttered in guttural Chinese, sliding himself down into the seat. After strapping himself in, he reached forward and flipped the switch that lowered the canopy. Then he studied the instrument array and illuminated controls, quickly deciding exactly what did what. The Chinese had stolen so much aeronautical technology from the West that getting the hang of things was embarrassingly easy.

He gave a hand signal to the crewmen below, lit the candle, and taxied into position behind the last jet in line for the center catapult. The blast shield had already risen from the deck behind the first jet in the squadron, and Hawke watched as the fighter was flung out over the ocean, afterburner glowing white hot.

He must have been daydreaming because he suddenly heard the air boss screaming at him in his headphones, telling him to get his ass moving. The aircraft in front of him had advanced into position and he'd not followed immediately. Now he added a touch of power and tucked in where he belonged. There remained only three planes ahead of him.

"So sorry, Boss," he muttered in the time-honored traditional communicative style of fighter pilots all over the world. On a carrier, the air boss is God himself.

"Don't let it happen again, Passionflower, or I'll kick your ass all the way back to Shanghai."

"Roger that, sir," Hawke said, advancing once more.

"You forget something in your preflight, Passionflower?"

"No, sir," Hawke said.

"Yeah? Check your fucking nav lights switch for me, just humor me."

Shit. He hadn't turned them on. Dumb mistake and he couldn't afford to be dumb at this point, not in the slightest.

"You awake down there, son? I'm inclined to pull your ass out of line."

"Sir, no sir. I'm good to go."

"Yeah, well, you damn well better be. I've got my eye on you now, honey. You screw up even a little bit on this mission this morning and your ass is mine. You believe me?"

"Sir, I always believe you. But I'll come back clean, I swear it."

"Damn right you will. Now get the hell off my boat, Passionflower. I got more important things than little pissants like you to worry about. You're up."

Hawke moved forward and engaged the catapult hook inside its buried track. He heard the blast shield rumble up into position behind him and looked to his left, nodding, a signal to the launch chief that he was poised and ready. The man raised his right arm and dropped it, meaning any second now. Hawke's right hand automatically went to the "oh-shit bar" on the right-hand side of the canopy.

Adrenaline flooded Hawke's veins as he gripped the bar with his right hand. Being launched violently into space by a modern carrier catapult was as close as any human being can come to the experience of being in a catastrophic fatal car crash and surviving. It was that intense.

Early on, after a lot of expensive hardware had gone into the drink, some aeronautical genius had figured out that most pilots instinctively grabbed the aircraft's controls too quickly after launch. It's scary to feel out of control when your wheels separate from the mother ship. Now every fighter had a handhold forward and to the right inside the canopy. You grabbed it just before they pulled the trigger. Thus its name, the oh-shit bar.

During a "cat shot," the time it took you to remove your hand from that bar and take hold of the controls was precisely, to the nanosecond, the right amount of time needed to elapse before you seized control after leaving the leading edge of the deck.

He was airborne.

He looked back down at the deck lights of the *Varyag*, the carrier growing rapidly smaller as he gained altitude. He suppressed any feelings of joy over escaping an agonizing death at the hands of the most sophisticated torturers on the planet. He wasn't out of the woods yet, he told himself, as he climbed upward to join "his" squadron's flight. Their heading was a northerly course that would take them over the Paracel Islands. Exactly the wrong direction. He needed to be headed south-southeast and he needed to get moving or he'd miss his rapidly diminishing window: the one chance he had to try to defuse a crisis with global implications.

The rim of the earth was edged in violent pink as he slipped into his designated slot at the rear of the tight formation. There was a minimum of radio chat for which he was thankful. There was normally a lot of banter at this stage and he didn't want to hear any questions or inside wisecracks over the radio that he couldn't respond to without sacrificing his cover. He needed precious time to remain anonymous until he could figure out how the hell to peel off and head for his mission destination without arousing the slightest suspicion.

He knew what he had to do now, although he didn't much like it.

—

Land on the island airstrip on Xiachuan Island. Meet with this Chinese Admiral Tsang and fulfill C's back-channel charge as best he could. Find a strategic way to avert the imminent showdown and eliminate another global flash point. He didn't much like the fact that a high-tech SAM had been launched at him streaking across some dinky little atoll in the middle of nowhere. And that a Chinese carrier just happened to be sailing the sea-lane where he went down? No. He simply couldn't shake the distinct impression that this might all be an elaborate setup. That the wily Chinese were going to use his violation of their airspace as proof positive that the West was being deliberately provocative.

They'd trot out his blackened corpse and twisted pieces of his American fighter jet on global TV. Use him to justify an even more aggressive posture in the South China Sea. Take retaliatory measures against Taiwan, Japan, or Vietnam. Next step, war. That's how he saw it, anyway. C might disagree. But C wasn't sitting in the hot seat with his ass on the line.

He now had little choice. He flew on with the formation, heading north toward the Pacific. He looked at his watch, calculated time and distance to his target. A long way to go and a short time to get there. And suddenly it came to him.

He thumbed the transmit button on his radio.

"Flight leader, flight leader, this is, uh, Passionflower, over."

"Roger, Passionflower, this is Red Flight Leader. Go ahead, over."

"Experiencing mechanical difficulties. System malfunctions, over."

"What's your situation?"

"I'm flying hot, sir. Engine overheat. It's getting worse. Running override system checks now. Doesn't look good."

"Are you declaring an emergency?"

"Negative, negative. I think I can throttle back and make it home to mother. Request permission to abort and return, over."

"Permission granted, over."

"Roger that, Red Flight Leader. Passionflower returning to the *Varyag*, over."

Hawke peeled away from the formation and went into a steep diving turn away from his flight. The sun was up now, just a sliver above the horizon, streaks of red light streaming across the sea below. When Red Flight was out of radar range, he corrected course and went to full throttle. By his latest calculations, he'd touch down just in time. He sat back and allowed himself his first smile in hours.

If he didn't get blown out of the sky, it promised to be another beautiful day in Paradise.

HARPER (LUXE)

THE NEW LUXURY IN READING

**Introducing a Clearer
Perspective on Larger Print**

With a 14-point type size for comfort reading
and published exclusively in paperback format,
HarperLuxe is light to carry and easy to read.

SEEING IS BELIEVING!

To view our great selection of titles in a
comfortable print and to sign up for the
HarperLuxe newsletter please visit:
www.harperluxe.com

*This ad has been set in the
14-point font for comfortable reading.

HRL 0307

BECAUSE THERE ARE TIMES
WHEN BIGGER IS BETTER